DYING TO TELL

DYING to TELL

A SLAUGHTER CREEK NOVEL

RITA HERRON

Text copyright © 2012 Rita Herron

Published by Montlake Romance
P.O. Box 400818
Las Vegas, NV 89140

ISBN-13: 9781611097450
ISBN-10: 1611097452

To Lindsay Guzzardo for liking my dark side!

Prologue

———— ◉ ————

From the moment I decided to kill him, I began to feel relief.
It had to be done. There was no other way to escape.

No turning back.

He had led me to the secret room so many times. He'd taken my soul and left me empty inside.

Ting. Ting. Ting.

The chimes began to ring. Crying. Shrill, grating sounds like a knife scraping bone.

No, he shouted.

Crying wasn't allowed.

I heard the tears anyway. Silent streams of pain. Pleas for help. Prayers to die.

But no one came.

Were the screams just in my mind? Or were they real?

It didn't matter.

I had to save myself.

The screech of the metal door echoed in the night. The bright light seared my eyes. The gruff sound of his voice whispering that he loved me.

My fingers curled around the knife as he walked nearer. So close, I saw the whites of his eyes.

The black pupils where his soul should have been, if he had ever had one.

The smell suffused me. Seeped into my pores.

The antiseptic. The cleansing soap. The faint hint of sweat. Sickening.

Then he leaned over me.

Ting. Ting. Ting.

Emotions left me, bleeding out like the crimson life force I intended to take from him.

I raised the knife and jammed it in his chest. His grunt of pain and shock echoed in the icy cold chamber.

His blood spurted onto my face.

Then his body collapsed against mine, and I waited for him to die.

It was the only way I could survive...

Chapter 1

———— ◉ ————

San Francisco, California, one week earlier

He *told me not to tell.*
   The little girl's voice echoed in Sadie Nettleton's head as the judge polled the jury for the verdict.

"Guilty."

"Guilty."

"Guilty."

"Guilty…"

As a forensic interviewer, Sadie had convinced the child to reveal the details of her abuse, and thankfully, now the jury had convicted the bastard. He would rot in jail.

But the child trembling in the seat next to her mother would have her own hell to live with. Maybe counseling would help, but would her internal scars ever heal?

Dammit, she knew about internal scars.

And secrets.

Lord, she had her own share of those.

Secrets she would never tell.

Two reporters rushed toward the DA and the family as they exited the courtroom. A third reporter, a clean-cut twentysomething who'd hounded Sadie for a personal interview after the last two trials in which she'd testified, made a beeline toward her.

"Miss Nettleton, you interviewed Melanie Norman." He pushed the microphone in her face. "What do you think about today's verdict?"

She cleared her throat and forced the rage from her voice, rage born on the child's behalf for the innocence that had been destroyed at the hands of a man she'd trusted. "The family can rest easier tonight. Justice was served."

"You've become quite the child advocate. Would you share with us what drove you to become a counselor and forensic interviewer?"

Not in this lifetime, she wouldn't.

Sadie's phone buzzed, and she pushed away the microphone. "I'm sorry. I really have to go."

Desperate to escape personal scrutiny, she hurried down the hall and out the door, then jogged toward her VW. She needed space, distance, time to regroup. Channel her emotions.

Bury the past that taunted her daily.

Her phone buzzed again as she slid into the seat, and she checked the number.

Slaughter Creek, Tennessee. Home.

The site of her worst nightmares. The town she'd left years ago and swore never to return to.

Ignoring the call, she peeled out of the parking lot and headed toward the pier. Five minutes later she parked, climbed out, and breathed in the fresh ocean air.

San Francisco: beautiful, scenic, full of life, vitality, and tourists.

And as far away from the East Coast as she could get.

The wind whistled. From a shop nearby, wind chimes tinkled. Musical, soft, restful. Then an almost violent symphony as the breeze picked up.

Her sister had an obsession with wind chimes, had hung them everywhere, on the porch, her bedroom ceiling, above her door…

Suddenly the hair on the back of Sadie's neck prickled. She glanced around, searching to see if someone was watching her. She'd had that feeling all her life, as if she was never alone.

And not just because she was a twin. Because she sensed someone watching her.

Music blasted from a group of teens nearby. A toddler squealed as his mother pushed him in his stroller. Two women jogged by. There were other locals on the street and several tourists snapping pictures. But no one that struck her as suspicious.

Yet the tinkle of the chimes echoed in her head again, reminding her of her sister. Poor Amelia had been diagnosed with DID, dissociative identity disorder, when she was twelve.

Honestly, her first episodes had started when she was only three. Amelia had talked about her friend Bessie, and Sadie played along, thinking Bessie was Amelia's imaginary friend. By the time Amelia was eight, and continued to talk about Bessie, her grandfather had become worried. Then at age twelve, her second personality, Viola—a flirtatious side of Amelia—had emerged. Psychiatrists had deemed that she was suffering from multiple personality disorder, DID. Then at fourteen, another personality had appeared, a sullen teenage boy who called himself Skid.

She shivered as her gaze strayed to Alcatraz. The prison stood alone, surrounded by frigid waters, weathered by time and storms…and evil.

Just as she was weathered by them.

Her phone buzzed with another call from home, and her heart hammered.

Something was wrong…

Bracing herself, she punched connect.

"Your sister…," a low voice rasped. "She's got a gun…"

Sweat beaded on Sadie's neck. The voice. Was it Amelia's? One of her alter egos?

Sadie's fingers tightened around the phone. "Who is this?"

"She's gonna kill Papaw…"

"What are you talking about?" A trembling started deep within Sadie. The voice sounded muffled, gruff. Male? Or a child's? Was this Skid, the teenage alter? Or had a new personality emerged from her sister's tangled mind? "Who is this?"

"I know what you did. What *she* did…" A choked breath. "You…you have to pay."

Thunder rumbled, the first splatter of rain hitting the pavement. A child's balloon floated toward the sky, lost, caught in the wind.

Sadie pressed a hand to her chest. "Amelia…"

But her sister didn't answer. Neither did the voice.

Instead a gunshot blasted the air, and a chilling scream filled her ears. A scream that seemed to go on forever.

Slaughter Creek, Tennessee

Sheriff Jake Blackwood had come back to Slaughter Creek to raise his daughter.

But now that he was sheriff, he might as well take advantage of the office, so he'd pulled the old file on his father's disappearance. Maybe he could finally get the answers he'd wanted for so long. Just being back in town stirred up his need for closure.

And his little girl had been asking questions about the family. He'd like to give her some answers, too.

He opened the file and rifled through the papers. Not much to go on.

Sheriff Bayler had checked out the family house, but there were no signs that Jake's father had packed a suitcase or planned a trip. No bus schedules or plane tickets, no note.

Nothing except that he was gone.

His father had been dating some woman from the neighboring town, but none of them, not him or his brother, Nick, had known her name or how to get in touch with her.

The trail had stopped cold.

He just hoped he wouldn't find out his father was dead.

But what other explanation could there be for him to desert his two sons?

Had his father run off with this woman?

Jake just couldn't make himself believe that, although Nick had accepted it a long time ago. But Jake figured that was because Nick and his father hadn't been close.

Hell, in the back of his mind, he'd even wondered if Nick and his father had gotten into it, and…

No, he wouldn't let himself go there.

But he would find out the truth.

The phone on his desk trilled, and Jake snatched it up. "Sheriff Blackwood speaking."

"You've got to come, Sheriff."

Jake tensed at the sound of the terrified voice on the phone. The minute he'd seen the Nettleton number, he'd known there was trouble. Ms. Lettie had a nursing background and had taken care of Amelia Nettleton for years.

Amelia Nettleton, who had mental problems and did crazy things when she went off her meds.

"What's wrong, Ms. Lettie?"

"Amelia, she got away from me, and then Sadie phoned—"

"Sadie?"

"Yes…," Ms. Lettie said. "She got a call, thought it was from her sister, but it musta been one of the *others*, and then she heard a gun go off, and Sheriff, I'm scared to death...Scared Amelia done killed her granddaddy."

"Wait outside, Ms. Lettie. I'll be right there."

"I will, but hurry, Sheriff."

Jake jogged to the squad car, jumped inside, and tore from the parking lot.

Trees flew past as he steered the vehicle up the winding mountain highway, the car spitting gravel as he veered onto the dirt road leading to the Nettletons' farm. His headlights panned over ruts and trees and then lit up the property ahead, and he silently noted how dilapidated the farm had become as it popped into view in the distance. Rotting fence posts. A broken-down tractor in an unplowed field. Hay that hadn't been cut.

Two quarter horses pranced gracefully in the pasture. Moonlight cast ominous shadows across the front yard, and as he screeched to a stop, he noticed weathered side buildings, a sagging front porch, paint peeling, and an overgrown yard.

Ms. Lettie hobbled from the edge of the porch and hurried toward him. Her gray hair had slipped from its bun and blew haphazardly in the wind, and she tugged a faded shawl around her bony frame as if the garment could protect her from whatever bad had happened here.

"Have you heard anything else?" Jake asked.

Ms. Lettie shook her head. "No...Jesus, this is all my fault. Amelia's been talking out of her head all day. I put her to bed, but she musta got up and snuck out."

"Shh, don't blame yourself," Jake said.

"But I shoulda known something was wrong. I found a bunch of her pills dumped in the ferns yesterday." Her voice cracked, then she glanced at the house again with worried eyes.

Jake removed his weapon from his holster. He hoped he didn't have to use it. "Go wait in the squad car till I return. I'll check out the house."

Ms. Lettie bobbed her head up and down, then clutched her shawl around her shoulders tighter as he raced inside.

The acrid scent of death, blood, and body waste filled Jake's nostrils as he entered. He nearly stumbled over a pile of newspapers. At first glance, he thought someone had ransacked the place. Then he realized that the piles of junk lining the wall to the den were semiorganized.

Walter Nettleton was a hoarder, he'd heard someone in town say. He bought boxes of junk from the salvage store and kept a stockpile of canned food, cleaning supplies, and other necessities in his house as if he were stocking a bomb shelter.

The floor squeaked above Jake, and he held himself still, senses honed as he listened for an intruder.

Then a low-pitched keening reverberated through the dark.

Holding his gun at the ready, he crossed the foyer and scanned the kitchen. Dirty dishes piled in the sink. An empty coffee cup along with other mugs sat on the counter. A cigarette burning in the ashtray. A bottle of Ezra Brooks, half empty. A broken glass on the stained linoleum floor, the bourbon spilled out.

And more piles of junk, file folders full of papers and receipts, supplies, plastic containers, mason jars that looked as if something was growing inside…There was barely a path through the mess.

But no one was on the first floor.

He moved to the left and stepped onto the winding staircase. The pine floors crackled beneath his boots, the acrid odors growing stronger as he climbed.

And so did the sounds. *The woman's cries.*

Sucking in a sharp breath, he paused at the threshold of the bedroom door and peered inside the room, alert for an attacker.

He had seen death before. Death from natural causes—his grandparents, God rest their souls. Other bodies twisted and mangled from car accidents—a teenager. A mother of four. Two truckers on Highway 9. A drunk.

But nothing had prepared him for the sight of the old man's body slumped on the floor beside the four-poster bed. Dammit. Walter's blood and brains were splattered all over the dingy whitewashed walls and the faded chenille spread.

Walter, Sadie's grandfather. Sadie, the girl he'd once wanted with a vengeance. The girl who'd run away from Slaughter Creek and left him when he'd needed her most. The girl with the twin who was so crazy she'd been in and out of a mental hospital half her life.

And judging from the bloodbath and the sight of Amelia crouched in the corner, clutching a sawed-off shotgun, the woman would be going back.

Knowing there was nothing he could do for Walter now, he lifted a warning hand to calm Amelia and slowly walked toward her, stepping over shoe boxes and more bins that held God knew what.

But Amelia didn't seem to notice that he'd arrived.

Then a scream pierced the air, and Jake turned to see that Ms. Lettie hadn't obeyed him and stayed in the car.

She had run into the room and was staring at the bloodbath.

And at Amelia, the girl who looked just like Sadie.

Except Amelia was covered in blood, with a gun in her hands.

———————— ′ ————————

San Francisco

"Your sister shot Papaw, Sadie…He's dead."

Sadie collapsed into the chair in her studio apartment, Ms. Lettie's words vibrating through her skull. Her hands were shaking so badly she had to prop her elbows on her knees to keep from dropping the handset.

Memories crashed back, one piling on top of the other. Her granddaddy stoop-shouldered and leaning on his horsehead cane as he'd been the last time she'd seen him. Sitting on his knee when she was four as he bounced her up and down.

Memories of him holding her while she cried at her grandmother's funeral when she was eight.

Memories of him pacing the floor when she was fifteen and Amelia was out of control. He'd tried everything, he'd said. The preacher at church. An exorcism. Doctors. Pills. Amelia had been institutionalized when she was twelve, then fourteen.

Nothing seemed to work.

When her grandmother was alive, she'd worried that Amelia's illness stemmed from the fact that their parents had been killed in a car crash when the girls were three.

She and Amelia had been in the car when it had happened and had luckily survived. Amelia couldn't possibly remember it…but doctors suggested that the impact of the crash might have somehow caused internal injuries to her brain that they hadn't detected on a CAT scan.

Gran thought it was the trauma of losing her parents so young. That trauma had manifested itself in a splitting of Amelia's personality—she'd adopted new personas to protect herself from the memory, inventing Bessie to play with her when she was three.

Of course, Skid had been surly and had a bad attitude, but he hadn't been violent.

Not until that night.

The night after prom.

The awful night Sadie and Amelia's lives had changed. Sadie could still hear the scrape of the shovel against rock and dirt, see the bulging eyes of the dead man staring up at her as she and her grandfather covered him with dirt…

Ms. Lettie's sniffle jerked Sadie out of her reverie.

"After you called, I got hold of Sheriff Blackwood—you remember Jake," Ms. Lettie said, "he went to school with you—well, he's sheriff now. He found your papaw's body on the floor in his bedroom, and poor Amelia was holding his sawed-off shotgun." Ms. Lettie broke down and started weeping. "Sheriff's with her now."

No...Amelia wouldn't kill their granddaddy. Not Papaw...

But other memories hacked at her consciousness, memories she'd tried so hard to banish.

Memories of meeting the others...

Amelia might not be capable of murder. But her alter Skid was.

"Did you hear me?" Ms. Lettie asked.

Sadie realized she'd zoned out while Ms. Lettie continued her rant.

"I said Jake is gonna put your sister in handcuffs and take her to jail." Tears clogged her voice. "She'll never survive there, Sadie. One of them will kill her, sure enough."

Ms. Lettie was right. Her sister was...sensitive. Delicate.

Sick.

Sadie had to drop everything and go home.

This was what she did—she interviewed traumatized victims for a living. She could handle this.

She'd talk to Amelia. Pretend she was just another patient. Use art therapy and interview techniques to access the alters.

Then she'd find out which one of the people inside Amelia's head had pulled the trigger.

———————— , ————————

That damn Sadie thought she knew everything. Everything about her sister and the alters.

But she didn't know about *him*.

No one did.

He lived inside Amelia's head. He had for years. And he ruled whatever she and the others did.

But they had served their purpose. And now it was time for all of them to go bye-bye.

Yes. One by one, they had to die.

And if Sadie got in the way, she'd have to die, too.

Chapter 2

———————— o ————————

Slaughter Creek

Jake's cop training kicked in. Even though he knew Amelia and Walter personally, he had a job to do, and this was a crime scene now. All personal feelings notwithstanding.

He had to assess the situation. Determine if Amelia was an immediate threat. Secure and process the scene. Take photographs. Call the coroner.

Notify the family.

No, Ms. Lettie was doing that now.

His gut tightened. He actually understood why Sadie had jumped at the scholarship offer she'd gotten for art school, a chance to leave this insanity. That was one reason he hadn't chased after her years ago. That and the fact that he'd been trying to find out what had happened to his father.

He hated to drag Sadie back into her family mess now.

Although there was no other choice.

But first he had to get the gun out of Amelia's bloody hands.

He narrowed his eyes and inched closer, watching for a reaction. "Amelia," he said quietly. "Can you hear me?"

No response. Just a flicker of her eyelashes and a trembling of her hands around the weapon. Her face was ashen, splattered with blood, her pupils wide, fixed on her grandfather's shattered skull and the insides of his brain splattered on the covers of the bed.

Good grief. He wished she didn't look so much like Sadie.

Another step forward and he became hyperaware of every sound in the house. The floor creaked. The wind screamed through the eaves of the old house. The furnace rumbled. Something—a cat or a tree branch?—scratched a windowpane downstairs.

Amelia suddenly startled. Her head jerked sideways as if she heard the sound.

Was he wrong about Amelia being the only one here? Could someone else have been in the house and fired the shotgun?

A siren wailed in the distance. His deputy on the way. Another sound—maybe the screen slapping in the wind? Or someone running out the back door?

Dammit, what should he do? He couldn't leave Amelia here with a weapon.

A mewling sound rent the air, and he saw Amelia's chest heaving for air. A swipe of her fingers across her cheek was meant to push the mop of hair from her face. Instead it plastered the strands down like glue, leaving a trail of bloody fingerprints across her cheek.

"Amelia, please put down the gun," he said in a soothing tone. "It's over now."

She didn't acknowledge that he'd spoken, simply heaved another breath as if it exhausted her just to live. He inched closer and slowly reached toward her. "Just give it to me, and Ms. Lettie can come back in here with you. She's calling Sadie now."

Her fingers were wrapped around the butt of the gun, but slowly she lowered it to her lap. He reached in his pocket, yanked out his handkerchief, and removed the shotgun.

She remained motionless as if someone had literally drained her of life. She looked so pitiful he wanted to wrap his arms around her and assure her everything would be all right.

But the stench of death in the air made him hold his tongue.

Nothing was going to be all right. Amelia was going to jail—or back to the mental hospital. Sadie would be tormented by the publicity, the funeral, and dealing with her sister.

And he would have to do his job.

Find the truth. Get justice for Sadie's grandfather. Lock Amelia up.

Outside, the siren squealed louder. Tires screeched as his deputy's car ground to a stop, tires slinging gravel.

Amelia's keening continued, low and rhythmic, and she stared listlessly into space, as if she were looking at some unknown monster in the room.

As if she had no idea she was the monster who'd killed her grandfather.

As the rental car ate the miles between the airport and the mountains where she'd grown up, Sadie's head reeled with the tasks she faced. Planning a funeral, burying Papaw, digging through his house and clothes.

Seeing her sister again…

For the past two years, Ms. Lettie and Papaw said Amelia had been stable. That the new medication coupled with therapy had kept her alters at bay. But something must have upset her enough to make her violent.

Would she be the hollow shell she'd been the last time Sadie had seen her? The night Sadie knew she had to run away?

The night she'd been sworn to silence.

She passed Whistler's Mountain, her grandmother's adage about the winds of change echoing in her mind. A weather vane stood at the top of the ridge, and Gran had sworn that when the wind changed directions, it was a sign of bad things to come.

The wind was shouting now, the weather vane fighting as it swiveled and bobbed back and forth violently, as if it couldn't decide which way to go.

Hulking pines and hardwood trees flanked the curvy road, throwing shadows across the black asphalt. Wet red, yellow, orange, and brown leaves lay in clumps on the road like a sodden blanket, adding to the dismal milieu, a reminder that winter would soon bring more death. Shades of gray streaked the sky, giving it the ominous look of another thunderstorm on the way.

A coyote howled in the distance, another sign that danger lurked in these rolling hills.

Dangers that she had met before. Some animal. Some human.

A shiver rippled through her, memories threatening. But she was well trained in denial and pushed them to the back of her mind.

A pickup truck pulled out in front of her, and she averted her face, hoping she wouldn't be recognized. At least not yet.

She wasn't ready for the gossip, the stares, the rumors.

Damn, the woods were suffocating. She missed the tranquility of the ocean, the bustling excitement of living in a big city.

The anonymity of walking among a sea of strangers, where no one knew her name.

Here in Slaughter Creek most everyone knew Sadie Nettleton and her crazy sister. Everyone pitied her, even as they whispered behind her back. Their words echoed in her head. They were identical twins, shared the same DNA. Would she turn out like Amelia?

She too wondered, though in her research she'd learned that DID often resulted from severe childhood trauma. Maybe the accident was the cause.

Still, just keeping her family's sordid secrets shamed her. If they spilled out, she'd lose any hope of keeping her sanity.

And her freedom.

The sign welcoming her to Slaughter Creek mocked her. "Slaughter Creek—where the great battle between the Cherokees and the Creeks was fought. Where people now live in peace and harmony."

Laughter bubbled in her throat at the irony.

Her instinct was to turn the car around and head back to the West Coast, far away from the lies she'd guarded for so long.

Far away from family. And from Jake Blackwood, the only boy she'd ever loved.

The boy she'd left behind without any answers.

The boy who had grown into a man and arrested her sister.

Reining in her emotions, she studied the scenery. The town square and antiques store that used to belong to her grandmother loomed ahead, stirring a wave of nostalgia. Even though Gran had been dead for years, Sadie still missed her warm smile and loving hands. She could smell Gran's lilac soap, the pine-scented candles in the shop, the dust and Lemon Pledge she used to make the antique wood shine.

She saw Gran tottering to the door with a plate of homemade gingerbread cookies and tea to welcome her customers. Heard her cry of anguish when Amelia came home as one of the *others*.

Was Papaw with Gran now? Were they looking down from heaven, wondering how Amelia could have taken her own grand-daddy's life?

She slowed the Honda and crawled toward the sheriff's office and the jail. She'd tie up the funeral arrangements, question her sister, and get the hell out again.

Then the past could stay buried where it belonged.

———————— ، ————————

Jake mentally rehashed the last twenty-four hours in his head as he entered the sheriff's office and dropped his notes on his desk.

This was his first homicide investigation, and he wanted to make sure he had the right person locked up.

Not that it appeared there was any question, but still...he had to be thorough for his own sake. For Sadie's. For Amelia's. For Walter Nettleton's.

His gaze fell to his father's file, and he pushed it aside. He'd get back to it later, once this mess was taken care of.

The notes and pictures scattered in front of him called to him now.

First he'd wrangled the gun from Amelia's bloody hands. She hadn't fought him at all. Hadn't screamed her innocence or even acknowledged his presence.

Neither had she cried for her grandfather, or exhibited any signs of grief.

She appeared to be in shock.

When he realized that Amelia posed no immediate threat, he'd called his deputy, then the coroner, Barry Bullock. His deputy had rushed over, and Jake had put him to work examining the perimeter of the house in case someone else had been present before or during the shooting.

Ms. Lettie had pulled herself together and phoned Amelia's doctor, Roy Tynsdale.

Tynsdale had been at a charity fund-raiser for the psychiatric hospital that had treated Amelia for years. The older man had been not only Amelia's doctor but a friend of Walt's, and the minute he received the call, he'd made his excuses and had raced to the crime scene like a bat out of hell.

One look at the bloodbath in the room, and he'd jumped into action, taking Amelia's vitals and making sure she hadn't injured herself.

Jake had searched the rest of the house; then his deputy came in, saying the drizzly rain had made finding any footprints around the house impossible, although he had noticed animal tracks—looked like a coyote's.

He'd have to mention it to Sadie if she decided to stay there.

His mind took a dangerous leap, and he found himself wondering what she looked like now. If she'd changed.

Dammit, of course she had. Ten years had passed since he'd seen or heard from her. She'd earned a degree, was some kind of children's advocate now, and she'd put thousands of miles between them, as if they'd never been friends.

Or lovers.

Meanwhile he'd worked Special Forces and served in Afghanistan, then been shot on a recon mission his fourth year. During his recovery, he had a one-night stand with one of the nurses at the rehab center, then married her six months later when he discovered she was pregnant with his baby. Two months after Ayla was born, Judy had announced that she wasn't cut out for motherhood and signed all rights over to him.

He hadn't known what to do then, so he'd stayed near her for a while, hoping she'd change her mind and at least have some contact with Ayla. But eventually he'd given up. Six months ago, he'd picked up his little girl and moved back to Slaughter Creek to raise her in his hometown.

Sheriff Bayler needed a deputy, so he took the training and signed on. When the man retired, Jake jumped at the chance to run for sheriff.

The job was flexible enough for him to spend time with Ayla, especially since until today, the town had been safe and virtually crime-free.

Jesus. He'd move heaven and hell to keep that little girl safe. And he'd kill anyone who ever tried to hurt her.

He forced his mind back to the investigation, making sure he'd covered all the bases.

He'd bagged the shotgun he'd taken from Amelia to send to the lab, and processed Amelia's hands while Mike photographed the house. At the jail, Ms. Lettie helped Amelia change into clean clothes, and he sent everything she'd been wearing to the lab as well.

So why did he feel as if he'd missed something important? That there was a clue right under his nose that had gone undetected?

The front door to the office swung open, and he glanced up from his desk as Mike loped in. He looked freshly showered and shaven, his short hair still damp and combed back from his forehead.

Rested, when Jake felt like shit.

"Awful quiet in here," Mike mumbled. "I figured Amelia would be pitching fits."

His deputy propped his butt on the edge of his desk, but didn't bother to take a seat. From the look of his dress shirt and his hair slicked back, he obviously had a date later on. Jake fleetingly wondered which one of the ladies in town he was seeing tonight. Not that he gave a damn. Mike could have a corner on the market. Jake's dating days were long gone.

"Doc Tynsdale sedated her," Jake finally said. "He's making arrangements to move her to the psychiatric hospital for observation."

Mike nodded. "Worried she'll off herself?"

Even though his comment hit the mark, Mike's callous tone irritated Jake. "Yeah. She's in a fragile state."

"Fragile?" Mike mumbled. "Holy cow, the freaking nutcase blew her granddaddy's brains out. They should have kept her locked up years ago. She's a menace to this town."

Jake's first instinct was to defend the woman in the jail cell, but there wasn't much he could say; Amelia's history was common knowledge.

Mike growled. "I even heard she'd committed other crimes, but the former sheriff covered up for her."

Jake frowned. That had to be gossip. He hadn't heard about any other crimes.

A low rasp made him jerk his head up toward the door. He hadn't realized it was open.

Sadie Nettleton stood in the doorway, her face pale and tortured.

Dammit. She was even more beautiful than he remembered.

And judging from the pain in her eyes, she'd heard every word his deputy had said.

Chapter 3

—————— ◦ ——————

Sadie had thought that long ago she'd toughened up. She'd built a wall of steel around her so that bitter words and gossip couldn't touch her anymore.

Hearing the stories of abuse, trauma, and illness her patients had suffered had also brought a reality check—she wasn't the only one who'd suffered hard knocks, and she refused to indulge in a pity party.

But the cruel comments about her sister sent her on a fast train back to her childhood, and she felt vulnerable again. Scared. Aching to be something she wasn't and would never be.

Whole again.

But she'd be damned if she'd show it.

A lean blond man with his back to her, the one who'd been speaking, suddenly pivoted. He raised his eyebrows when he saw her, and his jaw went slack. She was accustomed to people's reactions when they saw her and Amelia, especially together, but his was different.

The idiot had just realized he'd been trash-talking her sister.

The legs of the wooden chair the other man was sitting in hit the floor with a whack, then he stood and circled around in front of the desk.

"Sadie?"

Dear God. It was Jake.

His gravelly voice was so sexy and familiar, it nearly brought her to her knees with pain and longing for all she'd lost. All she couldn't have.

For a moment, she couldn't breathe. She simply soaked in the sight of her former lover. That don't-mess-with-me expression. That wide jaw darkened with beard stubble that made him look as if he should have been straddling a Harley instead of wearing a badge. Those high cheekbones that hinted at Native American blood in his background. And that mouth—lips that were thick and full, lips that made her body yearn for them to be on her.

Lord help her. He was even more handsome than she remembered. He'd always been athletic and muscular, but his body had become more defined, muscles more honed. His shoulders had broadened, he'd grown at least two more inches, and his arms were thick as he folded them across his chest.

She'd known him since they were in grade school, and he stuck up for her when other kids teased her because of her sister's erratic behavior. Then in high school, he played football and baseball, and all the girls wanted him. Although he dated around, he never seemed cocky or arrogant like some of the other popular kids.

She had admired him from afar, but never dreamed that he'd go out with her. He had his pick of girls, and dated Brenda Banks for most of his junior year.

That summer, Sadie had volunteered as a counselor at the local YMCA and taught the art camp. He volunteered there as well. He was so kind to the little kids and patient with the middle-schoolers learning to play ball that she couldn't help but fall for him. Still, she kept those feelings secret.

Midsummer, she enlisted the kids to put on an art show for their families and the town.

The day before the show, Jake brought his lunch over to sit with her. He told her that he had no artistic talent, and that he admired her creativity. After that day their friendship grew until one night, during one of the campouts, when the campers were asleep, he walked over to her tent.

They took a stroll in the moonlight, held hands, and talked for hours. He told her he'd broken up with Brenda and that he wanted to be with her. He even made a necklace out of a piece of flint by tying it to a piece of string, then put it around her neck.

They also shared their first kiss that evening under the twinkling stars.

When school started, she figured he'd drop her and go back to his crowd, but he hadn't. And she'd fallen hopelessly in love with him.

But she didn't see love in his eyes now. Instead, his dark coffee-colored eyes were intense, angry, filled with a coldness that made her stomach quiver.

The blond stared at her with avid interest. Curiosity. Then sexual interest. Then as if she were a bug he wanted to dissect.

As if he were comparing her to her sister.

She sighed in frustration. She'd hated that part about being a twin. Everyone thought they were supposed to be just alike. To think alike. To read each other's thoughts.

So they expected her to be crazy too.

Guilty or not, old instincts died hard, and she still had an innate urge to defend her sister.

But Papaw is dead...You have a mission here—to find out exactly what happened. What—or who—drove her to that point.

Sorrow gripped her for a moment at the thought of never seeing her grandfather again.

On the heels of that sorrow, the memory of breaking up with Jake taunted her. His father had just disappeared. Jake had been torn apart.

She'd had to leave because she knew the real story about what had happened to him.

It was the only way to protect Jake and her sister. And herself.

Of course he knew none of that.

And he never could. It would hurt him too much.

But judging from the anger sharpening his eyes, he remembered that she'd walked out. And he hated her for it.

———————— , ————————

Jake felt as if he was eighteen again, with his tongue tied to the roof of his mouth. Dammit, he'd hoped, prayed, that Sadie would have no effect on him now.

He was dead wrong.

The years fell away, and he saw her standing in the rain alone when she was eight and had missed the bus after school. Then the first day of high school, when she'd painted a picture of the sunset in art class that had made him realize that underneath that shy girl lay talent.

The night he'd first kissed her in the moonlight.

She'd been thin then, but feminine and sweet and so stand-offish that most of the guys were afraid to date her. That, and they were afraid of her sister.

The intensity was still there, but she wasn't thin now. Hell no. She'd developed curves in all the right places. Luscious curves that made his groin tighten.

He dragged his gaze from her eyes, torn by the well of emotions in them, and tried to wrestle in his reaction.

She might be Amelia's twin, but they looked nothing alike to him. Sadie had always had a life about her. A spark that her sister hadn't.

Her hair was a curly auburn mess now, spiraling over her shoulders in waves as if it had a mind of its own. Her clothes were nondescript—a plain black skirt, boots, and sweater—as if she didn't want to draw attention to herself.

But those eyes. Those damn blue eyes were like sapphires, dark and full of secrets and...pain.

They always had been.

That anguish had sucked him in once.

Never again.

"Hey, ma'am, you've got to be Amelia Nettleton's sister." Mike's deep drawl jerked him from his thoughts.

Sadie gave a curt nod, her gaze latching onto Jake.

Jake's throat hurt, but he cleared it and took charge. "I didn't know if you'd come or not."

Anger flashed across her face for a brief second before she plastered on her tough-girl face. One he recognized from years before.

He'd thought it had been a mask back then, but maybe she really hadn't given a damn.

She tightened her fingers around her big leather shoulder bag. "Of course I came. My grandfather just died."

"Holy mother," Mike said in a muffled voice. "You even sound like your sister."

Jake wanted to argue with that. Sadie's voice was lower, sexier. Especially when she'd whispered his name in bed.

Sadie shot Mike a belligerent look, then turned back to him. "Where is she, Jake?"

He hated to be the bearer of such bad news, especially considering the way they'd parted. "In the back."

Her expression didn't falter. Calm, cool, collected. Only he knew her better.

He knew she could lose control, that she was ticklish behind her ear, that she liked long, heated kisses and skinny-dipping in the dark at Slaughter Creek.

That she moaned long and hard when she came.

"Tell me what happened," she said, obviously oblivious to his thoughts. "Your version, before I talk to Amelia."

He chewed the inside of his cheek. So that was how she wanted to play it. As if nothing had ever happened between them. As if they'd never been friends. Or lovers. As if he'd never held her in his arms while she'd cried out in ecstasy.

Or cried over her miserable life with Amelia.

As if they'd never talked about running away together.

As if she hadn't run without him.

Well, two could play that game. He could be just as cold. He'd had lots of practice.

He gestured toward the double doors separating the reception area from his office, the interrogation rooms, and the holding cells. "Come on back to my private office, and we'll talk."

She nodded, and he led her to the small space he called his own. She glanced around the office as if noting the details, and he wondered what she was thinking. An apology for the tiny space, the mess, the lack of high-tech equipment, lay on his tongue, but he refused to apologize.

That would mean he cared what she thought, and he didn't.

He couldn't allow himself to.

The desk was a massive, scarred oak one that had belonged to his grandfather, the chair comfortable worn leather. He'd hung his military commendations on the wall, along with his diploma and a family photo of him and his brother, Nick. They were celebrating a win after a high school baseball game. Both he and his brother had been on the team. He was catcher, Nick, pitcher. Nick had hit a grand slam that day to win the game.

That was before his father disappeared and their life had fallen apart. He and Nick hadn't handled it well, hadn't been close since.

Another reason he had a picture of Ayla on the desk. Her sweet, innocent smile reminded him that once in a blue moon, good things did happen.

Sadie didn't comment on the room or even make small talk. Instead she fidgeted, then dropped into the wooden chair across from his desk.

He stopped at the coffeepot on the counter and poured himself a cup of coffee, then gestured an offering to her. She shook her head no, her lips pressed into a thin line.

He slid into his chair, listening for Amelia's sobs. She'd bellowed half the night, until Doc Tynsdale drugged her. But the cell block in the back was silent, and that made his nerves crawl in a different way.

He took a sip of coffee, his gaze locking with Sadie's. She remained all brave face and businesslike. A front? Or was she just trying to hold herself together for her sister's sake? She had to be upset over her grandfather's death.

Still, he wasn't exactly a stranger.

Did she not remember his touch? That he'd loved her once? Did she have any idea of the heartache he suffered when she broke it off with him?

Hell, he'd felt like a fool. All those times he'd driven by her house, by their favorite spot by the creek, pining for her. He'd even kept her painting of Slaughter Creek, although he stowed it in the attic so it wouldn't remind him of her.

She cleared her throat. "Tell me what happened, Jake. Did Amelia really kill Papaw?"

He drummed his knuckles on the desk. "It appears that way."

When she showed no response, he tacked his professional mask in place. He was a lawman. She was the sister of a suspect in a murder investigation.

If she'd talked to Amelia lately or to her grandfather, she might offer a clue that could help them understand this whole damn mess.

Then he could close the case; focus on finding out what happened to his father. She could leave, and he could forget about her all over again.

He had Ayla now. Ayla was the love of his life.

Sadie had deserted him. And so had Ayla's mother.

He would never trust another woman again.

—————————— , ——————————

Sadie dug her fingernails into the palms of her hands to control the trembling. She dealt with traumatized children, with detectives, with DAs, with violent angry defendants, all the time. She could do this. "Jake, please talk to me. I need to know Amelia's condition when you found her."

He hissed a breath, then leaned back in his chair. "When I arrived at the house, I heard crying from upstairs, in the bedroom. Walt was dead, gunshot wound to his head. Amelia was hunched on the floor with the shotgun in her hands."

Sadie gulped. "He was shot in the head?"

Jake nodded. "Yeah. It was a mess. Blood was everywhere…"

Sadie bit her tongue in denial. Her sister might be crazy, but she wouldn't kill Papaw…There had to be another explanation.

One of the personalities in her head?

But why? None of them had ever turned violent toward Papaw before.

To one other person, yes, but not to family…

Something wasn't right.

"Nobody else was there?" she asked. "Maybe someone else shot Papaw and put the gun in Amelia's hands."

"Amelia was the only one in the house." He spread his hands on the file on his desk, covering the folder that probably had photos of the crime scene. "After I took the gun away from her, I searched the house and perimeter."

Then Sadie spotted another file peeking from the stack and noticed it was labeled "Arthur Blackwood." A shudder coursed through her. Oh, God, was Jake looking into his father's disappearance?

Of course he would...

Had he found out anything so far?

A tense second passed, and she tried to pull herself together. "Did my sister say anything?" Sadie asked. "Offer any explanation about what happened?"

Jake shook his head, making a lock of black, wavy hair fall across his forehead. She had the insane urge to sweep it back with her fingers like she used to do. She could almost hear the way he groaned her name when she touched him.

When he touched her...

No, Sadie, you can't go there. Too many secrets. Too many lies.

Besides, hadn't she heard he'd married? She couldn't see who was in that photograph on his desk, but it was probably his beloved wife.

"I tried to talk to your sister," Jake said. "But she just stared into space as if she couldn't see me. As if she was lost in her own world."

Despair threatened...she'd seen her sister like that before. So many times.

Jake continued in a monotone, "I called the coroner for your grandfather, then Ms. Lettie phoned Dr. Tynsdale and he came right away."

"What did Dr. Tynsdale say?"

"That Amelia was traumatized. She'd slipped into a near catatonic state."

"But you arrested her and brought her here instead of the hospital?"

Jake's jaw tightened. "I had to, Sadie. She was holding the damn murder weapon in her hands."

Sadie felt panicky, as if the room, the walls, the years, were closing in on her. As if they were going to shatter and all the secrets would tumble out and she would crumble and blow away like dead leaves in the wind.

But she couldn't let Jake see her weakness. "Are you sure there was no one else around? It probably took you a few minutes to reach the farm once you received the call."

A tense pause. "I did everything by the book, Sadie. My deputy and I searched for footprints and signs of an intruder outside and inside, but found nothing. Then I processed your sister's hands, checked for powder burns, and collected samples. They're at the lab now." He leaned forward, so close she could see the scar above his right eye.

The one he'd gotten defending her in a school fight.

"Your sister fired the gun, Sadie. She killed your grandfather."

Sadie swallowed hard. If Amelia had shot Papaw, she had to have been confused. Thought he was someone else.

Or that *she* was...

"Have you talked to Amelia or your grandfather lately?" Jake asked. "Maybe one of them hinted there was a problem. Something going on between the two of them that could have triggered this."

Was that censure in his voice? Did he think this was her fault for not being here? "No..."

"No, you haven't talked to them," Jake asked, "or no, they didn't mention anything was wrong?"

Guilt clawed at her barely leashed control. Jake's mother had died when he was only four while giving birth to his little sister, who had died as well. Unlike her, he remembered his mother. She had told him that family meant everything.

According to him, Sadie had failed by deserting hers.

If only he knew the truth about his own.

No…he could never know. She would never hurt him like that.

So she squared her shoulders. "No, I haven't talked to either of them in a while. Ms. Lettie had my number and was supposed to call me if there was a problem."

"Well, you're here now. Maybe you can convince your sister to tell us what happened."

He folded his big hands into fists. Sadie saw the faint line where a wedding ring had once been, but it was gone.

Was he still married?

"You know Amelia doesn't belong here, Jake. She needs psychiatric treatment, not to be locked in jail like an animal."

Jake gave a clipped nod in concession. "The doctor is handling the paperwork to have her transferred to the mental hospital. I expect he'll be here shortly."

"Good."

Jake shuffled the file, and the edge of a photograph slipped into view. Blood dotted the carpet in Papaw's room.

She averted her gaze, her stomach revolting.

"Do you want to see your sister now?" Jake asked.

She couldn't avoid it any longer. But fear slithered through her. Persuading her sister to talk meant opening herself to the pain of meeting the *others* again.

But she had learned a lot on the job. She simply had to use her skills to unearth the truth.

Then she could get the hell out of Slaughter Creek before her whole world fell apart around her, and she ended up locked up like her sister.

Chapter 4

———— o ————

D read ballooned in Sadie's stomach, but she reminded herself that she wasn't five years old anymore. She wouldn't fall
apart now. She'd do whatever needed to be done.

Even if it meant lying to Jake.

Or to herself.

Lightning crackled outside, the sky opening to dump rain on
the earth, and thunder pounded against the tin roof. She tensed,
waiting for the trees to start snapping and for sparks to fly. For
the tornado to strike.

"Sadie, are you all right?" Jake asked quietly. "We don't have
to do this tonight if you'd rather wait."

The subtle note of sympathy in his voice almost brought tears
to her eyes. And Sadie hadn't cried in front of anyone in a long
damn time. She had to get a grip.

"No. I need to see her." She took a step toward the door. She
was a professional now, a counselor, an art therapist. She knew
tricks to coax people into opening up. But would they work on
her own sister? "Don't expect too much, Jake. If one of Amelia's
alters has taken over, she might not talk to me."

Jake's eyes held a sliver of compassion, and she realized she'd said too much. "I don't understand the alters. How many are there?"

"Amelia has three personalities. The first one that emerged was Bessie. She's the childlike personality, the innocent little girl. Actually, she appeared when Amelia was little, about three. At first, my grandparents and I thought she was just an imaginary friend, and we went along with it. But when Amelia was eight and she started showing signs that she really believed she was Bessie, Papaw got worried and took her to therapy. Then around age twelve, adolescence hit and Viola, the woman who likes sex, came out. A couple of years later, Skid, the angry belligerent teenage boy, appeared. He claims to protect the others."

"Does Amelia talk to them?"

"When she was younger, she had no idea the others existed. She completely blacked out when one of them took over. It's called a transition state. The goal is to merge the alters into one identity."

"And now?"

"Obviously she still blacks out sometimes, especially during a stressful situation like Papaw's death." Sadie ran a hand through her hair. "Although Dr. Tynsdale said she had progressed to the point that the other three personalities had met and started to talk to each other. Now at times Amelia can hear them. Hopefully she'll become strong enough to stand on her own, and she won't need them anymore."

"So you'll try to talk to each of them and find out what really happened last night?"

"Yes." Déjà vu struck Sadie, and she wanted to run again. To be back in San Francisco, where the temperature stayed the same all year. Where thunderstorms didn't rip apart trees...and lives. Where the ghosts of the past weren't waiting to choke her.

Where no one knew Sadie, and her twin, the crazy lady.

But she couldn't share any of that with this man.

She had to protect Amelia, just as she always had. "But first, I should call a lawyer."

"Tynsdale's already called Chad Marshall."

"Chad's a lawyer now?"

Jake's lips thinned, and she remembered that Jake and Chad had butted heads in high school. In sports and over girls. "Yeah."

"Good. Then I'll talk to Chad."

Jake gave a clipped nod, then gestured toward the door. "Come on, I'll take you to see Amelia now. But brace yourself. I just took over the job, and I haven't had time to clean up the cells."

They turned right out of his office, then walked through another set of double doors. She prepared herself for one of her sister's notorious, tearful outbursts, for a cuss fight from Skid, for the slutty voice of Viola, or for a stranger she might not recognize at all.

But an ominous silence reverberated off the dingy walls.

Two cells sat on the right, two more on the left. Basic prison decor—stained concrete walls and floor. The place reeked of dust, urine, sweat, and the musty odor of cigarettes. An odor she remembered from the first time she'd visited her sister in jail when she was fifteen, and Viola had gotten caught shoplifting lingerie at the local department store.

A thin thread of light from outside had managed to creep through the narrow windows, which had been carved out above eye level and were too small for a person to crawl through.

Jake stopped at the first cell on the right and reached for the keys jangling from the hook on his belt loop. Apparently Amelia had the place to herself.

Through the metal bars, she stared at the pitiful lump hunched on the cot.

The girl who'd played with her as a child and told secrets to her as a teenager lay curled in a fetal position facing the wall, a thin wool blanket pulled over her body and head, as if she'd disappeared inside it.

The sight reminded Sadie of the first time Amelia came back from the sanitarium. She'd talked about how awful it had been, about a friend she'd made named Grace. At first Sadie thought Grace wasn't real, that she was another personality.

But Grace had been real. She'd had as many problems as Amelia, and had been in and out of the hospital just as often.

The keys rattled as Jake twisted the lock, then the metal door screeched open. The concrete floor was cold and bare, the paint peeling off the pea-green walls. Foul words that would make her Gran roll over in her grave had been scratched above the bed, a disgusting figure of two people having violent sex etched above a dingy toilet, which had probably never seen Pine-Sol, much less bleach.

This was what her sister's life had come to. Locked behind bars. Forced to pee in the open and sleep with the roaches on a disease-infested cot.

A plastic tray from the diner next door holding a cold biscuit and rubbery eggs sat on the floor, untouched. The tray was devoid of silverware, and she assumed Doc Tynsdale had ordered Jake not to let her sister have anything that could be considered dangerous or used as a weapon. The first time Amelia had spent the night in a cell, she'd tried to kill herself with a fork, so they'd learned to be cautious early on.

Hysterical laughter bubbled in her throat. Nope. Didn't want the loony lady attacking the cops. Or killing herself before they could convict her and pronounce her death sentence.

"Sadie?" Jake asked quietly.

Her hysteria must have been showing through again. "Do you know what medication Dr. Tynsdale gave her?"

Jake placed one hand on the thick metal bars. "Whatever it was, it must have been strong. She conked right out, and I haven't heard a peep since."

Amelia was so still, so quiet that she looked dead. For a minute, Sadie held her breath, watching for her chest to rise and fall.

She blinked back tears. She wanted her sister back, talking, laughing...normal.

Then Amelia made a low moan, indicating she was alive. At least physically.

Sadie shuffled inside, not wanting to startle her, but worry made perspiration bead on her neck, and her hands felt clammy. "Amelia, it's me, Sadie." Just as she would approach a skittish colt, Sadie moved forward slowly, gauging her sister's reaction. Amelia still didn't respond, so she closed the distance, careful not to make any sudden loud noise.

Tension swirled in the musty air. The metallic scent of blood lingered on Amelia's skin and permeated her hair.

Papaw's blood.

Sadie felt the insane urge to ask for a damp cloth so she could wash the stench away.

Instead she scooted down on the side of the cot. "Amelia, it's me, Sadie. I came to talk."

She gently rubbed her hand across Amelia's back in a soothing gesture, then eased the blanket from her head. Her sister shifted slightly and released another low moan.

Her hair was wiry and straight now, the russet strands tangled and unkempt. Sadie brushed a strand from Amelia's cheek, as her grandmother used to do when she was little, and grimaced at the pale, bruised skin beneath her eyes. "Amelia, wake up and look at me. I need to know what happened with Papaw."

The lump beneath the blanket shifted slightly, and Sadie urged her to roll over. For a moment, the familiar pain and guilt overwhelmed her. Why had Amelia suffered so much, while Sadie, her twin, was normal?

Her lungs tightened at the streaks of dried blood on her sister's cheeks. Amelia's face looked gaunt, and more drops of something brown were splattered across her forehead and chin.

For a brief second, anger at Jake for not letting her sister clean up rolled through her. Then she sucked it back. No emotions here.

Suddenly Amelia jumped off the cot, crouched on the floor in the corner, and hugged her knees to her chest. Her hair fell over the bloodstained cheek as she rocked herself back and forth. Then she began to twirl her hair around her finger.

"Amelia?"

"Who are you?" a tinny voice whispered.

Sadie knotted her hands. That voice didn't belong to her sister, or to the person who'd called her from her grandfather's house to warn her that Amelia was about to kill her grandfather. It was a little girl's voice. A child about three. Sadie had met her before.

"Bessie," she said, "is that you?"

Amelia's head bobbed up and down, then she glanced around the dingy jail cell. "I wanna go home. I don't like it here." A lone tear rolled down her cheek, and she rubbed her nose with the back of a grimy hand. "I heard the chimes. One, two, three... they're singing."

The chimes—the wind chimes or the chimes of the clock? Sadie never was quite sure what her sister was talking about. She had an odd obsession with both, as if they were somehow connected.

"I'm trying to hear them, Bessie," Sadie said softly. "Tell me where they are."

But Bessie began to wail. "He took us in the dark. I don't like it, I hate the dark."

Sadie sighed. Dr. Tynsdale claimed Bessie was the innocent little child her sister had once been before her mind was fractured. Amelia resorted to Bessie when life became too traumatic for her to deal with the ugly reality. When bad things—violence—happened.

And her grandfather's murder was as bad as it could get.

———————— , ————————

Jake watched the scene between Sadie and her sister with a mixture of pity and frustration. If Amelia were any other criminal, he could throw the book at her and not lose a wink of sleep. And if she would snap out of it, confess, and explain why she'd killed her grandfather, it would make his job a helluva lot easier. Then everyone could understand and move on.

But she was a mentally ill woman, one who saw the world through a distorted lens. No telling what thoughts had been in her head when she'd pulled that trigger.

He'd hoped seeing Sadie might shake Amelia back to reality, but judging from the disturbing sound of the little girl's voice, this was one of the "others" Sadie had talked about years ago. He'd never met any of them, but Sadie had assured him they were real.

As real as an insane person could make them.

Sadie's face twisted with anguish for a brief moment. Then, with an effort, she set her face, her expression unreadable.

But when she spoke, her voice was soft and soothing, as if she were speaking to a child.

"Bessie," Sadie said, "do you know what happened with Amelia?"

Bessie frowned, the innocence of a child who was lost behind those steel bars. "She's sad."

"Yes," Sadie said matter-of-factly. "Because of Papaw."

Bessie wrinkled her nose. "This place smells. I want to go home."

Jake jammed his hands in his pockets, looking for signs that Amelia was faking the child persona, but if she was, she was a damn good actress.

"Do you know what happened to Papaw?" Sadie asked.

Bessie swiped at the tears streaming down her cheeks with the back of one hand. "No...Amelia said he's gone."

"Do you remember me?" Sadie asked. "We used to play together when I was a little girl."

Bessie's face brightened. "We had coloring parties."

"That's right." Sadie laid a hand on her sister's arm. She was trying to be patient, act unaffected, but the slight tremble of her fingers as she stroked Bessie's hand betrayed her suffering.

Jake retrieved his cell phone from the clip on his belt and stepped aside to phone the doctor. If Bessie was talking, maybe Tynsdale knew how to reach the alters.

He'd also heard Sadie was some kind of therapist. Maybe she could get Bessie to open up.

Still, he didn't stray so far that he couldn't watch his prisoner. Amelia had shot her grandfather. Who knew what she might do next?

She might attack Sadie. Or she might confess the crime and her reason for resorting to murder.

———— , ————

Sadie wished like hell that Jake wasn't watching. But he was the sheriff, and he'd be peering over her shoulder at every turn. Demanding to talk to her sister. Grilling her to confide whatever Amelia or the alters revealed.

She had to stay on guard every minute she was here.

Her cell phone vibrated in her purse, and she checked the caller ID. Her coworker at the clinic in San Francisco. Probably wanted to know if she was all right.

She'd have to lie to him, too.

"Can we have another coloring party?" Bessie asked.

Her heart broke for the child in front of her. For her sister, who had no idea what she'd done. For what would happen to

Amelia's fragile psyche when she realized she'd taken her own granddaddy's life.

"Yes, honey," Sadie said. "I'll find us some paper and crayons." Maybe Bessie had seen something.

Maybe she would draw a picture and give them some clues as to what had happened between her and Papaw, and who'd fired that gun.

And who had called her with the warning that Amelia was about to commit murder.

Chapter 5

———— o ————

J ake scrubbed a hand over the back of his neck. Sadie had always taken care of her twin. She'd admitted that she never knew who she might find in her house—a child, a scary teenager, or God knows who else.

Back in high school, she'd worried that her sister might get hurt while she was in one of her alter states. She'd never said Amelia was dangerous, though.

But if one of Amelia's alters had killed her grandfather, would that alter hurt Sadie if she pushed her too hard?

The thought sent a bolt of irrational fear through him that had nothing to do with the case.

"Bessie, let me get those crayons and paper." Sadie gestured toward the cell walls. "We can decorate your room here just like we did when we were little."

Bessie's cries grew quieter. "I like to draw."

"Me too," Sadie said. "I have my own studio at my apartment now."

Another pained look darkened her eyes though, making Jake wonder what kind of art she did.

"I want my dolly, too," Bessie whispered.

"I'll bring her next time I come to visit." Then she helped Bessie to lie down on the cot. "Why don't you rest a minute and think about what you want to draw while I get our supplies. Okay?"

"'Kay," Bessie said with a big yawn.

She stretched back out on the cot, and Sadie covered her with the blanket. "I'll be back soon."

"Promise?" Bessie whispered.

Sadie patted her sister's back. "I promise."

Sadie started to walk away, but Bessie lifted her head. "Sing 'Hush,' Sadie. Please."

Sadie paused, then sank back down on the cot and began to sing, "Hush little Bessie, don't say a word…"

Mike appeared through the double doors, and Jake threw up a hand to ask him to stop. It was difficult, witnessing Sadie playing parent to her twin. He doubted she'd want Mike watching the scene, too.

An image of Ayla flashed through his mind, and he grimaced. He'd hated his ex for her selfishness in abandoning their baby daughter. And sometimes he wished Ayla had a sibling to keep her company.

But Sadie might have been better off not having a mentally ill one.

Stop feeling sorry for Sadie. You have a case to wrap up, and she's the key.

Mike gestured toward the front, and mouthed the word *Chad*, and Jake grimaced again. Amelia's lawyer had arrived.

Now he would probably move Amelia to the psych ward, and any chance Jake had of hearing her side of the story would be lost between the doctors, her illness, and the red tape.

———————— , ————————

Sadie felt drained as she stepped from the jail cell. She might be a professional, but this case was her family, her past. Remaining objective was going to cost her, big-time.

Lord help her. She'd forgotten how exhausting it was to pretend everything was okay when *nothing* was okay.

Jake offered a half-sympathetic look, but she avoided looking directly into his eyes. She didn't want any kind of connection to him.

Still, just the sight of him tempted her to fall into his arms. "I need to see Dr. Tynsdale."

Jake nodded. "Thanks for trying to talk to your sister, Sadie."

A streak of anger shot through her. "I'm not trying to get you a confession. I want to see Amelia well, not in prison."

"I didn't mean it like that. I..." Jake shrugged, his eyes troubled. "Never mind. Your sister's attorney is here."

Chin high, she shouldered her way past Jake and headed through the double doors to the front. Mike was on the phone, laughing, leaning back in his chair as if he didn't have a care in the world, which irritated her even more, although she didn't take the time to analyze the reason.

Chad Marshall stood looking out the window at the rain, an expensive-looking briefcase in one hand. Pausing at the threshold, she took a minute to study him. His sandy brown hair was shorter now, combed back from his forehead in a *GQ* sort of way, and judging from his charcoal-gray suit, he must be doing well financially. He also looked trim and fit, but he'd never been the outdoorsy type, so she assumed he belonged to a gym.

The ladies probably loved him.

But she couldn't help comparing him to Jake. Jake was sexier—taller, gruffer, more masculine, with a thicker body, massive shoulders, a firmly set jaw. Not as cocky as Chad. No, Jake's smile didn't come as easy as Chad's, and there was no flirtatious gleam in his eyes. She pictured Jake living in a rustic cabin in the woods, while Chad probably owned one of the modern condos being built on the other side of Slaughter Creek.

For years she'd compared every man she met to Jake.

And none of them had measured up.

One of the reasons she was doomed to be alone.

The other—well, she couldn't think about getting close to anyone else. Or having a family—not when this horrible illness might be passed on to a child of her own.

Chad extended his hand. "Hey, Sadie. It's nice to see you again."

Not how she wanted to be reintroduced, but she shook his hand, her stomach roiling at the idea of having to share details about her sister with him.

All that mattered was that he was good at his job. "Thanks for agreeing to represent Amelia."

"Sure. Everyone is entitled to counsel."

She frowned at his unspoken words. *Even the insane.*

Chad released her hand, then reached inside his jacket and removed a piece of paper. "I have a court order from Judge Horner to move Amelia Nettleton to a psychiatric facility for evaluation and treatment until trial." He gave her a conspiratorial look. "That is, if there is a trial. I think we can cut a deal and keep this out of court."

Meaning a deal to lock her sister away in the mental asylum for the rest of her life.

Sadie shrugged. Maybe that was best. If Amelia was dangerous to herself or other people—and she obviously was—she shouldn't be on the streets. But she'd worked so hard in therapy to earn her freedom and live at home that Sadie wanted to know what had made her snap.

Jake accepted the papers, gave them a perfunctory once-over, then nodded. "Doc Tynsdale going to escort her?"

Chad nodded. "He should be here any minute. Of course, Sheriff, we realize you'll have to accompany Amelia until she's secured."

As if on cue, the front door opened, and Dr. Tynsdale appeared. He looked weathered and frazzled, and his hair had turned white. It was thinning now, and his glasses were thicker, wire rims that sat slightly crooked on his face. He'd also lost weight.

The stark scent of cigarettes still clung to him, indicating that he hadn't given up his habit of chain-smoking Marlboros, something Sadie had always thought was odd for a doctor who knew the risks. Judging from his yellow pallor, he must be paying for it.

"Sadie," he said, then reached to hug her. She stiffened, uncomfortable with his show of affection. That moat she'd built around her heart was built of steel.

"Thanks for coming," she said and eased away.

He gave a conciliatory nod. "You know I'm always here for you and your sister." He angled his head toward Chad. "You have the paperwork in order?"

Chad gestured toward Jake. "It's in the sheriff's hands."

"Good." Dr. Tynsdale adjusted his glasses. "Then let's transfer Amelia to the hospital so she can begin to recover from this ordeal."

Sadie forced herself not to react. She'd been down this road before. Her sister would never completely recover.

Only the broken pieces of her mind remained.

———————— , ————————

Jake pressed a hand to the doctor's chest before he could escape through the door. "I understand about patient-doctor privilege, but, Doc, this is a homicide investigation. I'd appreciate any information you glean from Amelia so we can tie up this mess."

Tynsdale's eyes flattened, the friendly smile he'd given Sadie dissipating. Jake's hackles rose. Good fucking grief. He wasn't the enemy here.

For all they knew, Amelia could have turned that shotgun on herself and committed suicide after she'd killed her grandfather, and he'd saved her damn life.

Besides, how could he put the case to bed if the doctor refused to share what he learned? Amelia certainly wouldn't open up to him.

"Amelia is mentally ill, Sheriff," Dr. Tynsdale said. "Don't expect too much."

Jake gave him a deadpan look. Then the psychiatrist and Chad pushed through the doors to the back. Sadie followed, obviously hoping she could help with Amelia.

The keys jangled in Jake's hands as he brought up the rear, and he remained alert in case one of Amelia's alters suddenly confessed.

Sadie's sister was huddled on the cot, clutching the blanket to her. Was the childlike Bessie occupying her body, or had Amelia returned?

"Amelia, my name is Chad Marshall," Chad said. "I'm a friend of Sadie's and an attorney. I'm going to be representing you. Can we talk?"

Amelia looked up at Chad as if she had no idea who he was. Of course Bessie wouldn't.

Dr. Tynsdale elbowed Chad aside and gripped the bars of the cell. "Open the door, Sheriff."

Jake jammed the key in the lock, twisted it, then pushed the cell door open.

Dr. Tynsdale moved inside. "Amelia, you've been through a terrible ordeal," he said in a soothing tone. "I'm going to carry you back to the hospital so you can rest."

Amelia scooted all the way to the back of the cot. "I heard the chimes...they're singing...no, crying..." She pressed her hands over her ears. "Make them stop."

Dr. Tynsdale placed a hand at the base of her neck and gently squeezed, then lifted her left hand and whispered something low in her ear. The fight drained from Amelia, and she accepted his outstretched hand and stood. Then she shuffled out behind him like a docile child.

Jake followed close behind as the doctor escorted her to the front of the jail, then outside. Chad climbed into his expensive silver Lexus, but the doc and Amelia slid into the back of the squad car.

Rain drizzled down, slapping the pavement, adding a miserable chill to the air. A handful of teenagers milling around the diner next door paused to stare and whisper.

Edith Swoony, sixty and counting, steered her thirty-year-old son Joe across a mud hole. Loony Swoony, the kids cruelly called him, because he was mentally challenged and had never progressed cognitively or behaviorally beyond age six.

Oblivious to Sadie's dilemma, Joe looked up at Sadie and gave her a crooked smile. She returned a smile, as if she felt a kinship with the boy. Jake supposed she did. They had both been the butt of gossip all their lives, and still were.

At least Joe's mother loved him and took care of him. Did Sadie have anyone now that her grandfather was gone? Maybe a boyfriend or lover?

The thought sent a seed of jealousy through him, but he forced it away.

Sadie had a tough road ahead of her here.

But he couldn't be the one to hold her hand. Not with his job and the history between them in the way.

A dark-haired woman in heels and a blue suit strode toward Sadie as she headed toward her rental car. Sadie tensed. She looked like a woman on a mission and had a camera slung over her shoulder. Probably a reporter.

As she grew nearer, Sadie grimaced. It was Brenda Banks from high school. Brenda had been on the dance team, had been beautiful and popular. And Jake's girlfriend.

Everything Sadie wasn't.

Then Sadie got Jake, and Brenda was furious. She made it her mission to make Sadie's life miserable by shunning her when she and Jake were together, and gossiping about Amelia in the school newsletter.

"Sadie Nettleton," Brenda said now in a falsely friendly voice. "Remember me—Brenda Banks?"

"Yes," Sadie said tightly. "How could I forget you?"

Brenda winced slightly, then pasted on a smile. "I'm with the *Gazette* now. I'm sorry to hear about your grandfather."

Sadie murmured her thanks, but Brenda didn't miss a beat.

"I thought you might give me a statement about your sister's arrest. Why did your sister shoot your grandfather?"

Sadie had dealt with plenty of reporters on the job, but this case was personal. Besides, the grapevine worked at lightning speed in Slaughter Creek. It wouldn't matter what she said; everyone in town had already formed his or her own opinion.

Jake stepped up beside her. "Brenda, I told you all I can on the phone. We're not at liberty to discuss the investigation yet."

She batted her eyes at Jake. "I know that, Sheriff, but I thought Sadie might want to give her side. Maybe we could do a personal profile piece about how difficult it is growing up with an emotionally disturbed relative. Might create some sympathy for Amelia."

"I'm not interested, Brenda," Sadie said matter-of-factly. "Now please, move so I can get in my car."

Brenda lifted her camera. "Come on, just a quick photo and a statement."

Sadie pushed the camera away. "Please, Brenda. I just lost my grandfather. This is not the time."

The woman pursed her red lips and feigned a hurt look. Sadie didn't care if she was rude. She didn't intend to have Amelia's or her picture plastered across the news, especially not her sister's. Not in her current condition.

And there was no telling what kind of spin Brenda would put on the story.

"Think about it," Brenda said. "I'm really on your side, Sadie."

Yeah, just like she was in high school.

Jake put a hand to her arm, urging her to move. "I'll let you know when I'm prepared to make a statement. Now please respect Sadie's privacy."

Brenda frowned, then jerked her arm from his grip. "You can't stop me from doing my job, Sheriff."

Jake's dark eyes narrowed. "But I can and will keep you from harassing other citizens."

Sadie wanted to hug him for defending her, but she climbed in her car and shut the door instead while Jake escorted Brenda to her BMW.

Sadie fell in line behind Chad's Lexus and Jake's squad car, their entourage reminding her of a funeral train as they headed toward Slaughter Creek Sanitarium.

The town hadn't changed much in the past few years. Buster's Barbeque still seemed to hold a crowd, as did Dougie's Diner. A new restaurant called the Station had been built beside the rail-road tracks in the center of the town, and a coffee shop called What a Grind sat on the corner. Had Slaughter Creek joined the twenty-first century with its wireless networks and latte and cap-puccino craze?

Ted's Hardware had a new coat of paint and awning. The Roll & Dye beauty parlor occupied the same space catering to the blue-hairs, and a Dollar Store had replaced the Five-and-Dime. In the middle on the other side of the square, the library adjoined City Hall and was flanked by insurance and real estate offices. Next to it, Fiona's Flower Shop showcased vases filled with festive flowers, and at the end of the row of buildings, a day care stood, with a colorful play yard boasting wooden cartoon characters surrounded by a fence.

At the edge of town, the trailer park sat like an eyesore with its add-on porches, weed-choked yards, and battered children's toys.

The Baptist church popped into view, dozens of cemetery markers standing in rows to honor the dead, faded flowers swaying in the wind.

Her parents were buried there beside her grandmother. She wished their images were more vivid, but she'd been so young when they died that all she could remember was her mother's voice singing a lullaby.

The trees rustled in the breeze, and another memory surfaced. She was twelve years old, shivering from fear as she was baptized in the cold creek water behind the tiny white building while the church members sang and prayed with all their might.

At every church service Preacher Bartholomew used to comb the aisles, determined that all the sinners repent before they let Satan steal their souls.

That day, as she'd stood in front of the parishioners in a soggy homemade dress, her Papaw had begged God to spare her the sickness that had possessed her sister's mind. Gran told her afterward that two months before, Papaw had carried Amelia to a shaman for an exorcism because he thought she was possessed.

Amelia had had nightmares for weeks afterward, which left her so terrified she would crawl into bed with Sadie.

Sadie had tried to reassure her sister, but the truth was that she herself lay awake, staring at the ceiling, for hours, unable to sleep, afraid the shaman would come for her. And when she fell asleep, images of a witch doctor dominated her dreams.

Night shadows plagued the winding mountain road, and a horn honked ahead, dragging her back to the present. A rumble of thunder reverberated through the spiny trees and the hollow below as she passed Slaughter Creek, which threaded through the hollow and between the hills. Worn, rotting shanties tilted lopsided on the ridges above, a few newer cabins interspersed among the ancient ones, a sign that maybe one day progress would come to this godforsaken backwater town.

On a cliff above, Sadie spotted a lone wolf silhouetted in the moon's light. Stories of werewolves inhabiting the forests, searching for prey, resurrected more old fears, reminding her of the stories her sister had invented about monsters living underground.

As she rounded the corner, she spotted the sanitarium, an ancient stone structure built miles from nowhere, surrounded by tall, craggy ridges, the creek, and an electric fence, all designed to keep the patients inside and safe.

Not for the first time, Sadie sensed that this building was more of a prison than the jail cell where her sister had just been.

Memories of visiting Amelia in the hospital as a child haunted her, and her stomach began to churn. She could hear the tormented screams of the patients who'd been trapped inside these walls, like the haunting cries of the Indian warriors at Slaughter Creek. She sensed their pain, their disconnect with the world.

Their shame.

Amelia had claimed that Satan was at the sanitarium. That he came in at night and hurt her and Grace. Sadie had told her grandfather, but he'd assured her that Amelia was simply making it up because she didn't want to go back for treatment. And she was delusional.

Jake stopped at the security gate to announce their arrival, and a second later, the massive steel gates opened. Giant oaks flanked the mile-long drive, the crooked branches bowing and overlapping in a tangle to create a natural tunnel.

The parade of cars parked in front of the building, and Jake climbed out. Doc Tynsdale led Amelia inside. Chad hung back, waiting for Sadie, and they walked in together.

Jake and the doctor paused at the receptionist's desk while Dr. Tynsdale conferred with the woman in charge. A moment later, Dr. Tynsdale introduced them all to Mazie, the head nurse, then instructed Sadie to wait while they settled Amelia into a room.

"Let's talk for a minute, Sadie." Chad indicated the sofa in the waiting room, and she claimed a faded plastic chair. He joined her, his hands clasped. "Did your sister explain to you what happened?"

"No." She gnawed on her lip. "How much do you know about her condition?"

Chad shrugged. "I understand she's been ill for some time, that her official diagnosis was DID."

"That's right." She paused, debating how much detail to offer, then decided to fill him in. He needed to know about the alters, in case one of them appeared to him.

Skepticism laced Chad's expression when she finished. "You've talked to them? Seen them?"

"Yes." She gripped her hands in her lap to keep from twitching. "When my sister transitions into one of her alters, she behaves and talks as if she's become that other person. Her voice changes pitch, her mannerisms are different."

Chad's frown deepened. "Dr. Tynsdale can confirm this diagnosis?"

"Yes. He's been treating her for years."

Behind them a loud beeping sounded. Footsteps pounded past, and nurses shouted and began running down the corridor.

Sadie rushed to the desk. "What's going on? Did something happen to my sister?"

The nurse shook her head. "She's settling in a room now, but Dr. Tynsdale had to leave her for a minute. Another patient flatlined."

"Which patient?"

"Grace Granger." The woman rubbed at a knot in her shoulder. "Odd, too. Yesterday she showed signs that she was coming out of her coma."

"When did she go into a coma?" Sadie asked.

The nurse frowned. "Two months ago. She tried to escape one night and fell and hit her head. She had some brain swelling, so they called Dr. Tynsdale in, and he induced the coma to allow her brain time to heal."

"Were they able to revive her?" Sadie asked.

The woman shook her head. "I'm afraid not."

Amelia's head swam with the voices. Ever since Dr. Tynsdale had opened the gates to them, they wouldn't leave her alone.

She was so exhausted all she wanted to do was crawl inside herself and sleep for days. Let the others run her life while she rested, for once.

But someone was talking about Grace. Said Grace was dead.

Grace her friend…the girl she'd met years ago when Papaw first brought her here. She'd heard Grace screaming…Then she'd looked through that glass and seen them tying Grace down… They'd hurt Grace so much…

Bessie's terrified sob echoed in her head. *I wanna go home.*

Shut up, kid, Skid barked. *I'll handle everything.*

I could help, Viola offered in her flirty voice. *Maybe cozy up to that sheriff. He's a looker.* Viola sighed. *I ain't been laid since I don't know when.*

No! Skid shouted. *Your whoring around won't help. Just be quiet.*

Well, you sure as hell aren't helping, Viola hissed. *Maybe we should let Sadie in on what went down.*

Fuck that shit, Viola, Skid snapped. *Nobody's gonna talk to Sadie.*

We have to protect her, Amelia shouted to them all. *I have to tell…*

Tell them what? Viola asked with a nervous twitter. *We haven't done anything wrong.*

Amelia felt as if she were drowning. As if the pain was tearing out her lungs. The others had her by the throat, choking her. She needed air. Needed someone to pull her up from the bottom of the well of darkness. Needed to remember everything.

But she was too weak…*Yes, we have to tell what they did to us in here…*

Won't nobody believe you, Amelia. Skid's sharp laugh rent the air. *'Case you've forgotten, they all think you're cuckoo.*

Amelia sank deeper into the quicksand. Her arms felt heavy, laden. Her lungs wouldn't work.

Skid was right. Papaw hadn't believed her when she'd told him. Neither had Sadie. And Dr. Tynsdale…he said she was delusional.

She closed her eyes. Willed away the image of her granddaddy's blood on her hands.

Voices sounded around her again. That loud, shrill beep. The hospital alarm.

The chimes…

Someone was dead.

Grace. Poor Grace…she'd gone away a long time ago. And she'd never come back.

They'd killed her. Amelia knew it.

The chimes began to ring in her head again. Then the incessant *ticktock*. Over and over and over…

She covered her ears and begged them to stop.

I wanna go home, Bessie whispered. *I'm scared.*

Bessie had a right to be scared.

I want a goddamn drink, Viola muttered. *Where the hell is the vodka?*

Amelia sank lower, so low she couldn't see the light anymore. So low she could drown out the sound of the chimes.

But Papaw's big eyes stared up at her from the black pit.

The crack of the gun firing split the air. And Papaw's choked cry.

Then the blood was everywhere. Splattering her clothes and hands and face. She tasted the coppery taste. Gagged and spit it out. She had to escape.

Had to forget.

Yes, forget. Go to sleep. Sleep for days.

Skid was young and strong and tough. He'd always been there for her. He'd take over for a while. He would protect Sadie and the others.

If he didn't, they'd kill her like they had Grace.

Chapter 6

———— o ————

Irritation plucked at Jake as he stepped back into the waiting room. Chad Marshall was standing way too close to Sadie. The rich jerk thought he could charm any woman he met with his money and fancy car.

And he obviously intended to wield that charm on Sadie.

Not that Jake gave a damn. They could do whatever the hell they wanted.

But he didn't trust Marshall, and he didn't like the idea of Sadie confiding her sister's secrets to the bastard.

Sadie jerked her head up as he approached; she took a step away from Chad. "Jake, that patient who died—Grace—do you know what happened to her?"

Jake shook his head. "No—why?"

Sadie worried her bottom lip with her teeth. "My sister... Amelia knew Grace. Amelia used to talk about her all the time." She paused, glancing at the nurses at the desk.

"A few minutes ago, I heard one of the nurses say that Grace had started to respond. They thought she was finally snapping out of the coma."

"And?" Jake said.

Sadie cut her eyes toward the door. "Amelia said they did bad things to Grace in here. She used to worry about her at night, and she begged Papaw to come and get her out."

Jake frowned. "Did she say who did those bad things?"

"The nurses, doctors, an orderly."

Jake narrowed his eyes. "Did anyone ever file a complaint?"

"No." Sadie lifted her chin. "No one ever took Amelia seriously."

Jake's sigh reeked of weariness. "Because she was ill?"

Sadie nodded. "Yes."

Suddenly a woman in her fifties rushed in, wiping tears from her eyes. She stopped at the nurse's station. "My daughter, Grace, you called...what happened? I thought she was getting better."

Mazie came around the desk and curved her arm around Mrs. Granger's shoulders. "I'm so sorry, Elma. Dr. Tynsdale will be here in a minute to talk to you."

Jake watched as Mazie tried to comfort the woman.

"I feel so bad for her," Sadie said.

Dr. Tynsdale rushed from the back a moment later to meet Mrs. Granger in the waiting room. Jake and Sadie stepped out of the way to give them some privacy.

A few minutes later, Dr. Tynsdale led Grace's mother back to see her body, and Mazie returned to the desk.

"Amelia's going to be upset about Grace," Sadie said quietly.

Jake refrained from comment. Amelia was so out of it, he thought, that he doubted she would even understand that her friend was gone.

———————— . ————————

Footsteps made Sadie jerk her head toward the doorway.

A smile of relief warmed Ms. Lettie's eyes as she rushed toward her. "I'm so glad you came, hon."

She pulled Sadie into a bear hug, her bony frame trembling against Sadie, then leaned back to study her as if she thought the younger woman's presence was an illusion.

Satisfied that Sadie wouldn't disappear, Ms. Lettie clacked her teeth. "How's your sister, sugar?"

"She's settled into a room now, and sedated."

"Did she say anything else about the shooting?"

Sadie shook her head. "I'm afraid not."

"The doctor suggested you all get some rest and let Amelia do the same tonight," Jake cut in. "You can talk to her tomorrow."

Ms. Lettie bristled. "I'm gonna stay right here with our Amelia. I don't intend to leave her side for a second."

Sadie stroked the older woman's arm. "That's not necessary."

Ms. Lettie threw her shoulders back, adding an inch to her height. Still, the little woman was only five feet tall and couldn't weigh more than ninety pounds soaking wet.

"Maybe not. But I can't stand leaving the poor child alone."

Sadie squeezed her arm, her voice hoarse with emotion. "You're so good to her. I don't know how to thank you."

"You know she's like my own. Besides, I'd feel better being here with her in case she wakes up and is scared." Ms. Lettie dabbed at a tear in the corner of her eye. "Especially seeing as this is all my fault. If I'd caught Amelia dumpin' her pills sooner and known she was off her meds, maybe she wouldn't have gone off the deep end, and your Papaw would still be with us."

Sadie swallowed hard. "Please don't blame yourself. You've been a godsend taking care of Amelia all these years."

Jake cleared his throat. "Ms. Lettie, did Amelia mention being upset with her grandfather recently?"

"No, not that I can think of."

"Amelia lived in the guesthouse while Walt stayed in the main house—is that correct?" Jake asked.

"Yes. She liked her privacy. Said staying in the studio made her feel independent, not like she was a burden." Ms. Lettie choked on the last word, then covered her mouth with her hand to stem the tears. "I kept tellin' her she weren't no burden. God gives us all kinds, and we just gots to love 'em however they are."

"How about Walt?" Jack pressed. "Did he mention that he and Amelia had any issues? Had something happened between them? Had they argued lately?"

"Not that I remember." She pursed her lips. "Although two nights ago, I saw Walt with some moonshine. Hadn't seen him like that in a while."

Sadie frowned. Her grandfather had a habit of drinking when he was upset. What had driven him to the bottle that night?

Dr. Tynsdale appeared from the hallway, his hand twitching at his lab-coat pocket.

"Is Amelia okay?" Sadie asked.

"Yes. She became agitated when she heard about Grace's death, but the medication kicked in, and she's sound asleep. Maybe she'll talk to us tomorrow."

"What did you tell her about Grace?" Sadie asked.

"Grace has been ill for some time now. Frankly, it's probably a blessing for her family to finally see her rest in peace."

"What caused her death?" Jake asked.

"The head injury caused swelling in her brain. The coma was supposed to give her time to heal, but there was too much damage," Dr. Tynsdale said.

Jake crossed his arms. "Is the coroner going to do an autopsy?"

The doctor frowned. "I doubt it. We know she took a fall a couple of months ago. One of the orderlies found her on a stairwell landing. Apparently she was trying to escape."

"Were you working here when she was admitted?" Jake asked.

"No. I believe she was first diagnosed a couple of years before Amelia by a Dr. Sanderson."

"What was her diagnosis?" Sadie asked.

"Schizophrenia," Dr. Tynsdale answered.

Mrs. Granger appeared from around the hallway, dabbing at her tears with a tissue. Grief lined her face, but she also looked angry as she strode toward them.

"Sheriff," Mrs. Granger said as she stopped in front of them. "I want an autopsy done on Grace."

Dr. Tynsdale lifted a hand to stroke her back. "Elma, I don't think that's necessary."

The woman stepped away from his comforting hand. "Well, I do, Doctor. Yesterday my daughter was coming out of that coma, and I had hoped to finally take her home with me. I want to know why she suddenly died."

Dr. Tynsdale looked surprised. "I told you—"

"I don't care what you said," Mrs. Granger cried. "I trusted you and all the other doctors that treated Grace for years, and none of you did a damned thing to help her. Then my daughter took a fall in here, you put her in a coma, and she suddenly dies?" She angled her head toward Jake. "That just doesn't sound right to me."

Sadie touched the woman's hand. "I'm so sorry to hear about Grace. She and my sister were friends."

Elma squeezed her hand. "I don't understand what happened to them, but it's time we found out." She gave Jake a pointed look. "You will request that autopsy for me, won't you, Sheriff?"

Jake nodded. "Yes, ma'am, I will."

Sadie considered the accusations Amelia had made. Could some of them have been true?

Jake hated to put the Granger family through the ordeal of an autopsy, but if Elma wanted it, he'd do as she asked. The poor woman had lived with the torment of watching her daughter withering away for years.

He understood the need for answers, for closure, and he would give her that.

Sadie turned to Dr. Tynsdale. "I'll be back in the morning. Thanks for everything."

He nodded, his eyes grave. "I'm sorry, Sadie. I really thought your sister had made progress. That she was stable."

Ms. Lettie sniffled. "I thought so too. But Amelia seems to have a mind of her own—one we may never understand."

That was true, Jake thought. He felt for Sadie. He'd contemplated releasing Amelia into Sadie's custody, but he couldn't do that—not knowing she was dangerous. "At least Amelia can't hurt herself or anyone else while she's in here."

Sadie's pained look made him wish he'd kept his mouth shut.

Ms. Lettie patted Sadie's back. "I went by Papaw's and cleaned up the blood, hon, if you want to stay there. But I have to warn you; his hoarding's been out of control."

"I guess I'll need to clean out some of his things," Sadie said with another flicker of anguish in her eyes. "And tomorrow I want to go over to the studio."

"What you lookin' for, child?"

"I don't know exactly, but maybe I'll find a clue as to what made Amelia snap."

Sadie turned to Dr. Tynsdale. "Did Amelia keep a journal?"

He jammed his hands in his pockets. "I encouraged her to, but I'm not sure you'll find one. Sometimes the alters ripped out pages or added others. Skid also hid it from your sister, and he burned at least two of them that I know of."

Sadie massaged her temple, where a headache pulsed.

"Where was she in her treatment before now, Dr. Tynsdale? I thought she was stable."

"She was better," he said. "She had reached the point where she had met the other personalities. Our next step was to get her to face the trauma in her past."

Sadie knew the event he was referring to, and was grateful he'd kept the family's secret. But he'd had to know the truth so he could treat Amelia.

"After that, I had high hopes she was going to be strong enough to start the unification process."

So she was making progress. "But she stopped taking her meds?"

Dr. Tynsdale frowned. "That's what Ms. Lettie said. Amelia said they stunted her creativity, but they did keep her calm."

"Obviously she needed them." Sadie rubbed her forehead. "Maybe I'll find something at the house to help me understand this mess."

Jake cleared his throat. "If you're ready to go, Sadie, I'll follow you home."

Sadie tensed. "You don't have to do that."

He gave her a flat look. *No personal involvement. By the book. Don't think about her staying in that house alone, not where the bloodbath took place.*

"Your grandfather's house was a crime scene. I wouldn't be doing my job if I didn't confirm that it's clear before you spend the night."

Emotions flickered in Sadie's eyes, and for a moment, Jake thought he read disappointment. But the moment disappeared so quickly, he was sure he'd imagined it.

"But first, let me speak to the orderly who found Grace," Jake said. "With Mrs. Granger asking questions, I need to find out exactly what happened to Grace."

Sadie stayed with Dr. Tynsdale while Jake crossed the waiting room to the nurse's station. He tapped on the glass. "Hi, Mazie. Can you tell me who found Grace Granger the night she took the fall?"

Mazie tapped a few keys on the computer, then glanced back up. "It was a temp named Herbert Foley."

"Is he on duty now?"

She shook her head, her short curls frozen in place with hair spray. "No, as a matter of fact, he only worked here a couple of weeks."

Jake shoved his hands in the pockets of his jeans. "Do you have an address or phone number where I can reach him?"

She jotted down the number and address on a sticky note and handed it to him. "Never met an orderly like him," she said in a low voice.

"What do you mean?"

"Something funny about him," she said. "He...was punctual, almost rigid in the way he handled patients, but he kept to himself. And he signed out that night right after Grace's fall and didn't show up for work the next day."

Jake frowned. "Thanks, I want to talk to him myself." He called the man's number, but the number was no longer in service.

"His number has been disconnected, Mazie." He gestured toward the security cameras. "How about surveillance cameras in the hall where she took the fall?"

Mazie shrugged. "Got cameras in the hallway but not the stairwell."

"Can I see the ones in the hall?"

She nodded, then pressed a button and spoke into it. A second later, a security guard appeared and escorted him to the central security center of the hospital. Jake explained what he wanted to see, and the man pulled up the feed for the specified day and time.

Jake's pulse hammered as he watched Grace Granger, clad in her hospital gown, running down the hall. She looked dizzy, disoriented, swaying back and forth, holding on to the wall. Twice she glanced over her shoulder as if she was looking for someone. Her choppy breathing echoed in the silence. She looked terrified, but he didn't see anyone following her.

She finally reached the end of the hall and threw open the door. A well of darkness bathed the interior of the stairwell, and then the camera lost sight of her.

A second later, a scream sounded.

Had one of the guards or staff been trying to catch her because she was trying to escape?

Was she trying to escape? Or was she running from someone who wanted to hurt her?

Mazie's comment about the man echoed in his head. Foley had seemed off, had left work the night Grace had fallen, and hadn't returned.

Had Grace, in her drug-induced state, simply fallen?

Or had he pushed her down the steps?

But why would Foley hurt her?

Jake requested a copy of the tape, waited while the guard copied it for him, then tucked it inside his jacket.

When he made it back to the waiting room, Sadie was pacing.

He gestured toward the elevator. "Let's go. I'll follow you home."

She started to argue, but his warning look must have caused her to change her mind.

The questions were still ticking in his head. Foley had supposedly found Grace at the bottom of a stairwell, where she was injured and unconscious; then the next day he stopped working at the hospital, without an explanation.

Jake checked the address in his pocket.

He'd stop by Foley's after he left Sadie. For Elma's sake, he'd make sure Grace's fall had been an accident and nothing more. Then he'd request that autopsy on Grace, to placate her mother.

And when Sadie accepted that her sister was a killer, she could leave.

Then his town could return to normal, and he could forget Sadie once again.

Regret that she had not come back to see her grandfather filled Sadie as she drove back to the farm. If she had visited, maybe she'd have figured out that something was wrong.

Images of her and Amelia playing in the yard flashed back, followed by a sequence of memories like a movie clip. Papaw teaching them both to groom the horses. Stacking hay in the back of the old wagon, then hitching it to his tractor and taking them for a hayride.

Decorating the farm for the pumpkin patch sale every year, then helping him collect money from customers who drove from miles around to ride in that same wagon and pick their own pumpkins.

The good memories were peppered with the bad, though. Each year she'd begged to carve a scary-faced jack-o'-lantern, but he always refused, saying Halloween was for Satan believers. Still, he'd sold the pumpkins to other families who did the same, which hadn't made sense to her.

He had loved the horses as much as she did. When she was six, he'd taught her how to ride. When her sister was in one of her more coherent states, she'd ridden, too.

One day stuck out in her mind. She'd been fourteen, and Amelia had just returned home from another hospital visit.

In a rare sisterly moment, they baked cookies together, then packed a picnic and rode on horseback to the creek.

They picked wildflowers, and Amelia sang songs and danced in the wind. Then Amelia laughed as they chased fireflies and caught them in a mayonnaise jar. Sadie had thought she finally had her sister home. Sane.

But then the wind picked up, and Amelia suddenly went still. She'd heard the chimes, she said. The chimes were calling to her, crying her name.

In a split second, Amelia vanished, and Skid appeared. He shoved Sadie into the creek, spooked her horse so it ran off, then rode away, leaving her alone.

Sadie sprained her ankle and had to walk half a mile to get back to the farm. By the time she made it, she'd been in pain, soaking wet, and chilled to the bone.

Of course, Amelia had remembered none of it.

It was one of her "nowhere" nights. Nights Amelia couldn't remember where she'd been or what she'd done.

Nights Sadie would never forget.

But she wasn't that frightened little girl anymore. She was a professional adult who would not let the insanity in her family break her.

The farm slid into view, and she grimaced. Her grandfather had aged, and she'd assumed he'd hired help to keep the place up. But judging from the overgrown pasture, the rotting fences, and the rusty, broken-down tractor in the field, he must have let them go long ago.

She pulled down the oak-lined drive, well aware that Jake was following her, relieved to see Chance trot toward the barn and a roan roaming the pasture as well. She wondered who had been taking care of the horses, but was glad to know that her grandfather hadn't sold them.

Parking the Honda beneath the detached overhang, she climbed out, retrieved her suitcase, and drew a deep breath as she faced the house. Jake swung the squad car to a stop and dragged his big body from the vehicle. Gravel crunched as he strode up beside her, and she had a sudden urge to reach for his hand and hold on tight.

But she tucked her hands in her pockets instead.

"Let me check the house first, then you can go inside."

Sadie was determined to remain strong. "That's not necessary, Jake. I can take care of myself."

"I'm sure you can." Jake slanted her a dark look. "But sometimes crime scenes draw curiosity seekers, vandals, teens who want to gawk."

"All right," Sadie conceded, but only because she didn't want to admit that being home spooked her. That ghosts were waiting for her...

He followed her to the front door and waited as she unlocked it. Sadie stepped aside and let Jake enter first. As soon as he flipped on the light, she noticed the clutter Ms. Lettie had mentioned. The hallway was full, the den overflowing with newspapers and assorted junk.

Jake strode through the downstairs, then climbed the steps two at a time while she waited in the foyer.

A musty odor permeated the air, and dust coated the furniture and walls, but the scent of bleach wafted down the steps. Ms. Lettie had said she'd cleaned up the blood.

Still, the stench of death lingered, and the empty house was a reminder of the violence that had happened.

And that her grandfather was gone forever.

"It's clear," Jake said as he jogged down the steps.

Sadie shoved her suitcase against the wall, suddenly feeling very much alone.

Jake's gaze skated over her, dark and intense. A sliver of something that looked like concern, like the old Jake, flashed in his expression, making her stomach twist. "Will you be all right here alone?"

Sadie lifted her chin. "Of course, Jake. I've been on my own for a while."

Anger replaced the concern in his eyes, making him look cold and harsh in the dim light. "Fine." He handed her his business card. "But here's my cell phone as well as the office's direct line, in case you need it." He headed toward the stairs. "Let me know what you learn from your sister."

Sadie shrugged. That depended on what her sister told her. She didn't intend to give Jake any rope to hang her with.

———————— , ————————

The thought of leaving Sadie alone in that big old house bothered Jake more than he wanted to admit. Dammit, she had left him high and dry years ago, and hadn't contacted him since.

But pain had darkened her eyes when she was with her sister. Pain he remembered seeing years before.

No wonder she'd run.

He pressed the accelerator, the rambling farmhouse fading in his rearview mirror as he headed toward home.

It probably wouldn't have worked if they'd left Slaughter Creek together, anyway. They'd only been teenagers, acting on hormones and lust. He'd been looking for…he didn't know what. A way to please his father?

No, he'd never done that.

And being with Sadie sure as hell hadn't helped. In fact, his dad had warned him to stay away from the whole damn Nettleton bunch.

Arthur Blackwood had been a tough-ass military man all the way. Rigid. Focused. Had trained him and his brother, Nick, to be the same way. And he'd had plans for them both to follow in his footsteps.

Until he'd left them without a word.

And Sadie…what had she been looking for? A way out of Slaughter Creek.

She'd found it, too. Only it hadn't been with him.

Was someone waiting for her back in San Francisco?

Not that it mattered to him. He had Ayla and his job, and that was all that mattered.

But he had promised Grace's mother some answers, so he turned into the entrance for the duplexes where Foley lived, noting signs of children in the tricycles, wagons, and bikes in the yards. Several units had cars parked in the driveways, and he checked the address, frowning when he noticed it was dark.

No vehicle in the driveway either.

He grabbed his flashlight, then strode up to the door and rang the bell. Shabby sheers hung on the front windows, and when no one answered the door, he shone the flashlight inside. Dammit, no sign anyone was inside.

Crickets chirped in the background, and a dog barked. He strode around the side of the duplex and looked in another window. No one there either.

And no furniture.

In fact, the place looked as if it had been cleaned out.

Mazie had said Foley was a temp, so Jake phoned the only temp agency in town. When it rolled to voice mail, he left a message for someone to call him about Herbert Foley.

He noted a rental sign in a neighboring yard and called that number.

"Logston's rentals," a man said.

"This is Sheriff Blackwood. I'm trying to locate one of your tenants."

"What's the name?"

"Herbert Foley."

"Foley...oh, yeah, a big guy, paid in cash for a month, then cut out."

Jake frowned. "Do you know where he went?"

"Nope, didn't even stay the whole month."

"When did he leave?" Jake asked.

"Just a minute, let me check my notes." Papers shuffled. "Okay, here it is. I went by to talk to him about mowing the yard the middle of the month, but the neighbor said she saw him load what little furniture he had in a van and drive away around midnight one night." He gave Jake the date, and the hairs on the back of Jake's neck prickled.

Herbert Foley had left town the same night Grace Granger took her fall.

———————— , ————————

He watched Amelia sleep. Her chest rose and fell in an even rhythm, all thanks to the drugs. But inside her head, the voices wouldn't die.

His was going to be the loudest.

He had lived inside her for years, ever since she was a child. But he'd lain dormant, bided his time, listened to the others bicker and argue, watched them torment Amelia.

Waited till the time was right for him to take over.

That time was near.

But not yet.

He had work to do first.

"The chimes are singing," he whispered in Amelia's ear. "Hear them cry…"

Amelia moaned and rolled over, restless.

Laughter bubbled inside him. Yes, his voice was going to be the loudest.

And when he finally killed her, it would be the only one she heard as he put her in the grave.

Chapter 7

———— ◦ ————

Mixed emotions pummeled Sadie as she watched Jake drive away.

How many nights had she lain awake dreaming about him after she left Slaughter Creek? Remembering the feel of his hands on her and the way he'd made her body hum with arousal.

Remembering the tender way he'd held her and the understanding in his eyes when she'd confessed her guilt over being the normal twin—her fear that one day she might be afflicted by the same mental disorder that had plagued Amelia. Her desire to run away from the terrible personality switches that had come upon her sister without warning as a teenager.

And then that one horrible night...

She tried to banish the memory, but the wind howled through the eaves of the old house, resurrecting it from the dead. It was dark tonight just like back then, a moonless night, the clouds obliterating the stars, rain pinging off the roof.

She locked the front door, willing the past to stay buried, but a tree branch scraped the window, and upstairs the floor creaked. The attic...

Was someone here?

No…Jake had searched the house. It was just the ghosts. Ghosts that had haunted her for years. They followed her everywhere she went.

She staggered away from the front door and collapsed on the steps. Her head was swirling, the room spinning, the darkness engulfing her and pulling her into that bleak tunnel she'd tried so hard to escape.

Then she was back there. Back to that haunting event.

She had just come home from prom. She and Jake had made out at Lovers' Peak, whispering promises to each other about forever and marriage and babies. But even as they made plans, she had an uneasy feeling that something was wrong at home.

She'd never been able to read Amelia's fragmented mind, but she'd had premonitions at times. And this one swept over her so strongly that she felt ill and asked Jake to take her home.

He wanted to come in with her, to make sure things were all right. But her grandfather had been drowning himself in the bottle too much that week, and she insisted Jake leave. The shame was too much.

She took off her prom dress and put on jeans, desperate to talk to Amelia and make sure she was okay. She hadn't been asked to the prom, and Sadie felt guilty about leaving her. But Amelia encouraged her to go, had said she was okay.

And she had seemed okay. She'd been taking her medication and had appeared stable for weeks.

Then Amelia's shrill scream pierced the night.

Amelia was in the guesthouse, in the studio they built when she and Amelia were teenagers so Amelia could exorcise her demons on canvas. Therapy, the doctors had said.

Her artwork was characteristic of whatever personality had assumed her body for the day.

Sadie began to shake, the fog of that night weighing so heavily on her that she had to fight for breath. It was as if she were reliving it all over again.

She raced outside...saw a man stumble from the guesthouse. Not just a man...Jake's father...he was hurt. Bleeding...

Then Amelia...no, not Amelia.

Skid.

Amelia was gone, and Skid was there. She could tell it was him because he was wearing that baseball cap. And he was limping.

Skid claimed he'd torn up his leg in an alley brawl.

He swung the rifle up and pointed it at Arthur Blackwood.

"No, put the gun down," Blackwood pleaded.

Sadie screamed and ran toward Skid, then grabbed his arm and tried to stop him from shooting.

But he fired, and Blackwood hit the dirt on his knees. He was coughing, choking, in pain.

Blood spewed...sprayed the ground...

Sadie ran to him. She had to help him.

But it was too late. Blackwood collapsed. Blood was everywhere. Coating him. Soaking his clothes. His face was pale. His eyes blank.

A cry caught in Sadie's throat.

Blackwood was dead...no...he couldn't be. Not Jake's father.

Skid was wild, cursing, swinging at her. "Get the fuck off of me, Sadie. I had to stop him!"

"Please go away, bring Amelia back," Sadie cried.

"You stupid bitch, I'm protecting her!" Skid yelled.

Then he turned on her with an evil glint, and fear paralyzed her. He was going to hurt her, too.

Trembling, she turned and ran toward the house. She had to get Papaw. Wind beat at her, and the sky unleashed a torrent of rain as she opened the door.

Papaw was slumped in his recliner, snoring softly, his breath reeking of whiskey. She raced over and shook him to wake him up.

"Papaw, help...Amelia killed Jake's daddy...I mean Skid did, he shot him."

Papaw jerked awake, his eyes wide in shock, then he staggered up and threw the bottle aside. "Jesus God."

The next few minutes blurred as they ran outside. Then she and Papaw were arguing. She wanted to call the sheriff. Papaw said no, they'd lock up Amelia forever.

Sadie was crying...she didn't want to lose her sister. Didn't want to lose Jake.

Jake...he would be devastated.

She grabbed Papaw's arm. "We have to call anyway. Jake has to know..."

But Papaw slapped her.

Slapped her so hard she hit the dirt on her knees and tasted her own blood. Then he shook her, yelled at her, told her everything would be okay. She just had to do as he said.

The next thing she knew, the sound of rain splattering the truck reverberated around her. Papaw had turned into someone else that night, too. He claimed he had to protect his granddaughters. He couldn't send Amelia to jail.

Sadie wiped at tears as she and Papaw and Skid loaded Blackwood's body into the back of Papaw's pickup truck.

Her stomach churned as the wheels rumbled over the graveled road by the river. Then the sound of the river gurgling...the mill spinning...Papaw's shovel hitting rock as they dug the grave...

Sadie jerked herself from the past, but the images remained in her head like a horror show, playing over and over.

What had Skid meant? He was protecting Amelia from what? From Arthur Blackwood?

And why had Blackwood been at the house?

She'd asked her grandfather, but he insisted they never speak about that night again.

And they hadn't.

But she'd never forgotten it.

She couldn't erase the cold, blank look of Jake's daddy's eyes staring up at her from the grave.

And she couldn't forgive herself for not calling the sheriff and being honest with Jake.

———————— , ————————

Jake took the shortcut to his house and made it there in five minutes. When he moved back to Slaughter Creek, he'd bought a fixer-upper not far from town and the local elementary school so he could pop home for lunch whenever possible.

And now Ayla had started kindergarten. His little girl was growing up.

He parked in front of the blue Victorian—Ayla had picked out the color—then stowed his gun inside his jacket and climbed from the sheriff's car. Thunder rumbled, the gray clouds rolling across the sky hinting at a storm.

He strode up to the back door, jangling his keys as he walked. He wished to hell he could erase Sadie from his mind. But she'd looked so small and lost, all alone in that house, that he couldn't.

Hell, he could smell the blood, the death, still lingering in the halls. How was she going to sleep there tonight?

Trying to smother the image, he forced himself to focus on what he needed to do as he let himself in the back door. He had to find out more about Foley and check on that autopsy of Grace Granger.

He didn't like the fact that Grace had fallen in the stairwell with no witnesses to corroborate that her fall was accidental, or the fact that the man who'd found her in the stairwell had disappeared.

The scent of homemade vegetable soup wafted through the kitchen as he entered, then the sight of Ayla, all smiles and pigtails as she jumped up from the kitchen chair and ran toward him, welcomed him with the kind of heartwarming greeting that could make a grown man cry.

Dammit, he'd been a hard-ass like his father until Ayla had come along.

"Daddy, Daddy, Daddy!" she squealed. "You're home."

His heart swelled with love as he scooped her into his arms. "Hey, baby girl."

She planted sloppy kisses all over his jaw, and he ate it up, squeezing her until she squirmed and wiggled and begged to get down. "Come see my grilled cheese. Gigi let me make a smiley face on it!"

Jake forgot about the murder and Sadie and Grace Granger as he lost himself in praising Ayla's creation, a face she'd carved into the bread before Gigi grilled it.

He gave the older woman who'd practically adopted the two of them as her family a grateful smile. Gigi, short for grandma, had lost her own son in a car accident before he'd had the chance to marry and have kids.

After Jake's mother's death, Gigi had babysat him and Nick while his father worked and when he went out of town. Which, come to think of it, had been often.

His father was in the reserves, so periodically he was called away on missions.

For a while after he disappeared, Jake had figured that was where his father was. But when he'd asked questions of the military, he'd come up empty.

Fortunately, when Jake had returned to Slaughter Creek, Gigi had eagerly agreed to watch Ayla and cook for him. In exchange, he gave her room and board and paid her salary and insurance. But he had a feeling she would have cared for Ayla free, just to have someone to love.

Gigi dipped him a bowl of soup and gestured toward the cornbread, and he nodded. "Thanks, it's been a long day."

"I know this case is difficult," she said, carefully avoiding the word *murder*. "And I heard that Sadie Nettleton is back."

Ayla plopped into her chair and took a bite of her sandwich. "Who's Sadie?"

Gigi gave him a questioning look, and he shrugged. "Someone I used to know a long time ago, pumpkin."

Ayla twirled a strand of her auburn hair around her finger, an endearing habit Jake had grown to love. "Is she pretty?"

Okay, his little girl definitely was growing up too fast. "Not that that matters, but yes, she is."

"Is she coming over to play?" Ayla asked.

Jake fought a smile. Now she was back to being his kid again. "No, sweetie. Her grandfather passed away, and she's here to bury him."

Ayla's face fell. "Oh."

Gigi placed a bowl of fruit on the table, sidetracking Ayla's probing as she dug into the strawberries.

But questions lingered in Gigi's eyes. Jake avoided those as well. The sweet woman had tried her matchmaking skills on him with the daughter of a friend. She thought he needed a wife, a mother for Ayla.

But he had insisted he was fine on his own.

Sadie's face flashed in his mind. Truthfully, he'd probably never gotten over her. Sadie had been the love of his life.

Back when he was foolish and young and believed in love.

Now she had her own life, and so did he. And the two would not mesh.

He wolfed down the bowl of soup and cornbread and, for the next two hours, lost himself in being a father.

The best part of his life. After Ayla's bath and a bedtime story, he tucked her in and hugged her tight.

"I love you, Daddy," she said with a gap-toothed smile.

He tweaked her nose. "I love you, too, sweet pea."

She scrambled beneath her pink ruffled coverlet, squeezed her baby doll to her, and closed her eyes. For a moment, Jake couldn't breathe as he watched her drift into innocent sleep.

For a little girl without a mother, she seemed surprisingly happy. Only occasionally did she question where her mother was, and why on Mommy & Me day at school, Gigi came instead.

Emotions clogged his throat, and he made himself leave the room. Gigi had retreated to her suite to read or watch TV, and he went to his office to check his computer for messages.

His cell phone buzzed before he could settle down, and he checked the number. A local one. The Grangers.

Sucking in a deep breath, he punched connect. "Sheriff Blackwood."

"Sheriff, it's Elma, Grace Granger's mama."

"Yes, Elma. I was going to call you tomorrow. I requested the autopsy, like you asked."

A sniffle sounded over the line. "Thank you, Sheriff. I...saw Grace the day before, and she squeezed my hand, and opened her eyes and said there was something she had to tell me."

"What was it?"

"She said they were hurting her in there."

"I'm sorry, Elma, but Grace did have some mental problems."

"I know that, but she also had some broken bones over the years. Once, it was her wrist. They said she twisted it too hard when they had to restrain her."

"Go on."

"Another time she broke her ankle. They said she tried to escape that time, too."

Jake grimaced. It was hard to tell if those injuries had been incurred as they'd said, or if there had been abuse. "Did you report it?"

"I talked to Sheriff Bayler, but he just wrote it off like everyone else. Said that she made it up."

"Did you question the staff? Did anyone see her being hurt?"

Elma made a choked sound. "No, but I still wondered, especially when she never got better in there."

"Why was she hospitalized to begin with?"

"Gracie cried all the time. She talked about people dying and made up stories, and her tests at school came back low."

"So she had emotional problems as well as learning difficulties?"

"It started when she was about three. I took her to that free clinic for her shots when she was a baby—thought it was a blessing, I did. But a few months after that, she started acting funny. Just stopped talking."

Jake considered her comment. Great strides had been made in diagnosing childhood problems, especially autism. For God's sake, once kids with hearing impairments had been dubbed mentally retarded.

Had Grace been autistic, or could she have suffered other problems that hadn't been detected?

"By the time she was twelve, she was starting to have paranoid delusions," Mrs. Granger said. "Dr. Coker, the doctor at the free clinic, said they could help Gracie at Slaughter Creek Sanitarium, so we took her there. But once she went in, she just shut down, and she never came out of her shell."

Jake frowned. "She didn't improve at all?"

"No, she got worse and worse." Elma's voice cracked. "So bad they even tried some of that treatment they called progressive for the time."

"What kind of treatment?"

"Well, they never really said. Except there were rumors about shock treatments and drugs that no one wanted to talk about."

Ayla's sweet face taunted him. If it were Ayla, he'd do anything to keep her safe. To help her if she was sick.

Elma had trusted the doctors, but they hadn't helped. In fact, she thought they'd made Grace worse.

And now Grace was dead.

It was up to him to find out the truth.

He scrubbed a hand through his hair. Just as it was up to him to unearth the reason Sadie's sister had killed her grandfather.

He assured her he would let her know what he learned, then ended the call.

Wanting to find answers for Elma, he logged on to his computer and signed in to the police database. Then he entered Herbert Foley's name. Three Herbert Foleys showed up. One was a ninety-year-old man in Memphis who'd never even had a parking ticket in his life; another, a sixty-two-year-old paraplegic.

The third was a thirtysomething man who had died six months ago of liver failure.

Jake frowned and decided to check a few other places. He searched databases for personal care assistants, medical technicians, and other related jobs, but found no Herbert Foley.

He phoned the hospital to ask if they had a photo of Foley, but the records department told him no. The man had presented a certificate showing his qualifications to be a patient care worker. Jake asked for the certificate number and where he'd received it, but when he checked, he found that the certificate bearing that number belonged to a woman.

Considering what he'd learned and the timing of Foley's departure from the hospital, suspicions rose in Jake's mind. Who was this man Herbert Foley? Did he really exist?

And if he'd stolen this woman's certificate, what else had he lied about?

Was Grace's accident really an accident?

But again, who would want to kill Grace Granger?

He studied the storm clouds choking the light from the sky. At least Sadie was safe at home tonight.

But what if somewhere in Amelia's crazy ramblings there had been some truth?

What if someone had hurt Grace?

What if they'd hurt Amelia too?

Sadie jerked awake, her heart racing.

The curtain was flapping in the breeze. A chill engulfed her, and her nerves fluttered.

She hadn't left the window open.

Wishing she had a weapon, she grabbed her cell phone from the nightstand, then scanned the space. At first glance, the room was empty.

But she sensed someone watching her, as she had for months.

The floor squeaked above, the furnace grumbling. She'd forgotten how much this house creaked and moaned, like an old person with brittle bones.

Then something skittered across the floor above her. Was someone in the attic?

Maybe a squirrel?

A squirrel hadn't opened her window...

She slid from the bed, stuffed her feet into her slippers, and rushed to shut the window. Her pulse pounded as she glanced at the guesthouse.

A light was burning, visible through the window.

The guesthouse had been dark when she went to bed.

Then a shadow moved, the silhouette framed in the window. Dear God. Someone was there now.

Chapter 8

———— o ————

Sadie gripped the phone with sweaty hands. She couldn't confront the intruder on her own. She had to call for help.

Jake…

He was the first person that came to mind.

God, she hated to call him. But he was the sheriff, and except for Ms. Lettie, she'd lost touch with everyone else in Slaughter Creek ten years ago.

Striving for calm, she took a deep breath and punched in his number. While she listened to the phone ring, she pushed the curtains aside, then peered out at the shadow in the guesthouse, moving through the living room.

What was he doing?

Searching for something?

Suddenly the shadow grew still. Turned toward the window.

Paused, as if he knew she had seen him.

For a long, tense minute, they seemed to lock gazes.

Then the shadow disappeared. Sadie blinked, wondering if she'd imagined it.

Jake's deep voice jerked her back to the phone call. "Sadie?"

Sadie grabbed her robe and yanked it on. "Yes, Jake. I'm sorry if I woke you—"

"What's wrong?"

Sadie glanced through the window again, scanning the door to the guesthouse, then the surrounding property. Where had the intruder gone?

"Sadie, dammit, talk to me. Are you all right?"

"Yes," she said in a shaky voice. "But someone was here... in the guesthouse. I woke up, and my window was open—then I looked out and saw a light in the studio."

"Stay inside with the door locked. I'll be right there."

The phone clicked off, and Sadie tried to compose herself. She flipped on the overhead light, hoping to chase the ghosts away, then slipped into the hall and flipped on that light as well.

The walls shook with the force of the wind, the house groaning again, and she tiptoed toward the steps, pausing every few feet to listen in case the intruder returned and tried to break into the house.

He'd seen her watching him.

What had he wanted in the studio?

Shivering, she tightened the belt on her robe and slowly walked down the steps. The possibilities clicked through her head.

Maybe some teenagers had heard about Amelia's arrest and thought the farm was vacant, so they'd broken in to steal what they could sell.

Or maybe it was some vagrant looking for a warm place to hide for the night.

Nothing else made sense.

She flipped on the light at the bottom of the steps, blinking to adjust her eyes as she scanned the den. The room adjoined the kitchen, and looked empty as well.

Papaw's gun case was open, the shotgun missing. The one that had killed him...Amelia had taken it.

Now Jake had probably confiscated it as evidence.

Headlights from a car beamed down the graveled drive from the road, and she exhaled the breath she'd been holding.

Jake was here. Everything would be all right.

Relief flooded her, reminding her of all the times he'd come to her rescue during her senior year. No matter how late it was or how upset she'd been, he'd rushed over like a knight in shining armor.

Guilt assaulted her. When he'd needed her, she'd left and never come back.

He cut the lights, coasted to a stop in front of the house, then unfolded his big body from his car. Sadie unlocked the front door and met him on the steps.

Jake's hair was ruffled from sleep, the shadow of his beard stubble darkening his jaw. Her heart stuttered. He looked fierce and protective and commanding as he strode up the steps.

"Are you okay?"

Sadie nodded and gestured toward the guesthouse. "I think he's gone, but I'm sure someone was inside."

Jake removed his gun from his holster, and she followed him to the front door, her heart in her throat. The wind sent the chimes clinking and tinkling from the porch, a grating sound that tested Sadie's nerves.

When she reached for the doorknob, Jake shook his head and gestured for her to wait behind him. Then he pushed open the door and played a flashlight across the interior of the living area. The guesthouse was small, a living room/kitchen combination, bath, and one bedroom. The art studio occupied the left side of the living area.

Sadie's gaze automatically strayed to the studio, where several canvases were stacked and scattered along the floor. One in particular drew her eye.

It was a dark, morose painting of twin girls who looked just alike. One sat in the corner facing a drab gray wall. Red paint depicting blood was splattered across the floor, the wall, and the little girl's hands.

The other girl was locked in a cage with bars surrounding her, a sea of black engulfing her.

Sadie's chest throbbed. The painting looked eerily similar to the one she had sketched at her own home, the one of her trapped in Alcatraz.

But Amelia had never been to her apartment or seen it.

Could they possibly have more of a connection than she'd thought?

Jake quickly scanned the interior of the guesthouse, noting the assortment of hodgepodge furniture, the macabre paintings, and the kitchen, which was cluttered with a mixture of ceramic cats, posters of heavy metal bands, and erotic art.

Nothing went together, yet Jake realized that in a strange way, it made sense. Amelia hadn't lived here alone; her alters shared the same house.

He bypassed a sinister, almost frightening rendition of two little girls, one in prison, the other shrouded in darkness and blood. Images of Amelia and Sadie?

Shaking off the disturbing thought, he eased into the bedroom and bath to check them out.

At first sight, no one was inside.

For a moment he studied the room, hoping to gain insight into Amelia and the reason she'd shot her grandfather. His conversations with Sadie about her DID diagnosis echoed in his mind. Amelia'd had three alters: Bessie, a three-year-old child; Skid, a snarly, sinister teenager who protected her; and Viola, an older woman who liked booze, men, and sex.

Stuffed animals filled one corner shelf, and baby dolls were seated at a child's table, with a tea set arranged as if they were having a tea party. Obviously Bessie's.

On the opposite wall, heavy metal posters with skulls and crossbones covered one section, and a collection of crudely carved wooden pieces—all birds of prey—filled two shelves. A collection of books on guns were stacked on the floor by a guitar and men's boots. Obviously Skid's.

The oak four-poster bed was covered in a bright-fuchsia-and-green-striped coverlet, and a lacy teddy and a pair of sheer black thongs were draped over its foot.

Hmm...Viola's.

Then a random thought nagged at him. Amelia was a young woman—could *she* possibly have had a boyfriend or a lover?

Tucking his gun back inside the holster, he spied several perfume bottles on the vanity, an assortment of makeup, a hairbrush, and a pack of condoms. All things a sexually active female would own.

His mind took a detour down that road. What if Amelia or Viola'd had a boyfriend? Maybe her grandfather had found them together. Maybe he'd tried to break up the relationship, or accused the man of taking advantage of Amelia in her diminished mental state? Amelia—or the man—could have killed her grandfather, so they could be together...

But if that were the case, what had happened to the lover?

Had he run?

Jake crossed the room, looking for a computer or day planner on the small desk, but found neither. Then he noticed some kind of wooden box protruding from beneath the bed.

Sadie must have spotted it at the same time, because she cleared her throat just as he reached for it.

"Let me have that. It's Amelia's," Sadie said behind him.

Jake tensed, remembering how panicked he'd been when Sadie had called.

She looked pale, shaken—vulnerable—in her robe and slippers. The instinct to pull her into his arms and comfort her hit him.

But he had to keep his distance.

So he stooped to retrieve the box anyway. But Sadie grabbed it before he could. "Please, Jake, this is a keepsake box." She gestured toward the rose carved on the top. "Gran gave them to us on our sixth birthday. Mine had a lily on it, and Amelia's the rose."

Jake frowned. For some reason, he sensed, Sadie was afraid of what that box held. Which made him even more curious.

"You called me for help, remember?"

Apprehension flickered in her eyes. "Because of an intruder, not so you could snoop through Amelia's personal belongings."

"I'm the sheriff; it's my job to snoop," he said with an edge to his voice. "In fact, I probably should have searched the guesthouse already."

"Why?" Sadie asked. "You seemed certain that Amelia killed Papaw. You said she had the gun in her hand, blood all over her."

"That's true," Jake said. "But I would like to understand her motive. I'd think you would, too."

Sadie hugged the box to her. "I do, and I plan to talk to her and find out."

"Then let me see what's in that box. It might be love letters from some boyfriend who helped her kill your grandfather."

Sadie shook her head. "I doubt that, Jake. It's probably some therapeutic assignment the doctors gave her."

"We can't find out what was going on in her mind unless we explore every angle—"

"If there's anything in the box that explains what drove my sister to shoot Papaw, I will tell you. All right?"

Jake knew he shouldn't relent. That he could get a warrant and confiscate the box.

But Sadie had lost her grandfather, and her sister was locked up for murder. Why would she hide anything from him?

It wasn't like she could prove Amelia innocent...

Still, it looked as if someone had broken into her house. "I could stay tonight," he offered.

Sadie took a step back. "I...don't think that's a good idea."

Jake suddenly realized Sadie thought he was suggesting more. Obviously she didn't want to rekindle a relationship with him. "Nothing personal, Sadie," he said, his voice tight. "Just in case the intruder returns."

"No," Sadie said quickly. "I've been on my own for a long time, Jake. I'll be fine."

But she didn't look fine. She looked nervous and wary. And if he didn't know better, there were secrets in her eyes.

———————— · ————————

Guilt crowded Sadie's throat for playing off Jake's sympathy, when she had lied to him for years.

But what if Amelia had stowed something in the box about the night Jake's father died?

She didn't understand what exactly had happened between Blackwood and her sister, only what Skid had told her—that Blackwood had hurt her—but he'd never explained what he'd done. Bessie claimed he'd hurt her, too, but she'd resorted to crying, and they couldn't get anything more from her.

And Amelia couldn't remember.

She sighed. She might never know the truth about why Amelia had killed Papaw either. Unless she or Dr. Tynsdale could persuade her or one of the alters to open up.

Still, she needed to sort through this box alone. To spend some time with Amelia and try to understand her.

To keep their secret, because telling Jake now would only hurt him.

If only she knew why his father had come to their house that night.

Arthur Blackwood had served as the hospital administrator at the sanitarium. He had access to the patients, could come and go at will without question. But he wasn't a doctor or a counselor. Still, he'd known Amelia from the sanitarium.

And he'd known that Sadie was dating Jake.

Every time she was around him, he'd made her feel uneasy. He scrutinized her as if he were trying to pick her apart.

Dissected her to see if she were demented or sick like her sister.

He hadn't approved of Jake dating her. She'd heard him mutter warnings to Jake when he thought she'd left the room. Of course, half the town had been skeptical of her because she was Amelia's twin sister.

Jake's phone buzzed, startling her, and he checked the number. "Let me get this. It's the medical examiner."

Sadie nodded and carried the wooden box to the living area while Jake stepped out onto the porch. She traced a finger over the rose, remembering the day her grandmother had given the boxes to them. They were having a mother-daughter day at school. She had wanted her mother with her so badly that day.

Then Gran had dressed in her Sunday best. She had bought her and Amelia pretty dresses and attended the luncheon with them.

Later, when they got home, she'd given them the keepsake boxes, each with a photograph of their parents inside.

Sadie opened the box, looked at the picture, traced her finger over it. Would her sister have been normal had it not been for the accident that had taken her parents' lives?

A second later, Jake stepped back inside, and she snapped the box shut.

Jake checked his watch. "I'm going to meet the ME," he said.

Sadie noticed the early-morning sunshine flickering through the sheers. "It's about Papaw's body?"

Jake shook his head. "No—Grace Granger. But he did say he plans to release your grandfather to the funeral home this morning, if you want to start making arrangements."

Sadie's mind raced with the tasks ahead. How was she going to make the arrangements all by herself?

Jake laid a gentle hand on her shoulder. "Are you okay?"

Sadie nodded. Of course she was. She had to be.

"I'm fine—thanks for coming out. I'll call the funeral home in a little while."

"If you need help with the arrangements, with…anything, call me."

Tears burned the backs of her eyelids, but she blinked them back. How could she keep relying on Jake when she'd kept such a horrible secret from him?

He deserved to know the truth…to have buried his father. To have said good-bye.

But the truth—the fact that she'd lied to him—would only hurt him. And it wouldn't bring his father back.

So she watched him leave, and waited until he'd driven away before she opened the box again.

She examined two of the envelopes and recognized her name on the outside. Curious, she quickly rifled through the stack. They were all written on stationery from the mental hospital.

And all addressed to her.

But she'd never seen them.

Nerves tingled along her spine as she removed one of the envelopes and began to read.

Dear Sadie,

Please help me. Get me out of here. You don't know what they do to us at night. It hurts…

Tears blurred Sadie's eyes as the writing changed. At first it had been Amelia's, then a childlike scrawl. Then Skid's angry slanted writing. Then Amelia's again.

She snatched up another letter and skimmed it. This one from Skid, full of anger, hate, vows of revenge. A plan to help Amelia escape.

Sadie choked back a cry.

Amelia had been pleading for help.

She swiped at the tears streaming down her face and read another letter and another. All desperate cries.

Some described being punished. Tortured. Kept in a dark room for days. In a closet. A box. Being deprived of food and water. Of light.

Dear God. Were these ramblings from her twisted mind, or had something happened to Amelia in the sanitarium?

———————— , ————————

Dammit, Sadie had found that box.

He had looked for it before, and he'd almost had his hands on it when Sadie spotted him. What if she figured out what was going on?

He gripped the knife handle and studied the guesthouse. Maybe he should finish her off tonight.

No...that would draw suspicion.

And he didn't need anyone, especially the law, sniffing around.

Especially since his assistant had fucked it up with Grace. And Jake Blackwood was asking questions.

Hell, he'd keep an eye on Sadie like he always had.

And if she got out of hand, or if Amelia spilled her secrets, he'd take care of both of them.

Chapter 9

———— ◦ ————

J ake stewed over leaving Sadie alone as he drove toward the medical examiner's office, but he'd checked the guesthouse, and whoever had been inside was gone. Of course, the intruder might come back, but most likely not during the day.

Not now that Sadie was there, and whoever it was knew the house wasn't deserted.

Several instances of teens breaking and entering to steal computers and other small electronics had been reported in town, and then there were the curiosity seekers who might have heard about the murder and come snooping to see if anything valuable had been left behind. Others might just be interested in seeing the scene of the murder.

But what if it was something else? What if Sadie was in danger?

Who would want to hurt her, though?

It wasn't as if he didn't know who'd killed her grandfather. It had been Amelia—he'd caught her red-handed.

A truck pulled in front of him, nearly cutting him off, and he considered flipping on his siren, but honked his horn instead. He didn't have time to chase down the jerk. A minute later, the truck turned down a side road, and he drove on. He had to get to the morgue.

A couple of early-morning joggers made their way along the sidewalk as he wove through town, and the diner had already opened, with truckers and workers staggering in for breakfast and coffee. Jake phoned his deputy to tell him to open up.

"I'm going to the morgue about the autopsy on Grace Granger," he told Waterstone. "Call my cell if anything comes up."

"I've got it covered," Mike said. "I'll do rounds in the town before I go to the office."

Jake disconnected, then drove through the doughnut shop and ordered a cup of coffee to go. Candy, the twenty-three-year old bundle of flirtatious energy, threw in his usual glazed dough-nut and waved to him as he rushed on.

She'd acted interested in him before, but she didn't stir his blood. Not like Sadie Nettleton did.

He sipped his coffee. He'd thought ten years would have diminished his lust for her, but it hadn't. One look at her, and he was wound up so tight his body was in knots.

Irritated at himself, he glanced at the clock, mentally taking a reality check. Ayla would be getting up for kindergarten soon, munching on her Cheerios and arguing with Gigi about whether to wear her hair in pigtails or a braid for the day.

He hated that he was missing it. Hell, he'd learned to do a pretty damn good braid himself over the last few months.

Maybe if he got the results from the ME and everything looked good, he could make it home and give her a kiss before she caught the school bus. A little sugar from his darlin' would remind him that his future was about being a father.

Not looking for some woman to complicate their lives.

Forcing his mind back to work, he wolfed down his dough-nut as he veered onto the street leading to the main hospital. The morgue was housed in the basement, so he parked, took a sip of his coffee, then carried it with him across the parking lot.

As customary, he checked in at the desk when he entered, then rode the elevator to the basement.

Dead bodies were just bodies, he told himself. Except that Sadie's grandfather, a man he'd known most of his life, lay in one of the drawers, his life drained away. Although Sadie tried to act tough, she was grieving.

Her quiet display of courage and strength was one reason he'd fallen for her so long ago. Her home life was hell, but she put on a brave face and stood up to the taunts the kids threw at her, even defending her sister to the point of being pushed around. He had stepped in a time or two himself to shut them up.

The metal door screeched as he opened it, the dim light casting shadows on the gray walls. No surprise the morgue was housed in the oldest section of the hospital, tucked away as if the people were already forgotten.

Dr. Barry Bullock, a rail-thin thirtysomething guy with a receding hairline and an obsession with bugs, odd biological evidence, and particulates, shoved his protective mask up and waved him into the exam room.

The stench of blood, body waste, formaldehyde, and other chemicals permeated the room, forcing Jake to take a deep breath and blow air out to expel the stench.

"What is it?" Jake asked. "You made it sound as if you found something important, something abnormal."

Dr. Bullock adjusted his goggles. "I don't know exactly what happened to this woman, Sheriff Blackwood, but judging from the samples and tests I've run so far, there is nothing normal in what I've found."

"What do you mean by that? What was the cause of death?"

"That's complicated." Bullock led him over to a series of metal trays lined up on a table, then gestured toward a computer screen and a series of X-rays. "Certainly Grace had problems stemming from her head injury, but everything I've discovered so far only raises more questions."

Jake scrubbed a hand through his hair. He'd yet to finish his coffee and hadn't had a shower, and this man was talking in circles. "Just get to the point, Dr. Bullock. What happened to Grace Granger?"

"She sustained several broken bones over the years." Dr. Bullock pointed to the series of X-rays. "Bone breaks start healing immediately. There's a rounding or blunting of the edges of fractures that occurs as early as a week after a break. A callus begins to develop six weeks after injury to cover the broken ends. It's irregular in shape, raised, with a disorganized surface. A healed bone never looks the same as the sleek, smooth unbroken bone. It will always look different on X-rays. It has a mild lumpiness where the break was." Dr. Bullock lifted his gaze to Jake. "It makes me wonder if there might have been some family abuse."

Jake frowned. "Her mother mentioned that she had broken her wrist and ankle in the hospital."

"That might explain the broken bones, but there's something else that disturbs me."

"What is that?"

"There are also scars on the cranial skeleton that indicate that she was subjected to severe shock treatment, and there are surgical scars indicating that she had a lobotomy."

Jake grimaced. "I thought that happened only in science fiction novels."

"No, at one time the lobotomy was practiced to treat patients with aggressive problems and other disorders. But"—Bullock paused—"most states banned its use in the 1970s."

Jake contemplated Bullock's comments. If the lobotomy had been banned, why had it been used on Grace?

Anger mounted inside Sadie as she realized the implications of the letters she'd found. Poor Amelia had tried to reach out to her, tried to tell her that something wasn't right in the hospital.

But she'd been selfish, lost in her own world of pain and shame, and had trusted the adults around her to take care of her sister.

Had Papaw seen these letters?

Probably not. They had been in Amelia's treasure box. She'd have to ask Amelia about them. Why had no one mailed them for her? Or why had Amelia never mailed them herself?

A noise sounded outside, limbs cracking beneath the weight of the wind. She stuffed the letters back inside the box. She hadn't read them all, but she would.

But first she wanted to see her sister.

She wondered if Ms. Lettie knew about the letters.

Ms. Lettie had worked at the sanitarium as a nurse before retiring to tend to Amelia. The first part of Amelia's therapy had focused on the doctors earning her trust and making her feel safe. For some reason, Amelia had latched onto Ms. Lettie as that safety net. Since then, she'd been like family.

And Dr. Tynsdale had treated Amelia since she was a child. He and her grandfather had been good friends long before he'd taken Amelia on as a patient.

If someone had mistreated her, one of them might know.

Although if they had detected foul play, why wouldn't they have reported it or told her?

Because you were a child. And as soon as you came of age, you ran...

She knotted her hands together. Well, she wasn't a child anymore. And she didn't intend to run.

She had come home for answers, and she refused to leave until she got them.

Tucking the box beneath her arm, Sadie strode to the door, but she paused to study Amelia's dark, morose painting. Maybe there were clues in her sister's artwork. Some piece Amelia had painted recently that would give Sadie an idea what had gone on in her sister's head when she'd taken Papaw's gun and pulled the trigger.

If she'd hidden this box, there might be other things hidden in the house, too.

Curious, she quickly searched the kitchen, then the bedroom and closet, but she didn't find anything unusual. Just more paintings that her sister must have painted when she was depressed.

Knowing that Amelia needed her, she closed and locked the door, then hurried over to the main house, raced inside, and placed the box on the desk in the den. Then she threw on a pot of coffee and jumped in the shower.

Her cell was ringing by the time she dried off, the screen displaying her work number. She ignored the call, dressed, then sent her boss a quick e-mail, telling him she needed at least a couple of weeks at home to sort through her grandfather's affairs.

Her clients and patients would have to wait. Parker, her coworker, had offered to take over her caseload. She had hedged before she'd left, but she sent him an e-mail asking him to cover for her.

Anxious to leave, she ran a brush through her hair, tucked a couple of the letters in her purse to show Amelia, then hurried out to her rental car. As she started the car, she surveyed the property, the driveway, the woods beyond, in case someone was watching.

Early-morning shadows flickered in the trees, winter setting in.

Mentally, Sadie ticked off her tasks for the day.

After she met with Amelia, she needed to go to the funeral home. Sometime today she'd stop at the grocery store and stock the cupboards as well. Most of the canned goods her grandfather had stockpiled had expired.

She also wanted to find out what Jake had learned at the autopsy. If Grace's autopsy proved suspicious, then Amelia's mindless rantings might have held some truths.

The problem would be sorting them out from the delusions.

Her phone buzzed again, and this time she saw Brenda Banks's name on the screen. She was not going to answer that and give Brenda fuel for the fire. God knows she'd been misquoted enough in her work to be wary of any reporter. They could twist your words and give them an entirely different meaning, especially when they were taken out of context.

The sun struggled to fight its way through the gray clouds as she drove to the sanitarium. Winter was definitely making its arrival; the dismal chill of an impending snowstorm lurked on the horizon. The bare branches of the trees swayed, the last leaves drifting down to create a blanket of brown, orange, and red.

She passed a few cars, but once she turned off toward the sanitarium, the road was virtually deserted. Towering trees shadowed the road, giving her a chill as she crossed through the security gates. Barbed wire topped the fence surrounding the property, again making her think more of a prison than a hospital, the spiked turrets of the ancient stone building adding to its gloomy, ghostly look.

As a child, she'd heard rumors that those who'd died within these walls haunted the place, and she'd been terrified to visit Amelia. She'd begged Papaw to bring her sister home, but he'd promised her that the doctors were helping Amelia.

After seeing those letters, she wondered if that was true.

She tugged her coat tighter around her as she strode up to the front door. When she entered, the sound of heels clicking on the floor echoed. Then she heard someone crying down the hall.

Tension thrummed through her, but she crossed to the nurse's station and asked to see her sister.

The nurse glanced at the visitor log, then stood. "Dr. Tynsdale is supposed to check on your sister this morning, but he hasn't arrived yet."

"Good—I'll stay with her until he gets here," Sadie said. "I need to speak to him about my sister's condition." If anyone knew about Amelia's treatments, he would.

The nurse escorted her down a hallway into a more secure ward where an armed security guard stood watch. Sadie assumed this was where the dangerous patients were kept, and noted that three of the rooms were empty, two locked and dark.

"This is your sister's room," the nurse said.

Sadie braced herself as the door opened. Ms. Lettie was sitting by the bed in a recliner, her head lolled to the side as she snoozed. Amelia's arms and legs were in restraints, her face pale as she writhed in her sleep.

Ms. Lettie stirred, lifted her oval wire rims and rubbed at her eyes, then adjusted her glasses and looked up at Sadie. "Mornin', child."

"Good morning. Did you rest at all?"

The little woman nodded. "Some. Amelia settled down and slept a good bit, too."

"Good." Sadie turned to the nurse. "I'd like the restraints removed so I can visit with my sister."

"We'll have to get Doc Tynsdale's permission."

Sadie nodded. The nurse left, and Ms. Lettie pushed herself from the chair. "I'm glad you're here."

Sadie removed two of the letters from her bag. "Last night I found a box of letters under Amelia's bed. They were addressed to me, but they were never mailed." She showed her the envelopes. "Did you know about them?"

Ms. Lettie rubbed at her lower back as if it was aching. "No, darlin'. Maybe it was just something she wrote for herself, for therapy."

"I thought about that," Sadie said.

"Anyway, if your Papaw had seen them, he wouldn't have sent them to you. He wanted you to have a good life, a normal one."

While her sister suffered in silence.

Had Amelia thought Sadie'd deserted her?

Sadie chewed her bottom lip. "Amelia made some accusations in the letters that worry me." Of course, that was the perception of a confused mind.

"What kind of accusations?"

"That she was given some strong psychopharmaceutical drugs."

"Well, hon, of course she was. She was exhibiting signs of schizophrenia."

"But it sounds like more than that." Sadie hoped she was wrong. "In one letter she describes being in pain, as if she was subjected to shock treatments."

Ms. Lettie sighed. "It was a long time ago, Sadie. Doctors don't know what they do now. They were desperate, trying new things."

Sadie frowned. "What are you saying?"

"That they did try electroshock therapy." Ms. Lettie took Sadie's hands in hers. "But, honey, they had to. Your sister was lost, and your papaw was desperate."

"So he knew about it?"

She nodded. "Yes. You know ECT is still used today in certain cases."

"Yes, I know." Although she wasn't sure she agreed with the practice.

She stroked her sister's hair, brushing it away from her cheek. The treatments sounded radical, but her grandfather wouldn't have agreed if he hadn't believed Dr. Tynsdale was trying to help Amelia.

Maybe her sister had been getting closer to unification.

But would her grandfather's murder set her back?

———————————

Someone was asking questions. Questions none of them wanted to answer.

He let himself inside the doctor's custom-designed cabin, pausing to listen. Sanderson had done well, had accumulated wealth and success.

All thanks to their arrangement.

But he'd called in a panic last night because of Grace Granger. Because of Amelia.

Irritation needled him. Damn doctor. Death had been knocking at his door for months, but the fucker had hung in there. Even worse, he'd decided to grow a conscience.

Opening old wounds wouldn't help anyone. They'd done what they had to do back then.

And he would do the same now. He would protect their secrets.

He slid the knife from his pocket and tiptoed toward the man's office. Relying on years of training, he knew how to move silently. How to carry out orders.

He knocked, then let himself in, a smile creasing his face when Sanderson pivoted in his desk chair.

Sanderson had aged dramatically since their last meeting. Lines fanned his eyes and mouth, his yellow-tinted skin was sagging, and his breathing sounded labored. He was on his deathbed...or close enough to it that a few days or weeks wouldn't matter.

"What are you doing here?" Sanderson said, then broke into a cough.

He gave a nonchalant shrug. "I came to make sure you kept our agreement." Thankfully, the other doctor involved, Jonas Coker, had already succumbed to dementia.

A chuckle caught in his throat. Of course, *he* had helped that along. And he'd considered drugging Sanderson. But he'd decided to make this one look like a random robbery in case police suspected a connection between Sanderson's death and Coker's illness...

Sanderson raked a hand through his thinning white hair. "You have to stop this. No one else needs to get hurt."

His body tightened, coiled like a viper ready to strike. "I agree."

One lunge, and he sliced the man's throat. Sanderson yelped, his eyes widening in shock as blood spurted down his neck.

Then the doctor's body jerked, and he collapsed face-first on his desk.

Relief spilled through him. One more problem taken care of.

He quickly tossed the office, took the man's wallet and Rolex, then cracked open his safe and grabbed his cash. Sanderson's iPad, smartphone, and computer went into his bag as well. All to make the scene appear to be a home invasion/robbery.

Now he just had to search the cabin and get rid of any incriminating evidence Sanderson had left behind.

Chapter 10

———— o ————

Questions filled Jake's head as he studied the results of the ME's report. "I still don't understand why doctors would perform a lobotomy on Grace Granger if the practice had been banned."

An eagerness lit the ME's eyes. "In the first half of the twentieth century, the lobotomy, also known as a leucotomy, was used to treat serious mental disorders. António Egas Moniz was actually awarded half of the Nobel Prize for Physiology in 1949 for his discovery of the therapeutic value of leucotomy in certain psychoses. It was used in the forties and fifties, but its use was reduced once the antipsychotic drug chlorpromazine was introduced in 1954."

Jake frowned. "How old was Grace when she died?"

"Thirty."

"How long had she been at the sanitarium?"

The ME consulted the file. "She started treatment when she was five years old. But she wasn't hospitalized then. According to her medical records, she received outpatient therapy and was diagnosed with schizophrenia as a teenager."

"How long was she hospitalized?" Jake asked.

"The first time at thirteen, she stayed about six months. She went home for a while, but had to be admitted again when she was eighteen. That time she stayed another few months. At twenty-one, she started having bizarre mood swings. The doctor diagnosed her as bipolar. According to her mother, she cut up the bedsheets. Another time she took her car and crashed it. Then last year, she completely broke down."

"What do you mean?" Jake asked.

"She became violent toward her mother." Dr. Bullock said. "She attacked her with a butcher knife. That's when her mother decided to commit her."

Jake rubbed the back of his neck. "Did her mother ever report that she'd used recreational drugs?"

"No. Because of her problems, her mother monitored her very closely. But tissue damage does indicate she suffered from long-term drug use."

"What kind of drugs?"

"Psychotropic drugs."

"What about the head injury? Were there any signs that her fall wasn't accidental?"

Bullock pinched the bridge of his nose. "Actually, judging from the X-ray, it appears that she was struck over the head with a blunt object. That blow disoriented her and caused bleeding to the brain, which in turn caused her to fall."

Jake contemplated the ramifications of Bullock's statements. Grace had been intentionally hit her over the head; then she was found by a temporary employee with a fake identity who had disappeared the night of the fall.

Jesus. Had Grace been murdered?

———————— ⹁ ————————

Sadie's cell phone buzzed from her purse as she walked Ms. Lettie to the door. "Please go home and rest," she said. "I appreciate you staying with Amelia last night, but I need some time with her now." A pang of sadness squeezed her chest as she glanced back at her sister. "I think we both need it."

Ms. Lettie gave her a hug. "I understand, sugar. But remember, the doctors will take good care of her."

Would they?

Sadie hated to doubt them, but she couldn't help it.

Still, she said nothing as Ms. Lettie left. Instead, she checked her phone log as she settled into the chair beside her sister.

Jake had called, so she listened to his message. "Sadie, call me. It's about Grace Granger. We need to talk."

She pressed redial and waited while the phone rang. "Jake?"

"I just talked to the ME about Grace Granger's autopsy."

Amelia began to stir and tug at her bindings. "What did he find?" Sadie asked.

"Some disturbing stuff. She definitely underwent radical treatment."

"What kind of radical treatment?"

"There was evidence of severe shock treatments on Grace's brain. And she received a lobotomy."

The air in the room thickened as nausea climbed to her stomach. "My God, Jake." Sadie took a deep breath, her mind racing. "Lobotomies were performed in the forties and fifties, but they were shown to have serious side effects. Why would they do one on Grace?"

"Good question," Jake said. "There's more, too. Her fall wasn't accidental. She sustained a sharp blow to the head with a blunt object. That blow caused her fall, along with bleeding to the brain."

"Which is what killed her?" Sadie asked.

"Yes. I tried to find the orderly who discovered her lying at the foot of the stairs after the fall, but he left Slaughter Creek."

"What do you mean?"

"He worked for a temp agency, paid cash for a rental unit, then moved out the night Grace fell."

"That doesn't sound right, Jake."

"I know. I ran a search on his name, but it looks as if the man used a stolen identity and false credentials to land his job at the hospital."

Sadie tried to assimilate the information. "So you're saying Grace was murdered?"

A tense heartbeat passed. "It appears that way."

Tears blurred Sadie's eyes, and she placed her hand on top of Amelia's. Amelia's fingers felt cold and clammy, and her skin was so pale her veins were clearly visible beneath the surface.

"I'm going to question Dr. Tynsdale," Jake said.

"And I'll talk to Amelia," Sadie whispered.

And this time she'd listen to whatever her sister said.

———————— , ————————

Jake didn't like the way this was looking. First Walt Nettleton had been murdered by his granddaughter, who had been a patient at Slaughter Creek Sanitarium.

And now another patient had been murdered inside those same hospital walls.

His gut tightened as a nagging thought hit him. Hell, his father had been the administrator there ten years ago, and he had disappeared.

No…it couldn't be related, could it?

He phoned Dr. Tynsdale. The phone rang three times before the doctor answered it. "I need to talk to you, Doc."

"What's going on?"

"It's about Grace Granger. Can you meet me at the sheriff's office in half an hour?"

"Sure."

Jake drove to his office, wondering what in the hell was going on. He'd moved Ayla to Slaughter Creek to raise her in a safe place, and now there had been two murders in a matter of days.

His deputy was gone, so he grabbed the file on his father's case and studied it while he waited on the doctor to arrive.

Just as Sheriff Bayler had told Jake the first time he asked after he moved back, Bayler had investigated his father's disappearance. He had questioned neighbors, the staff at the sanitarium, and family members.

Both Jake and Nick.

According to Bayler's notes, his brother had been cold and uncooperative. But Bayler had chalked his behavior up to the fact that he was a scared teenager.

Jake pulled a hand down his chin, a memory surfacing. Nick and his father going off for one of his father's campout/survival exercises. Nick shouting at his father when they'd returned.

Jake had tried to ask his brother about it, but Nick refused to talk.

The door opened, and Jake looked up to see Dr. Tynsdale enter. He stood and greeted him, then offered him a cup of coffee, but Tynsdale declined.

"What's going on, Sheriff?" the doctor asked.

Jake explained about Grace's autopsy. "She had a lobotomy, Doctor. Did you know anything about that?"

"Yes, I was aware of it, but I didn't perform it," Dr. Tynsdale said. "I only took over Grace's care about four years ago, when her original doctor retired."

"What was his name?"

"A psychiatrist named Dr. Sanderson. I think he still lives outside Slaughter Creek."

"But you induced the coma after Grace's fall?"

Dr. Tynsdale nodded. "The CAT scan showed severe swelling of the brain. I thought it was the only way to save her. Even then, we couldn't be sure there wouldn't be brain damage."

"Were you at the hospital when she fell?" Jake asked.

"No, but I was told that one of the patient care workers found her lying at the bottom of a stairwell, unconscious. Given the fact that she was prone to outbursts, they said she must have tried to escape and fallen."

"She didn't just fall," Jake said. "The ME said that she suffered a blow to the head before she fell."

Dr. Tynsdale's eyes widened. "You're saying someone caused that fall?"

Jake nodded. "That's exactly what I'm saying."

Sadie was still stewing over her phone conversation when Brenda Banks poked her head into the hospital room. Anger surged through Sadie, and she stood and pushed Brenda back into the hallway. "What are you doing here? Trying to get some smutty photo of my sister to humiliate us?"

Brenda's face blanched. "Listen to me, Sadie. I know I wasn't your friend ten years ago, but I'm not that same girl. I've seen all you've done as a children's advocate, and I admire you for that."

Sadie didn't know what to say.

But she didn't have to speak. Brenda seemed intent on doing the talking. "I really want to help you now."

"Help me?" Sadie whispered. "All you want is a story."

"It's true that I want a story," Brenda said, straightening her suit jacket. "I'm tired of writing about the dog and pony shows in town. And I think I'm on to something now."

Sadie scrubbed a hand through her hair. "What are you talking about?"

Brenda pulled her into a corner, then glanced around to make sure no one was watching. "I have a source, someone inside this hospital who contacted me and told me some things. So I've been investigating on my own. When I heard that Grace Granger died, I knew I had to talk to you."

Sadie leaned closer. "Go on."

Brenda lowered her voice. "My source said that some patients were being mistreated," she said. "That they have been for years. That they were given experimental drugs as children, that it was part of some research project the patients and their families knew nothing about."

Sadie's skin crawled. "Really?"

Brenda nodded. "There's been long-term abuse and drug misuse," Brenda whispered. "That's all I know for now, but I thought your sister might be able to tell you what happened in here."

Sadie sighed. As wary as she was of Brenda, she sounded sincere. And in her work she had read about abuse in nursing homes and health-care facilities. "I don't know how she can help. Amelia is traumatized from my grandfather's death."

A long-drawn-out moment passed; then Mazie, the head nurse, looked up.

"I have to go," Brenda said. "But remember, Sadie, I am trying to help."

"Wait." Sadie grabbed her arm. "Who told you this?"

Brenda shook her head. "I'm sorry but I can't reveal my source."

"Then how can you trust them?"

"Oh, this person is trustworthy," Brenda said. "I never would have said anything if I doubted that."

Brenda raced toward the elevator without another word.

Sadie nodded, shocked that the girl who had been her enemy was on her side now. But if what Brenda said was true, then some of Amelia's ranting might also be true.

She reached into her pocket for her phone to call Jake.

Jake listened to Sadie relay her conversation with Brenda Banks, his head spinning. "These sound like rumors, Sadie. You know how small towns are."

"I don't believe they are," Sadie said.

"But coming from Brenda?"

"She said her source is inside the hospital. She also said that she's working on a bigger story, so I think she really believes there's something wrong here."

Jake didn't know whether to trust Brenda or not. She had hated Sadie when he dropped Brenda for her.

But that had been ten years ago, and Brenda had moved on. She'd married, although that hadn't worked out.

Brenda was smart and ambitious, and she was dedicated to her job.

Hell, in light of Grace's mother's concerns about her daughter's treatment, Grace's murder, and now Brenda's comments, he had to investigate.

Sadie slipped inside Amelia's room, grateful to see her sister open her eyes.

Amelia seemed disoriented, then angry as she realized she was handcuffed to the bed. "Sadie?"

"I'm here, Amelia," Sadie whispered.

Amelia was clinging to her hand, squeezing the life out of her fingers. "Sadie," she moaned. "Help me."

Sadie rubbed Amelia's hand with her free one. "Shh, it's okay, I'm here, Sis."

"Help me," Amelia whispered. "They're trying to kill me."

"Who's trying to kill you?" Sadie asked.

"*He* is…he's going to kill the chimes."

Frustration knotted Sadie's stomach. "Amelia, I am here to help you," she said as she freed her hand and pulled the chair up next to the bed. "But if someone's trying to hurt you, I need you to tell me who it is."

"*They* are," Amelia said, agitation edging her voice. "They're trying to kill me and make me forget."

"Forget what?"

"Forget what they did to us in here, in the dark."

"What *did* they do to you?"

Amelia's eyes went wild, then a moan erupted from deep inside her. "Tied me up, then took me into that dark tunnel... hurt me...it hurts. Help me, Sadie. Get me out of here!"

"Shh," Sadie murmured. "I'm here, and I'm not going to let them hurt you. But you have to talk to me. Tell me who hurt you, so I can stop them."

"He did, he did, he did," Amelia wailed. "He's back, I hear him in my head..."

Sadie stroked Amelia's hair again, trying to soothe her. "Tell him to go away," she said. "That I need to talk to Amelia."

"No, he's here...he's smothering me..."

"I won't let him," Sadie whispered. "I'll save you this time, Sis. I promise."

The metal cuffs clanked against the bed rail as Amelia kicked and fought to get free.

Sadie couldn't stand it any longer. And she couldn't wait for Dr. Tynsdale or waste time arguing with the nurse.

She released the restraints herself.

Amelia rubbed at her wrists and sat up, frantically looking around the room, as if she was searching for an escape.

Sadie intentionally lowered the pitch of her voice to a soothing tone. "It's okay, Amelia. We're going to figure out what happened together."

"Sadie?" Amelia said in a tinny voice.

"Yes, I'm here. Stay with me." She removed one of the letters from her bag. "Amelia, do you remember writing letters to me?"

Her sister took the envelope and studied it, then opened it and looked at the handwriting. "I...I did write this."

"I found them in your keepsake box," Sadie said. "Did you put them there?"

Amelia nodded. "I wanted Papaw to mail them to you—I thought he did." Her face turned ashen. "But he didn't send them."

Sadie tensed. "Did you and Papaw fight about it?"

Amelia ran her finger over the lines of her own writing. "Yes. I was mad 'cause I found them in his desk. I thought he sent them to you a long time ago."

Sadie squeezed her sister's hand. "No, I'm sorry, Sis. I wish he had."

Her gaze met Amelia's, but wariness flashed in her sister's eyes.

"Where's Papaw now?"

Sadie winced.

"Tell me what you remember about the night you and Papaw argued about the letters."

Suddenly Amelia went stone still; then a shudder rippled through her. She closed her eyes, rocked herself back and forth, then murmured something Sadie couldn't understand. A second later, she opened her eyes, and her mouth tightened.

Then she jumped off the bed, paced to the window, and squared her shoulders. When Amelia turned back to face her, a belligerent expression stretched across her features.

Sadie braced herself as she realized what had happened. Amelia was gone. This wasn't the innocent, terrified little girl named Bessie either.

Skid had surfaced, and he looked mad as hell.

Jake wanted to know what exactly had happened at the sanitarium. Another local about the same age as Amelia and Grace had been treated at the hospital. If there had been foul play, Joe Swoony's mother, Edith Swoony, might know.

He parked at the Swoonys' house, noting the neatly kept yard and the pickup truck parked beneath a pine tree, its hood covered in dead pine needles.

He tugged on his leather jacket, secured his weapon, then strode up to the front porch. The flowerbeds flanking the porch were empty now, but judging from the lawn work, Edith probably kept them full in the spring. A mutt lay panting in the corner, chewing on a tennis shoe that had probably belonged to Joe at one time.

He knocked on the door. "Edith, it's Sheriff Blackwood. I need to talk to you."

The sound of a TV game show blared in the background, and smoke curled from the chimney. He knocked again, then heard Edith holler that she was coming.

A minute later, she opened the door wearing a flour-dusted apron, drying her hands on a dish towel. On the floor in the den, he spotted Joe playing with some Hot Wheels, while on the television a man and woman in Raggedy Ann & Andy costumes jumped up and down to get attention on *Let's Make a Deal*.

"What can I do for you, Sheriff?"

Jake tilted his hat. "Can I come in, ma'am?"

She frowned and gestured for him to follow her inside. The furniture was old and worn, but clean, and other than a few toys scattered across the floor, the room was tidy.

Joe didn't even look at Jake. In fact, he continued to make truck sounds as if he didn't realize they had a visitor.

"We'll be right here in the kitchen," Edith told her son. Sadly, Joe didn't acknowledge her either.

"Have a seat." She gestured toward an oak table. "Would you like some coffee?"

Jake slid into the wooden chair. "Yes, ma'am, that sounds good."

She busied herself getting him a mug, then poured them both a cup, and they settled at the kitchen table.

"You heard about Grace Granger's death?" Jake asked.

A sad look flashed in her eyes as she glanced at her son. Joe continued playing cars, pretending they were drag racing. "Yes, news travels in Slaughter Creek. I hate it for Grace's mama. There's nothing worse than watching your child suffer."

She stirred sugar into her coffee. "But why would you want to talk to me about Grace?"

Jake hedged. He couldn't divulge the results of the autopsy, or he might jeopardize the investigation. Not that the ME had ruled murder, but still, Grace's death raised suspicions.

"She died the day Amelia Nettleton was admitted to the hospital."

"I heard about that, too," Edith said, fidgeting with the bobby pins holding her bun in place. "Amelia killed her granddaddy. Poor Walt. He loved those girls and tried to help Amelia, but nothing worked." She paused, her eye twitching. "I heard her sister's come back to town."

"Yes, ma'am. She's here to bury her grandfather."

"That family's sure had their share of bad times," Edith said in a pensive tone. "But I still don't see what this has to do with me."

Jake took a deep breath. "It may not, Edith, and I don't mean to pry, but I'd like to ask you about Joe. About his treatment at the sanitarium and what happened when he was young."

Edith stiffened. "Now, I really don't understand," she said, growing defensive.

Jake covered her hand with his. "I'm sorry to bring up a painful subject, but I have reason to believe that Grace might have been hurt, maybe mistreated, in the hospital."

Edith heaved an exasperated breath. Joe threw the little cars in a pile, making crashing sounds as if the cars were involved in a big pileup, and another wave of sadness passed over Edith's face.

"Joe seemed okay when he was born," Edith said. "Perfectly normal, I mean. Back then, we didn't have much money, and there was this clinic this Dr. Coker had opened up years before to help out folks like us. He took care of the needy, said it was his callin'."

"A free clinic?"

"Yes. Well, folks who could pay did. But lots of us couldn't."

Jake nodded, encouraging her to continue.

"Joe was just a baby when we started. Dr. Coker gave him all his immunizations," Edith said. "And for a while, he was growing and walking, and starting to talk."

"When did that change?"

"When he was about five."

Jake narrowed his eyes. "What happened?"

"He suddenly regressed. He was potty-trained, then he started wetting his pants. He threw his food on the floor and woke up screaming at night. In fact, he threw these awful temper fits all the time." A faraway look settled in her eyes. "He screamed for no reason, just sat and rocked himself back and forth. He wouldn't make eye contact, and he couldn't stand for me to touch him or pick him up."

"What did Dr. Coker say?"

"He ran some tests and said Joe was showing signs of autism. I didn't know what that meant, but Dr. Coker had read some research on it and said Joe's behavior fit."

"What kind of treatment did he prescribe?"

She sipped her coffee. "He referred us to the doctors at the mental hospital. They had a wing designated for children with various disorders."

"Tell me more about this Dr. Coker," Jake said.

"Some folks called him a saint the way he helped the poor." She toyed with her hands in her lap. "He was a charmer, too. Turned the women's heads." Edith rubbed her temple in thought. "I think there was another doctor who worked with him. Don't recall his name right offhand though."

Jake swallowed a sip of the tepid coffee. "Who else did Dr. Coker treat?"

"Let me see. The Nettleton twins' mama was struggling financially herself, being a single mama and all. She carried Amelia and Sadie there when they were babies. I met her in line while we waited to get their shots."

An uneasy feeling gnawed at Jake. "How about Grace?"

"She was there, too, with Elma."

"Do you know where Dr. Coker is now?" Jake asked.

Edith shrugged. "He retired a while back, but I believe he still owns that old place near the river."

Jake stood. "Thanks for the coffee."

Edith caught his hand, worry creasing her face. "Sheriff, you think Dr. Coker did something to my boy?"

"I don't know, ma'am. But I intend to find out."

"Amelia?" Sadie said, bracing herself for one of the "others."

Her sister straightened, then paced across the room. Her movements seemed jerky for a moment, her face agitated.

Sadie waited, giving her time to purge her restlessness.

Amelia's alter patted her chest, then her waist, as if she were searching for pockets. "Where's my damn cigarettes?"

Sadie forced herself to remain calm as she recognized the deep voice of her sister's male alter. Skid was the tough teenage boy who had surfaced years ago. The one with all the rage.

The one who had shot Jake's father.

"I'm sorry, but you can't smoke in here, Skid."

Amelia's alter glanced around angrily. "Goddammit, I can't believe Amelia got us locked up in here again."

"Did she? Or was it you?" Sadie asked.

Amelia paused, crossed her arms, and leaned against the window edge. Everything about her demeanor suddenly screamed male, from her gait to the antagonistic attitude in her folded arms to the snarl on her face.

"Not me. I'm too smart to get caught."

"Where's Amelia?" Sadie asked.

"She's sleeping." The alter made a sound of disgust. "She can't handle what happened to your granddaddy." Amelia tilted her head to the side, her mouth curled into a grimace.

"Then why don't you tell me what happened."

"Why should I talk to you?" Skid said. "What the hell are you doing here anyway? Thought you didn't care about Amelia anymore."

"I've always cared about her," Sadie said, her anger mounting. "As a matter of fact, I'd like to talk to her now, let her tell me what happened with Papaw."

Skid gave a dismissive headshake. "Amelia don't know shit about that night."

"But you were there?" Sadie asked, keeping her voice even.

Skid cut his eyes to the side, a cold look marring his face. "Not till later. Till afterward…"

"You mean until after she shot Papaw?"

Skid folded his hand into a fist and rapped on the wall. "I heard her screaming, and I tried to save her," he said, his voice taking on a razor edge. "But someone else beat me there."

"Was someone else in the room?"

"Fuck, yes, someone else was there. Are you deaf?" His movements became more agitated. "That's what I've been telling you. *He* killed Papaw."

"Who are you talking about?" Sadie asked. "Another person? Or is there a fourth alter?"

Skid's eyes darted back and forth as if he was searching for someone in the room. "I don't know. I told you I wasn't there. But Amelia didn't shoot that gun. She'd never believe anything bad about your granddaddy."

"What do you mean? She wouldn't believe anything bad about him?" Fear slithered through Sadie. "Did Papaw do something?"

"I told you, I don't know." Skid clawed at his arms. "But Amelia's scared. She said *he* killed your granddaddy, and that he's gonna kill her next."

———————— , ————————

The chimes were ringing. *Ting. Ting. Ting.*

Then the clock. *Ticktock. Ticktock. Ticktock.*

He was there.

Whispering in her ear.

Time to go, Amelia. Close your eyes and it won't hurt.

But she was crying again…Bessie was scared…

He had lied.

It did hurt. She could hear the others scream. The cries resounded through the hollow walls.

The terrified pleas to let them go. To stop the pain.

Then Bessie was gone, and she was drowning, the darkness swallowing her into its abyss.

"No more Amelia," he murmured. "No more weak girl."

No! He couldn't kill Amelia.

She had to tell Sadie. Sadie would come, she'd help her.

Only the black curtain fell over her again. Dark. It was so dark.

The pain was back. He was choking her…

She tried to scream, but there was no sound. Where was Sadie?

Sadie is gone.

She can't help you now, he murmured.

"I'll tell," she cried.

His voice rumbled in her ear, sinister and low this time.

No, you won't.

Tell and you die…

Chapter 11

───────────── ◦ ─────────────

S kid's words reverberated in Sadie's head. *Amelia is afraid.*
"Tell me more, Skid," Sadie said. "Who is Amelia afraid of?"

Skid's eyes glazed over. Then he dropped his head forward and closed his eyes. Sadie recognized the shudder that usually accompanied one of her sister's transitions into an alter.

Just as she expected, a second later Amelia opened her eyes, and the sullen teenage boy with the bad attitude had vanished. In his place, her docile, frightened sister appeared. "Sadie?"

"I'm here, Amelia. I came to help you."

Amelia's shoulders were slumped, her posture timid, her expression confused as she glanced around the room. When she saw the restraints on the bed and looked down at her gown, terror darkened her eyes. "What happened? Why am I here?" She gripped Sadie by the arms. "Why are *you* here?'"

A knock sounded on the door, and Dr. Tynsdale poked his head in. His bushy eyebrows rose when he realized Amelia was no longer restrained.

"How is our patient this morning?"

Amelia's eyes widened in terror. "Why did you put me back in here? You promised you wouldn't."

"We had to admit you," Dr. Tynsdale said. "Ms. Lettie said you stopped taking your medication."

Amelia rubbed at her temple. "I did? No...yes...maybe...I don't remember..."

"You had an episode," Dr. Tynsdale said gently.

Amelia angled her head toward Sadie. "That's why you're here? But you've never come home before."

Sadie flinched at her accusatory tone. But she couldn't argue. Ten years ago, she'd walked away and hadn't been able to face coming back.

Obviously her sister thought she'd abandoned her.

You did. You ran as far away as you could.

"I'm sorry, Amelia, but I'm here now, and I need you to talk to me." Battling a surge of guilt, Sadie squeezed her sister's hand. "We were talking about you and Papaw before you transitioned."

A desperate look flashed across Amelia's face, her eyes flitting back and forth.

"Do you remember anything about yesterday?" Sadie asked. "Did something happen with you and Papaw? Is that when you found the letters?"

"No...oh, God...no, I found those a while back." Amelia wiped at her tears with a shaky hand. "Where is Papaw? And where's Ms. Lettie?"

Sadie cradled her sister's hands between hers. "Ms. Lettie spent the night here with you. But Papaw...Amelia...he's gone."

"What do you mean, gone?" Amelia asked in a haunted whisper.

Dr. Tynsdale gave Sadie a warning look. She knew Amelia was fragile, but how would she find answers if she kept the truth from her sister?

Sadie coaxed her toward the bed. "Come here and sit down, and I'll explain."

Amelia pushed at her hands. "You're not going to tie me back down. Please…"

Emotions clogged Sadie's throat. "I won't, I promise, Sis. Just sit down so we can talk."

Amelia spotted the round table in the corner and reluctantly allowed Sadie to lead her to a chair. When she settled into it, she began to pick at her fingernails. "Where did Papaw go?"

Sadie swallowed hard, well aware Dr. Tynsdale was watching.

"He died, Amelia," Sadie said, her voice cracking. "That's the reason I came home. I have to plan his funeral." She pulled Amelia's hands into hers to stop her nail biting. "We have to bury him."

Tears filled Amelia's eyes and trickled down her face. "No… no. Papaw…he's not dead…he wouldn't leave me…"

"I'm sorry, honey, but it's true," Sadie said gently. "When was the last time you saw him?"

Amelia tugged her hands away. "I…don't remember." She bounced up and down, making the chair legs clang against the floor.

"Please try," Sadie said.

Amelia rocked more fiercely, the banging echoing in the sterile room.

"What about Papaw's shotgun?" Sadie asked. "Do you remember taking it?"

Distress lined her sister's face, then a shocked glaze settled over her eyes, and she started trembling uncontrollably.

Sadie braced herself for one of the alters to appear. "Stay with me, Amelia. It's important that you tell me if you took Papaw's gun."

Amelia rocked harder. "Blood…blood…so much…everywhere."

"Yes, there was blood," Sadie said. "Papaw's blood, because he was hurt. And you were in the room—"

Amelia shot up from the table. "I have to save Papaw...get the gun from the bad man...make him go away."

Sadie caught her arms, forcing her to look at her. "What bad man, Amelia? Did you shoot Papaw, or was someone else there?"

"He did it," Amelia cried. "He shot him, and he's going to kill me." She wrenched away from Sadie, ran toward the door, and grabbed the doorknob. "I have to get out!"

Dr. Tynsdale caught her by the arm. "I'm sorry, Amelia, but you can't leave right now."

She shook the doorknob with a piercing scream. "Yes, I have to. He'll find me here like he did before."

"Who'll find you?" Sadie pressed.

"He will," Amelia shouted. "You can't make me stay here, Sadie!" Amelia jerked at Sadie's arms. "You promised you wouldn't lock me back in here!"

"Amelia," Sadie said, lowering her voice. "Calm down, sweetie. I'm here. I won't let anyone hurt you."

"They will," Amelia cried. "They're going to kill me and bury me in the basement, and I won't ever get to go home again."

Dr. Tynsdale reached in his bag for a hypodermic, but Sadie shook her head. "I can't work with her if you keep her drugged and incoherent."

"Sadie," Dr. Tynsdale said, "you have no idea what you're doing."

"Maybe not," she said with a challenging look. "But I want to see what my sister says when she's lucid."

"You can't make me stay!" Amelia cried. "No, no, no..." She doubled over, hugging her arms around her middle. "Get Papaw, he's not dead, he's not dead..."

The door swung open, and two orderlies rushed in. A heavyset one took one look at Amelia, wrapped his arms around her waist, and dragged her toward the bed.

"Let me go, let me go!" Amelia cried. "I have to get out of here before he finds me!"

"Amelia, please," Sadie said softly. "Who is he?"

"No, don't lock me up. He'll find me and kill me, and then he'll come after you."

Dr. Tynsdale checked the hypodermic. "I'm sorry, Amelia, but we have to stabilize you."

Sadie winced as he gave her the injection. A second later, Amelia sagged in his arms, the fight slowly fading from her.

Sadie fisted her hands in frustration. "You didn't have to knock her out. I wanted to talk to her."

"You've upset her enough for today," Dr. Tynsdale hissed. "She needs to remember slowly, or we could damage her psyche permanently."

Sadie watched as the orderly reattached the restraints.

Amelia would never hurt her.

Then again, she'd never imagined that she'd hurt their grandfather either.

Although she could hurt herself.

A frown of disapproval furrowed Dr. Tynsdale's brow. "Amelia has been my patient for years, Sadie. You have to trust me."

Anxiety knotted Sadie's shoulders. That was the problem.

She didn't trust anyone anymore.

———————— , ————————

Jake was antsy to talk to Dr. Coker about the free clinic as well as to Dr. Sanderson, the doctor who'd treated Grace, but he decided to check on Sadie and her sister first, so he drove straight to the sanitarium.

By the time he arrived, Sadie and Dr. Tynsdale were standing outside Amelia's room. Sadie looked agitated, her shoulders slumped as she rubbed her arms with her hands. They were talking in hushed voices, Dr. Tynsdale's expression troubled.

"What's going on?" Jake asked.

A flicker of relief crossed Sadie's face when she spotted him approaching. "Let's go to the coffee shop and talk."

Dr. Tynsdale worried his hand across his chin, then the three of them walked down the hallway and rode the elevator to the second-floor cafeteria.

Jake frowned at the dingy walls and smell of burned food. Why didn't someone at least update the drab, dark curtains and add some lighting to create a cheery atmosphere for the staff and the patients' families and friends?

Except for a couple of workers behind a grill and another lady at a cash register, the room was essentially empty. In the center, a hot bar offered meats and vegetables in warming trays while the grill offered sandwiches, burgers, and pizza.

Jake filled his cup. "This looks worse than the sludge at the jail."

"I'd give anything for a Starbucks," Sadie said.

Dr. Tynsdale simply shrugged. "You get used to it."

"I can't imagine visitors lingering in here," Sadie commented, mirroring Jake's earlier impression of the place.

"Sadly, most of the patients have very few visitors." Dr. Tynsdale took his coffee black and gestured toward a corner table. "And when they do, they tend not to hang out or eat here."

Sadie stirred sweetener in her coffee and sipped it, then dumped the cup in the trash.

"So how is Amelia?" Jake asked as they seated themselves.

A pang of sadness flickered across Sadie's face. "She's sedated again. But I talked to one of her alters."

Dr. Tynsdale's eyes shot to Sadie. "You didn't tell me that. Which one?"

"Skid, the teenage boy." Sadie exchanged an odd look with the doctor. "He kept saying that Amelia didn't kill Papaw, that someone else did. Has another alter surfaced that I don't know about?"

Dr. Tynsdale shook his head. "No, not to me anyway."

"Who did this Skid character say killed Walt?" Jake asked.

Sadie made a frustrated sound. "He didn't say. But he was adamant that a man killed Papaw." Sadie massaged her temple the way she always did when she was worried. "He also said something else that troubled me."

"What?" Dr. Tynsdale asked.

"That Amelia would never believe anything bad about Papaw."

Jake drummed his fingers on the table. "What did he mean by that?"

"I have no idea." Sadie sighed. "When I pushed for answers, Skid disappeared and Amelia returned. She was agitated when she realized she was in the hospital."

Dr. Tynsdale fidgeted with his glasses. "Sadie tried to coax her into talking about her grandfather's murder, but she got so upset, I had to sedate her."

Sadie glanced out the window. "I hate seeing her restrained like she's some kind of animal."

Jake wanted to comfort her, but it wasn't the place or time. Not with Dr. Tynsdale watching and with questions ticking through his head.

Besides, technically Amelia was a suspect in a homicide.

"Dr. Tynsdale, how long have you treated Amelia?"

The doctor sipped his coffee. "I've known the girls since they were little, but I started treating Amelia when she was twelve."

"Were you the doctor who admitted her to the sanitarium?"

"No." Tynsdale stared into his coffee. "Walt said this doctor from the free clinic in town did. Said Amelia exhibited signs of schizophrenia, that she claimed she was hearing voices in her head."

"That was about the time her second personality emerged?" Jake asked.

"That's right," Dr. Tynsdale said.

"Was the doctor named Coker?" Jake asked.

Tynsdale scratched his head. "I believe so."

Brenda Banks's conversation with Sadie echoed in Jake's head. "You've been working at the hospital for years now. Have you ever noticed any patients being mistreated?"

Tynsdale's brows furrowed. "No—if I did, I certainly would have reported it."

"I'd like to see records of Amelia's treatments," Jake said.

Tynsdale scowled. "You know patient-doctor confidentiality laws prohibit me from showing them to you."

"I'm her only family, and now that Papaw's gone, I'm her guardian," Sadie said. "You can show them to me."

"All right," Dr. Tynsdale said. "I'll get a file to you ASAP."

"How about files from the free clinic?" Jake asked.

"I'll see what I can find out. But that clinic was closed a long time ago. As a matter of fact, there was a fire, and the records burned. That's why I don't have records of that time."

"Just get Amelia's together," Jake said. "I'm going to request a warrant to have Grace Granger's medical records released to me."

Again, Tynsdale shifted, and Jake wondered if the man knew more than he was telling.

After all, Tynsdale had been treating Amelia for years. He could easily have manipulated her meds or treatment to cover up inappropriate activities.

Worse, Sadie had trusted him with her sister's life, just as her grandfather had.

And he had ended up dead.

———————— . ————————

He studied the pictures of the "chimes."

All the innocent faces. The ones who'd given themselves for the cause.

A laugh bubbled in his throat. Well, maybe they hadn't exactly given themselves freely.

But they had been such an important part of the plan.

Dammit, Amelia was starting to remember.

That was dangerous. She had to be stopped.

He knew how to do it, too. She was weak. She always had been.

The key to controlling her was the others.

He'd use them to smother her voice. To make her forget.

Sadie was the opposite though. Tenacious. A fighter. She wouldn't give up.

She had her devious side, too. A side no one in town knew about.

But if she didn't leave the past alone, they would know.

Everyone would.

And Sadie would be sorry she'd ever returned to Slaughter Creek.

Chapter 12

———— o ————

Sadie hated to leave Amelia, but her sister would probably sleep for hours. Still, she gave orders for the nurse to phone her if Amelia woke up and was agitated, no matter what the time of day or night. Ms. Lettie had also called to say that she was on her way back to the hospital to stay with Amelia so Sadie could stop by the funeral home and arrange for her grandfather's memorial service.

Jake walked her outside. "I'm going to question Dr. Coker," he said as they paused by her car. "I didn't want to mention this in front of Dr. Tynsdale, but he also treated Joe Swoony at the free clinic."

Sadie frowned. "So three people who had mental disorders were treated as children at the clinic before they became seriously ill?"

Jake nodded. "It may be nothing, but considering Grace's murder and Brenda's accusations, I'm curious."

Sadie caught his arm. "Thank you for doing this, Jake."

Jake stiffened, his dark eyes meeting hers. Tension stretched between them, the urge to lean into him tugging at her. She had been alone so long, had missed him, yearned for him, for his touch, his understanding.

His love.

But she had no right. Not after what her family had done to him.

"I'm just doing my job," Jake said.

Her heart lurched. Of course he was. It was nothing personal to him.

"I need to stop by the funeral home," Sadie said. "But I'd like to go with you to see Dr. Coker first."

Jake frowned. "I don't think that's a good idea. You're too close to this."

Sadie stood her ground. "I am a psychiatric counselor, Jake. I might be able to help."

He reluctantly agreed, and they dropped her car by the funeral home.

Determined to steer her mind away from Jake, Sadie studied the scenery as he drove down the winding road. The mountains rose above them, the sharp ridges jutting out, the trees shivering beneath the weight of the wind. Late-afternoon shadows plagued the highway, clouds rolling in from the north, threatening more flurries.

She needed to put the horses in the barn when she got home. Make sure they had food and water and were warm.

They wound through a series of back roads, then veered onto a road near the river, resurrecting haunting memories and taking Sadie back to the night that had ruined her life.

She fought the images, but they flew at her like a sea of bats in the dark. The sounds of the shovel hitting dirt and rock, Skid's constant curses, Papaw's incessant cough, her own silent cries of horror at what they were doing.

At all that had been lost.

Papaw's cold slap on her face, ordering her not to tell anyone what had happened. Then her guilt as she followed him in the truck while he drove Arthur Blackwood's car to the airport and left it.

By the time they reached the dirt road leading to Dr. Coker's hideaway, sweat beaded her skin, and she felt dizzy with guilt and shame.

Oblivious, Jake parked and turned to her. "You sure you want to do this?"

No. She wanted to run again.

At the same time, she wanted to hug Jake and confess how much she'd loved him.

To beg his forgiveness for the lies she'd told.

For leaving him behind.

But Papaw was gone now, and Amelia was locked away, needing help. She had run before, and it hadn't done any good. No matter how far she'd gone, the secrets, lies, and pain had followed her.

So she grabbed the door handle and climbed out. The secrets had to stay buried deep in the ground—just like Jake's father.

———————— ˌ ————————

Jake knocked on the door, and Sadie drew a deep breath, as if she needed it for courage. An elderly woman in a pink double-knit suit opened the door, her face weathered but kind.

"Ma'am, I'm Sheriff Jake Blackwood, and this is Sadie Nettleton."

"Dora Mae Coker," the little woman said. "Come on in. We don't get many visitors out here."

"We'd really like to speak to your husband," Jake said.

The woman pinched her lips together, accentuating the lines bracketing her mouth. "What's this about, Sheriff?"

"Just a patient he had a long time ago," Jake said.

"All right, but I'll warn you. He's not having a good day."

Sadie frowned. "What do you mean?"

"He took the Alzheimer's awhile back," Dora Mae said. "Half the time he doesn't even know my name, and we've been married fifty years."

Frustration knotted Jake's insides. "Well, ma'am, we'll try not to upset him."

"Good, 'cause that nosy reporter Brenda Banks got him all riled up when she came out here."

Jake and Sadie exchanged a look.

Mrs. Coker gestured for them to follow her. The house was riddled with homemade throws, pillows, and needlepoint wall hangings. Three cats lay in fur balls around the fire, and dust coated everything in sight.

Dora Mae led them to a sitting room that overlooked the river, the dim gray light spilling in, casting shadows on the chipped, faded walls. Her husband was slumped in a rocking chair with an Afghan spread over his legs, staring out the window. He looked feeble and weak-eyed, his age-spotted skin pale.

"Jonas, the sheriff and this nice lady are here to see you," Dora Mae said.

The man's bushy white hair stuck up in disarray, his skin leathery and sagging, his eyes vacant as he turned to look at them.

"I'll get y'all some coffee," Dora Mae said, then disappeared from the room, her orthopedic shoes clicking on the wood floor.

Sadie and Jake seated himself across from him in two wing-back chairs. "Dr. Coker," Jake said. "We need to talk to you about the time when you ran the free clinic in town."

His eyelids fluttered as he moved his mouth from side to side.

Jake leaned forward in the chair. "You had several patients, children you treated, who were referred to the Slaughter Creek Sanitarium."

"One of them was my sister, Amelia Nettleton," Sadie said. "Do you remember her?"

Other than a slight twitch of the man's eyelids, he showed no response.

"You also treated a boy named Joe Swoony," Sadie said. "His mother said he presented with symptoms of autism and schizo-phrenia."

Coker's glazed eyes shifted slightly, as if for a moment, the name registered.

"And you took care of a patient named Grace Granger. Later she had a lobotomy."

This time Coker gripped the edges of the rocking chair with his gnarled hands.

"Did you perform the lobotomy?" Jake asked.

Coker's eyes twitched, flashing to him. But he clamped his lips shut and didn't answer.

"Were you giving them some kind of experimental drug?"

"Drugs?" he muttered. "Not time for my drugs."

Sadie gently touched his hand. "Were the patients mistreated?"

Coker mumbled something indiscernible, and both Sadie and Jake leaned forward to decipher his words.

"If you didn't perform the lobotomy, you knew about it, didn't you? Who did it?" Jake continued.

"Did things we shouldn't have," Coker said in a raspy voice.

"What kind of things?" Jake asked.

Coker curled his fingers into Sadie's hand. "You...look just like her."

"Like Amelia," Sadie said with a nod. "Yes, she's my twin sister, Dr. Coker. You immunized us when we were little."

Coker's bushy eyebrows shot up for a moment. "Like your mama..."

"You knew my mother?" Sadie said in a hushed whisper.

"I told them not to hurt her and your daddy," he said in a choked voice. "I told them she didn't know..."

Sadie's face turned a chalky white. "What are you talking about? My parents died in a car accident."

Jake frowned. Granted the man was suffering from dementia, but in that moment he seemed perfectly lucid.

"Tell me," Sadie pleaded. "Did someone cause their accident?"

But Coker turned back to the window, a shuttered look passing across his face as if he'd closed the curtain on those memories.

Dora Mae tottered in, and Jake stood. "Mrs. Coker, did you know anything about your husband's work at the free clinic years ago?"

"Yes, of course," she tittered in adoration. "My husband was a generous man. He felt sorry for all the folks that couldn't pay, and he refused to let a child go untreated. Folks called him their savior."

Jake shoved his hands in his pockets. Had Coker been a savior?

Or had he taken advantage of poor families and innocent kids?

Dammit, he wished he knew who Brenda's source was.

And what kind of experimental project she was talking about.

By the time Jake drove Sadie back to the funeral home, her head was swimming with worry for Amelia.

Coker had also raised questions about her parents' deaths.

She struggled to remember her mother, but she'd been tiny when her mother died. Papaw and Gran had taken her and Amelia in, and then Amelia had started having horrible nightmares.

Sadie massaged her temple, desperate to recall the years before Amelia had started having episodes. Talking about the voices and the other people who lived in her head.

A faint memory of their grandfather carrying them for a hayride in the back of the wagon when they were four surfaced, and tears pricked her eyes. She and Amelia had been like two peas in a pod, inseparable. They'd slept together, eaten together, shared their own secret language.

That night they'd laughed and giggled and whispered stories about the silly faces they wanted to carve on their pumpkins and the scarecrow Papaw had erected in the pumpkin patch.

Amelia had seemed perfectly normal.

Had she been normal at one time? And what exactly caused that to change?

She desperately wished she could turn back the clock. Wished she could change what had happened to steal her sister's life.

Jake parked at the funeral home and leaned against the seat. "I understand you're upset about Coker's comment about your parents, but remember he's suffering from dementia, Sadie. He could be confused."

"I know."

"I'll find out who worked with Coker at the clinic," Jake said. "Another doctor, nurse, receptionist—maybe someone else knew what was going on."

Sadie twisted her hand together. "Thanks, Jake."

For a moment, he looked at her with such longing that Sadie yearned to spill the truth.

But she didn't think she could stand to see the look on his face when she told him that his father was dead, and that she'd helped cover up his murder.

So she fought her instincts as she climbed from his car and headed into the funeral home, a two-story Georgian house that had been renovated years ago.

Dr. Coker's comments about her parents' deaths not being an accident and about her mother taunted her. What if her mother had discovered that Amelia was being mistreated? Her natural instinct would have been to protect her daughter, to report the abuse…

Had someone killed her to keep her quiet, then made it look like an accident to stave off suspicion?

The scent of roses and some flowery air freshener, sweet and cloying at the same time, lingered in the air as she entered, reminding her of her grandmother's funeral. She'd been irritated at the people who laughed and chatted around her coffin as if they were having a family reunion or a tea party.

As an adult, she realized that sharing stories and memories of loved ones and friends comforting one another was a natural part of the grieving process.

But at the time, her grandmother dead of a sudden heart attack, she'd wanted to scream at everyone to shut up. How could they laugh when her gran would never smile again? When she'd never make homemade apple pie or hang the sheets on the clothesline to dry so they smelled fresh, like spring rainwater?

"Sadie Nettleton," a thin man with a bad comb-over said as he approached her, leaning on his cane, "I'm George Pelverson, the director of Slaughter Creek Funeral Home. I'm so sorry about your loss."

Sadie accepted his extended hand, swallowing her distaste at the cold, slimy feel of his skin. Was it her imagination, or did he smell like formaldehyde?

"Thank you." Her gaze swept across the foyer, from its cozy seating nooks to the two viewing rooms on the left and right. A small chapel was attached, with access off the hallway and outside. "Did you know my grandfather, Mr. Pelverson?"

"Of course." The old man coughed into his hand. "You don't remember me, do you, Sadie?"

Sadie frowned and studied his face.

"I'm sorry. I'm afraid not."

He patted her shoulder with a gnarled hand. "That's understandable. You were just a little girl when your gran passed."

"You ran the funeral home then?" Sadie said, a distant memory tickling her conscience. The man who'd helped her grandfather had been robust, dark-haired.

But age had robbed him of his girth and hair.

"I knew your grandfather from church. We sang in the choir together. He and your grandmother brought both of you girls to

Slaughter Creek Baptist when you were children." He adjusted his glasses with a trembling hand. "People couldn't get over how much you two looked alike."

And how crazy Amelia was.

But she was determined not to revisit that part of the past. "Mr. Pelverson, you probably heard that my sister shot Papaw."

He pursed his thin lips as if trying to hold his tongue. "Yes, I'm sorry. Walt did everything he could to help little Amelia. He grieved his heart out that she never got well."

Sadie frowned at his wording. "Did he discuss her treatment with you?"

"What do you mean?"

"Did he mention anything specifically about the hospital? Maybe a doctor or nurse he didn't like? Or that he was worried Amelia was being mistreated?"

A tense second ticked by, as if he were contemplating his answer. Somewhere in the background a telephone rang, and Sadie heard a woman answer. The front door opened, and a deliveryman from a florist shop entered with a cross-shaped wreath made from yellow roses.

"Slaughter Creek Baptist sent these for a Mr. Walt Nettleton," the deliveryman said.

The director signed the slip, then directed him to the viewing room to the right.

Sadie thought she detected relief on his face that they'd been interrupted. "Mr. Pelverson," Sadie said more firmly. "Was my grandfather upset about something before he died?"

"Just Amelia." He wheezed for a breath. "He said he blamed himself she was the way she was."

Sadie swallowed hard. "What did he mean by that?"

"I don't know," Pelverson said. "Mental illness was something to be ashamed of back in our day. I suppose he meant it ran in his family."

Sadie stewed over that possibility. As far as she knew, no one else in her family had a history of mental illness.

A headache pulsed behind her eyes, and she rubbed her temple, afraid one of her notorious migraines was setting in.

"We're working on your grandfather, but I'm afraid we can't fix his face." Pelverson's weary sigh rattled through the room like bones creaking, dragging her from her thoughts. "If I were you, I'd keep the casket closed. You can put a nice framed photograph of him on display so folks will remember him the way he was."

Sadie grimaced.

Papaw might have had a few friends, but Amelia's illness had always scared people away.

"A closed casket it is," she said, keeping her emotions at bay.

"Let's choose a coffin, then we can select a time for the service and post it in the paper. Then you can run home and bring us back some clothes, whatever you want to bury him in."

Realizing she'd gleaned all she could from the funeral director at the moment, she let her questions slide. Maybe the people who attended the funeral would shed some light on her grandfather and the past.

A numbness settled over her as they discussed the details for the service. She asked him to have one of her grandfather's friends choose the hymns to be sung and the Bible verses to be read.

Then she thanked him and stood, her nerves frayed. "If you think of anything that had upset my grandfather, please let me know."

He adjusted his bifocals. "Sometimes we just have to accept things, Sadie."

But she couldn't accept it without trying to understand the situation. She'd done that when her sister killed Jake's father, and she'd regretted it ever since.

She wouldn't do that again, no matter how painful the truth was for her or Amelia.

Unease nagged at her as she left the funeral home and drove back to the farmhouse. Storm clouds had darkened, gathering in packs, so she stopped at the grocery and picked up some staples, then hurried home. The wind had picked up, the temperature dropping, leaves swirling across the withering grass.

She rushed the groceries inside, then remembered the horses and dragged on her coat and boots to take care of them.

But the hair on the back of her neck prickled as she stepped outside. She pivoted, searching the property, the porch, the hills behind the house.

A second later, her cell phone rang. She checked the number, but didn't recognize it. Still, it could be someone local—maybe someone who'd known her grandfather and could answer some questions.

"I'm watching you, Sadie," a low, gruff voice mumbled. "I know what you did. And if you keep asking questions and poking into the past, everyone else will know, too."

Chapter 13

———— o ————

Sadie clutched the phone with a white-knuckled grip. "Who is this?"

The line went dead. She peered around, shivering.

Someone was watching her. She hadn't just imagined it this time.

And he knew what had happened years ago.

But how?

Her mind swirled as she raced inside the house. She flipped on the light as she entered, shutting the door and leaning against it, as if she could block out the harsh reality of the man's threat.

The old house moaned as the wind shook the thin walls, the wind chimes outside clanging wildly with the force of the gale. The urge to tear down those chimes and dispose of them hit her.

The events of that night ten years ago bombarded her. She and Papaw and Amelia—no, it was Skid who'd shot Blackwood and helped them drag his body into the back of Papaw's old pickup truck. Papaw had thrown a tarp on the bed of the truck first to soak up the blood, then another over the body, while Skid had grabbed a shovel and covered up the bloody trail on the ground.

The sound of the truck bouncing over the ruts in the road as Papaw drove to the river churned in her head. She felt sick, in shock, as she watched Skid.

Her sister had retreated into her mind for days after that. Not just a "nowhere" night but a month of them, the alters ping-ponging in and out of her daily life like a carnival freak show. Skid disappeared after they buried Blackwood, but Bessie came in his place—timid, terrified, vulnerable little Bessie, who had cried for her mother.

A mother who was already dead.

Then Viola, with her desperate need for attention from men.

Sadie jerked herself from the memories, her resolve strengthening. If someone had hurt Amelia and killed her parents, she had to know.

And she wouldn't allow this man's threats to stop her from looking for the answers.

But what about Jake?

If she kept searching, Jake might learn the truth. Then he would be devastated, and he would hate her.

Amelia would spend the rest of her life in the sanitarium. Which she might anyway.

And Sadie would go to jail.

A sudden sound made Sadie jump. She searched the room, then sighed in relief as she noticed a tree branch scraping the window. Remembering the horses, she raced to Papaw's closet for his rifle, but it was gone. He must have gotten rid of it after she'd left; probably he didn't want reminders that Amelia had killed a man with that gun. Or maybe he'd wanted to hide it in case someone looked for evidence some day.

She shuddered, grabbed Papaw's pistol from the nightstand, tugged on her jacket, then stuffed the gun into a pocket. The storm clouds had robbed the day of any remaining sunlight; night was setting in under a starless sky. The house lights suddenly flickered off, then on, then off again.

She fumbled her way to the laundry room, found a flashlight and carried it with her, then rushed outside. Her nerves on edge. She searched the yard, the woods, and the pasture. It was so dark she could barely see, but she used the flashlight to light a path.

Chance was acting up, racing around the pen, and the other horse, Amos, was pawing the dirt by the edge of the gate as if he were trying to claw his way out. "Shh, fellows," Sadie said as she inched toward the animal. "Let's go in the barn where it'll be warm and dry."

Amos rose on his back legs with a whinny. She rushed inside the barn, grabbed a rope, and returned. She held up a hand, speaking in a low voice to soothe Amos as she approached, then tossed the rope around his neck. He balked at first, pawing the dirt again and neighing, but she calmed him with soft words and led him into the barn. She put him in the first stall, then returned for Chance.

"Come on, buddy," she said, cautious as he backed up against the railing. Thunder clapped, lightning zigzagging across the tops of the trees, and Chance reared back again.

"It's okay, bud, come on." Using a calming voice, she inched toward him. "Remember me? It's Sadie. We used to ride together when I lived here."

Suddenly he dropped his head forward and studied her as if he finally recognized her, then leaned his head into her palm. Tears blurred Sadie's eyes. Chance had been her best friend when she was younger, her escape from the chaotic, ugly world in her house. When she was upset, she'd ride the trails, the wind blowing her hair off her shoulders, and feel free, at least for a little while.

Chance nudged his nose into her palm and followed her into the barn. She gathered food for the horses, then filled their water buckets.

She patted Chance's back, remembering all the times she used to hide out here to escape Amelia's moods and rantings. She'd needed the peace and quiet.

But even then, she'd heard Amelia crying out for her as if she were in the same room. Amelia pleading with Sadie to save her…

Only she'd let her down.

She wouldn't let her down now.

More determined than ever, she headed back to the house. That box of letters was waiting for her.

Maybe she'd find some answers in Amelia's pleas for help.

———————— , ————————

After leaving Sadie, Jake stopped by his office. His deputy was on the phone when he arrived. Jake settled at his own desk and called Judge Horner.

"I need a warrant for some medical records," Jake said without preamble.

"On what basis?" Judge Horner asked.

Jake explained about the investigation into Walt Nettleton's and Grace Granger's deaths, that he was investigating a report of abuse at the sanitarium.

"Accusing a hospital of mistreatment is a serious claim," the judge said. "Are you sure you want to go down this road?"

"Both Grace's family and Joe Swoony's said their children were referred for tests, but their conditions worsened after treatment instead of improving. And all three—Grace, Joe, and Amelia—were treated at the free clinic in town when they were children."

"So were dozens of other people, but not all of them ended up with mental problems," Judge Horner said.

Jake crumbled an old message slip in his hand and tossed it into the trash. "True. But Grace Granger was murdered in that hospital. And I want to know who killed her and why."

"You think it has something to do with the sanitarium?"

"I have reason to look at that possibility. I'd like a look at the clinic's records, too."

"It burned down years ago," Judge Horner said. "Without computers, the files are lost."

Just as Tynsdale had said. "Then I'll dig around. Maybe someone in town worked there or knows something."

"All right, I'll sign the warrant. But be careful, Jake. These families have suffered enough. Don't go making more problems for them."

"I'm not. I just think they deserve to know the truth." And so did Sadie.

Jake hung up, then strode back to Waterstone's desk. He was leaning back in his chair with his feet propped up, still on the phone. "Yeah, seven sounds good, baby."

Jake crossed his arms, and Mike dropped his feet to the floor with a thud. "I'll see you then."

Mike's face was smug, a sure sign Jake's deputy was going to get lucky tonight.

Sadie's luscious body floated in Jake's mind, but he banished it. She was a case, nothing more.

She couldn't be more. She'd leave as soon as the investigation ended, and he would not pine over her as he had years ago.

Jake snatched the fax as it came in. The phone records he'd requested from the Nettleton house, to verify who had called Sadie about the shooting. Sweet-talking Lula Bell into sending them to him without a warrant had sped the process along. "Did you do rounds today?" Jake asked.

Mike nodded. "Yeah. Going to do another ride through town before dinner."

"Anything I need to know about?"

Mike shook his head, then Jake filled him in on his request for a warrant. "You and that chick had a thing back in the day, didn't you?" Mike asked.

Jake's jaw tightened. "What makes you say that?"

"People in town talk. They say you and her were an item in high school, but then she had enough of her crazy sister and left town."

Jake didn't like the fact that the town was talking about his personal life—or to be reminded of that part of his past. "Just stick to business," he said curtly. "And let me know when those warrants get here."

His deputy looked curious, but Jake refused to say more. Then he glanced down at the fax, skimming over the numbers. Ms. Lettie'd said that Amelia, or one of the alters, had called Sadie in San Francisco to tell her Amelia was going to shoot her grandfather.

He studied the date and time to verify the call. The call to Sadie had come from the home phone.

The 911 call showed up as well. But as he skimmed the print-out, he recognized another number on the list. His deputy's.

He slammed the printout down onto the desk in front of Mike. "What the hell is this? I wasn't aware that you knew Amelia Nettleton."

Mike's eyes flared with worry. "It's not what it looks like, Sheriff."

"Then you know what it looks like," Jake said tightly. "That you knew her and hid that information."

Mike vaulted up, his chair banging the wall. "I didn't mention it because it was a while back."

Jake didn't believe him. "There are several recent phone calls between you two."

Mike paced across the floor. "Look, I'm not proud of it, but this is what happened. One night about a year ago, I met this woman at a bar. She was sexy, hot. She came on to me."

"Shy Amelia came on to you?" Jake asked, a bad feeling in his gut.

"Trust me, this woman wasn't shy." Mike raked a hand through his hair. "She told me her name was Viola. I…we hooked up that night."

"Viola?"

"That's what she said," Mike insisted. "I had no reason not to believe her."

It was a small town, but Mike was new. It was possible he hadn't heard about Amelia's illness.

Jake chewed the inside of his cheek, a memory tickling his consciousness. In high school, Amelia had come on to a couple of the teachers. Sadie said that was her Viola alter.

Amelia was attractive. Hell, she looked just like Sadie.

Except they were nothing alike. He couldn't imagine Sadie hooking up in a bar.

Then again, what did he know about her now? It had been ten years...

"Go on."

"I saw her two, maybe three, times after that." Mike paused in his pacing to face him. "Honest to God, I had no idea who she really was. Then I ran into her in town one day. And this time she looked different."

"How so?"

"She wasn't dressed provocatively, not in a miniskirt and tube top like she wore to the bar. She had on a plain dress. No makeup. Hell, her hair was barely combed."

"What happened then?"

"I spoke to her, but she acted like she didn't know me, like she'd never even met me. She said her name was Amelia and ran off." Mike heaved a sigh. "Then someone at the diner gave me an earful, and I realized I had to stay clear of her."

"When did you last see her?"

"About six months ago. She called me a few times though. As Viola, I mean." A frown marred his face. "I told her to leave me alone, but she even sent me flowers a time or two. Another time, one of those lacy teddies. It was spooky as shit."

"She was stalking you?"

"I wouldn't exactly call it stalking." Mike shrugged. "But after a while, I threatened to get a restraining order against her. I haven't heard from her since."

Jake stewed over Mike's declaration. Mike was such a ladies' man, he probably didn't want anyone knowing that he'd been dating a mentally ill woman.

What if Walt had found out? "Did you know Amelia's grandfather?"

A muscle ticked in Mike's jaw. "No. I mean, I'd seen him in town, but we never really met." He smirked. "Although this is the reason I didn't mention it. I figured you'd jump to conclusions." Mike snatched his coat. "And before you ask, no, I didn't have a run-in with him about Viola. *And* I have an alibi the night the old man was killed."

Then he turned and stalked toward the door.

"Wait a damn minute," Jake said. "I have an assignment for you."

Mike hesitated, his look wary. "What?"

Jake explained about the questions surrounding Grace Granger's death. "Go to the hospital, talk to some of the nurses on staff, and see if they saw or heard anything out of the ordinary." Mike's charms could come in handy there. "Find out if anyone saw Grace fall, and if anyone talked to this guy Herbert Foley."

"Who's he?" Mike asked.

"The orderly who supposedly found her after the fall."

"You think he might have been the one to push her?"

Jake nodded. "He disappeared that same night."

Mike's brows arched. "I'll get right on it, boss."

Jake glanced down at the phone log as his deputy left. Maybe he and Waterstone would learn to work together after all.

Still, he didn't like the fact that Mike had kept information from him. But knowing Viola had been sleeping around raised more questions.

What if Walt had discovered she was taking lovers? Maybe Walt confronted her and a man, and they killed Walt in the heat of the argument.

———————— , ————————

Sadie settled on the sofa with a cup of hot tea and skimmed through several more letters in the keepsake box. Each one disturbed her more. It was as if Amelia had left a box of darkness behind.

Still, she had to read them to help her understand her sister.

Dear Sadie,

You have to get me out of here. Last night it happened again. They took us in the night.

Ting. Ting. Ting.

It's time for the chimes to ring.

They line us up all in a row. Like robots, they make us follow them into the long dark corridor. One of the chimes is crying so loud the walls shake. Another one pounds his feet up and down like he's marching to death camp. Another one makes a hideous noise, over and over and over…

It's cold and damp and something claws at my arms.

I try to hang on, to tell myself to be strong. But I hear Bessie crying somewhere inside me. And I'm scared…

The door creaks open, and it's a sea of black.

They're going to kill us this time.

The awful humming starts in my head. The hollow sounds echoing through the tunnel.

No one knows about this place but us.

I tried to tell one of the nurses, but she said I made it up.

It's not real, a voice inside my head whispers. But if it's not, then why am I here? Why can I feel the metal snapping around my wrists when they force me to lie down? The prongs poking into my chest and head. The tightness around my ankles when I struggle to get up.

The sharp sting of the needle as it pierces my skin.

The light they shine in my eyes is so bright I close my eyes and shut it out. But I can't close my eyes. They hold my eyelids up with wires.

Ticktock. Ticktock. Ticktock.

Seconds tick by as the darkness swallows me.

The medicine burns as it seeps through my veins. I fight it, but it swirls inside me so I feel its warming lull. My head swims, my throat feels dry, then the colors come.

And the voices.

Don't fight it, Amelia.

You belong to me now.

It's another man's voice. He's in my head. He won't go away.

I'm the Commander, he says. *I can bring the others back to you, or I can make them disappear.*

No! I scream. But the sound comes out a hoarse, pitiful sound instead of a scream.

I don't want the others to leave. Then I'll be all alone.

I need them.

Viola tries to make a deal with him. She offers him our body in exchange so she can live. Bessie cries and cries and says she's going to hide.

Skid cusses and flails to shake off the restraints, but the Commander tightens them and Skid collapses. I try to shake him and wake him up, but he's so quiet and still I'm afraid he left me for good.

No...

I can't do it alone.

But they're gone.

And I'm left alone with the Commander...

Chapter 14

———— ○ ————

Winter had definitely set in, the chill forcing Jake to crank up the heater as he drove home. When he reached his house, the scent of fried chicken and gravy wafted through the kitchen, and he forced himself to leave the investigation at the door.

Ayla jumped from the table where she'd been working a Cinderella puzzle and raced toward him. "Daddy, Daddy, Daddy!"

He swung her up in a hug and nuzzled her neck, planting kisses all over her face until she squealed and giggled for him to put her down.

Gigi laughed and set a pan of biscuits on the table with butter and honey. Jake's stomach growled, and he and Ayla practically jumped into their seats. Ayla chattered all during dinner, her sweet voice sidetracking him from the troubling case.

He spent the next two hours playing with Ayla, then they read bedtime stories and said prayers.

Ayla threw out her arms in a bear hug. "I love you this much."

He grinned and threw his arms around her, once again kissing her until she laughed and begged for him to let her go.

But he never wanted to let her go. He wanted her to stay his baby so he could protect her forever.

"Daddy!" she cried. "You're squeezing me too tight!"

He laughed, then tucked her in.

Finally, she settled back on her pillow and hugged her rag doll to her. "Don't leave me, Daddy."

Jake tweaked her nose. "Don't worry, I'll be right down the hall."

Her lower lip formed a pout. "I mean, don't go away like Mommy did."

Jake took a deep breath. Damn his ex for cutting all ties with Ayla. He didn't understand how a mother could abandon a child.

"I'm not going anywhere." He would never do that to his daughter. "You and I are a family, and no one will ever change that." He tucked her in tight, kissed her again, and then made a show of hugging her doll, earning him another giggle. But as he left the room, his mind drifted back to Sadie and Amelia.

Amelia had been a child when she was first treated at the sanitarium. Her family had trusted the doctors.

How would he feel if someone had mistreated his little girl?

He balled his hands into fists. He'd kill them...

Gigi was finishing the dishes when he entered the kitchen. "Gigi, you've lived in Slaughter Creek all your life, haven't you?"

She nodded, dried the cast-iron frying pan, and stowed it in the cupboard. "Yes, why?"

He couldn't tell her everything, so he hedged. "I'm trying to help Sadie figure out why her sister killed her grandfather. Both the twins were treated at the free clinic in Slaughter Creek as babies. So were Grace Granger and Joe Swoony."

Gigi's penciled-in eyebrows narrowed. "All so sad. Those kids having trouble so young."

"Do you remember the doctor who ran the clinic, Dr. Coker?"

She sat down at the table with a cup of coffee. "Yes, he seemed like a real caring man. At least, he was when I lost my Pearl."

Jake frowned. "What do you mean?"

"Pearl, my baby girl." Gigi's eyes blurred with tears, and she wiped them away. "She was born with a heart defect and only lived a few days."

"I'm sorry, I didn't realize you lost a baby."

"It was a long time ago," Gigi said.

"Do you remember anyone else who worked at the clinic?"

Gigi tilted her head in thought. "There was a nurse. Patty Mandolin. Real sweet and caring woman."

"Where is she now?"

"Lives in the retirement community in town."

Jake squeezed Gigi's hand. "Do you mind if I go out for a while? I'd like to talk to her tonight."

She agreed, and retired to her room while Jake rushed to his squad car.

He'd pass the Nettleton farm on the way. Maybe he'd stop by and check on Sadie. She might even want to go with him to see the doctor.

Hopefully the nurse could give them the answers they needed.

———————— , ————————

The sound of a knock on the door jarred Sadie from the letter. She tensed and glanced at the clock. Eight p.m. Who would be coming to see her?

Maybe someone wanting to offer condolences over her grandfather's death?

Or maybe it was the person who'd made that threatening call?

She stuffed the letter back inside the box, hurried to the door, and checked the peephole. Relief whooshed through her when she saw Jake. But the memory of that threatening call made her anxious as she opened the door. What if the person who'd phoned had called Jake?

"Sorry to bother you this late," Jake said, "but I talked to Gigi tonight—"

"Gigi, the woman who babysat you and Nick when you were little?"

He nodded. "Yes, she keeps my little girl now."

Sadie's heart fluttered. "You have a child?"

Jake's expression closed. "Yes, she's five."

Sadie released a breath. "I…heard you were married—"

"Not anymore," he said gruffly. "But I got Ayla out of it."

Sadie didn't know what to say to that. Jake was a father…

Irrational jealousy traipsed through her. Years ago, she'd dreamed of the two of them getting married, having children—but that dream had died…

She wanted to tell him about the threatening phone call. But then he would ask questions about what the caller had meant. Questions she wasn't ready to answer.

"Where is Ayla's mother?" Sadie asked. "Does she live close by?" Was he still in love with her?

"No," Jake said in a clipped tone. "She left when Ayla was just a baby. Said she wasn't cut out for motherhood. She doesn't see Ayla at all."

Sadie's heart suddenly ached for the child.

"Anyway," Jake said, "Gigi mentioned a nurse who worked with Dr. Coker at the free clinic. I thought she might know something about what happened years ago. Do you want to go with me?"

"Yes," Sadie said. "Let me grab my coat." She snatched it from the coatrack on the wall, then grabbed her purse and followed Jake.

"This nurse's name is Patty Mandolin," Jake continued as Sadie fastened her seat belt. "She lives in a retirement community close by. Gigi said the records from the clinic were destroyed in the fire that burned down the building a few years ago. Hopefully, Patty remembers something about the patients' treatments."

Sadie twined her hands together. "I found some letters in Amelia's keepsake box."

"What kind of letters?"

"Letters to me. She was begging me to rescue her from that hospital."

Jake cut his gaze toward her as he drove from the farm. "Of course she wanted out, Sadie."

"It's more than that, Jake. I never received any of those letters. She asked Papaw to mail them, but he never did. She told me she found them, and she and Papaw argued about them because she thought he'd mailed them to me."

"You think that's the reason she shot him? The argument got out of control?"

Sadie ran a hand through her hair. "I don't know what to think now."

"What was in the letters?" Jake asked.

"Amelia described different episodes that sounded like abuse. In one of the letters, she wrote about being taken into a dark tunnel, tied down, and drugged." Sadie's voice cracked. "She described having a bright light shining in her eyes, and that she tried to close her eyes, but that they held them open."

"Jesus." Perspiration beaded on Jake's forehead. "Still, Sadie, you know your sister was ill. How can you believe anything she wrote?"

"That's the problem. Sorting out the truth from her delusions." Sadie sighed. "But with what you learned about Grace and Brenda's information, it makes me wonder if there's some truth to it."

"It's still hard to swallow."

Sadie's eyes darkened. "I know it sounds crazy, but if the doctors were doing something underhanded to the patients, they had built-in protection. Everyone assumed the complaints were just the crazy rantings of the mentally ill."

Jake turned into the parking lot for the retirement community, a series of small white brick units that looked bright and cheery in contrast to the stormy night. When he parked, he turned to her. "There's something else I have to tell you."

Sadie didn't like the sound of his gruff voice. "What?"

"Earlier I received a copy of the phone records from your grandfather's house and Amelia's phone." He paused, concern flaring in his eyes. "My deputy's phone number was on the list."

Sadie twisted in her seat. "I don't understand."

"Mike admitted that he met Amelia in a bar...well, no, not Amelia, Viola."

Another disturbing memory surfaced. Viola coming home drunk, smelling like men's cheap cologne when she was seventeen...talking about sex and how she used men to get what she wanted.

"He didn't mention it when I met him," Sadie said. "And at the jail, Amelia didn't act as if she knew him." Because she'd lapsed into her Bessie alter.

"I know. Mike said they hooked up a few times, then he ran into her in town one day and she looked different. She didn't recognize him."

"Because it was Amelia," Sadie said, realization dawning.

He nodded. "He found out about her mental instability that day and broke it off. Viola called him a few times after that." Jake sighed. "Then he threatened to get a restraining order against her, and she left him alone."

"What are you saying? That Papaw might have found out Viola had a lover and confronted her?"

"It's a possibility." Jake hesitated. "Mike has an alibi for that night. But if Viola slept with him, she might have had other lovers."

Sadie sagged in her seat. "You're right. She and Papaw could have argued over one of them."

Jake gave her a sympathetic look, then stroked her arm. "I'm sorry, Sadie, I didn't mean to upset you."

The touch of his fingers on her skin made her body tingle. Made her ache for more.

For things she could never have. Like Jake in her arms, in her bed.

In her life.

He squeezed her hands to comfort her, and Sadie blinked back tears. Still, humiliation ate at her as memories of Amelia's episodes flashed through her mind.

One day at school, her sister, as Viola, had tried to seduce their history teacher in front of the entire class. Another time she'd come on to the gym coach. And one night at a football game, she'd snuck up on Jake and kissed him.

Sadie's heart had broken at the sight.

But Jake had realized Amelia wasn't she, unlike most people, who couldn't tell them apart, and he'd pushed Amelia away.

She had fallen even more in love with him for knowing the difference.

Their gazes met, tension thrumming through the air between them, electric with the closeness they had once shared.

Before her life shattered around her, and she lost Jake.

———————— , ————————

The shiver that tore through Sadie made Jake ache to pull her into his arms.

If Amelia hadn't killed her grandfather, and her lover had, then she had either blocked out the traumatic event, was too afraid to tell, or didn't want to implicate her lover.

Which meant that she might be a witness.

She also might be in danger.

"When you visit Amelia tomorrow, can you access Viola?" Jake asked. "Maybe she can tell you what happened between Amelia and Walt."

"I'll try," Sadie said, looking shaken, as if she too realized that her sister might be in danger. "But if Viola's lover killed Papaw, then looking into mistreatment at the hospital may be a wild goose chase."

Jake shrugged. "It's still my duty to find out what happened to Grace Granger. Someone at the hospital might have witnessed what happened." He turned in to a driveway. "I sent my deputy over there to see what he could find out from the staff."

Sadie reached for the car door. "If someone hurt Amelia at the hospital, I want them punished. Especially if my parents died because of it."

Sadie climbed out, anxious to question the nurse. Cold air engulfed them as they walked up to the door, and Jake rang the bell.

The sound of a radio echoed from inside, then feet shuffling. "Who's there?" a female voice asked.

"Sheriff Blackwood, ma'am. I need to talk to you for a minute."

The lock clicked from inside, then the door opened. A heavyset woman, probably in her seventies, with short gray curls stood in a jogging suit. "Yes?"

Jake introduced Sadie, and Patty invited them in. She offered tea, but they declined. "What can I do for you?"

Jake cleared his throat. "Tell us about the time you worked for Dr. Coker at the free clinic."

The woman sipped her own cup of tea. "What about it?"

"My sister and I were treated there as children," Sadie said. "Do you remember us? We were twins."

Patty's hand fluttered to her cheek. "Uh…yes, of course. Your sister had some emotional problems."

"That's right," Sadie said. "But we're investigating the possibility that Dr. Coker or another doctor might have mistreated her at the clinic."

Patty fidgeted. "Dr. Coker was a good doctor. He…gave free health care to the needy."

"Did you ever see him do anything medically inappropriate?" Jake asked.

"No," the woman said. "I told you he was a good man."

Sadie cleared her throat. "We spoke to him, and he admitted they did things they shouldn't have at the clinic. He even hinted that my parents' deaths weren't an accident. It made me wonder if they discovered some impropriety and were killed because of it."

The woman gasped. "Dr. Coker would never have hurt your mother. And I certainly wouldn't have." She stood abruptly. "Now, I think you should leave."

"Please, Patty," Sadie said. "Joe's mother claims he was normal when he first visited the clinic, but after a few visits, he stopped talking and his behavior changed."

"I...don't know what you're implying," Patty said. "But I don't like it. Often kids with problems don't exhibit signs until they're around two or three, when parents notice that they aren't progressing normally. In fact, autism often becomes apparent around that age."

"That's true," Sadie said. "But please talk to us. We have reason to believe that some of the children were given experimental drugs. Maybe the doctors tried a new medication on my sister and Joe and Grace."

"I don't recall anything like that," Patty said.

"Was there anyone else at the clinic who had access to the patients?" Jake asked. "Another nurse, another doctor?"

The woman picked at a loose thread on her sweater. "Now that you mention it, there was another doctor who worked at the clinic for a short while. Only a couple of days a week."

"What was his name?"

"Dr. Sanderson," Patty said, her voice low, distant, as if the memory had just surfaced. "I almost forgot about him."

Jake had heard that name before. Sanderson had treated Grace. "Do you know where he is now?"

Patty shook her head. "I think he retired somewhere near Byrne Holler."

"Thank you for your help, Patty." Jake removed a business card from his pocket and laid it on the table. "Call me if you think of anything else."

Her eyes flitted toward the card, then she twisted her hands together again.

Jake took Sadie's elbow and led her to the door. A minute later, they settled back in the car. "Dr. Tynsdale said that Dr. Sanderson treated Grace."

"Then let's talk to him," Sadie said. "Should we call first to make sure he's home?" Sadie asked.

"No," Jake said. "I want the element of surprise on our side."

Jake grabbed his tablet and accessed the police database, then plugged in a search for Sanderson. Just as Patty had said, he now lived in the hollow.

Sadie lapsed into silence as he started the engine and drove away. The temptation to pull her up against him and soothe her tugged at Jake. He had dreamed about seeing her for so long, about having her return home and confess that she'd always loved him, that an ache started deep in his chest, burning through him.

Dammit, she'd bled him dry when she left years ago. Loving her had destroyed him.

He could not travel down that dangerous path again.

Thunder rolled across the sky, lightning streaked over the mountain ridges, and the wind beat at his car as he drove into the hollow. A dirt road veered off from the main highway, leading into a wooded area that seemed deserted, and so dark that Jake nearly hit a deer that raced in front of the car.

Sadie gasped as the deer fled into the woods to safety, and he glanced at her. She looked small and lost in the seat beside him, her breathing echoing in the awkward silence. Ten years ago, she would have crept over to his side and laid her head on his shoulder, and he would have wrapped an arm around her and whispered that he loved her.

But everything had changed.

His headlights swept across the woods, finally lighting up a log cabin situated on the river. But it wasn't a rustic cabin; this one was gigantic, custom-built, with skylights and a deck that spanned its width at the back, overlooking the river. A Cadillac was parked to the side, and a low light burned in the front room, evident through the Palladian windows.

Jake checked his weapon inside his jacket before he opened the car door, and he and Sadie wove their way up the rocky path to the front porch. The boards of the porch steps squeaked as they climbed.

Jake raised his fist and knocked while Sadie glanced off the side of the porch at the river. The sound of water rushing over rocks filled the air, and a tree limb snapped off and flew against the side of the house.

Jake listened for sounds inside but heard no movement, so he knocked again. Sadie walked up behind him, tugging her coat more tightly around herself.

He tapped his boot on the porch floor and gave the man another few seconds to answer, but again nothing.

Still, a car was outside.

Sensing trouble, Jake decided to check out the house. Glancing through the front windows into the den and kitchen, he saw no one inside.

He twisted the knob, and was surprised when it turned and the door opened. Instinct warned him to be careful, and he threw up a hand, urging Sadie to wait outside.

"Dr. Sanderson," he shouted as he eased in the door. "It's Sheriff Blackwood." He scanned the front room. Newspapers were stacked by the fireplace; a pair of worn house shoes rested in front of a leather recliner; and a dirty coffee cup sat on the coffee table.

Sadie eased up behind him, but he whispered for her to stay close so he could shield her in case of an attack.

Suddenly a loud noise rent the air, and a cat tore past them. Startled, Sadie clutched Jake's arm. He sucked in a sharp breath at the sight of dried blood on the cat's nose. Earlier, its paws had left a bloody trail across the floor.

"Jake?"

"Stay here." He removed his gun from his holster and held it at the ready.

"No," Sadie whispered. "I feel safer with you."

His heart swelled at that, although worry niggled at him that they might be walking into a trap. Another step, and he checked out the kitchen, which was empty. He glanced at the office to the right. It had been ransacked, the safe open.

A home invasion/robbery?

Then he spotted Sanderson. His back was to them, but he was slumped over, his head on the desk. The scent of death, of blood and body odors, hit Jake. Behind him, Sadie gasped and clutched his arm.

Jake inched closer, then lifted the man's head. Dammit.

Sanderson's throat had been cut, his clothes soaked in blood.

Chapter 15

"Oh, my God," Sadie whispered.

"Stay back and don't touch anything, Sadie." Jake motioned for her to move against the wall. "Judging from the body's decomp, the killer is long gone, but I'm going to take a quick run through the house just to make sure."

Sadie nodded, then held her breath as he left the room, his gun drawn.

Who had killed the doctor? And why?

The timing of their visit disturbed her even more. Had Dr. Coker called and warned Sanderson they were coming? No…he hadn't been coherent enough to do that.

The threat she'd received echoed in her head.

Could his death have something to do with them nosing into the past?

Jake's footsteps pounded above, on the second floor, then down the steps, and he met her at the edge of the office door. "It's all clear. I'm going to call a crime unit from the county to process the scene. But you really need to stay clear, Sadie. Your sister's arrest makes you being here a conflict of interest."

"Jake," Sadie said, her voice cracking, "do you think he was killed because we've been asking questions?"

"I don't know. It looks like a home invasion, but like I said earlier, too many coincidences arouse suspicions." He made a phone call, explained what they'd found, and said he'd secure the crime scene and wait until the forensics unit arrived.

He hurried to his car and returned with his crime kit, then pulled on latex gloves and began to rifle through Sanderson's desk drawers.

"What are you looking for?" Sadie asked.

"Anything related to the research and the sanitarium."

"Can I help?"

Jake shook his head. "I can't let you do that, Sadie. We don't want to compromise the investigation."

Sadie frowned but agreed and watched him work. All of the rooms looked as if they'd been combed through.

Jake checked the counter by the phone, the kitchen cabinet drawers, then the small desk in the corner. All he found though, were advertisements and assorted mail—oddly, no phone bill.

When the kitchen turned up nothing, he searched the end tables in the den, and noticed a pad on the table, which was blank. Then he returned to Sanderson's office and rummaged through his file cabinet. Seconds later, he slammed it shut with a bang.

"The only thing I see are housing expenses and personal financial records. Nothing about the clinic or patients."

A siren wailed in the distance. "How about his computer?"

Jake pivoted and scanned the room, and Sadie did the same. There was no computer in the room. Hmm, surely the man had one.

Had the killer stolen it to sell?

Or had he taken it with him because it held some incriminating evidence?

Jake didn't like this turn of events. What had started out as a domestic murder had spiked into a major investigation.

Now there were three suspicious deaths—Walt's, Grace's, and Sanderson's.

Five, if you counted Sadie's parents.

All connected in some way.

He rushed outside and checked Sanderson's Cadillac for a computer and cell phone, but came up empty. Then he hurried back inside and checked Sanderson's pocket for the phone. Again, no luck.

"Did you see a cell phone?" he asked.

Sadie shook her head no. "Maybe he didn't have one," Sadie said.

"He had one," Jake said. "Just look at this place. A man with this kind of money has expensive toys."

A siren wailed as the police and coroner's vehicles pulled up. Sadie stepped into the foyer, her face haunted, as he greeted the crime unit and coroner.

"I haven't found a computer or cell phone," Jake said. "So if you find either of those, send it and his home phone records to my office. I also want to be notified of any forensic information."

"Certainly, Sheriff," the crime tech said. "Did you find the murder weapon?"

"No. The killer probably tossed it in the river, but have your guys search the trash and the property just in case."

The tech nodded, and Jake went back to Sadie. "Come on, I'll take you home, then follow up with them later."

Sadie looked exhausted as she sank into the seat.

"Did you make the arrangements for your grandfather?" Jake asked as he drove toward the farm.

A sadness passed over her face. "Yes."

Jake wanted to reach out and hold her so badly that he held the steering wheel in a white-knuckled grip. "I know it was difficult for you to come back here. That you had your own life."

Sadie's troubled gaze met his. "My work has been my life," she said so quietly that it tore at his heart.

"You…never married?"

Pain slashed across her face, then she turned to look out the window. "No, Jake. Amelia is the only one I have left."

The realization that Sadie was alone in the world made him ache for her even more.

But he couldn't let himself want her again. Losing her once was all he could bear.

Sadie's chest throbbed. She wanted Jake, but there was no way she could reach out and hold him the way she once had.

The way she'd yearned to do for years.

It was hopeless for her to even dream of a future with him. He had a daughter by a woman he might still love.

And he would never forgive her if he learned the truth about why she'd left Slaughter Creek.

He parked in front of her house, and she grimaced at the thought of going inside alone. No Papaw to wrap her in a hug.

No Ms. Lettie and Amelia to breathe life into the place.

No matter how much trouble Amelia had been, she was still Sadie's sister. And at one time, when they were little, they'd been so close they could finish each other's sentences.

"You're going to the hospital to see Amelia tomorrow?" Jake asked as he cut the engine.

Sadie nodded. "I'll see if I can access Viola, find out about her and your deputy." She paused. "And if she had any other lovers Papaw might not have been happy about."

She started to open the car door, but Jake laid his hand over hers. The moment his fingers touched hers, a warm tingle spread through her, and the temptation to lean into him hit her.

But she couldn't do that. She had to stand on her own.

So she reached for the door instead.

"Call me if you need anything," Jake said.

She needed *him*.

But that could never be.

So she dragged herself from the car, tugged her coat around herself, and hurried inside. Maybe she'd find more answers in Amelia's letters.

But when she went to the desk to retrieve the keepsake box, it was gone.

———————— , ————————

Jake's chest constricted as he watched Sadie disappear inside the house.

She'd had a rough couple of days, and that big farmhouse had to be lonely tonight. The urge to follow her and make sure she was okay made him hesitate before he pulled out of the drive.

But what would happen if he did?

Would she fall into his arms? Let him hold her?

Walk away when the funeral was over and Amelia had settled down?

Dammit, she looked so small and vulnerable and...sad.

He checked his watch. Eleven thirty. Ayla would be in bed, sound asleep, and so would Gigi.

He might as well stop by the Tavern, where Mike had met Viola, and see what he could learn. Rain began to drizzle down, turning to sleet pelting his windshield. He flipped on the defroster and wipers, driving slowly through town to the bar.

Grateful he'd changed from his uniform, he secured his weapon inside his jacket, then strode inside.

Country music blared through the speakers; a group of people were line dancing, while others lounged at tables over beer and drinks.

A young bartender with a sleeve of tattoos and a name tag reading "Beau" slapped a napkin down in front of him as he approached. "What will you have?"

"Whatever you have on tap," Jake said.

The bartender filled a mug, then handed it to him. Jake took a sip, slid onto the bar stool, then removed the photograph from his jacket. "Listen, man, have you seen this woman?"

The potbellied guy next to him slid off his seat and lumbered toward the restroom.

Beau glanced at the picture. "What are you, a cop?"

Jake gave a clipped nod. "Sheriff."

The bartender's eyes darted around as if he was nervous.

"Don't worry, I'm not here to bust anyone," Jake said. "I just need some information." He gestured toward the photo again. "Do you know her?"

Beau thumped the edge of the bar in tune with the music. "Yeah, I've seen her a few times. Why? Something happen to her?"

Jake maintained a calm facade. "Actually, she was arrested for allegedly shooting her grandfather."

"Man, oh, man," the bartender said with a whistle. "I saw that in the paper. Didn't know it was the same chick though. She looked…different."

"How so?" Jake asked.

"When she came in, she was all dressed up, you know, sexy like. Wore miniskirts, halter tops, a real flirt with all the men."

"You hook up with her?" Jake asked.

Beau averted his eyes. "Naw, I got a steady."

Jake sipped his beer as he considered his approach. "She met up with a man named Mike Waterstone a couple of times." He didn't add that the son of a bitch was his deputy.

"Yeah, she left with Mike once or twice. But he wasn't the only one."

Another customer leaned over the bar. "Can I get a refill, buddy?"

"Sure." The bartender poured him a whiskey, then glanced across the room. "Like I said, she was friendly."

"Who else did she leave with?" Jake pressed.

Beau gestured toward a cowboy in the corner with a blonde draped across his lap. "Wade."

"Thanks." Jake tossed down enough bills to pay the tab along with a hefty tip, then laid his card on top. "If you think of anything else, give me a call."

Then he strode over to the cowboy and stopped by his table. "Name's Sheriff Blackwood. I need to talk to you."

Wade's mouth twisted sideways, then he patted the woman's butt. "Sugar, go powder that nose and give us a minute."

She planted a sloppy kiss on his face, then sashayed toward the ladies' room.

"What's going on, Sheriff?"

Jake showed him the photo. "You know this woman?"

Wade grimaced. "Yeah, that bitch is nuts. She came on to me, then when we went in the back room, she started crying and talking like she was a little girl. I mean, baby talk. It freaked me out."

So Viola had picked up the man, then Bessie's personality had emerged. "She has a mental disorder," Jake explained. "You didn't know that?"

"Hell, no. Not at first, anyway. She was all over me, whispering dirty words and shit. But when she started that kid talk, I lost it. I mean, I'm not into kinky stuff." He narrowed his eyes as if he suddenly realized he might have said too much. "Why? She say different?"

Jake crossed his arms and gave him a deadly stare. "Would she have?"

"I don't know, she was crazy." Wade looked defensive. "Thought she might be one of those nut jobs that play up to a man, then cry rape to get attention."

Jake contemplated his suggestion. What if Amelia or Bessie had told her grandfather that some man had tried to hurt her? He might have confronted the man, and they could have fought…

Although Walt knew Amelia was ill, and probably wouldn't have believed her. Unless he'd caught the man with her at the house.

Then Walt might have done something. And if he confronted the man, things could have spiraled out of control…

He rubbed his chin. But he had no proof that anyone else had been there.

Only Amelia and her grandfather, and Amelia with the gun.

―――――――――― , ――――――――――

Sadie searched the house, afraid that whoever had stolen the letters was still inside, but the house was empty. Who would take Amelia's letters?

Other than Jake and Ms. Lettie, who had even known they existed?

She should probably call him and tell him…but what could he do? Report stolen letters?

No use in calling him tonight. She'd tell him later. Her nerves were too raw to see him again. If he came over, she might give in and beg him to stay.

She checked to make sure all the doors were locked and secure, then grabbed her grandfather's pistol again and carried it to bed with her.

For hours, she lay staring at the ceiling, the image of the dead doctor floating through her mind. She had left Slaughter Creek because of one man Amelia had killed, and returned because of another.

Ten years ago, she had put as many miles between her and this insanity as she could, thinking distance would chase away the memories. But they had dogged her everywhere she'd gone.

And now she'd returned to more death and madness.

Finally she drifted into a restless sleep, but she jerked awake at dawn, her heart drumming. Arthur Blackwood's face taunted her.

She rubbed her eyes, mentally ordering his image away, but just as it had done for years now, it refused to leave her.

Shivering, she grabbed her robe and tugged it on, anxious to talk to Amelia. While she showered, she struggled to recall the details of the night Skid killed Arthur Blackwood. Had someone been in the woods by the house?

Or had someone been at the old mill by the river?

She hadn't noticed any cars or heard anyone nearby. But she'd been horrified at what her sister, or rather Skid, had done, and terrified they'd get caught, and she hadn't exactly been looking around.

Shaking off the tremors that accompanied the memories, she dried off and threw on some clothes, then made coffee and ate a bite of toast. By the time she reached the hospital, she'd formulated a plan.

Hopefully she could talk to Amelia, then access Viola. Maybe Viola knew something about the night Papaw had died.

She checked in at the nurse's station, then peeked in on her sister. Ms. Lettie had dozed off in the chair, so Sadie woke her.

"Go on home, Ms. Lettie. I'll stay with Amelia now."

Ms. Lettie rubbed her eyes, stood and stretched, then hobbled over to Amelia and squeezed her hand. "I'll be back later, sugar."

As soon as she left, Sadie remembered the letters. She should have asked Ms. Lettie about them. She made a mental note to do so later.

Weary, she settled down beside her sister and watched her sleep—a restless sleep that Sadie knew was riddled with the voices of the others.

Finally, in the early afternoon, Amelia stirred and opened her eyes. "Sadie?"

Sadie scooted her chair closer to the bed. "I'm here, Sis."

Amelia's eyes looked clearer today, as if the medication had taken effect.

"Sadie, I'm scared," she whispered.

Sadie moved the chair closer to the bed and cradled Amelia's hands in hers. "I know, but I'm here. And we're going to figure things out together."

Amelia bit down on her lower lip. "Is it true? Papaw's...dead?"

The anguish in her sister's voice wrenched Sadie's heart. "Yes, I'm afraid so."

Tears trickled down Amelia's cheeks. "I...they...they say I did it?"

Sadie swallowed back her own emotions. "You were there, Sis, but we're not sure what happened. That's why we need to talk."

Amelia blinked back more tears. "But I don't remember..."

Sadie nodded. "Ms. Lettie said Papaw had been drinking a lot lately. Was he upset about something?"

Amelia tried to push herself to a sitting position, but the restraints snapped tighter around her wrists and ankles, and she cried out in frustration.

This time Sadie didn't bother to call the nurse. "Hang on, I'll get these things off of you." Amelia calmed slightly as Sadie unfastened the restraints. Then her sister sat up, rubbing at her wrists where they were red and bruised.

"Now," Sadie said, using the same low soothing tone she used with her patients, "let's talk about that night. I understand it's painful, but it's important you remember what happened."

"I would never hurt Papaw," Amelia said in a raw whisper. "I loved him, Sadie."

"I know you did, Sis, and that's why this doesn't make sense," Sadie said, struggling for answers. Had one of her sister's alters felt differently about their grandfather? "Was Papaw upset about something?" she asked again.

Amelia pulled at the sheet. "I don't know...I don't think so."

"Please, Amelia." Sadie captured her sister's trembling hands in hers. "Trust me. I want to try a therapeutic technique on you. Now close your eyes and relax."

Amelia looked panicked, but she nodded, and Sadie squeezed her hands to reassure her.

"That's right—close your eyes and think of a safe place. It can be anywhere. Your bedroom. The studio." She lowered her voice to a soothing pitch and continued talking about Amelia's art and her paintings until her sister calmed, slipping into a hypnotic state.

"You feel safe, don't you?"

Her sister nodded.

"Now we're going back to the other night. You're at home, and Papaw is there. Are you two alone, or is someone else there with you?"

"I...don't know...I'm coming in the house, and it's dark."

"Where's Ms. Lettie?"

"She went home," Amelia whispered, as if she was recalling the details. "She was mad at me, because I hid some of my pills in the flowerpot, and she told Papaw he should put me back in the hospital. Papaw said no, but she said if I didn't take my meds, I'd have to go back."

Sadie squeezed her fingers to reassure her. "That's good. Then what happened?"

Amelia's lower lip quivered. "I didn't want Papaw to be mad, but the pills...they make my head so fuzzy I can't think. I can't paint..."

She was getting agitated again, so Sadie rubbed her hands. "It's okay, Amelia. I understand. Then what happened? You went inside to talk to Papaw—"

Amelia sighed, a pained, troubled sound. "He...yes, he wants to talk to me about the sanitarium. And about that n...ight."

Sadie went perfectly still. "What night?"

Amelia stiffened. "You know...*that* night. The one we never talk about."

A coldness swept over Sadie. That night—the one that had changed her life forever. After they'd buried Blackwood's body, her grandfather had forbidden them from ever discussing it.

"Why did he want to talk about it?" Sadie asked.

"I don't know." She put her hands over her ears. "The voices started then, and I got upset...and I don't remember what happened."

"Did you hear the gun fire?"

Amelia began to rock herself back and forth, tears trickling down her face. "The shot...Papaw, there's blood..."

Sadie drew Amelia into a hug. "I know, it's so sad," Sadie whispered. "But you did good, Amelia. Really good."

Amelia clung to her. "I miss Papaw, I...what's going to happen to me, Sadie?"

Sadie gripped her sister's arms and forced her to look at her. "Nothing. I'm going to take care of everything." Which meant she had to access the alters. "I realize this is difficult, Sis, but I need to talk to Viola."

"Viola?" Amelia straightened, clenching the sheets tighter. "But I don't want to go away."

At one time Amelia couldn't call upon the alters or switch at will, but part of her therapy had been learning to talk to them so she could merge them into one. "It's just for a few minutes. She might know something that could help us," Sadie said. "Then I'll call you back, Amelia. I promise."

Amelia clawed at her hand. "Wait, Sadie—first I have to tell you something."

"Tell me what?"

An odd look darkened her face. "No...they don't want me to tell you."

Frustration knotted Sadie's stomach. "Tell me what?"

Her sister angled her head to the side, then dropped it forward and closed her eyes. Sadie watched her body jerk; then Amelia opened her eyes again, and Sadie realized her sister had transitioned.

Amelia stroked her hair down, as if primping, then crossed her legs and raised her fingers as if she were holding an invisible cigarette. "You wanted to talk to me?"

"Yes, Viola," Sadie said. "Do you know why Amelia's in the hospital?"

Viola rolled her eyes. "Of course, we all know. She's a mess without us."

Sadie remained calm. "Losing Papaw is hard on her. Can you tell me what he was upset about? Did he and Amelia argue?"

Viola jerked her eyes away.

"Or was he mad at you, Viola?" Sadie asked.

"Why would he be mad at me?" Viola asked with genuine shock in her expression. "Me and your granddaddy got along just fine."

Sadie arched a brow. "He didn't mind if you brought boyfriends back to Amelia's house?"

She looked offended. "It's my house, too."

"So he didn't mind?"

Viola shrugged, but a devilish gleam lit her eyes. "What he didn't know didn't hurt him."

"He never found you entertaining a man?"

Viola smoothed her hair down. "No, darling. I...was always discreet."

Not like she'd been in high school.

"Do you know what happened the night Papaw was shot?" Sadie asked.

Viola's eyes widened, as if she was remembering. "They were arguing," she said in a low whisper. "Your granddaddy was beside himself, said he was scared for Amelia. Said that *he* was back."

Sadie frowned. "What do you mean, he's back? Who's back?"

"*He* is," Viola whispered. "He's back, and he's going to kill Amelia. We have to stop him."

"I don't understand. Are you talking about another alter?"

Viola's hand trembled as she stood and paced to the window. For a moment, she gripped it, looking out as if she was terrified of something outside.

Then Viola disappeared, and Sadie watched as Skid assumed her body. "Shut up, Viola!" Skid instantly slicked Amelia's hair behind one ear, threw his shoulders back with an attitude, and cocked his head sideways like a belligerent teenager. "Viola talks too damn much."

"Then you talk to me," Sadie said. "If you want to protect Amelia, tell me what happened the night Papaw died."

Skid spun around, eyes spewing venom. "Stop asking questions, Sadie. You're gonna get your sister killed."

Sadie choked back her anger. "Me? I'm trying to save her from going to jail."

"No, you're causing more trouble!" Skid snarled. "Just go back where you came from and leave us the hell alone!"

"You want me to leave because you don't want me to find out that you killed Papaw just like you killed Arthur Blackwood. Isn't that right?"

Skid punched the wall. "You don't know what you're talking about. All your nosing around is making things worse."

"I know you're the violent one," Sadie said, forcing herself not to react. "That you think you're protecting Amelia, just like you did years ago. But the only way to help Amelia is to tell the truth."

Skid glared at her. "Who are you to talk? You ran out on her. *We* stuck around and protected her."

The nurse poked her head inside with raised brows, and Sadie positioned herself between Skid and the nurse.

"Everything's fine," she said, hoping to diffuse the situation.

Fortunately, Skid remained silent while the nurse stood at the door. "All right, Dr. Tynsdale is on his way up. But any more commotion, and she goes back in the restraints."

Sadie nodded. "There won't be any problems."

Skid paced to the window and turned his back to her, shutting down, and a sense of defeat nagged at Sadie.

A second later, Dr. Tynsdale appeared at the door. "How's my girl today?"

Amelia shuddered, then turned around, and Sadie realized Amelia had transitioned back into herself. "I…Sadie, you talked to the others?"

Sadie nodded. "To Skid and Viola."

Amelia clasped her hands. "What did they say?"

"Nothing much that helped," Sadie said. "Viola said she and Papaw got along fine. Skid insists he's been protecting you all along."

"Sadie, I really wish you wouldn't talk to the alters without me being present," Dr. Tynsdale said.

Sadie frowned at him. "I'm trying to help her," she said.

"Can we talk for a moment?" Dr. Tynsdale said.

Sadie glanced at her sister, who looked lost and forlorn. "I'll be back, Amelia."

She stepped into the hallway, and Dr. Tynsdale followed.

"I wanted to talk to you about Amelia's treatment. We were making progress before this thing with your grandfather."

Sadie sighed. "Had she talked to you about the night with Arthur Blackwood?" Her grandfather had confided in him as Amelia's doctor, knowing he was bound by doctor-patient confidentiality.

"Not yet, but I was going to broach that in our next session. Then this happened."

Sadie tucked a strand of hair behind her ear. "Do you know what Papaw wanted to talk to Amelia about that night?"

Dr. Tynsdale shook his head. "We had just discussed the subject. I really felt that Amelia needed to deal with the trauma of what happened before she could fully heal."

Sadie sighed. "That makes sense. Did Papaw agree?"

"Yes," Dr. Tynsdale said.

"Do you think that's what triggered Amelia to kill Papaw? That he tried to talk to her about it, and she couldn't handle it, then transitioned to Skid, and he shot my grandfather?"

His eyebrows crinkled. "I don't know, but I'd like to work with her and find out."

Sadie had always trusted Dr. Tynsdale. She hated having doubts now.

"Did you ever notice Amelia being mistreated while she was at the sanitarium?"

His eyes widened. "Of course, not. My God, I would have reported it and removed her immediately."

But he hadn't treated Amelia when she'd first been admitted. Dr. Sanderson had.

And now he was dead.

So was Grace, another one of Sanderson's patients.

Dr. Tynsdale removed a file from his bag. "I understand that you're worried, but here is your sister's medical file. You can see the medication she's taken, and there's documentation of her treatment."

"Thank you," she said. "I appreciate this."

"We both want Amelia to get well," he said with a smile.

Her cell phone buzzed, and she saw that it was the funeral home. "I'm sorry, I have to get this. I'm going to grab some coffee and look at the file. I'll be back in a few minutes."

She hurried out the door before he could respond.

But Skid's warning taunted her.

What had Skid meant, when he said she was going to get Amelia killed?

Skid had to get them out of this nuthouse.

He'd told Sadie *he* was back, and he was. Viola had seen him, and so had Bessie.

He had come back to torture them. To hunt them down like animals.

The chimes...*Ting. Ting. Ting.*

He would kill them all and stop their ringing.

Then it would be the end of him too.

He waited quietly, biding his time while Amelia whined to the doctor. Finally the old man left to talk to that nurse, then the fat bitch who had been ugly to Amelia during the night waddled in, a hypodermic in her hand.

"I hate to do this to you, Amelia, but we can't let you get worked up again."

Worked up? Hell, the stupid cunt didn't know the meaning.

He grabbed her wrist, jerked the needle from her hand, and stabbed her in the neck with it before she could yell for help. She fell to the floor with a loud clatter, banging the rolling cart holding that crap they'd called breakfast.

Fuck. He had to save Amelia and the others before Sadie came back. Before the Commander found them and ended them for good.

He rifled through the nurse's pockets and took her keycard, then tiptoed to the door and peeked out. The hall was empty. Somewhere down the corridor, a food cart rattled. Someone hummed. A patient was crying.

Screams echoed in his head.

He drowned them out as he slipped from the room and headed down the hall toward the back stairwell. He'd find a way out of this hellhole.

And no one would ever lock him up again.

Chapter 16

———— o ————

Sadie took a deep breath as she stepped into the hallway. "Yes, 'Amazing Grace' is fine." A pause. "Yes, 'Shall We Gather at the River' will be good."

Mazie passed her as she ended the call, and Sadie followed her over to the nurse's station. "Mazie, can I ask you something?"

The woman looked around, wary, then nodded. "What is it?"

"Were you working here when Arthur Blackwood was the administrator?"

A flash of some emotion Sadie couldn't quite define lit Mazie's eyes. "Yes."

Sadie leaned over the nurse's desk and lowered her voice. "What was he like?"

"Why would you ask about him?"

Sadie shrugged. "I just wondered if he took an interest in patient care."

"Well, yes," Mazie said in a low voice. "He used to hold weekly staff meetings with the doctors for updates."

"Did he ever visit patients in their homes?"

Mazie glanced around again. "No, not that I remember. But that was a long time ago."

"Right." Sadie debated on how much to push. "Do you remember a doctor named Coker?"

"Yes," Mazie said. "He worked at the free clinic."

"What about Dr. Sanderson?"

"He was here until a few years ago," Mazie said.

"What did you think of them?" Sadie asked.

Mazie stiffened. "I like keeping my job, Ms. Nettleton, so I never gossip about doctors." She turned to her computer. "Now, if you'll excuse me, I have work to do."

"If you think of anything you want to tell me, I'd appreciate it," Sadie said.

Mazie cut her a stern look. "You'd best be careful poking around."

Sadie nodded, although she wasn't about to be scared off. Her stomach growled, and she decided to grab a bite of lunch while she reviewed the file Dr. Tynsdale had given her.

She walked to the cafeteria, chose a turkey sandwich, a cup of soup, and iced tea and settled at a table in the corner. But her appetite had vanished, and she was nowhere closer to the truth than she had been the day she'd arrived in town.

When she returned to Amelia's room, she'd use her art therapy techniques to tap into Amelia's subconscious.

The others might be protecting Amelia, but she'd have to convince them that helping Sadie learn the truth would help her sister. Of course, that meant accessing their memories.

Between the three alters and Amelia, maybe she could piece together the facts.

Her resolve renewed, she managed to eat a few more bites, then opened the file.

She noted the date and realized that the file only contained information on how Dr. Tynsdale had treated her; it held nothing prior to the date he took charge.

Nothing about Sanderson or Coker and what they might have done.

She skimmed the first part, which focused on the three steps of treatment for DID:

1. Stabilization and symptom reduction
2. Treatment of traumatic memories
3. Reintegration and rehabilitation

Dr. Tynsdale had tried hypnotic techniques to access the memories, but Amelia still hadn't dealt with the night Blackwood died.

Another hypnotic session had focused on accessing early childhood memories, but there was nothing about sexual or physical abuse, as was often found. He had tried to discuss her parents' car accident and deaths, and Amelia had become agitated. She had commented that she remembered hearing her mother scream and seeing blood flying against the glass.

Sadie pressed her hand over her mouth to stem the tears as the same memory surfaced for her. She'd had nightmares about it.

But had it caused Amelia's psychotic break?

A chill slithered through her. What if Coker had given some of the children a bad vaccine?

But *she* hadn't reacted. Unless she'd received medication from a different batch.

She put that thought on hold and finished reading the file.

Dr. Tynsdale had prescribed a battery of psychopharmacological drugs, antidepressants and anxiolytics, serotonin reuptake inhibitors, and anticonvulsants, including Neurontin.

Sadie shook her head. All that therapy, and her sister was no better off than before. And now this shooting had caused a setback.

Her nerves prickled as two patient-care workers strolled in, talking in hushed voices.

Suddenly an alarm sounded, the intercom bursting to life. "Code red, code red. The hospital is in lockdown."

Lockdown. That meant a patient had escaped, or that one of the patients had attacked a staff member or other patient.

Sadie froze, her throat tightening as one of the order-lies turned and stared at her. He said something to the other man, then spoke into his radio, his gaze remaining fastened on her.

A bad feeling crept up her spine. Something was wrong. Why were they looking at her like that? Like she was some kind of... criminal?

Then an image of Grace flashed into her mind. Grace had been pushed down one of the stairwells.

Dear Lord, had something happened to Amelia?

She stuck the file under her arm, left her tray, and headed toward the door, but a guard stepped in front of her. "Amelia Nettleton?"

"No, I'm her sister, Sadie. Is something wrong?"

He gripped her arm. "Good try, lady, but I've seen you before."

"Listen to me, I'm Amelia's sister." Sadie tried to push away from him. "Did Amelia get out of her room?"

His fingernails dug into her arms as he half dragged her down the hallway toward her sister's room. "You can't escape here."

Sadie dug in her heels and tried to reach for the file. "You're making a mistake. Just look at her file. I'm Amelia's twin."

He ignored her protests and jerked her forward, then took the file from her. Sadie winced in pain. For the first time in her life, she understood the blinding panic that Amelia felt when people didn't believe her.

"Call Dr. Tynsdale—he can verify who I am." He yanked her so hard, she bit her tongue to keep from cursing him. She couldn't let them drug her before she found someone to straighten out this mess. "Check with the head nurse. She saw me in Amelia's room."

"Right," he muttered. "And you're the sane sister, not the one who attacked one of our nurses."

Sadie gasped. Dear God…Amelia must be desperate.

The alarm was still sounding, people scurrying up and down the hall, and another guard appeared with a radio, then spoke into it. "Patient has been located. We're escorting her back to her room now."

"No," Sadie cried. "Call Dr. Tynsdale, call Sheriff Blackwood. They'll tell you I'm not Amelia! If she's escaping, we need to find her."

But the beefy guy who had been manhandling her shoved her into the hospital room and onto the bed, then reached for the restraints.

Reality hit her with the force of a fist, and she fought him, but he was too big and strong, and he pressed his knee into her chest and held her down. Sadie struggled to breathe as he clamped the restraints around her wrists.

"You have the wrong person," she said in a choked cry. "You have to find my sister."

Ignoring her protests, he pulled a hypodermic from his pocket and stabbed her arm with it.

Tears filled her eyes as she fought to explain. If the drugs took effect and no one realized the mistake they'd made, she might be here for hours.

By then, Amelia could be anywhere.

And if her sister was in danger, she might not be able to save her.

———— . ————

Jake spent the morning at his office, fending off calls from curious residents. Brenda Banks had called, and this time he returned her call. "It's the sheriff."

"Jake," Brenda said. "I'm assuming Sadie told you about our talk."

"Yes," Jake said. "Why don't you fill me in?"

"I don't know any more than what I told Sadie," Brenda said. "Someone contacted me and told me that there was abuse in that hospital, that it had been going on for years."

"Who was this?"

"I can't divulge my source, Jake."

"I know you have that reporter-informant privacy thing, but this is important, Brenda."

"Listen, Jake, the person who called me was scared. She was afraid of retribution if she was identified."

"You mean she was afraid of getting fired?"

"I sensed it was more than that," Brenda said.

Jake chewed the inside of his cheek. "Did she say anything else? Mention any specific doctors?"

A slight pause. "No, just that she thought that two doctors conducted some kind of experimental research there about twenty, thirty years ago, that the patients and their families had no idea what was happening. And that it caused terrible side effects in the children."

About the time Grace, Amelia, and Joe started treatment.

"Are you sure about this?" Jake asked.

"My source is reliable," Brenda said.

Jake rubbed his chin. "Why did you come to Sadie with this?"

Brenda sighed. "Because I didn't think you'd believe me if I came to you."

"And you thought Sadie would."

"I figured she wanted answers about her sister."

"So what do you get out of this?" Jake asked.

Brenda cleared her throat. "I want an exclusive if you find something."

"That figures."

"Listen, Sheriff, I am trying to help, but I also want to do my job."

"All right. If there turns out to be some truth in this, the story's yours."

He hung up, then studied the forensics reports. So far, they hadn't discovered any extraneous prints at Amelia's studio.

And none at Sanderson's house. They also hadn't found a computer or cell phone, which made it appear to be a home invasion.

Unfortunately, CSU had also found no files, nothing to link the cases.

Which made him even more uneasy.

Only a pro would be as meticulous in his cleanup as this killer had been. The slice to Sanderson's throat had been quick and lethal, neatly severing his jugular artery. It hadn't been done by a first-timer. There were no tentative marks, no struggle.

Which suggested that Sanderson had known his killer.

And that the killer had known what he was doing.

But why murder Dr. Sanderson? What enemies had he made over the years?

According to Coker's wife, Coker had been considered a saint, and if Sanderson had been giving free services, people thought the same about him.

Unless someone had discovered that the doctors had been mistreating patients, using them as research guinea pigs.

The doctor's statement about Sadie's mother echoed in his head. What if Mrs. Nettleton had stumbled onto the fact that Amelia had been mistreated? Had her and her husband's deaths been an accident or murder?

He'd have to talk to the coroner back then, and to Sheriff Bayler.

He tapped a few keys and looked for complaints filed against Sanderson with the medical board, noting two names: Bertrice Folsom and Emanuel Giogardi.

Mike strode in, tucking his cell phone into his jacket pocket.

"Did you find out anything at the hospital?" Jake asked.

Mike shrugged and sank into his chair. "No. A couple of the nurses thought Foley was handsome, said he was a big guy, short haircut, he had some tat that looked like it was military." Mike handed him a crude sketch. "One of the women drew this."

Jake leaned forward in his seat to examine it and frowned. It was a scorpion with a number etched below it. It looked like one of the tats he'd seen on some of the Special Forces teams—a symbol that they were bound as one.

So why hadn't the man's name shown up when he'd searched for it?

"Research that tattoo and see if you can find out what unit had it," Jake told his deputy.

"If it was Special Forces, we might not find it," Mike said. "You know they're pretty secretive."

"I know, but we have to explore every lead we have." He sighed. "Did anyone see Grace Granger trying to escape? See Foley rescuing her?"

Mike shook his head. "Happened during the shift change. People coming and going. Probably how she slipped through that locked door at the end of her ward."

And a good time to cause an accident while no one was looking, Jake thought.

"Thanks, Mike. I'm going to plug this sketch in and see if it pops. But we have another problem."

Mike crossed his arms. "What?"

"Another murder." He explained about Sanderson. "Would you canvass the neighbors who lived near the old man and see if anyone heard anything suspicious?"

"No problem." Mike rubbed a hand over his chin. "What do you think's going on? Three murders in one week—that's a lot for Slaughter Creek."

"Sure as hell is."

Mike left to question Sanderson's neighbors, and Jake called the judge and asked him to amend the warrant. He wanted a list of all of Dr. Sanderson's patients, especially those who'd been treated at Slaughter Creek Sanitarium.

And he wanted to question Folsom and Giogardi, the patients who'd filed complaints.

But first he planned to talk to the coroner about Sadie's parents' deaths.

Dr. Thad Grimes had worked as the country coroner for twenty years; four years ago he'd retired and moved to Nashville. Jake found his address and home phone and called the number. Five rings later, it rolled to voice mail, so he left a message.

"It's important I talk to you about a case you worked a few years back," Jake said. "Please call me back ASAP."

Antsy for information, he headed to the door to drive out to Bayler's house.

A second later, his phone buzzed, and he answered it.

"Sheriff, this is Dr. Grimes. What can I do for you?"

"Did you do autopsies on Mr. and Mrs. Nettleton when they had their car accident about twenty-five years ago?"

"Yes—why the interest?"

"Just tell me what you found. Anything unusual?"

"That was a long time ago, and I don't have the files with me, but I don't remember anything odd," Dr. Grimes said. "Both their injuries were consistent with the impact of the car crash."

"What about a tox screen?"

"That I can't say. I'd have to look back at the files."

"Would their records still be at the ME's office?"

"Should be, although they'll be in the basement. We never did get them all inputted into the computer system."

Jake thanked him and ended the call, then called Bullock. "I know you're busy, but will you have one of your assistants pull this file for me?"

"All right, but it might take a while. I'll have to call you back."

"No problem."

He disconnected, then rushed to his car.

Maybe Sheriff Bayler had some answers.

———————— . ————————

Amelia trembled as she hid in the linen closet down from her hospital room. She had to be strong, had to get her head clear. Skid had attacked that nurse, and now she was out of that room.

She couldn't go back.

But she'd heard Sadie's voice in the hall. She'd peeked outside and seen that orderly dragging Sadie toward her room. Sadie was trying to tell them who she was.

Amelia's throat clogged with a scream.

She couldn't leave Sadie here. What if they hurt her?

She left you, Bessie whispered. *Please, just get us out.*

She doesn't care about you, Skid said.

It's time for us to live, Viola chirped.

Amelia clawed at her arms, hating the drugs. The sounds in here. The nurses and orderlies and smells…

Her ears were ringing with the noises, with the memories.

She'd tried to tell Sadie. Papaw. Ms. Lettie.

But no one believed her.

They'll put us back in here for good if you don't run, Skid said.

He was right. It was up to her to find some proof. But how? She was so confused…She didn't know what day it was. Couldn't remember what happened with Papaw…

A sob caught in her throat, but she heard footsteps outside in the hall, then Ms. Lettie's voice.

"Oh, my dear, she tried to escape," Ms. Lettie cried. "I'd better go sit with her."

Panic tightened her stomach, and she clawed at her arms again. Would Ms. Lettie know it was Sadie in that bed instead of her?

All the more reason for you to get us out of here fast, Skid said sharply.

He was right. She couldn't think straight or remember with all those drugs clouding her mind.

Her head throbbed, nausea rising, and her hands trembled. More side effects of that stuff they pumped through her.

Just like years ago.

She snapped her head up.

Ting. Ting. Ting.

She heard the chimes ringing.

That was it—she had to find the room where they'd done those awful things to her. If she could show it to someone, maybe they would believe her.

She reached for the doorknob, but Viola's voice stopped her. *You can't go out in that hospital gown.*

She was right!

Then she spotted the hospital scrubs on the shelf. Yes, no one would stop her if she was dressed like a doctor…it was the perfect escape.

Then she'd finally be free of this place, and maybe she could remember how she'd gotten here.

Jake passed over the steep mountain ridge to the east side, the hills giving way to farmland and apple orchards. Winter advisories warned there might be sleet, but at the moment it had held off. Still the wind whipped the trees into a frenzy, scattering leaves like a thick rainfall.

Bullock phoned just as he neared Bayler's house, and he answered the call. "Sheriff, my assistant pulled that file like you asked."

"Did Grimes note anything out of the ordinary?"

A pause. "Both victims were killed instantly, bruises and contusions all over their bodies. Hmmm."

"What?"

"Looks like Mrs. Nettleton had some scratches on her arm that weren't consistent with the accident, but considering the impact of the crash, he let it go."

Scratches, as in, she might have fought with someone?

"What about the tox screen?"

"Mrs. Nettleton was driving, and no drugs were found in her system. The husband had some alcohol, but not enough to have impaired him."

"I realize this is the ME's report, not the sheriff's, but does the report mention anything found in the car?"

"Just a note with the name *Coker* in the mother's hand."

Had she been on her way to see him? "Where did the accident take place?" Jake asked.

Bullock muttered something, and Jake realized he was skimming the file. "Says here it was out on Blindman's Curve."

"The one going out of town?"

"That's it."

Jake drove down Bayler's drive with a frown. He had passed Blindman's Curve on his way here. Could the Nettletons have possibly been coming to Sheriff Bayler's house? "All right, thanks."

Bullock hung up, and Jake noted that the silo and barn to the right of Sheriff Bayler's house looked a little run-down, although a decent herd of cattle grazed in the pasture.

Then he saw the former sheriff sitting on the front porch. He tugged at the straps of his overalls and stood as Jake climbed out and walked up the steps toward him. He looked different out of uniform, like an old man who'd never even worn a badge.

"What brings you out this way, Sheriff?" Bayler asked.

"I wanted to talk to you about some things that happened when you were in office."

Bayler scratched his graying beard, then gestured toward the metal chair on the porch, and they both sat down. Bayler once again settled into the glider.

"What things?"

"The Nettleton family."

Bayler murmured his regrets. "Heard about poor Walt. A bad way to go, getting shot by your own granddaughter. Especially after all he did for that girl."

"That's partly the reason I'm here," Jake said. "I'm trying to find out why she killed him."

"The fact that she was unstable isn't enough?"

"Yes, but there are some things about that hospital where she was that are bothering me," Jake admitted. "Another patient at Slaughter Creek Sanitarium died, and I started asking questions. Those questions led to more questions."

Bayler worked his mouth from side to side. "I don't understand where you're going with this."

Jake explained about Grace's suspicious death, then her connection to Dr. Sanderson, and his murder.

"Jesus Christ," Bayler said. "We haven't had a murder around here in twenty years."

Jake sighed. And they had all happened on his watch.

"I'm investigating the possibility that there was abuse at the sanitarium. Also that some doctors used patients in an unsanctioned research project."

Bayler rocked back and forth. "What? Where did you hear that?"

"A source," Jake said. "Did you ever hear suggestions of abuse or misconduct there?"

"Hmm, seems like someone mentioned the possibility once, but after considering the source, I didn't see reason to look into it." Bayler pressed his hands on his legs. "Besides, your father was the administrator. He was extremely detail-oriented and micromanaged. If something was wrong, he would have taken care of it."

The sheriff's comment set Jake's teeth on edge. That was true. If his father had discovered abuse or an illegal project, he would have reported it.

Unless…what if his father had discovered some impropriety? What if he'd decided to handle it himself, and he'd been killed because it?

That would explain his sudden disappearance.

Then again, maybe he was jumping to conclusions.

"What else did this doctor say?" Bayler asked.

"Dr. Coker implied that they did things they shouldn't. He also commented that the accident that killed the Nettleton couple wasn't an accident."

He watched for the sheriff's reaction, but Bayler didn't show one.

"You investigated their deaths?" he asked when the sheriff didn't comment.

Bayler rubbed a hand over his leg. "Nothing to investigate that I remember. It was a cold night, sleeting. Mrs. Nettleton hit a patch of black ice and ran off the road."

"Her husband was with her. What were they like?"

Bayler nodded. "They had been separated for a few months. Walt said she was upset, said it had to do with Amelia. She said she had to talk to the girls' father."

"Sadie never talked about her father."

Bayler shrugged. "She was so little she probably didn't remember much about him. The Nettletons had some marital problems, but I heard they were trying to work them out." He pushed the swing back and forth, the metal creaking. "Then we found the two of them in that car, both dead, so everyone assumed they were going to reconcile. After the funeral, the girls went to live with their grandparents."

Jake shifted, glancing across the farm at the mountain ridges. Amelia and Sadie had been around three. Amelia hadn't exhibited full-blown signs of mental illness at that point.

But her mother had scratches on her. She'd been upset about Amelia, had connected with her estranged husband, and had Dr. Coker's name on a piece of paper in her hand. Had she gotten the scratches from her ex?

Or…What if she had discovered that Dr. Coker had given Amelia some kind of experimental drug? Perhaps they had argued, and she'd gotten the scratches during their altercation. Then she'd called Sadie's father to go with her to see Sheriff Bayler.

Maybe the drug had caused Amelia's alter Bessie to appear.

"Did you have the car examined to make sure there wasn't a malfunction of some kind?"

Bayler shook his head. "Like I said, didn't see any reason."

Jake gritted his teeth. "What happened to the car?"

"Wrecker hauled it to the dump."

It had been twenty-five years since the accident. Could it possibly still be there?

Dammit, he'd find out. Forensics had come a long way since the couple's deaths.

If the car was still there, he'd have someone look at it and see if there was any evidence of foul play.

———————— · ————————

Sadie drifted in and out of a fog of dreams. Colors flashed in front of her eyes, imaginary creatures dancing, the drone of machines splitting the air.

She struggled to hold on to reality, but the crazy dreams wouldn't stop.

"Amelia, dear, don't worry, I'm here."

Sadie blinked in confusion. Why was Ms. Lettie calling her Amelia?

Then a sliver of reality returned, and panic made her yank at the restraints. Amelia had escaped, and everyone thought she was her sister.

"Ms. Lettie," she cried. "Help me."

"I'm here, hon," the kind woman's voice murmured. "Now you really shouldn't have tried to escape. That's what happens when you go off your meds. You do things you shouldn't."

Sadie tried to talk, but her mouth was so dry she couldn't make it work.

"The nurse said you attacked her," Ms. Lettie said. "I assured her that you didn't know what you were doing."

Sadie tried to lift her head, but it was so heavy, she collapsed back on the bed. "Not me," she said, although her voice sounded far away. Distant.

Or had she spoken out loud at all?

"Here, sugar, take your other pill." Ms. Lettie slipped a tablet between her lips. Sadie tried to spit it out but choked.

"Take a sip of water," Ms. Lettie said. "Then you'll feel better. After you sleep we can talk."

Ms. Lettie held a straw to her mouth and Sadie drank, but she felt water running down her neck. Ms. Lettie dabbed at it, drying her off.

Then the room began to spin, and Sadie slid deeper and deeper into the tunnel of darkness.

The same darkness where her sister must have lived for years.

———————— , ————————

Amelia pulled the scrub hat lower on her head, ducking her face as she passed one of the orderlies. If he recognized her, it would be all over.

They'd drag her back to that room and drug her, and she'd never remember what happened to Papaw.

The thought that she'd killed him sent a spasm of panic through her.

But Skid yelled at her to keep moving, and she did. She made her way past the section of rooms where she'd been kept. The ones that felt like prison.

Then she stopped at the corner of the next unit, trying to remember. Voices echoed from down the hall, and a cart clanked.

She jumped behind the doorway of an empty room until they passed. Sweat soaked her hands, the rumble of the ancient furnace taking her back to when she was a child.

She closed her eyes and pictured the hallway. The stairs. The hidden entrance.

Yes, it was there. She knew it.

Her body began to tremble, her chest hurting as she struggled for air.

Just get us out of here, Skid barked in her ear.

But Amelia wanted more than to escape. She wanted to find a way to make Sadie believe her. She wanted to remember the night Papaw died.

She had to know if she'd killed him.

Chapter 17

---○---

Jake phoned the local junkyard where Bayler had said the Nettletons' car had been sent, hoping the car hadn't been demolished in the past few years or the parts sold for cash.

"Cordelle Boone speaking, Cordelle's Auto Parts."

"Cordelle, this is Sheriff Blackwood. Do you still have that Chevy from the Nettletons' crash? It happened about twenty-five years ago."

The guy had been there for ages. If anyone could help him, it was Cordelle.

"I believe it's still here," Cordelle said.

"You haven't sold off parts?"

"Naw, it was too damaged to do much with. It's pretty rusted out now, way at the back of the junkyard."

"I have a favor to ask." He explained that he wanted it checked to see if anything had malfunctioned.

"What's this about, Sheriff?"

"Just some questions that cropped up about that accident that's related to another investigation I'm working on."

"I don't know what I'll be able to tell, but I'll give it a look-see," Cordelle said.

Jake thanked him and disconnected, then checked the address for Bertrice Folsom's family. Apparently the aunt who had raised her was still living in the trailer where Bertrice had grown up, down in the hollow.

Frannie Folsom would be in her late sixties now, but she might shed some light on Bertrice's condition.

Twenty minutes later, Jake was sipping iced tea on the porch of her trailer. Given its dilapidated state, he was surprised the mobile home had survived tornado season.

"Bertrice killed herself five years ago," Frannie said. "Why are you asking questions now?"

"Because she was in the same mental hospital as Grace Granger, and I'm looking into her death," Jake explained. "Did you ever have any concerns about her care at the hospital?"

The ice in Frannie's tea clinked as she took a sip. "It was a sanitarium," Frannie said. "That place used to scare me to death. But I never understood what happened to Bertrice, why she was the way she was, so I didn't know where else to turn."

"Tell me about her," Jake said.

"She seemed fine till she was about eight. Then her daddy died, God rest his soul. And she just went away herself."

"What happened to her father?" Jake asked.

"Killed in a hunting accident."

"Did Bertrice ever talk about what happened at the sanitarium?" Jake asked.

"She never talked about anything," Frannie said. "After I took her there for outpatient treatment, she became sullen. The doctors said she'd work through it, but she never did."

"Who was her doctor?"

"Dr. Sanderson," Frannie said. "He was always so kind to us. Gave me a break on the bill."

Jake refrained from comment. First the free clinic, then giving patients breaks on their bills at the mental hospital? Not incriminating in itself, but linked with other things, it could mean he'd taken advantage of needy families who would be so appreciative of his help that they wouldn't ask too many questions.

"How was she as a teenager?"

"She suffered from severe depression and anxiety disorders, paranoid delusions, then turned to drinking. Eventually to drugs."

"Did she have ongoing treatment at the hospital?"

Frannie seemed to think about that for a moment. "I know she took some medication. Prozac and Klonopin, I believe it was. But they didn't help that much. A few times when I tried to reach out to her, she got so angry she scared me."

"What do you mean?"

"One time she picked up a knife and threw it at me. Another time she took one of my husband's old rifles and shot a hole in the ceiling. That's when I committed her."

"How about right before she died? Was she depressed then?"

Frannie took a long drink of her tea. "Yes, she had been for weeks. Had been saying crazy things. Come to think of it, that Nettleton girl, Amelia, she had just visited Frannie in the hospital. Frannie called me that night, hysterical, talking out of her head, making all kinds of accusations."

"What accusations?"

Frannie released a loud breath. "Said they gave them LSD. That the doctors were brainwashing them. I tried to calm her down and told her I'd come and see her the next day. But..." Her voice cracked. "They called me at six a.m. Said my little girl had slit her wrist." Frannie knotted her skirt in her hands. "She didn't even leave a note telling me good-bye."

So Bertrice had died at the mental hospital, just as Grace had. And after Amelia had visited her, and after she'd made accusations against the doctors.

Of course, both Bertrice and Grace had severe mental issues, but for two of them to die in the hospital still made him wonder.

Either they had been mistreated, or the hospital was just plain negligent.

His phone rang as he climbed back in his car. He checked the number, then picked up the call when he saw it was Cordelle.

"Sheriff, I did what you asked."

"That was fast," Jake said.

"It's been a slow day," Cordelle said. "But you're not gonna like what I found."

Jake tensed as he turned onto the main highway. "What?"

"The brake lines on that car had been cut," Cordelle said. "That accident wasn't no accident at all."

Jake hissed. Sadie's parents had been murdered.

Sadie forced her eyes open as the nurse led her into the shower. She blindly remembered the woman removing her clothes and pushing her into the stall.

Then the shower water blasted her, and she shivered, her breath catching at the unexpected cold. She looked down at her naked body, then at the woman watching her, and wanted to scream.

But screaming wouldn't get her out of here. It would only reinforce to everyone around her that she was unstable.

Still, her skin crawled as the chubby woman thrust a sponge into her hand. "Wash, lady. I don't have all day."

Sadie's vision blurred, the past few hours tangled in her mind. How long had she been in this room?

How long had Amelia been gone?

"Hurry up," the nurse said. "It's not like you're primping for a damn date."

Sadie shuddered, then ran the sponge over her body. Her mind became fuzzy, her movements slow, her arms so weighted she could barely reach her hands above herself to shampoo her hair.

Then the woman grabbed her arm and jerked her out of the shower stall, scrubbing her body roughly with a towel.

"Put the gown on," the woman ordered with a sneer. "You thought you were smart, stealing your sister's clothes. Or did she give them to you?" She cursed beneath her breath. "Next time we'll search her before she pays you a visit."

"But I'm Sadie," she said, although her words sounded slurred, the room spinning again. What in the hell had they given her?

The same drugs they'd given Amelia...

No wonder her sister had been incoherent.

She stuffed her arms into the sleeves of the hospital gown, humiliation mingling with nausea as the nurse tied the back of the gown together.

Panic hit her as the woman dragged her back toward the room. She took one look at the restraints on the bed and knew she couldn't go back.

She had to find Amelia.

Her head throbbed, but she mustered up her anger and shoved the nurse back into the bathroom. The nurse bellowed, but she closed the door, then pushed the chair in front of it.

Dizzy again, she had to pause to catch her breath. But there was no time to wait. Someone would hear that damn nurse any minute...

Frantic, she ran to the door, then peeked outside. Noise from down the hall echoed loud and clear—an orderly and a nurse laughing about some stupid joke. Then the clank of the medicine cart. And footsteps.

She waited until they grew quiet, then eased open the door. When she saw the hall was empty, she ran down the hall, her vision blurring in and out of focus. For a moment, she saw double, then threes, and she clutched the wall, groping her way until she found the stairwell that led down to the bottom floor.

A voice made her freeze; then she realized it was another patient screaming for help. A shudder rippled through her, and tears burned her eyes.

That could have been Amelia.

Or she.

But she couldn't help whoever it was until she escaped, herself, and the drugs wore off.

Blinking to refocus, she turned the corridor, hugging the hall as she went. One step, two, three…a few more, and she'd reach the next hall. It led to the front.

No…she needed to find a side exit. Too much security up front.

Another step, and she nearly stumbled, then felt her way around the corner and headed down the hall. No, the wrong way.

Tears of frustration burned her eyes. *Dammit, Sadie, you don't have time to cry.*

She ducked into a corner when a nurse walked by, then glanced left and right. Another nurse down the hall. A patient strolling with a family member.

A security guard.

Her heart started to flutter, panic setting in. She fought for breath, then bolted the other way and rounded a corner, spotting a neon orange exit sign above the door at the end.

Summoning every ounce of strength she possessed, she ran down the hallway toward the sign. Her feet felt heavy, paranoia reminding her to hurry.

She was going to make it. She was almost there. Just another few feet.

Then suddenly a loud noise boomed over the intercom.

"Code red, patient missing from the west wing."

Alarms pealed all through the hospital, lights blinked wildly, footsteps pounded the floors. She was slowing, her lungs squeezing for fresh air.

Her mind scattered, fear taking over. She could not get caught. She could not.

She had to run.

One more step.

Her fingers touched the door. Another alarm boomeranged, blasting so loudly that she had to cover her ears, and her knees went weak.

Dammit, she needed a key to get through that door.

She turned and tried to run the other way toward the stairs, but suddenly something hard slammed against her skull.

She tried to scream, to fight. She called out for Jake.

But the world faded away and she slipped into the darkness.

———————— , ————————

Skid pulled on the scrub suit and hat, tucked Amelia's hair beneath it, and ducked his head as he eased down the corridor. He had hidden out while the fucking guards had searched the hospital, waiting on the alarms to die down.

Amelia had almost gone into that basement, but he'd saved her from that.

Just like he'd saved her back then.

Still, Amelia had tried to claw her way to the surface, begging him to go back and save her sister, but he quickly vetoed that idea.

It was too risky.

Besides, that damn sheriff who had his head up Sadie's ass would probably figure out the truth.

Hell, he'd be long gone by then.

Another alarm pealed, the intercom blasting that a patient was missing. Fear clogged his throat. Had they already discovered they had the wrong twin?

He had to hurry.

He grabbed a chart from the door of one of the rooms, pretending interest in it as he made his way to the back exit. Two security guards rushed past, obviously on the hunt. He kept his face in the chart; he had to be cool, not draw any attention to himself.

He swiped the key through the locked door, then made it down the hall to the emergency exit. Sweet relief filled him as he opened the door and stepped outside, The sky was dark, though, storm clouds bullying their way across and turning it a dismal gray.

He turned in a wide arc, scanning the parking lot and mountain ridges. This fucking stink hole was miles and miles away from town.

And from the farm.

He needed a ride.

He ditched the chart in the trash can, then strode toward the parking lot. Shit. He should have taken Sadie's keys, then he could have had her car.

But it was too late to go back now. He couldn't chance getting caught.

A male orderly exited the front door and headed the same direction. Maybe he could steal the man's car.

He felt in the pockets of the scrub suit for a weapon, but the pockets were empty. Shit. He should have thought to snatch a scalpel.

He'd have to use his hands, put the guy in a chokehold. He could knock him out within seconds.

You don't need a weapon, Viola whispered. *I can get him to give us a ride.*

Shit, he hated that doc had made it so they could all talk to one another. He was the boss. They needed to know that. *No*, Skid said. *We don't have time for you to fuck this guy.*

All right, but we don't need you racking up more charges against us either. So don't get any ideas about hurting him.

He hated to admit it, but she was right.

Hell, he didn't want to fool with the guy anyway. He'd just hot-wire a ride. He'd done it plenty of times before. And when he got close to the farm, he could ditch it and no one would ever know.

He loped toward a beat-up sedan on the opposite side of the lot from the orderly and waited until the guy climbed in his Honda and took off.

Then he found a rock at the edge of the woods and used it to smash the window on the passenger side.

I told you not to rack up more charges! Viola shouted.

Stop being a nag. I didn't hurt the fucker, Skid said as he reached inside and unlocked the door.

Stealing is a crime, too, Viola argued.

Since when did you get to be fucking Mother Teresa?

I'm not, but I'm trying to be good.

A laugh escaped him. Viola was too far gone to be good. But she had been useful.

That could end any minute.

He yanked on the sterile gloves he'd stuffed in his pocket and wiggled his fingers into them. *No worries. No one will ever trace the car back to us.*

He raced around to the driver's side, slid into the seat, and hot-wired the vehicle.

I told you I could have handled him, Viola said. *Why don't you ever listen to me?*

Skid grinned to himself, then told her to shut the fuck up. He was the boss now. He would do what he damn well pleased.

The others could go to sleep with Amelia.

Then he could take over forever.

———————— , ————————

Dr. Sanderson's face stared at him from the newspaper. The bastard was dead, just as he should be. The police were hunting for his killer.

That damn reporter Brenda Banks cited the doctor's accomplishments. Sanderson had volunteered at a free clinic for years. He had treated numerous patients for mental disorders.

Folks claimed he'd been a damn saint.

But *he* knew differently.

It's time for you to go, too, the voice inside his head whispered. *Write the note now, just as I ordered.*

Outside, rain pinged off the roof. Thunder rumbled. Lightning struck, zigzagging across the mountain ridges as if God had screamed his wrath upon them.

He had to obey the Commander.

The darkness caved in around him, sucking him into its vortex. The voices...the cries of the others...the screams and pleas, begging the doctor to stop.

Begging the Commander to free them from the agony.

It had all happened so long ago.

But the legacy had followed him, shaped him into the man he'd become.

He glanced at the commendations on the wall. Remembered the oath he'd taken.

Sworn to silence.

He would keep their secrets to the grave.

The Commander's voice reverberated in his head again. Quiet. Calm. All-knowing.

He sat down at the kitchen table, then picked up the pen and began to write.

I pray God will forgive me for my sins. I took Dr. Sanderson's life because he hurt me when I was little. He hurt so many of us that I had to end it.

He signed his name, Emanuel Giogardi, then took a sip of his coffee and ran his finger over the .38 the Commander had given him. He had so many guns. Had used them so many times.

Weapons far more powerful than this one.

The M24 was his favorite. He liked the way the cool, sleek metal felt in his hands. The way it emitted that clean shot.

The faces of targets blurred in front of his eyes. Targets he had willingly killed.

Because disobeying the Commander was not an option. Disobeying brought punishments. Punishments he could not bear.

Slowly he lifted the gun to his head.

Do it now, and all the pain will end, the Commander whispered.

His hand shook slightly, but the Commander was right. He was always right.

Resigned, he pressed the barrel of the gun to his temple and pulled the trigger.

Chapter 18

J ake's conversation with Frannie Folsom still bugged him two days later. He had called Emanuel Giogardi and left messages, but hadn't heard from him since. He might just have to make that drive after all.

Even more disturbing was the fact that he hadn't heard from Sadie. He'd called her several times and left messages, but she hadn't called him back.

He told himself that he needed distance between them, that she was probably sorting through her grandfather's things, spending time with Amelia.

Besides, what could he tell her? That he now believed her parents had been murdered?

That would only torment her with more questions.

Sheriff Bayler had always seemed like a straight shooter, but had he been blind to what was happening in his town?

Needing to analyze all he'd learned so far, Jake assembled a stack of note cards and began jotting down all the information relating to Walt Nettleton's death and the sanitarium, using a separate card for each detail. One for his murder. Another for

Grace Granger. Another for Bertrice Folsom. One for Dr. Coker and Dr. Sanderson—and the free clinic.

Then Sanderson's death.

He tacked each card up on the bulletin board and studied them, drawing links to connect them. At the heart of them all lay the sanitarium.

Sadie was probably there now, working with Amelia.

He glanced at the clock—eleven at night. No, surely she was home now.

Dammit, he wanted to see her.

Not a good idea.

Seeing her only made him want to hold her and be with her.

Still, he dialed her number again. A second later, her voice came on the line. "Hello, Jake."

He breathed a sigh of relief. Yes, he could sleep easier tonight, now he knew she was safe.

———————— , ————————

Amelia's hands trembled as she answered the phone.

Jake had been calling for two days. She had listened to the messages while she hid out in her studio, but she'd been too afraid to answer.

Afraid he would know she wasn't Sadie.

Now she was afraid not to answer.

Afraid he'd get suspicious and come out to see her. Then he would know.

Jake had always been able to tell them apart.

"Sadie?"

Amelia cleared her throat. She was stronger now that the drugs were wearing off. She was more coherent, her mind clearer. She could do this.

"Yes, Jake."

"Thank God," Jake said. "I was starting to get worried when you didn't return my calls."

Don't tell him anything, Skid whispered in her head.

She wanted to scream at him to shut up and leave her alone. She couldn't think when the voices bombarded her.

"Sadie?" Jake said gruffly. "Are you okay?"

She had to pull it together, or he'd know something was wrong. "Yes," she said, searching for a lie that he would believe. "I've just been staying at the hospital with Amelia. Trying to help her remember."

"That's what I figured," Jake said. "Have you made any progress?"

Amelia closed her eyes. Saw her sister strapped down in the hospital, screaming for help.

Saw herself screaming for help for years, but no one had listened.

"I think so," she said. "But nothing concrete yet." In fact, she still couldn't remember what happened that night. Except that Papaw had been upset and wanted to discuss Arthur Blackwood's death...

Had he wanted her to come forward and tell everyone what she'd done that night?

"I talked to Bertrice Folsom's mother," Jake said. "Like Grace and Joe's family, she went to the free clinic when she was little. Her problems started after her father died."

Amelia's mind raced back in time. The chimes...*Ting. Ting. Ting.*

Line up and follow the Commander. Down the hall. To the secret room.

The bright lights. The darkness.

The electric bolts running through her body.

The children's screams for help.

Joe Swoony's. Grace's. Bertrice's.

But no one could hear.

Because the room had been built that way. Soundproofed to drown out their cries.

She closed her eyes, rocked herself back and forth, her head dizzy with the terror.

"I think we're on to something, Sadie. See if Amelia can identify one of the doctors in charge."

Amelia bit back a cry. The doctors, nurses…the Commander. He owned them all.

She struggled to see past the darkness. She had to look at his face. Tell Sadie.

But the world faded, and then she was launched back to that other night. The night they buried Jake's father.

To the grave…

"Anyway, I'm headed home, but I'll follow up tomorrow," Jake said. "Let me know if Amelia tells you anything."

Amelia's head spun.

"Sadie?"

Tell him good-bye, or he's going to get freaked and come over here, Viola whispered.

"I will," she said.

A tense heartbeat passed, then he said good night, and she dropped the phone.

You almost blew it, Skid said.

I could take over and sweet-talk that sheriff, Viola said.

Shut up! Amelia shouted.

Skid and Viola must have been startled, because they grew quiet. Still, the images flew at her. Jake's father, the gunshot blast…the blood everywhere.

Then she and Skid and Sadie and Papaw were dragging him through the rain and digging the grave.

She grabbed a clean canvas from the stack against the wall, then picked up her paints and began to sketch out the scene. The dark colors, the terror in the brushstrokes, the ghosts hovering by the grave watching them.

Following her wherever she went. Back to the hospital. To her studio.

He'd haunted Papaw, too. And he told her he'd followed Sadie.

Or was she crazy?

Was that all in her mind?

The strokes became fast and furious, reds and grays and blacks.

Then the bones rising from the grave, the skeleton's eyes reminding her that she couldn't outrun him.

That he was going to kill her one day.

A panicked feeling seized her. Everyone thought she was still strapped down in the sanitarium. What if he went back there to kill her and killed Sadie, thinking she was Amelia?

Sadie faded in and out of consciousness, the days blurring into endless terrible dreams and confusing snippets of people coming in and out of the room.

She blinked back tears of frustration. She had almost escaped.

But someone caught her and knocked her unconscious. When she stirred, she'd tried to see who it was. For a hazy terrifying moment, she thought she'd been looking into the face of Arthur Blackwood.

But then she blinked and realized an orderly was dragging her back into the room.

Despair overcame her as he chained her back to the bed.

No wonder Amelia had sounded incoherent half the time. Even though she was sane, the medications were distorting her thoughts.

She held the last pill the nurse had given her beneath her tongue, sipped the water she offered, and pretended to swallow it.

Her mind was such a mess that she felt dizzy again, but she willed herself to fend off the effect of the drugs.

Somehow she had to get out of here.

Ms. Lettie hobbled over to her and placed a hand on her arm. "It's going to be okay, hon."

How could it be okay if she was unconscious? If Amelia was missing, and no one even knew it? Where was her sister?

Finally Ms. Lettie sat down beside her, and Sadie turned her head sideways enough to spit out the pill. It landed on the sheet, and she wiggled enough to cover it with her body. If the nurse saw it, she'd force another shot into her, and then she'd lose hours, maybe days again.

She couldn't let that happen. She had to think.

As long as she cried and pleaded with them to believe that she was Sadie, not Amelia, they would keep her drugged sense-less.

Her mouth was so dry she had to clear her throat twice to speak. "Ms. Lettie?"

"Yes, dear, I'm right here."

"Where's Sadie?"

Ms. Lettie smiled slowly, as if she was glad that Amelia'd stopped trying to convince her they had restrained the wrong sister. "I don't know, Amelia. I thought she'd be by today to visit."

"I need her," Sadie said, choking on the word. "Please, I need to see Sadie."

Ms. Lettie's face grew pinched. "I know you do, and I'm sure she'll be by sometime. She's probably just cleaning out your grandfather's things."

"No," Sadie cried. "I need her now. Please, Ms. Lettie, call Sadie, tell her to come and see me."

"It's late now, hon. We'll call her tomorrow."

Sadie jerked at the restraints. "No, I need her now. She's the only one I can talk to. Make her come."

"I called her earlier, and she didn't answer," Ms. Lettie said. "Maybe she's just busy with the funeral arrangements."

"No, try her again," Sadie cried. "I'm scared something's happened to her."

"Amelia, dear, that's just your paranoia."

"No, it's not," Sadie whispered. "She promised to come back, and she hasn't. I know something's wrong."

"Amelia—"

"Please, just call again, and if she doesn't answer, call Sheriff Blackwood. Ask him to ride out there to make sure she's okay."

Ms. Lettie studied her for a moment, her eyes puzzled, then gave a nod. "All right, I'll try again. Just try to stay calm." She stood, then toddled toward the door.

Fatigue threatened to suck Sadie back into the dark pit where she'd lived since that orderly had caught her, but she fought it. Surely Ms. Lettie would start wondering why Sadie hadn't visited.

How long had it been? Days? A week maybe?

She felt isolated, alone and terrified.

Just as her sister must have felt for years.

Where was Amelia?

Had one of her alters taken over and decided to leave Sadie here to rot because she hadn't saved Amelia?

The door closed behind Ms. Lettie, and Sadie glanced at the window, trying to judge the time of day. Through the thin blinds, a stream of moonlight shone through, indicating it was night. Tears of frustration burned her eyes, but she blinked them back. Crying hadn't helped before, and it wouldn't help now.

She just hoped her plan worked. That Ms. Lettie would realize something was wrong when Sadie didn't answer.

Despair threatened, the narcotics blurring her mind again, and as much as she fought it, the darkness pulled at her again, sucking her into its tunnel.

Suddenly the door screeched, and she jerked her eyes open. Confusion mixed with fear as a figure in a scrub suit approached her.

Not Ms. Lettie or Jake.

She tried to sit up, but the restraints yanked her wrists painfully. Then the figure picked up the pillow Ms. Lettie had been using and walked toward her.

Shadows darkened the man's face, the scent of sweat permeating the room. It wasn't Dr. Tynsdale. He wouldn't dress in scrubs.

Suddenly the man lunged toward her and pressed the pillow over her face.

Fear struck her, and she tried to scream. But he pressed it so hard over her face that she couldn't breathe.

She kicked and fought, bucking her hips up to push him away, but he was too heavy, and she was restrained. No matter how hard she shook her head and jerked her body, she couldn't shake him off. Stars spun in front of her eyes, mingling with the black emptiness.

Then a low, gruff male voice echoed in her ear. "I warned you not to tell."

Sadie gulped for air.

He was going to kill her.

Jake saw Ms. Lettie's name on the caller ID and snatched the phone. "Sheriff Blackwood."

"Sheriff, it's Lettie. I hate to call this late, but I phoned Sadie's cell and the house phone yesterday and today, and she's not answering. Amelia's really distraught and has been asking for Sadie nonstop. She's afraid something's happened to her, but I think that's just her delusions. Still, maybe Sadie could calm her sister down. Is she with you?"

Jake tensed. "What do you mean, Amelia's asking for Sadie? I talked to Sadie earlier, and she said she's been staying with Amelia day and night."

A second passed, fraught with tension. "But Sadie hasn't been to the hospital in two days. I went by the house and studio a few times too, and she wasn't there."

Jake's heart hammered. "You left messages?"

"Yes, but she hasn't returned my calls." Worry edged her voice. "I don't know what to tell Amelia. She's had a rough couple of days, and if she thinks Sadie left town, she'll be even more agitated."

Sadie would not abandon her sister right now. Not until she had some answers.

He stood, grabbed his keys, and jogged outside to his car. "I'll check around town and go by the house and see if I can find her."

It was late, and the town was quiet as he sped away from the sheriff's office. He checked the diner but didn't spot Sadie's car, then headed out of town toward the Nettleton farm. He tried the home number as he drove, but the message machine kicked in, so he tried Sadie's cell. Again, no answer.

Traffic was minimal, allowing him to make it to the farm in minutes. Shadows flickered in the trees, the farmland eerily quiet as he wound up the drive.

Anxiety knotted his shoulders when he noticed that both the house and guesthouse were dark. He didn't see Sadie's car anywhere around the farm either.

Of course, Sadie could be tucked in bed asleep. Maybe she'd simply needed some time alone to grieve, some time away from Amelia.

But why had she lied to him? And where was her damn car?

He checked to make sure his gun was secure in his jacket, then strode up to the house. If Sadie was asleep, she might be angry that he woke her.

But he had to know that she was safe.

He punched the doorbell and waited, but seconds passed, and he heard nothing from inside. He rang the bell again, then pounded on the door. "Sadie, if you're in there, please open up."

He banged again, but no lights came on, and the house remained dark. Worry knotting his stomach, he rushed to his car and retrieved his lock-picking kit. Once he got the door open, he flipped on the light, but other than the furnace rumbling and the wind whistling through the eaves of the old house, it was quiet.

Panic gnawed at him, and he raced from room to room, calling Sadie's name.

But the rooms were empty. In fact, Sadie's bed didn't even look slept in. Her suitcase was still on the chair, though; it looked as if she hadn't left town.

So where was she sleeping? And why hadn't she been to visit her sister?

Antsy, he jogged down the stairs, then over to the guesthouse. He knocked on the door, but there was no response, so he picked that lock as he'd done the other one.

Instantly the quiet hit him. He flicked on the light and glanced around the studio, a macabre painting of a grave catching his eye. Had Amelia painted it, or had Sadie?

It didn't matter. He didn't have time to dwell on it.

He rushed into the bedroom, but it was empty, too, although the bed looked mussed, making him wonder if Sadie had slept out here instead of in the house.

His phone buzzed again—Ms. Lettie. He quickly picked up. "Sheriff, did you find Sadie?"

"No, she's not at the house or studio, and neither is her car."

"Her car is in the hospital parking lot," Ms. Lettie said, her voice odd.

Something definitely wasn't right. "When was the last time you saw her?"

"Two days ago, when she came to see Amelia. It was the same day Amelia tried to escape."

A cold wave of fear washed over Jake. "I'll be right there." Not waiting for her to respond, he ran to his car and sped down the road to the sanitarium. His mind churned with various scenarios.

None of them good.

Trees blurred as he sped up the mountain road, the seconds dragging. He spotted Sadie's car in the parking lot, pulled up next to it, jumped out, and examined it.

But it was locked, and nothing looked amiss.

He glanced around the area but saw no signs of a struggle. No purse.

No blood.

Thank God.

He jogged toward the hospital entrance. Just as he entered, a loud voice boomed over the intercom, indicating that a patient was in distress.

His gut clenched. Was it Amelia?

He didn't bother asking. He just raced toward her room. When he neared it, he heard a scream, then shoved open the door and saw Ms. Lettie and a nurse trying to calm Amelia.

"Someone tried to kill me," she cried. "He was in my room, and he tried to smother me."

"You must have dreamed it," Ms. Lettie said.

"No, he was here, I tell you. He tried to smother me with that pillow."

Jake spotted the pillow on the floor. But it was the voice that made fear choke him.

That wasn't Amelia crying.

It was Sadie.

Sadie fought the panic closing her throat. She hadn't dreamed it. She had seen the man.

And he had tried to kill her.

"What's going on?" Jake asked.

She bit back another sob at the sound of his voice. Thank God he was here.

"Amelia had a nightmare while I was out of the room," Ms. Lettie said.

The nurse backed toward the door. "I'll call her doctor for another sedative to calm her."

"No," Sadie cried. "No more drugs."

She had to make Jake believe her. The narcotics were fogging her mind, distorting everything.

She had to fight her way back to reality. Amelia had escaped, and she could be anywhere now.

She might be in danger.

"Jake…," she whispered. "Please, it's me, Sadie. We have to find Amelia."

Jake's eyes hardened with anger, then he strode from the room, slamming the door behind him.

A sense of desperation filled Sadie. He hadn't believed her, hadn't recognized her. He was going to leave her here to the drugs and staff.

Terrified, she twisted and bucked, desperate to escape the restraints, the metal bed rattling with the force. This must be how her sister had felt, tied down like an animal.

"Help me!" she screamed. "Get Dr. Tynsdale!"

A deadly silence fell across the room, the only reply her sobs bouncing off the sterile walls.

She gulped them back, reminding herself of hospital protocol. Behaving irrationally would only make them believe she was crazy, and they would drug her even more.

Finally the door swung open with a bang, and footsteps pounded on the floor.

"You have the wrong twin," Jake bellowed as he strode in with the head nurse, Mazie. "This is Amelia's sister, Sadie. Release her immediately."

Relief flooded Sadie. Thank God, Jake had recognized her.

Mazie suddenly appeared by the bed, looking skeptical and frightened. Ms. Lettie stumbled backward, obviously shaken. "It really is you, Sadie?"

"Yes, I tried to tell you," she whispered.

"Oh, dear Lord." Alarm flickered in the older woman's eyes.

Then Dr. Tynsdale burst into the room, his hair sticking out in a dozen directions. "I was paged. What's going on?"

"I don't know what happened, but obviously Amelia escaped," Jake said. "Someone mistook Sadie for her and put her in here." He glared at Ms. Lettie. "Couldn't you tell the difference?"

Ms. Lettie paled. "I…don't know how this happened."

"I was here, visiting Amelia," Sadie said. "She escaped while I was in the cafeteria. An orderly saw me there, thought I was her, and drugged me—" She choked on the words. "Then no one would listen."

Jake stepped closer and brushed her cheek with the pad of his thumb. "It's okay, Sadie," Jake said gruffly. "I'm here now. I'll take care of you."

She latched on to his voice, desperately wanting to believe him.

"Jesus," Dr. Tynsdale said. "That means Amelia is out there alone, and off her meds."

"I…don't feel well," Ms. Lettie said. "I have to go to the restroom." She rushed out, and Dr. Tynsdale approached the bed.

He tilted Sadie's face toward him. "I'm sorry, Sadie. I'll get you out of here immediately."

Jake's dark gaze met hers. The promises she saw there sent a wave of relief and love and…pain through her.

"Remove those restraints now," Jake snapped.

The nurse unfastened the restraints, then Dr. Tynsdale checked Sadie's eyes and her heart rate. "I'm sorry, Sadie. It'll take a while for the narcotics to work their way out of your system."

Tears pricked her eyes again, but she blinked them back. "It doesn't matter. We have to find Amelia."

Jake reached for his phone. "I'm going to issue an APB."

Sadie struggled to retrieve her clothes, but she was unsteady and swayed. Dr. Tynsdale eased her back down to the bed. "Take it slow—you're bound to be dizzy and disoriented."

"I don't have time to waste," Sadie said, frustrated. "Hand me my clothes. I have to find Amelia."

"We will find her," Jake said.

Sadie gripped the bed to keep the room from tilting sideways. "Jake, you have to tell the police not to hurt her when they do."

"I will," Jake promised.

Sadie's hand shook as she pushed the hair from her eyes. If one of the alters took over and attacked an officer or someone else, there was no telling what Amelia might do. Skid might assume her body and provoke them into hurting Amelia.

"Do you have any idea where she might go?" Jake asked.

Sadie shook her head. It had been so long since she and Amelia were close that she had no idea.

Although Amelia loved her art studio. And she did like riding the horses, and had once loved being at the river.

But the river was the last place she'd go now. Not after what had happened that night.

"Home, maybe," she whispered.

"I just checked, and no one was there," Jake said.

Terror streaked through Sadie. Where was her sister?

Chapter 19

———— o ————

Sadie tugged on her clothes, swaying as she stuffed her arms in her shirtsleeves. The room was spinning so badly she had to sit back on the bed to pull on her boots, but she had insisted she could dress herself, and she wanted some privacy.

The past two days had been a nightmare. The medication had made her crazy, but it was probably nothing compared to the psychopharmaceutical cocktails they injected into Amelia.

A knock sounded, and Jake asked if he could come in. "Yes," Sadie answered, although her voice sounded slurred, and colors danced in front of her eyes.

Jake poked his head in. "Are you ready?"

Sadie nodded and pushed herself off the bed. But the room swayed again, spinning crazily.

Jake grabbed her around the waist. "Dammit, Sadie, I can't believe they did this to you. Let me get a wheelchair."

"No, I can walk," she said, clinging to the last remnants of her shredded dignity.

"You are still as stubborn as you were ten years ago," he muttered as he helped her toward the door.

Sadie clung to him for support as they left the room. Her legs felt heavy and unsteady, her feet like dead weights, and she had to remind herself to put one foot in front of the other as she made the trek down the hall. They passed Mazie in the corridor, and the nurse frowned, then looked away. The few feet to the front door seemed like a marathon.

Finally they stepped outside, and she inhaled the fresh air, hoping it would alleviate the nausea climbing to her throat. The last thing she wanted to do was throw up in front of Jake.

She hated that she had to lean on him now, when she was still keeping secrets. The parking lot was another obstacle, and her legs wobbled with each step. He opened the car door, and she sank into the seat and leaned her head back, gulping in more air. But voices echoed in her head, and her vision blurred.

She closed her eyes to shut out the images. But they bombarded her anyway—dead bodies floated in front of her. A river of them. Then ghosts flew at her. Ghosts with sharp claws.

Had the nurse given her a hallucinogen?

She gripped the edge of the seat, struggling to hold on to reality. The images were just a bad dream. They weren't real. "I can't believe this is happening," she whispered.

Jake covered her hand with his. "I'm so sorry, Sadie."

Emotions welled in her throat as the hospital disappeared behind them, and the car ate the miles to the farmhouse. The storm had gathered, rain pinging off the car so loudly it sounded like rocks hitting metal.

The world grew foggy, monsters creeping from the woods around them.

"I don't know how Amelia escaped," Sadie said as they rounded a curve and turned onto the road leading to the farm. "Or where she would go."

"Maybe she'll come home," he said.

"I hope so."

Sadie closed her eyes again, mentally battling the monsters coming at her. But the same face kept tormenting her. Arthur Blackwood's.

"What happened when you last talked to your sister?" Jake asked.

Sadie sifted through the fog, latching on to the comforting sound of his familiar voice. "I asked her about the night Papaw died, but she didn't remember. Then Viola appeared, and then Skid. He was angry."

"What did they tell you?"

Sadie blinked, seeing double for a moment. She couldn't hear, couldn't even think straight. "I…my head is so fuzzy."

"It's okay," Jake said softly. "We can talk after you sleep for a while."

Sadie nodded, the trees passing by in a blur.

If one of Amelia's alters was in control, there was no telling where he or she might go. Viola might look for a man to soothe her with a night of hot sex.

But Skid had a mountain of pent-up rage inside him. He might be dangerous.

"Wait," Sadie said, Skid's comment echoing in her head. "Skid said that my nosing around was going to get Amelia killed."

Jake hissed between his teeth. "What did he mean by that?"

"I don't know," Sadie said in a strained voice. "That maybe we're on to something."

A shudder coursed through her. Skid had warned her that he had to protect Amelia. And he had killed Arthur Blackwood to do just that.

If he thought *she* was endangering Amelia, would he come after her?

———— · ————

Jake felt powerless as he parked in front of the farmhouse and helped Sadie inside. Dammit, she was suffering and frightened, and he wanted to alleviate her pain.

He parked and rushed around the side of the car to help her out. Her pallor and listless eyes worried him. Independent and stubborn as ever, she tried to stand, but her legs gave way. He scooped her up into his arms, ignoring her feeble protests, which faded as she lapsed into tears.

"Shh, it's okay," he whispered as he unlocked her door and carried her upstairs to her bedroom. The room looked the same as it had when she was a teenager.

How many times had Walt wished she'd return? She had probably left as big a void in the old man's life as she had in Jake's. It was a damn shame it had taken his death to bring her home.

And now her sister was missing...

What was Amelia doing now? What would happen if someone found her and tried to bring her in? What if she resisted or fought the police?

Determined to take care of Sadie, he yanked down the homemade quilt Sadie's grandmother had made and gently deposited her on the bed.

Sadie rolled sideways on a sob, and his heart wrenched as she began to bat at some invisible demon. Dammit, the hospital ought to be sued for making such a colossal mistake.

Perspiration beaded on her face and neck. "They're attacking me," she cried. "Stop them, Jake. The bones...the dead people... they're flying at me."

Jake frowned, his heart drumming as he realized the narcotics must be causing her to hallucinate.

She swung her hands out again and screamed; then he realized she was trembling uncontrollably. Jake couldn't take it anymore. He slid down beside her and folded her into his arms.

"Shh, it's okay, I'm here now." Just as he had when they were teenagers, he rocked her in his arms and stroked her hair, soothing her and holding her while she cried.

For a moment, his professional voice kicked in. He should focus on questioning her. Locating her sister.

On not getting involved.

But hell. He had called in the APB on Amelia, and there was nothing else he could do right now.

So he stretched out on the bed and comforted her, willing away her fears. "I promise I'll make this right," he whispered into her hair.

Slowly her sobs subsided, but her breathing was choppy as she drifted into a fitful sleep. Each time he tried to leave her, she jerked and started trembling again, another cry escaping.

He thought of all the nights he'd held her like this when they were young. How badly he'd wanted to slay her dragons and bring joy into her life.

And he had tried.

But somehow his love hadn't been enough.

She curled her hands up against his chest, hanging on to him, and he squeezed her tight and pressed a kiss into her hair.

God, he'd understood that the college scholarship was a good opportunity for her. But the timing had been horrible. His dad had just gone missing the week before.

And the way she'd broken it off—she'd been so cold. Had written him a letter and left the flint necklace he'd given her. The one he'd made out of the arrowhead they'd found at the river. It hadn't cost much, but it had been a symbol. The flint had lasted through storms and battles; so would they.

But in the note she'd said it was over, that she wanted a clean break. No phone calls. No visits. No trying to make a long-distance relationship work.

He had been devastated.

But he'd never forgotten how she'd felt in his arms. Or how much he wanted her back there again.

He kissed her hair again, savoring her feminine scent. He had failed her before. He'd be damned if he'd fail her again.

Even if she didn't love him, he couldn't deny what he'd known all along. That he still cared about Sadie.

He always had, and he always would.

———————— , ————————

Sadie battled the dead for hours. The voices, the dark tunnel, the sounds of bones creaking, the image of Arthur Blackwood's face glaring down at her.

"Murderer. Liar. Leave my son alone."

Sadie jerked awake, terrified that Jake's father was really in the room.

But Jake lay next to her instead. He had drifted asleep beside her, his arms around her, his face so near that his beard stubble grazed her cheek.

He was so handsome he took her breath away.

Tears threatened again, the urge to kiss him making her ache with desire. She had tried dating a few times, but her heart just hadn't been in it.

Because she'd given her heart to Jake when she was seventeen.

And she'd been terrified of loving again.

Besides, no other man had ever touched her the way he had. Not just physically but emotionally.

She had loved him as a young girl.

She loved him now.

Her heart pitched. But loving him meant she had to keep her secrets. And continue the lies.

Thankfully, the worst of the narcotics seemed to be dissipating, but fatigue still pulled at her limbs, so she curled back into

Jake's arms. She wanted to kiss him, to make love to him, to feel his naked body pressed against hers.

She couldn't act on that hunger, but she could savor his arms cradling her while she slept.

His breath bathed her face as she drifted away again. This time she dreamed that she had never left town, that her sister wasn't ill, that Amelia hadn't murdered Arthur Blackwood, that she and Jake had married and had a baby of their own.

They'd never stopped loving each other and had made love night and day for years. Her body tingled as his thigh brushed hers, her heart fluttering as she lifted her lips and pressed them to his neck. He moaned softly, and she placed one hand against his cheek and nibbled at his mouth.

This time he groaned, then dragged her against him. His body felt hard and so masculine that heat seared her, and she deepened the kiss. He threaded his hands into her hair and claimed her mouth with his, whispering her name as he teased her body to life.

She eased the buttons on his shirt open and raked her hands across his chest. Another moan erupted from him, and he wrapped one leg around hers, pulling her so tightly against his body that his arousal pulsed between her thighs. He was thick and big and hard, eliciting memories of the first night they'd joined their bodies and become one.

The hot need thrumming through her intensified, and she trailed kisses along his chest, desperate for more. For any morsel of love Jake had left to give.

Suddenly Jake's hands were everywhere. On her face, her body, pulling at her shirt. She urged him on, begging him with her body to take her as she gasped for breath.

"Jake…"

"Sadie, God, I've missed you."

"I missed you too," she whispered.

He slid one hand inside her shirt and cupped her breast, and she groaned, needing him naked and closer to her. Wanting him with every fiber of her being.

But suddenly a door slammed somewhere in the distance. A voice yelled her name.

Jake must have heard the voice and the footsteps as well, because he tensed. The voice again.

Ms. Lettie was home.

Shivering with unspent desire, she looked up into Jake's eyes. He was watching her, his breathing erratic, his shirt half open, his chest damp and red where her mouth had been.

Sadie struggled between reality and the fact that her body was still humming with need, and that she didn't want him to stop.

Jake's eyes darkened with a charged kind of animal hunger that she hadn't seen from a man since she'd been with him.

But she also recognized other emotions in his eyes.

Regret. Anger. Denial.

Then he pushed himself off the bed and hastily buttoned his shirt. "I'm sorry, Sadie."

"Jake—"

He pressed his finger over her lips. "Don't say anything."

Footsteps pounded on the wood floor below. "Sadie, are you up there?"

Sadie froze, rattled as she heard Ms. Lettie storming up the stairs. "I just wanted to see if you were okay, and if you've heard anything about Amelia."

Sadie hurriedly straightened her clothing, and Jake moved to the door. Ms. Lettie hobbled in, her eyes widening when she spotted Jake in the doorway and Sadie on the bed.

"Oh, dear, I didn't mean to interrupt." She backed out of the doorway, but Jake caught her arm.

"No, don't go. I was about to call you to stay with Sadie."

Ms. Lettie frowned, then glanced at Sadie. "So you haven't found Amelia yet?"

"No," Sadie said. "I thought she'd come back here."

Sadie tucked an errant strand of hair behind her ear, hoping she didn't look as shaken as she felt.

"How are you doing?" Ms. Lettie asked.

"Better. The drugs are finally wearing off."

"Ms. Lettie, do you have any idea where Amelia would go?" Jake asked.

The older woman tugged her shawl around her shoulders. "The only place I could think of was here."

Jake shifted, back in work mode. "What about Viola? Did she have a lover that she might turn to?"

Ms. Lettie pursed her lips. "Viola didn't bring men back to the house."

"Not even to the studio?" Sadie asked.

Ms. Lettie shook her head no. "Not that I knew of."

Jake's phone jangled, and he jerked it from his belt and checked the number. "I need to take this. Ms. Lettie, can you take care of Sadie? I have to go back to work."

"Of course," Ms. Lettie said.

Jake paused at the door, his gaze meeting Sadie's. "Call me if you hear from your sister."

Sadie didn't want him to go. But she couldn't stop him.

Without another word, he rushed from the room. Sadie's heart sank as he left.

For a moment when she'd been in his arms, the two of them loving each other, she'd thought that he still loved her.

But that had just been a fantasy.

She had to find Amelia and settle things with her, make sure she was safe. Then she had to leave before she confessed her true feelings to Jake.

Because even if he did love her, once he found out the truth, she would lose him.

Jake tensed as he stepped onto Sadie's porch to take the call.

His deputy's voice boomed over the line. "Sheriff, we just got a nine-one-one call from a couple of kids out at Wells Valley. Said they think a man's dead. They sound pretty shaken up."

Wells Valley—why did that sound familiar?

He snapped his fingers as it hit him. That was where Emanuel Giogardi lived.

"You want me to check it out?" Mike asked.

"No, I'll go. Did you find anything on that tat?"

"Nothing specific, but it's similar to some Marine Corps ones that popped up. I'll keep looking."

"Thanks. I have another assignment for you."

"What?"

"Amelia Nettleton escaped the mental hospital," Jake said. "I want you to go to that bar in case she shows up there."

Mike cursed under his breath. "You've got to be shittin' me."

"No, I'm not," Jake said. "She's on the loose, and she might be dangerous."

"Hell, yes, she's dangerous," Mike muttered.

"Then do your job and protect the citizens in town," Jake said. "And Mike?"

"What?"

"Don't sleep with her this time."

Mike hissed. "You don't have to worry about that."

"Don't hurt her either," Jake added as he climbed into his car.

He didn't give Mike time to comment. He hung up, hurried to his car, and left Sadie's, desperate to forget what had just happened between them.

Because he wanted to go back and finish what they'd started. Forget the pain between them, forget her sister, forget this case, and make love to her all night.

The rain had stopped, but the wind had intensified, the temperature dropping, making the mountain roads hazardous with black ice.

Weather advisories urged people to stay off the road, but a few people were still out, crawling along the highway. He flipped on his siren, weaving around them and passing over Slaughter Creek Bridge. A deer ran in front of his car as he neared Wells Valley, and he braked, then swerved and skimmed the guardrail to avoid hitting the animal.

Needing to ground himself, he phoned home, but Gigi said Ayla had already gone to bed. He grimaced, hating that he'd missed dinner and bedtime with her. "I'll be there for breakfast with her in the morning," he said.

Gigi assured him it was no problem, but guilt still nagged at him as he hung up. Ayla's mother had deserted her. He didn't want her to ever think that he had.

He turned down a dirt road, noting how desolate and dark the area was. A couple of run-down shanties sat on the side of the mountain, and another one was visible in the valley, exactly where he needed to be. A rusty Jeep on three wheels was parked in the yard, a black pickup beside it.

Tension knotted his shoulders as he wove down the mountain toward it, then slowed to a stop and climbed out. He felt for his gun, hoping he wouldn't need it, then eased up the stoop. A porch swing creaked in the wind, and he glanced over and saw two teenage boys on the porch.

"I'm Sheriff Blackwood," he said. "You boys made that nine-one-one call?"

The boys nodded.

"What's your name?"

"Billy Marvin," the tall, lanky one said. "This here's my brother, Dewey."

"What were you doing out here?" Jake asked.

The boys looked sheepish and exchanged a look, as if they knew they were in trouble.

"Look, you'd best be honest," Jake said. "Did you know the man who lived here?"

The boys shook their heads, then Billy piped up. "No, but we heard he was a hunter, that he had a bunch of guns, and we wanted to look at them."

"And did you?" Jake asked.

"No, sir," Billy said.

Dewey was shaking all over and looked pale, and Jake realized that the younger boy had thrown up over the railing.

"We heard he kept the guns in his garage," Billy said. "So we snuck around to the side. That's when I saw the blood through the window."

"But you didn't go inside?" Jake asked.

Billy shook his head. "No. Dewey got scared and started to run, but I was afraid someone would see us, so I made him wait in the bushes."

"Did you see anyone around the house when you got here?"

"No," they both said.

"What happened next?" Jake asked.

Billy pointed to the house. "I saw the body—a man's, slumped over."

Jake gave them a stern look. "Wait here, guys. I'll check out the inside."

Jake entered cautiously, the scent of blood and excrement filling the air as he inched inside.

Billy was right. Blood was everywhere. On the floor, the walls, the kitchen table. The man's brain matter had been splattered along with it.

The stench was almost unbearable.

The body was stiff too, in full rigor, already starting to decay.

Jake spotted a notepad on the table, speckled with blood as well. Careful not to touch it, he leaned closer to take a look.

It was handwritten. A suicide note.

Jake heaved a sigh. What the hell was going on?

He noticed something on Giogardi's arm, then pushed up his shirtsleeve. He had the same tattoo as Herbert Foley.

Dammit. Slaughter Creek had once been a safe little town, but in the past week, it had seen more deaths than there had been in years.

Deaths that were all connected to the clinic and sanitarium. To Dr. Coker and Dr. Sanderson.

Deaths that all led back to Amelia and Sadie.

Sadie missed Jake already. But she had to be strong. Had to find Amelia before something bad happened to her.

"Honey, are you sure you're all right?" Ms. Lettie asked.

Sadie sipped the tea Ms. Lettie had brought her. "Yes, I'm feeling much better now." Except she couldn't stop thinking about how wonderful it had felt to be with Jake.

And how much she wanted to kiss him again. To make love to him.

"Ms. Lettie, you've been with Amelia and Papaw for the past few years. How did Amelia seem lately?"

Ms. Lettie tugged at her shawl. "As long as she was on her meds, she was okay. A little depressed, but not violent." She gestured toward Sadie's teacup and the plate of toast she'd made her. "Can I get you anything else, hon? How about something more to eat?"

"No, thanks, my stomach couldn't handle anything but toast." Sadie stretched, feeling marginally better. "I just want to rest tonight. Why don't you go on home?"

"But what about Amelia?"

Sadie tried to swallow her fear, but images of Amelia in trouble, desperate, hurt, taunted her. "Jake is looking for her. And if she comes back here, I'll be waiting."

"But I should be here to take care of her if she shows up," Ms. Lettie argued.

Sadie squeezed the woman's hands. "Thanks, Ms. Lettie—if I need you, I'll call."

Ms. Lettie studied her for a long minute, then conceded and tottered toward the door. Sadie climbed from bed and peeked through the window, watching as Ms. Lettie drove away. For once, she was glad the woman had kept her own small house in town and wasn't here hovering over her.

She went to the bathroom and washed her face, then yanked on her shoes and jacket and tiptoed down the stairs. She grabbed a flashlight to light her way along the stone path to the guest-house.

The moment she entered, she knew that Amelia had been there. The scent of her lavender bath gel filled the air, mingling with the strong odor of her oil paints.

Was she still here, hiding and waiting for Sadie?

"Amelia?" she whispered.

She flipped on a lamp on the side table, bathing the dark room in a soft golden glow. But her gaze latched onto the painting in the studio, one that hadn't been there before.

It was a morose rendition of the river and the old mill where Jake's father was buried. Only this was much more disturbing. Not only were the colors dark, drab grays and blacks, but the grave had been dug up, and bones were scattered along the riverbank.

Was this her sister's way of working out her guilt?

The threat Sadie had received earlier taunted her.

Or had someone witnessed them burying Blackwood's body ten years ago?

———————— , ————————

They were all getting too damn close to the truth.

Now Amelia had escaped, and that fucking Sadie was poking around.

Jake was crawling in bed with the bitch, getting suckered in by her again. He wouldn't give up until he uncovered the truth.

He couldn't let that happen.

Amelia and Sadie had to die.

Chapter 20

———— o ————

Jake studied the suicide note, debating on whether or not to believe it. Emanuel could have been forced to write it.

And to blow out his own brains.

But how?

He lifted the man's hands. Examining them for powder burns, he saw residue. The gun had definitely been in Giogardi's hands when he'd fired it.

Of course that didn't necessarily mean Giogardi'd shot himself.

He'd have to wait on the autopsy to be sure.

After he conducted a preliminary search in the house, he'd request a forensics team to make sure he didn't miss anything.

But first he needed to take care of the boys who'd discovered the body.

He strode back to the porch and saw them huddled together, looking scared and shaken now that the adrenaline was waning. "We need to call your folks, guys."

"We ain't got no daddy," Dewey said.

Jake chewed the inside of his cheek. "What about your mother?"

"She was working, but she oughta be home now." Billy dug his hands in his coat pockets. "You gonna tell her what we were doing?"

Jake handed the kid his cell phone. "No, you are. And I hope this taught you a lesson. Guns are dangerous, and so is sneaking around someone else's house."

Dewey's teeth were chattering as he inched closer to his big brother. Billy nodded and punched his mother's number.

"Mama," he said. "We need you to come get us." A pause, and Jake heard her asking questions, so he took the phone and explained where they were.

"I'll be right there," the woman said with a huff.

She hung up, and Jake called the county forensics team.

Five minutes later, headlights beamed down the drive, then a Ford rolled to a stop. A thin brunette in a waitress uniform pulled herself from the vehicle, her hair tied back in a ribbon, her makeup a little too heavy, her expression furious as she walked toward them.

"I can't believe you boys," she said, lighting into them. She turned and wagged a finger at Billy. "You are supposed to be watching your brother at home, and instead you're out here sneaking around other people's houses."

"Tell her why," Jake said, giving Billy a sharp look.

Billy bit down on his lip. "We heard the man who lived here had a bunch of guns," he said. "We just wanted to look at them, Mama."

The woman looked horrified. "You two are grounded forever," she said firmly. "We'll talk about this some more when we get home. Now get in the car."

The boys dropped their heads and shuffled toward the car, looking contrite and shaken.

"Did you know Emanuel Giogardi?" Jake asked.

"Who?"

"The man who lived here," Jake replied.

She pursed her lips in thought. "No. We live down the road." She glanced back at the car. "I can't believe they did this. They're really good boys, Sheriff, honest they are."

"They need supervision," Jake said, not cutting her any slack.

Anger flared in her eyes. "I do the best I can. I'm a single mother. I have to make a living."

"I understand that," Jake said. "And I'm sure it's difficult, but look into your local YMCA. They have programs for kids, even scholarships."

"I don't take charity," she said haughtily.

Jake grimaced. "Don't let your pride keep you from making sure your children are safe. If they'd gotten hold of those guns, you might have been looking at one of them in there dead, not taking them home with you tonight."

Fear darkened her face for a moment. Then she clamped her mouth closed and headed to her car, but she was wagging her finger and fussing at the boys as they drove away.

Jake retrieved a kit from his car, strode back inside, and snapped photos of the crime scene. Other than the bloody mess from the shooting, the house was meticulous. Everything was neat and orderly—towels hung at equal intervals, canned food was organized alphabetically, white shirts hung exactly an inch apart, and sheets were tucked in military style.

Either Giogardi was an obsessive-compulsive neat freak, or he'd had military training. Maybe both.

So far, the other patients who'd been treated at the clinic and the sanitarium had suffered serious mental disorders—ones that had impaired them to the point that they needed medication or inpatient treatment.

But Jake didn't find any medications in this house. An array of professional medical journals, history books, and two awards on Giogardi's wall indicated that the man was intelligent, and had excelled in the army.

But when Jake searched for a computer and cell phone, he came up empty, just as he had at Sanderson's house.

Remembering the boys' comment about the guns, he strode to the attached garage. He picked the lock, then opened the door, surveying the assortment of weapons lining the walls.

Like everything else, they were meticulously arranged. But these weapons didn't look like hunting guns.

In fact, the M24 rifle was used by snipers.

———————— , ————————

Sadie searched the guesthouse, willing Amelia to appear, but no one was inside. She had to have been there earlier. So where was she now?

Raindrops pinged against the tin roof, sharp grating sounds like fingernails scraping across a chalkboard.

Thunder rumbled outside, and brittle tree limbs scraped the window as if they were alive, trying to claw their way in. The cuckoo clock burst into song with the shrill screech of a sick bird announcing the time. Midnight.

The wind chimes outside rattled like bones, catapulting Sadie back to her teenage years and another one of her sister's "nowhere" nights.

Sadie had been in her own bed, waiting on Amelia to get home. But it was midnight, and she hadn't called or shown.

Suddenly the sound of the door opening rent the air. A gust of cold air swirled up the steps all the way to her room.

Footsteps scraped the floor. One of the wood chairs in the kitchen banged against the wall. A glass shattered.

Was Amelia home?

Sadie threw off the quilts and tiptoed down the stairs. A keening noise echoed from the kitchen. The clock finally grew quiet.

Nerves knotted Sadie's stomach as she peeked through the crack in the door to the kitchen.

A single naked lightbulb dangling from the ceiling burned dully, casting shadows across the cold room. Dust motes danced in the dark like tiny ghosts welcoming the monsters inside.

Where had Amelia been this evening?

Who had possessed her mind?

Would the police come knocking before dawn this time?

Amelia dragged her mud-coated Keds across the floor, her shoulders hunched as she sank to the floor. Her face looked gaunt, pale as buttermilk, slick with sweat. Her hair was a tangled spider-web around her face, and there was a black smudge on her cheek. She drew her knees up, then tugged the hooded sweatshirt over her head as if to hide her face.

Then she slowly raised her hands. Stretched out her fingers. Turned her palms over.

Dirt caked her hands, and mud streaked her clothes.

For a moment, her sister looked up at her, but it wasn't her sister looking back at her.

It was one of the others.

She ran to her, knelt, and took her sister's hands in hers. "What happened, Amelia?"

Rage flashed into her sister's eyes, then suddenly her shoulders slumped and the anger was gone. Fear took its place.

"The monsters were chasing me," Amelia cried.

"What monsters?" Sadie asked.

"The bad ones," Amelia said. "They're everywhere."

Assuming the monsters were a product of Amelia's delusions, Sadie helped her up and washed her hands and face. She had to take care of Amelia, put her to bed again.

And hope that when she woke up, the others had gone and her sister had returned.

Sadie jerked out of the memory, trembling with the force of the fear crowding her chest. That was years ago, and her sister was still troubled.

Tomorrow she would have to bury Papaw. Too restless to sleep, she hurried back to the main house to gather his clothes for the funeral.

But as she walked back to the house and the wind swirled around her, she thought she heard Amelia crying out her name.

She looked around, suddenly on edge. Was someone watching her?

"Where are you, Sis?" Sadie whispered. "I need to know so I can help you."

But the silence made her even more uneasy.

Sadie went to her grandfather's room to pick out his clothes. Stacks of magazines leaned against one wall, and his dresser was overflowing with junk. She opened the top drawer and found some socks and underwear, then went to the closet for his suit and tie. She chose a dark blue tie to go with his gray suit, then glanced down at the shoe rack and picked out his Sunday dress shoes.

His *National Geographic* collection was stacked beside the closet, and as she shut the door, she noticed the edge of a folder sticking out from the middle of the stack.

She laid her grandfather's clothes on the bed, then went to straighten the stack, which looked as if it was going to fall over.

Curious, she pulled the folder out and opened it. She was shocked to see that it contained medical records.

Records of Amelia's treatment by Dr. Sanderson and Dr. Coker.

Sadie sank to the floor to skim the contents, her heart pounding as she flipped the pages. The incidents Amelia had described suddenly made sense.

According to the notations, her sister had been given a cocktail of drugs over the years, including LSD and an improved version of Metrazol that they had hoped wouldn't cause seizures, as Metrazol had. The drug was experimental and hadn't yet been approved by the FDA, but doctors were hopeful they could use it in biowarfare to terrorize the enemy.

They also thought it might have therapeutic uses in treating overly aggressive behavior.

Sadie trembled at the implications. Why would they give Amelia LSD?

She glanced at the top of the page and noted the heading—"Subject #3."

Bile rose to her throat.

Dear God. Was Brenda right? Had Dr. Sanderson and Dr. Coker used Amelia as part of an experiment? And had that experimental drug caused adverse side effects?

Could it have triggered her multiple personalities?

———————— , ————————

It took hours for the crime unit to process Emanuel Giogardi's house. Jake waited until they were finished, which was almost morning, then rubbed his bleary eyes and drove home just in time to have breakfast with Ayla and Gigi.

Ayla giggled over pancakes, then talked nonstop about the birthday party she'd been invited to that afternoon. "We have to buy a gift this morning," she said.

"Thanks," Jake told her. "I need to go to Walt Nettleton's funeral."

"I figured as much," Gigi said.

Ayla climbed in his lap and looped her arms around him. "Your face looks like a grizzly bear's!"

He ran a hand over his face. "I guess I do need a shave."

Gigi gave him a worried look. "And some sleep, from the looks of it."

"I'll sleep tonight," Jake said.

Ayla planted a sloppy kiss on his cheek. "We gots to go, Gigi. I don't want to miss the party!"

Jake squeezed her hard, then swung her to the floor, and she raced off to get dressed. His cell phone jangled, and he snatched it up.

"Sheriff Blackwood?"

"Yes?"

"This is Brenda. Can you give us the details on that body you found in Wells Valley?"

Jake silently cursed. How had she found out about it so quickly? Granted, he'd made a deal with her, but he wasn't ready to discuss details yet.

"It's an ongoing investigation," he said in a clipped tone. "I can't comment further."

"I thought it was a suicide," Brenda said. "The man left a note, didn't he?"

"Where did you hear that?" Jake asked.

"You know I can't divulge my source, Jake."

Jake growled deep in his throat. "And I really can't discuss the case until I investigate further."

"Does it have to do with the lead I gave you?" Brenda asked quietly.

So she must have known Emanuel had been treated by Sanderson. "I honestly don't know yet, Brenda. But I haven't forgotten our deal, all right?"

"Thanks, Jake." She ended the call, and he smiled as Ayla ran through and waved good-bye. Then she and Gigi rushed out the door. He jumped in the shower, then dressed and drove to his office. His deputy was on the phone when he arrived.

"Any luck at the bar last night?" Jake asked.

Mike gave him an irritated look. "I could have gotten lucky if I hadn't been working."

"Jesus, Mike, if you don't want to work, I'll be glad to let you off the hook. Permanently."

"Sorry." Mike raked a hand through his hair. "Viola—I mean Amelia—never showed. I told the bartender to call me if she did."

"Good. Who was on the phone?"

"That damn reporter. She's trying to get some dirt on you and Sadie."

Jake scowled at him. Just when he'd begun to halfway trust Brenda... "What did you tell her?"

"Nothing."

"Keep it that way." Jake turned to business and explained about finding Giogardi.

"You think it wasn't a suicide?" Mike asked.

"Hell, I don't know. Too many dead people in my town." Jake sighed. "Can you cover the office? I'm heading to Walt Nettleton's funeral. Maybe Amelia will show up there."

Mike agreed, and Jake checked the fax machine for the forensics reports he had asked the team to send over, but the files hadn't arrived yet.

Restless, he grabbed a cup of coffee and drove to the funeral home. Sadie was already there, along with Ms. Lettie, who looked grief-stricken in her plain gray dress.

Sadie looked pale as well, her eyes anguished as she stood beside the closed casket. The funeral director leaned over and said something to her; then Sadie and Ms. Lettie claimed their seats in the front pew of the small chapel.

Knowing Walt had been murdered by his own granddaughter made the service even more awkward. Several people from town filed in and settled in the seats, and Jake noticed Mazie, the head nurse from the sanitarium, in the back.

A lady he recognized as Betty Dodger sang, and then a man from the church gave the eulogy.

"Walt was a good man, an honorable man," Daryl Farmer said. "He had his share of troubles over the years. He lost his daughter too soon, then mental illness struck his family, and he lost his precious wife. But he believed in the good Lord and never gave up. Walt told me once that he loved his granddaughters and would protect them with his life."

That statement jump-started more questions in Jake's head. What if someone had threatened Amelia, and Walt had been trying to protect her, and he'd gotten shot in the process? What if Amelia hadn't pulled the trigger?

Dammit, Jake, you found her with the gun in her hand and blood all over her. No one else was there.

He heard a sniffle, and realized that Sadie was crying quietly. The fact that she was alone while she was grieving made his chest tighten. He wanted to slip into the seat beside her and hold her.

But of course he couldn't do that. Not here, in front of half the town.

Not and keep his sanity in check. Holding her earlier had only resurrected the lust and love he'd once had for her.

And made him yearn for the life with her that he had lost.

The preacher ended with a prayer; then the pallbearers lifted Walt's casket to carry it to the cemetery, while Sadie and the other mourners followed. He noticed Mrs. Swoony and her son Joe, along with several women from the church who'd raised money for the police department, Dr. Tynsdale, and a few of the older men who sang in the church choir and had played checkers with Walt on Saturdays at the country store on Route 9.

Jake followed them out to the graveside and stood at the edge, his gaze scanning the graveyard for Amelia.

If she showed, he'd have to take her in.

Sadie felt empty inside as they lowered her grandfather's casket into the ground. Amelia should be here with her, two sisters grieving together over their grandfather's loss.

Instead Amelia was out there somewhere, hiding, scared.

Alone.

Fortunately the rain had dwindled, but the darkening sky promised another storm, casting inky shadows across the faded tombstone markers. Sadie took a rose from one of the arrangements and placed it on her parents' graves, beside her grandfather's.

Dr. Tynsdale approached and shook her hand, then moved on, allowing the line of guests to offer their condolences.

Joe Swoony's mother gave her a conciliatory hug. "Your granddaddy was a good man, God rest his soul." Then she took Joe's hand and led him away.

Sadie remembered the file she'd found and the numbers, and her lungs squeezed for air. If Amelia had been Subject #3, that meant there were more. Had Joe been one of the subjects? And Grace?

Betty Dodger patted her hand. "We'll miss Walt, hon, but remember, the people at the church are here for you."

Sadie nodded, numb, as she shook hand after hand. Most of the people who'd come were her grandfather's friends from church. Odd, but she really had no friends from when she'd lived here before, no one she'd been close to.

Except for Jake.

Mazie walked up and squeezed her hands. "I'm so sorry about Walt. I got to know him from his visits with your sister." She leaned closer. "I sure hope you find her, and that she's okay."

"So do I." Sadie noticed Brenda approaching. Luckily, she didn't have her camera this time.

"Let me know if you need anything," Brenda said.

Sadie frowned. She still wasn't sure about Brenda, but she nodded.

The small crowd dispersed as they began to cover the casket with dirt, and Sadie broke out in a cold sweat as the memory of burying Jake's father flashed in her mind.

The ping of the shovel...the dirt...the dead man's eyes staring up at her.

Suddenly the wind shifted, and she sensed someone watching her. She angled her head and studied the woods.

Was Amelia out there, hiding in the bushes?

Amelia hid behind the trees and watched as they lowered her grandfather into the ground. "Papaw, no—you can't be dead. What will I do without you?"

You have us, Skid barked. *You don't need him anymore.*

The chimes began to ring. *Ting. Ting. Ting.*

Then the voices came, the cries, the screams...just as they had years ago. She covered her ears, begging them to stop.

Just rest, Amelia, Skid murmured. *I'll take care of you.*

But Amelia didn't want to go away. Sadie was here. She wanted to talk to Sadie, to share her secrets with her.

She wanted to be strong, not fade and die, the way Skid wanted her to.

Skid and Viola—sometimes she thought they were plotting to get rid of her for good.

Then no one would ever know the truth. And she would be dead.

"I have to tell," she said, struggling to battle her way through the haze of voices clouding her mind.

How can you tell when you don't even know what happened? Skid asked.

Amelia bit her tongue to keep from lashing out. Skid was right. The pieces of the night Blackwood died were so disjointed that she couldn't make them fit.

The world grew fuzzy. Then she was catapulted back in time. Blackwood was in the room with her. Doing things...threatening her...hurting her...

She cried out for help, but no one came.

No...Bessie had come. Bessie had cried and cried. Then Skid was there...Skid, who took care of her.

Skid had to make him stop. Kill Blackwood. End her pain.

She'd reached for the gun—no, it wasn't she. It was Skid. Skid, yelling at Blackwood, accusing him of torturing Amelia... then the world went black.

She had disappeared into that tunnel...

Then Sadie was outside with her in the rain, crying, asking questions. Questions Amelia couldn't answer.

Sadie and Papaw, both screaming at once.

And Blackwood...Blackwood was dead.

But that had been years ago.

What about Papaw? How had he ended up in the grave?

She closed her eyes, willing back the memories she'd tried so hard to forget. She'd stopped taking the drugs because they made her sleep all the time. They dulled her senses, clouded her mind. She couldn't even paint; they drowned the Amelia that wanted to live.

A fleeting image suddenly appeared behind her eyes.

Papaw had come to her that night, they'd argued...he'd told her something. What?

He wanted to tell everything, Skid said.

Amelia turned cold inside. Skid was the one who insisted they keep quiet. Skid had shot Blackwood to protect her.

Fear assaulted her. Papaw had wanted to come clean, said he had to before he met his Maker. That he had to purge his sins to get in the pearly gates.

Had Skid killed him to keep him quiet?

Chapter 21

———— o ————

Sadie tossed a rose on her grandfather's grave, forcing herself to picture the way he looked when he was alive. "I'll find Amelia and take care of her, Papaw," she whispered. "I promise."

Chad Marshall slid a hand over her back. "Do you know where she is?"

Sadie tensed. Chad was supposed to be on her sister's side, but for some reason she sensed he wanted her locked back up. "No, I wish I did."

"I'd be lying if I said that assaulting that orderly and running away doesn't look bad. It makes her look—"

"I know, guilty," Sadie said. "But she's sick and scared, Chad."

"Just let me know if you hear from her," Chad said. "I'll do whatever I can to help."

Sadie mentally chastised herself for her earlier thoughts. Being here was making her paranoid, distrustful. "Thank you, Chad. I appreciate that."

"Sure. Do you want me to hang around and keep you company for a while?"

Sadie noticed Jake watching and shook her head. "Thanks, I appreciate the gesture, but I'd really like to be alone." And she needed to talk to Jake about that file she'd found in her grandfather's things.

Chad gave her a hug. "Okay, but call me if you need anything."

"I will."

Chad stopped to talk to Ms. Lettie. Hmm, she didn't realize they knew each other. Then again, Chad could have visited Amelia in the hospital when Ms. Lettie was there. And it was a small town. Their paths could easily have crossed before.

Dr. Tynsdale patted her shoulder next. "This is a sad day," he said. "Walt was a good man."

"Yes, he was," Sadie said. "I really miss him."

"He missed you, too, dear," Dr. Tynsdale said. "And so did Amelia."

Guilt suffused her again. Had she hurt her grandfather by staying away? "I should have come back more often. Maybe if I had, I would have known something was wrong, and I could have prevented this from happening."

"Or you might have gotten hurt yourself." He adjusted his glasses. "Your grandfather wanted to protect you."

Sadie frowned, sensing a deeper meaning behind his statement. "Do you think Amelia is okay?"

"She's off her medication and frightened. But that makes me think she'll show up at the house." He touched her hand. "Besides, you're there, and it's the safest place she knows."

"Sadie?" Jake approached her, his big body robbing her of breath again.

"I'm sorry you're going through this," he said in a gruff voice. "I...wish I could do more."

She wished he could, too. That he could hold her and make all the pain go away. That she could turn back time and change all that had happened to tear them apart.

"You know I was tracking down the patients Dr. Sanderson worked with at the free clinic."

She nodded.

He explained about Bertrice Folsom's suicide. "Last night the second name on my list, a man named Emanuel Giogardi, turned up dead."

Sadie pressed a hand to her racing heart. "What happened?"

"He shot himself in the head."

"Oh, my God," Sadie whispered. "Why did he do it?"

"He said he'd hurt too many people. I'm not sure what he meant by that, but I found an arsenal of guns in his garage. One, specifically, was a sniper rifle.

"Sadie, that makes three of Sanderson's patients that are dead."

"Did you find drugs at his place?"

"No, but the ME will run a tox screen, so we'll see."

Sadie folded her hands. "Jake, there's something I need to tell you."

"What?"

"Walk me to the car, and I'll show you," Sadie said. "It's something I found at home, in my grandfather's room."

Jake nodded. After he walked her to her car, Sadie reached inside the briefcase in the backseat and retrieved the file. "This may be the connection we've been looking for between all these deaths."

Jake opened the file and read the first page, then began skimming. The notes described Amelia's treatment and her symptoms, starting at age three, when she'd attended the free clinic.

Then he noted the reference to "Subject #3."

"What is this?" he muttered.

Sadie's face was pale. "Read on and see what they did to Amelia when they hospitalized her."

Jake read the notations about giving Amelia LSD, using sensory deprivation and ECT on her, then saw references to the experimental drug and the effects it had had.

"Amelia always talked about the monsters," Sadie said. "Now I know who they were. The doctors who were taking care of her."

Jake jerked his head up toward her. "You found this in your grandfather's room?"

Sadie nodded. "It was hidden between some of his *National Geographics*."

"Do you think he agreed to Amelia being used as a subject?"

Sadie shrugged. "I don't know. He could have thought it was a legitimate study, and that this new drug they were using could cure her."

"That makes sense," Jake said.

"But what if later he realized that it wasn't?" Sadie asked. "Maybe he told Amelia that night, and they fought about it."

"What is this drug, Paxolomine?"

"That's the experimental one Brenda's source must have been talking about."

"What does it do?"

"I don't know for sure, but if you look toward the end of the file, it says it was believed to be a cross between Paxil, which is used for panic attacks and depression, and chlorpromazine. But the dosage they gave Amelia is twice what a doctor might order for the other drugs. And as you see from the doctor's notes, it causes seizures and hallucinations."

Jake focused on one section of the notes. "It mentions that the drug was used in conjunction with studying mind-control techniques, that they tried to create different personalities so they could use them in the military."

"I don't understand why they would conduct this experiment on children," Sadie said.

The breeze blew her hair into a tangle around her face, and she pushed it back. "But according to this file, they did. And my sister was subject number three, which means there are others."

Jake nodded. "Giogardi, Bertrice Folsom, Joe Swoony, and Grace—they all might have been part of it."

Sadie glanced back at the grave, then at him. "Your father was the hospital administrator. Do you think he knew what was going on?"

Anger slammed into Jake. "No. He would never have let this happen." An image of the two of them hiking flashed back, and pain hit him.

But he had to consider the possibility that his father had discovered what was happening. "Maybe, though, he found out, and someone killed him to cover up what they were doing."

———— · ————

Sadie's heart stuttered. Jake wanted to see his father as a hero, but she didn't think he was.

But what if he was right? What if Blackwood hadn't known about the experiments? What if he'd found out, and come to talk to Amelia about it? In her confused mental state, she could have seen him as one of the monsters.

Oh, God, she felt sick just thinking about it.

Jake's phone buzzed, and he said he had to go, so she climbed in her car and drove back to her grandfather's.

She had to pack up his things. After discovering that file, she wondered what else she might find.

She spent the afternoon sorting through her grandfather's clothes—his well-worn overalls, flannel shirts, the pair of work boots he'd had since she was a little girl.

Nostalgia washed over her as she touched the cigar box where he kept his loose change. The pocket watch his own father had given him. The picture of him and her grandmother on their wedding day.

She packed the pictures she wanted to keep in a separate box, desperately needing to hold on to what little she had left of her family.

His clothes, socks, underwear, shirts, and ties all went into a box for Goodwill. She stripped the bed where he'd slept and threw the bedding into the wash. She'd give that to Goodwill as well.

But when she removed the fitted sheet, a journal fell from beneath the mattress. She'd almost forgotten that her grandfather liked to write down his thoughts when he was troubled. He'd encouraged Amelia to do the same, just as the doctors had.

She sat down on the bed and thumbed through the first few entries. There were notations from when she and Amelia were little, when they first came to live with him and Gran. Tears blurred her eyes as she read how much he'd worried about them losing their parents at such a young age.

Shortly after the accident, Amelia had started having bad nightmares. Dr. Coker had suggested she was suffering from a psychological disorder. The doctors had prescribed medication, which had helped with her nightmares, but Amelia had insisted monsters were coming for her in her bed.

Sadie frowned. Later, her grandfather had become convinced Amelia was possessed. The description of the exorcism sent a shiver up her spine, as did the page where he'd poured out his grief-stricken heart over Gran's death.

Sadie flipped forward to their teenage years and located an entry about the night Blackwood had died.

It was another one of Amelia's nowhere nights. Sadie heard Amelia scream and ran out to the studio to her. Then everything went wrong. Blackwood was dead, and there was so much blood. I didn't want my granddaughter to go to jail.

I pray Amelia and Sadie never remember the details.

But we had to bury Blackwood; I had to protect my girls.

That secret lies like a heavy burden on my soul though. I pray that one day God will forgive me...

Sadie's chest ached. She flipped forward to the last entries, skimming.

Doc says my ticker's about to give out, so I'll probably be meeting my Maker soon. Going to glory. But I have to confess my sins to receive forgiveness.

My sins are many.

I pour them out at night in prayer, but God wants more from me.

He wants me to confess everything. To purge the lies I've told for so long.

Only doing so will hurt Sadie...

Sadie turned to the next page, searching for answers. Obviously, her grandfather had become increasingly guilt-ridden and burdened by their secret, by that night.

Amelia is starting to remember things. Asking questions. I want her to get stronger, to fend off the alters, but what if she remembers everything about the night Blackwood died?

She flipped further to see if he said anything else, but that was the last entry.

A cold knot of fear tightened Sadie's throat.

Papaw'd written that Amelia was starting to remember details, things about that night...

According to psychologists, facing the trauma would help Amelia heal.

So why had he been so worried that she would remember?

Jake's pulse hammered as he drove back to his office. Amelia was still on the loose, and he had a handful of other suspicious deaths.

All related to Slaughter Creek Sanitarium. And all seemingly connected to Dr. Coker and Dr. Sanderson.

Even his father's disappearance might stem from their research experiment.

As soon as he arrived at his office, he checked the fax and found the information he'd been waiting for regarding Giogardi. He was interested in that tox screen.

He phoned Bullock.

"I'm sorry, I'm working on it," Bullock said.

"One more thing, Doctor—I want you to compare the tox screen for Grace Granger to Giogardi's. See if there are any similarities."

"What are you looking for?"

"Specifically, an experimental drug called Paxolomine."

"I've never heard of it," Bullock said.

"It was a research drug," Jake explained. "Just see what you find and let me know."

"All right."

Jake disconnected, then grabbed the medical files he'd requested, which were on his desk.

Grace Granger. The dates for her admission were listed; all of the notes on her treatment were reports from Dr. Tynsdale.

None from when Dr. Sanderson and Dr. Coker treated her—those files had supposedly been lost in that fire.

Dammit.

Although Walt had gotten hold of Amelia's. What if Sanderson had had a guilty conscience and had kept copies of some of the files at home or in a safe place, then given Amelia's file to Walt?

But if he had, why wouldn't he have done the same with the other patients?

Maybe Walt suspected something and had approached Sanderson...

Hell, he was just guessing now.

Tynsdale's name was listed as the primary doctor, and Jake realized that he could have been part of the experiment. He'd taken over Sanderson's cases, so he could be covering for the man.

Jake skimmed the file—a lot of medical jargon—but he didn't see anything radical—nothing about the lobotomy, LSD, sensory deprivation techniques, mind control, or the experimental drug.

He checked Amelia's and found the same—none of the information that Sadie had shown him was in the file.

That meant either that Tynsdale didn't know about it, or that he had intentionally omitted it.

Questions churning through his head, Jake studied the ME's report. Giogardi had definitely bled out from the gunshot wound. Powder burns and the angle of the shot supported suicide versus murder. The handwriting in the suicide note had been analyzed and was definitely Giogardi's.

Whether or not another party had been in the room and had forced him to write the note and pull the trigger was another question.

However, there was no evidence to substantiate that theory. Again, the investigators had found no phone or computer.

That in itself fueled Jake's curiosity.

The report listed each weapon discovered in the garage, along with notations designating which ones had been fired and which ones hadn't.

Tissues in Giogardi's body also hinted at long-term drug abuse.

At the age of twelve, Giogardi had spent six months at Slaughter Creek Sanitarium.

Jake stood, then crossed the room to his whiteboard, and jotted down everything he knew so far, placing the sanitarium and Coker's and Sanderson's names in the middle.

Next he listed the people he suspected had been subjects.

Amelia had been Subject #3. How many were there?

He drummed his fingers on his desk, the scope of the investigation hitting him. This was bigger than Slaughter Creek.

Bigger than him.

He needed someone with access to more information. Someone who'd tell him the truth.

Dammit. He didn't know anyone in the CIA, but he did know an FBI agent.

His brother.

He pinched the bridge of his nose, emotions pummeling him. The last time he'd seen Nick, it hadn't been pretty. They'd both been young men, both grieving, both angry.

Nick had been glad his father was gone, had shouted that he hated him, that he hoped he was dead.

Jake had been so angry he'd slugged Nick. He hadn't understood how Nick could say such a horrible thing when they didn't know if their father was dead or alive.

A month later, Jake had enlisted. He'd come back for holidays that first year, but Nick had been sullen, and the distance between them had grown.

Would Nick help him now if he called?

———————— , ————————

Sadie had to go to the river. If Amelia was trying to remember what had happened that night, she might go back to the mill.

She rushed down the steps, flipped off the lights, grabbed her coat and keys, and ran to her car. The storm that had threatened earlier had broken through the clouds, and sleet pelted her windshield as she drove. She slowed, flipped on the defroster, and negotiated the winding mountain road, haunted by the night shadows dogging her from the woods.

Nervous energy made her antsy as she neared the river. Ten years ago, when she and Papaw and Skid had left this place, she'd sworn she'd never return. The temptation to turn the car around and drive away hit her, and she braked.

But Papaw's journal entries nagged at her. Had Amelia remembered the details about that night? If she had, maybe it meant that she was growing stronger. That she might one day be healed.

She pulled down the graveled road to the mill, which had been shut down for years, and parked, looking out at the water through the foggy glass.

She squeezed the steering wheel and closed her eyes, the sounds and smells launching her back in time. It was raining outside, the raindrops pinging off the roof.

The sound of a car engine sputtering nearby, rising above the whistle of the wind, jarred her, and she opened her eyes. Suddenly the eerie sensation that someone was watching her returned. She pivoted, glanced around at the mill and the river, then saw a dark sedan approaching.

That threatening call taunted her again. Had someone been watching her?

Why had she come out here? It was the last place Amelia would come. Amelia would want to be safe.

The only safe place for her was her studio.

Trembling, she started the engine, swung the car around, and headed back home, her tires slinging gravel. The sleet intensified, forcing her to crawl down the highway. The headlights of an oncoming truck nearly blinded her, and she skidded, fighting to keep the car on the road.

The mountain ridges towered above, sharp ridges jutting out like hands trapping her. She thought she saw something in the road.

A man...no, a ghost.

It was Arthur Blackwood.

Choking back a sob, she hit the brakes, but the shimmering image faded, and the road was black again.

God—she was losing it.

She slowed and tried to hang on to her sanity as she turned off the road onto the driveway and parked by the dark guesthouse, the night sounds echoing around her.

Then she noticed a light glowing in the main house—the lamp in the den. But she'd turned it off before she'd left.

Adrenaline surging through her, she opened the car door and climbed out. Maybe Amelia needed to be close to her grandfather tonight.

Certain her sister had come home as she expected, she slipped inside the house.

But what if it wasn't Amelia?

Her earlier paranoia kicked in, and she removed her cell phone from her purse, ready to call Jake if it was an intruder.

"Amelia?" she whispered as she tiptoed inside. "Amelia, it's me, Sadie."

She scanned the room in search of her sister, but instead she saw pictures lying on the coffee table. Ghastly pictures of her grandfather's murder. Of the bloody floor, the bloody walls, her grandfather's body slumped in the corner, his head...blown apart.

Then a deep low voice echoed behind her.

I know what you did that night. I warned you.

Now you have to die.

That voice...who was it?

Sadie pivoted to see, but something hard struck her over the head, and she collapsed on the floor.

The room swirled; then the scent of smoke began to fill the room as she sank into unconsciousness.

Chapter 22

———— ○ ————

J ake had Nick's number somewhere in his phone history. He was surprised when his brother answered on the third ring.

"Nick, it's Jake."

His brother's breathing echoed over the line. "This is a surprise."

Jake hated the cynicism in Nick's voice. Then again, maybe he deserved it. He should have tried harder to reach Nick, to understand him. But Nick had been so full of rage, and Jake had been brokenhearted over losing Sadie, and terrified about what had happened to his father.

"Jake, why did you call?"

He took a deep breath. "I need your help."

Another pause fraught with tension, then Nick cleared his throat. "What kind of help?"

"Your professional help," Jake said. "I'm the sheriff of Slaughter Creek now, and I've uncovered something that I think the feds might be interested in."

"Really?"

"Yes," Jake said. "Listen, Nick, I know this isn't easy, that you probably don't want to work with me, but this is about Slaughter

Creek Sanitarium." He paused. "It involves an experiment I think took place there years ago. At the time Dad worked at the hospital."

Nick sighed. "You've been investigating what happened to Dad?"

"Yes," Jake admitted. "But there's more."

A tense pause. "I'm listening."

Jake started from the beginning with Walt Nettleton's murder, then went on to tell Nick about Sadie's return, about the two doctors and what they'd uncovered, and about the suspicious deaths of Grace Granger, Bertrice Folsom, Emanuel Giogardi, and Dr. Sanderson.

"Sadie found a file in her grandfather's closet that had notes in it from when Amelia had been treated by Dr. Sanderson. She was referred to as 'subject number three,' and there were descriptions of experiments using drugs and mind control."

"You're sure about this?" Nick asked.

"I'm looking at the file right now." Jake ran a hand through his hair. "So far all the patients involved were from low-income families or immigrants who needed free treatment."

"But if Sanderson is dead, then it's over."

"Maybe, maybe not," Jake said. "I think someone else may have been behind this. And it looks like they're getting rid of everyone who had anything to do with the project."

Another pause, then he heard Nick's muttered curse. "All right. Let me talk to my superior and explain what you found, then I'll be there as soon as I can."

Jake hung up, his stomach churning. If someone bigger was behind the experiment and cleaning up, then Amelia was definitely in danger.

And since Sadie had been asking questions, so was she.

He tucked his weapon inside his holster, grabbed his jacket, and headed to the door. Cold air pelted him as he stepped outside, and anxiety tightened his shoulders as he drove toward Sadie's.

He phoned Gigi to check on Ayla, and Gigi assured him that Ayla was enjoying the birthday party. He'd been afraid she was too young to spend the night, but Gigi said she'd danced off with her friends, excited at the thought of a sleepover.

He turned onto the old road leading to the farmhouse, his gut pinching when he spotted smoke curling into the sky in the distance. Was the farmhouse on fire?

Panic surged through him, and he stepped hard on the gas, skidding slightly on the black ice. He swerved around the curve, his fears confirmed as he realized the house was ablaze. He grabbed his phone and punched 911.

"Get a fire engine out to the Nettleton farm," he ordered. "The house is on fire!"

Orange, red, and yellow flames shot toward the dark sky, smoke billowing in a thick cloud.

Terrified, he threw the car into park, jumped out, and ran toward the house. He took the steps two at a time, heat striking him as he pushed open the front door. Flames crackled along the interior, eating the floor and walls. Wood snapped and cracked, plaster from the ceiling raining down. He frantically searched the foyer, then the living room, dodging falling debris and flames. The furniture was ablaze, the curtains engulfed.

Then he spotted Sadie lying on the floor, unconscious, blood trickling down her forehead.

A board cracked and fell behind him, the whoosh of flames sweeping up the newspapers stacked on the floor. He had to hurry.

Kneeling beside Sadie, he checked her pulse. Low and thready—but at least she was alive.

Heat seared his neck as he checked her for other injuries. There was nothing visible, so he scooped her up into his arms. Sadie moaned, and he whispered her name as he raced outside to safety.

Sadie's head throbbed, and her lungs churned for air as she regained consciousness. Jake was murmuring to her while fire crackled and boards splintered around them.

She clung to him and tried to open her eyes, but the room was so full of smoke, her vision blurred and tears stung her eyes.

"Don't leave me now, Sadie," Jake murmured. "Come on, we're going to make it."

She nodded against his chest, a whiff of cold air assaulting her as he raced onto the porch and down the steps. A siren wailed in the distance, its chilling sound mingling with the thunderous roar of the roof collapsing.

Jake rushed her away from the burning structure and carried her to his car.

He swung open the back door and eased her inside, then leaned over her. "Are you all right, Sadie?"

She nodded as she blinked back more tears.

Jake raked her tangled hair from her cheek. "What happened?"

Sadie gripped his hand, her memory foggy.

"Your head—it's bleeding. Did you fall, or did someone attack you?"

Sadie gasped as the sound of the man's voice echoed in her head. "A man...he was in the house. There were pictures."

"Pictures?"

"Of Papaw's murder," Sadie said in a bleak whisper. "I found them in the den, on the table. Then I heard someone behind me, and something hard hit me in the head."

Jake examined the cut, dabbing at it with his handkerchief. "Dammit, Sadie. Did you see who it was?"

She shook her head, then pushed herself up, straining to see. Horror filled her at the sight of her childhood home completely engulfed in flames. The siren wailed closer, tires screeching as the fire engine raced down the drive and screeched to a halt.

"Are you all right?" Jake asked.

"Yes, go talk to them," Sadie said, fighting for breath.

"I'll be right back." Jake squeezed her hand, then hurried toward the firefighters.

The firefighters quickly rolled out the fire hose and began to spray water at the flames. A moment later the porch caved in, the sound of the siding splintering telling her it was too late. There was no way they could save the house, or anything inside it.

In spite of the heat rolling off the house, a chill engulfed her.

Someone had tried to kill her tonight.

I warned you, the man had said.

Then he'd knocked her out and left her there to die.

———————— , ————————

Jake met the paramedics as they arrived and directed them to Sadie while he watched the firefighters work to extinguish the flames. Given the wind, saving the main house was futile; so they focused on containing the blaze and preventing the fire from spreading to the guesthouse and woods beyond.

"Sadie was assaulted before the fire started, so consider this a crime scene," Jake told the lead firefighter. "We need to know the point of origin, what type of accelerant was used, and I want the debris searched for evidence."

"I'll alert the chief to get in touch with our arson investigator ASAP," the firefighter said.

Jake thanked him, then walked over to check on Sadie. "How is she?" he asked the medic.

"I'm fine," Sadie said, pushing away the oxygen mask the medic had placed on her face.

A female who introduced herself as Judy offered him a smile. "She inhaled some smoke, but her lungs sound clear."

"How about the cut?"

"A butterfly bandage should do it, although she'll probably have a headache tonight."

"I told you I was okay," Sadie said.

Jake crossed his arms. "You should go to the hospital for observation."

"I don't need a hospital," Sadie said in a tone that brooked no argument. "I have to be here in case Amelia shows up."

Jake made a low sound in his throat. He understood her concerns. Burying their grandfather today had to have been painful. And if Amelia was coherent enough to realize what had happened, tonight she would want to be with Sadie.

But Sadie broke into a coughing spell again, and she looked so damn pale against the soot streaking her face that he didn't want to take any chances. For God's sake, when he thought he was going to lose her in that fire, it had scared him senseless.

"Stay with her for a few more minutes," Jake told the medics. "Then if she's breathing normally, you can go."

The next two hours passed in a blur as he helped the firefighters extinguish the last embers. A light rain began to fall, aiding in the task, and finally the firefighters packed up. The arson investigator was supposed to come in the morning to examine the scene.

Jake marked it off as a crime scene, knowing he had to stay close by in case Sadie's assailant returned.

Not that he would have left her anyway. She had almost died tonight...

After the paramedics drove away, Jake helped Sadie into the guesthouse.

Her legs trembled as they entered, the sight of her sister's gory, manic paintings a reminder of her troubled mental state.

"I have to shower off the smoke," Sadie said, then she quickly disappeared into the bathroom. Jake phoned Gigi to explain that he had to keep watch over Sadie during the night in case her attacker returned.

The shower water kicked on, and images of Sadie naked, water sluicing over her body, taunted him. Then he heard her crying, and guilt slammed into him.

What kind of man was he, lusting after her when she'd just suffered a trauma? Not only had she been attacked, but she'd buried her grandfather and lost her home in the same day.

He paced the living room, studying the pieces of art while he waited. Anything to distract him from Sadie's sorrow and the fact that he wanted to go to her and comfort her more than ever.

One of the paintings was a childlike sketch done in crayons, depicting two little girls holding hands. In the next one, a black wall had been drawn, dividing them.

Another drawing showed one of the little girls locked in a small room that looked like a box. She had scribbled the words to the childhood rhyme, "Take the key and lock her up, lock her up, lock her up…," below the picture.

He moved on, to a charcoal drawing that was so morbid and so real that it made his skin crawl. This one was of a graveyard, but the grave had been exhumed, and a shadowy figure stood like a ghost, looking out at the river.

The water shut off, and he willed himself to be strong. He was here to protect Sadie, nothing more.

But when she left the bathroom and entered the room wearing nothing but a big terry-cloth robe, her damp hair tangled around her shoulders, she looked so lost and vulnerable and alone that he walked toward her.

"Sadie?" He tilted her chin up with the pad of his thumb, and his heart lurched at the need and want reflected in her eyes.

He had loved her with all his heart ten years ago.

Hell, he had never stopped loving her.

She had left because of her tormented family, and now had returned to be drawn into their drama again.

The image of her lying unconscious on that floor with flames billowing around her zapped through him, and he couldn't fight his feelings any longer.

Someone had almost killed her tonight.

Had almost taken her from him forever.

A lone tear trickled down her cheek, and he wiped it away with his finger, then dragged her into his arms and held her. The feel of her slender body pressed against his and the low murmur she emitted brought all his senses alive, reminding him of how she'd felt years ago and how much he'd missed her, and he lowered his head and closed his mouth over hers.

———————— . ————————

Sadie had never wanted anything more than she wanted to be with Jake. Ten years ago, when she'd walked away, she had left her heart here with him.

It had always belonged to Jake, and it always would.

She threaded her fingers through his hair, pulled him closer, and kissed him with all the passion pent up inside her.

"Sadie...," Jake whispered. "We shouldn't do this—you're hurt."

She shook her head in denial. "Please, Jake, I need you tonight." Even as she spoke the words, guilt clawed at her.

But for once, she pushed it away. She would deal with it later.

She had almost died tonight, and she couldn't tear herself away from his arms. They deserved one night together again—didn't they?

Yes, they had both been hurt, had both suffered. They had to live in the moment.

So she parted her lips and moaned as his tongue slid in to dance with hers. He teased her with his loving, his big hands sliding down to cup her bottom and pull her up against him. She felt the thick bulge of his arousal pressing against her heat, and desire fluttered inside her.

Jake walked her backward toward the bedroom, his lips blazing a trail along her throat. She whispered his name in a plea for more, raking her hands over his muscled shoulders, then downward to tear at his shirt.

His breath fanned her skin in an erotic rush as he emitted a hungry moan against her throat. An ache burned deep within her, and she pressed a kiss to his chest, sighing as he slid his fingers inside her robe and slipped it off her shoulders.

Cool air brushed her skin, and her nipples hardened to stiff peaks as his gaze skated over her.

"I'd forgotten how beautiful you are," he whispered.

And she'd forgotten how wonderful it felt to be held and loved.

And love her he did.

He lowered his mouth and closed his lips over one turgid peak, suckling her until she buckled and cried out his name. Then he pushed her onto the bed, stripped off her robe, and traced his fingers and mouth over every inch of her.

Sadie returned the favor, kissing him with all her heart and opening to him as he climbed on top of her. He caressed her breasts, suckling her again, then planted kisses along her abdomen and thighs as he parted her legs and plunged his tongue inside her heat.

But Sadie was hungry for more. She flipped him onto his back and rose above him, her breasts swaying, teasing his chest, as she lowered her head and planted erotic kisses all over his mouth and jaw, then down his chest.

"Sadie…," Jake groaned.

She didn't stop though. She had craved Jake for so long that she wanted to taste every inch of him. His bronzed chest was muscular, the fine hair dusting it so soft that she raked her fingers through it, then lowered her hand to cup his sex.

He was hard and big, throbbing in her hands, and she wanted him inside her, filling her, loving her, remembering how good they were together.

Wanting her as desperately as he had back then.

Another groan erupted from deep in his throat, and he threaded his hands through her hair and wound his legs around hers.

Sensations pummeled her. She raked her hands across his chest, then licked her way down his belly.

His sex hardened in her hand, and he thrust himself toward her, then moaned as she trailed kisses down his thighs, then flicked her tongue over his thick length.

Jake grabbed her arms and threw her on her back, a guttural groan of pleasure rumbling from him before he told her that was enough.

Then he climbed on top of her, kissed her so deeply that she thought her heart might explode. She was trying to catch her breath when he dipped his head, pushed her legs apart, and thrust his tongue into her soft folds.

Sadie had only known such exquisite pleasure at Jake's ministrations. And Jake remembered exactly what she liked, the slow flick of his tongue along her inner thighs, the gentle strokes, the mind-numbing feel of his tongue swirling against her skin, teasing and torturing her until she thought she was going to come.

She curled her hands into his hair, erotic sensations assaulting her as he greedily loved her. Another flick of his tongue against her core, and her body convulsed, shuddering with sweet relief as her orgasm rippled through her.

One delicious sensation followed another, and then he rose above her and cupped her face in his hands. "Sadie, I—"

"Just love me," she whispered. "Please, I need you tonight, Jake."

RITA HERRON

Jake's heated gaze met hers, and a smile tilted his handsome face, then he thrust himself inside her. She arched her back and cried out his name again as he filled her and took her to oblivion.

———————— , ————————

Jake made love to Sadie over and over during the night. It had been so long since he'd touched her, kissed her, held her, that he never wanted to let her go.

Sadie seemed just as eager to make love with him as he was to keep her in bed. Her skin seemed softer, her body more in tune with his touches, her womanly curves even more perfect as she nestled in his arms.

"I missed you," Jake whispered against her ear. "I've missed this."

Sadie curled into him. "I missed you too."

He nibbled at her neck. "When you left, I didn't know what to do."

Sadie tensed slightly. "Jake, please, can we not talk about the past tonight? Let's just enjoy holding each other."

He hugged her tighter. "I do love holding you." And this time he wanted it to last. But Sadie obviously wasn't ready for promises.

She traced her finger down his abdomen, pausing to run a finger over the scar that stretched across his belly. "What happened here?"

"I joined the military after you left town," Jake said, remembering that dark time. "Got injured on a recon mission and was given a medical discharge."

"What branch were you in?"

"The marines. I thought it would bring me closer to my dad, that I might find out what happened to him through some of his contacts."

Sadie's body went still, but he pulled her closer.

"What did you find out?"

"That the military is closemouthed," Jake said. "Then I had to deal with the injury and rehab." He hesitated. That had been a bleak time too, another low point in his life.

"That's how you wound up back here as sheriff?" Sadie asked.

"Not at first. I met Ayla's mother in rehab. She was a nurse," he said. "But that didn't work out. I stayed in Virginia where she was for a while, hoping she'd change her mind and spend time with Ayla, but she didn't. Then I got custody of Ayla, and I felt like she needed a home and stability, so eventually I moved back to Slaughter Creek."

And maybe he'd hoped Sadie would eventually return and they would end up like this.

Only being with her tonight was temporary.

And when everything was settled and her sister was found, she would fly back to her life in San Francisco without him.

Unless he could change her mind...

He brushed her hair back from her cheek. "I dreamed about this." And so much more.

Sadie looked up at him with such longing in her eyes that he realized he couldn't push her. "Sadie— "

"Shh." She pressed a kiss to his chest, teasing his nipple with her tongue, and he forgot about talking and made love to her again. He touched her with all the love he had in his heart, thrusting inside her until he felt her muscles clench around him and her fingers dig into his back.

And when she cried out his name again and fell asleep in his arms, he whispered how much he loved her and hoped that one day they could be together.

———————— , ————————

Take the key and lock her up, lock her up, lock her up, take the key and lock her up. My fair lady.

Bessie's voice wove into Sadie's dream, the rhythmic rocking back and forth of her body as it hit the wall, grating on her nerves. Then she heard the scream.

Amelia.

"No, help me, stop!"

Sadie raced to the guesthouse, peered through the window. Amelia was there...screaming, a shadow above her. A man. He was going to hurt her.

The man turned, glared at her with evil eyes. He had a needle and something else in his hand.

Sadie screamed at him to stop and grabbed his arm to pull him off her sister...

Then everything faded. The world turned black. The gunshot sounded. They were outside, the three of them in the rain. Blood was everywhere—on Amelia's hands and clothes, on her, on the man who lay on the ground.

Her head spun, the world faded again, and she found herself slipping into the mud. Sinking into the dirt, water soaking her face, she was in a hole...a grave...

Sadie jerked awake, panting for air. The room was dark, the faint glow of the moon shimmering through the blinds. Her gaze fell on Amelia's painting of the river, the ghostly shadow beside it.

She knew who it was.

Blackwood.

A shudder coursed through her as she climbed from bed. She lifted the canvas to see another rendition of the same scene—only this time the figure wasn't a ghost. He was reaching for the little girl, pushing her into the grave.

Papaw's journal entry taunted her. What had Papaw meant about her not finding out the truth about what happened? Was Amelia trying to send her a message?

There was something different about the memory, too. She had been inside the guesthouse when she'd first seen Blackwood, not outside in the yard in the rain.

Horror struck her as she studied the painting again. Someone had threatened her, had told her they knew what she'd done that night.

But the only people who knew were she, Amelia, their grandfather, Dr. Tynsdale, and Arthur Blackwood.

She contemplated the sketch of the grave and the ghostly figure. It was Blackwood. He was a ghost...

Or was he?

What if Amelia's sketch was meant as some kind of message? A warning?

That he was back? No, that was impossible.

But what if someone connected to him knew what had happened? Maybe Amelia wanted to meet her at the river to tell her what she'd remembered.

She glanced at Jake, her body still yearning for his. God, how she loved him.

But she had to know the truth.

Hands trembling, she quietly dressed, slipped on her boots, jacket, and gloves, and sneaked out to the storage shed behind the house, which now sat in ashes. She grabbed the shovel, then tiptoed to her car, careful not to turn on the lights until she had backed away from the house and made it halfway down the drive.

She didn't want to wake Jake.

But she had to see this thing through. She had to make sure his father was still buried where they'd left him, ten years ago.

Chapter 23

––––––– o –––––––

Jake stirred from sleep, then heard Sadie sneaking out, and threw on his clothes. At first he thought she might be going to search the ashes of the farmhouse, or that she just needed some air.

But then he'd feared she was abandoning him again, so he looked out the window.

She climbed into her car, then started the engine. It was still dark outside. Where would she be going this early in the morning?

Hell, he didn't care. He wouldn't let her run away.

Not this time.

He snatched his keys, grabbed his gun and jacket, then rushed outside, jumped in his car, and followed her. Keeping a safe distance behind her so she didn't spot him tailing her, he tried to guess her destination.

The logical explanation was that Amelia had contacted her, and she was going to meet her.

But why hadn't she woken him up and asked him to go with her?

She wound around the mountain, then veered down the road leading to the old river mill, and he turned, slowing and keeping his lights on dim. He kept his eyes trained, searching the area for another car waiting to meet her.

Or someone else who might want to do her harm.

She bounced over a rut, then drove to the right side of the mill and parked along the river, near a wooded section that was overgrown with weeds.

Why would Amelia choose to meet Sadie out here in this deserted area? Had she been hiding out in the old mill?

Irritated that Sadie hadn't confided in him, he turned onto the dirt road that led to the mill, then parked a few feet down, on the shoulder of the road.

Moving as quietly as he could, he eased himself from his car, retrieved a flashlight from his trunk, then crept through the woods toward the mill. Twigs and leaves snapped and crackled beneath his boots, moisture raining down from the trees as the wind shook the leaves.

He paused next to a group of pine trees, shock bolting through him. What in the hell was Sadie doing?

She had a shovel and was digging a hole in the ground.

A hole that looked like a grave.

———————·———————

Sadie jammed the shovel into the wet dirt next to the homemade marker Papaw had made to indicate the location of the grave.

Not that she would ever forget the exact spot where they'd left Blackwood's body.

Papaw had said it was bad enough that they were disrespecting Blackwood by not giving him a proper burial; they had to at least mark the grave.

Her grandfather had been a drinker, but he'd also been a religious man, and he had insisted on praying for Blackwood's soul once they'd put him in the ground.

She jammed the shovel deeper, tossing dirt to the side, her chest aching with the effect the memories had on her own soul. She had helped protect Amelia to keep her from prison, but she'd felt as if she'd lived in her own private prison for years.

Never getting close to anyone for fear of being hurt again. Never loving, because she didn't deserve love.

Not after she had betrayed Jake.

The scent of wet earth, red clay, and moss rose around her as she poured her frustration into digging up the grave. Perspiration dampened her face and neck, and her hands felt clammy as the hole grew deeper. She found the four stones Papaw had used to mark the grave's corners, her stomach lurching as she imagined what condition Blackwood's body would be in after ten years in the ground.

Papaw had rolled Blackwood up inside a blanket for protection, and seconds later, the shovel hit the worn, frayed fabric. Twigs snapped in the distance, and the wind howled.

Her nerves prickled, and she glanced around the mill.

What was she doing out here? Blackwood was dead. There was no way he could have survived the shooting.

What could she accomplish by digging up his bones?

But the doubts that had assailed her earlier bombarded her again. Someone knew about that night and had threatened to expose her.

But Amelia was the only other person alive who had been there.

Had one of her personalities, a new alter, made the threat? Perhaps a guilty conscience pushing Amelia to remember and tell the truth?

The urge to run nagged at Sadie, but she had come too far now to turn back. She had to know if Blackwood was still here.

Shaking with the force of her emotions, she knelt to touch the blanket. Bile rose in her throat, just as it had that gruesome night, guilt eating at her like a live beast.

Leaves crackled in the tense silence, the wind tossing her hair around her face as she lifted away the folds of the blanket.

She staggered backward. Dear God.

The grave was empty.

———————— . ————————

Dread balled in Jake's belly as he watched Sadie kneeling by the grave. Her face was ashen, the low cry that ripped from her throat raw and anguished.

What the hell was going on? Why had she dug up a grave? Who had been buried here?

Dammit, he wanted some answers. And Sadie would damn well tell him the truth.

He stepped from the edge of the woods, his boots squishing through the damp leaves as he bypassed the pile of dirt Sadie had shoveled aside.

She seemed to be lost in her thoughts, and didn't realize he was there until he spoke. "Sadie?"

Her head jerked up, her eyes wide and wrenched with guilt, shame, and something else…fear.

He forced himself to take a deep breath, battling a feeling of impending doom. "What are you doing?"

Shock strained her features.

"Who was buried there?" he asked in a gruff tone.

"I…oh, God, Jake," she murmured. "He's not there."

Jake had no idea what was going on, but obviously Sadie had been keeping a secret from him, one that was so important to her that she had sneaked away to come out here alone.

He pulled her to a standing position and gently shook her. "What's going on, Sadie? Who was supposed to be buried there?"

The emotions in her face twisted his gut. Something was very wrong.

He shook her again. "Sadie, tell me. Who was buried there?"

Her shaky breathing rattled out, but she didn't answer him.

He cupped her face in his hands. "Sadie, who was it?"

"Y-our father…"

Shock slammed into Jake with such force, it took a minute for her words to register. "What? What are you talking about?"

"It was awful," Sadie said, another sob escaping. "He… Amelia…God, Jake, please forgive us…"

Jake stumbled backward, her declaration like a knife in his chest. "What about my father?"

She shoved a strand of hair from her face. "He…was hurting Amelia. I heard her screaming, crying out for help, then the gun went off…"

Jake shook his head in denial. Sadie couldn't be saying this.

His mind raced back to the past, to holidays when he and his father and Jake had cut down Christmas trees. To other times when his dad had taken him hiking, to the missions he'd gone on when Gigi had come to stay with them. To the awards in his father's office. "My father was a war hero," he said between clenched teeth. "He wouldn't hurt your sister."

Sadie gripped his arms. "He did, Jake, she said he did, and Amelia shot him. I ran outside. There was blood everywhere, and he was dead, and she was hysterical. I tried to talk Papaw into going to the police, but he was afraid for Amelia, so we…we brought him out here…"

Anger mingled with disbelief, fueling his temper, and he jerked away from her. "What are you saying, Sadie?"

Sadie's face paled in the darkness, but he couldn't feel sorry for her.

Why was she lying to him now? Making these horrible accusations?

"Sadie?"

"I'm so sorry, Jake, so sorry, but Amelia killed your father, Jake, and…" Her voice cracked as she pointed to the grave. "And Papaw and I helped bury him here."

Sadie shuddered, clawing at her arms to hold herself upright. She had kept her secret so long that telling it had unleashed the shame and guilt that had festered inside her for ten years. She felt raw, exposed, terrified.

Relieved.

But the pain in Jake's eyes also made her heart wrench in agony.

"Jake—"

His jaw hardened. "You're lying. Why would you make up something like this?"

"I'm not lying," she said, choking out the words. "I wish I was, Jake. God, how I wish I was, but it's true."

"Your sister was crazy, Sadie," he said tightly. "She *is* crazy. If she said my father hurt her, she lied to protect herself. She shot him in cold blood." He raked his hand through his hair as he paced, and Sadie shook her head.

Although doubts assaulted her. Hadn't she repeatedly asked herself if her sister had been confused about the attack?

But one look into the empty grave, and she remembered why she'd come here tonight. "I know what I heard, Jake—I heard her screaming, saying that he was hurting her."

He spun toward her. "No, she murdered him, and you and your grandfather covered it up."

"I'm sorry, I wanted to call the police," Sadie cried. "But Papaw was too worried. He knew Amelia would have to go back to the hospital, but he didn't want her to go to jail."

"You could have called for help," Jake said angrily. "Called an ambulance."

"I told you he was already dead," Sadie shouted.

Jake gestured toward the grave. "If you buried him here, where's his body?"

Sadie shrugged as she struggled to make sense of it. "I don't know." Her mind raced. "Maybe someone found him and moved the body."

Jake knelt and examined the blanket as if he was desperate for some sign his father was alive.

Rage flared in his eyes when he looked back up at her. "I can't believe you did this. You let me think he ran off, that he deserted me. You left me wondering and looking for him for years." He stood and balled his hands into fists. "Then you left town, abandoning me, too."

"I had to leave," Sadie whispered. "I...couldn't tell you, Jake. I—"

"You had to protect your sister," he said, his tone so cold that Sadie felt as if she'd been punched. "You chose her over me."

"It wasn't like that, Jake. Please try to understand. Amelia was sick and scared, and I really thought he'd hurt her."

"My father was hard on us boys, but he would never hurt an innocent woman," Jake argued.

"Maybe, maybe not. But why was he at my house?"

Jake's eyes widened, disbelief simmering in the depths. "I don't know."

"I don't know what to think anymore either," Sadie said as she grappled for answers. "But I do know we buried your father here. His face has haunted me for years. And someone called and threatened me when I got to town, Jake. A man. He said he knew what happened that night, and he threatened to tell if I didn't leave the past alone."

Jake narrowed his eyes. "When did this happen?"

"Right after I arrived in Slaughter Creek."

A hollow emptiness darkened his eyes. A sense of betrayal and hurt flickered there, so harsh that it nearly brought her to her knees.

"You've lied to me for years, Sadie. How can I believe anything you say now?"

"Just look at the grave," Sadie said, her voice strained. "Someone must have moved his body."

Probably the person who'd seen them burying him. So what had they done with him?

"I can't believe you betrayed me like this," Jake said, his voice brittle. "You of all people, Sadie. I loved you, I trusted you."

"I loved you, too, Jake, I still do. I…didn't want to hurt you."

"But you did," Jake said. "You, the girl I tried to protect, the one I loved and made promises to. And you made promises back."

"I know, Jake, and believe me, I'm sorry."

"I am such a fool." A bitter laugh rent the air. "I can't believe I fell for you again."

A mask slid down over his face, erasing any emotion as he grabbed her arms, spun her around, and snapped handcuffs around her wrist. "You are under arrest as an accomplice in the murder of Arthur Blackwood." He pushed her toward his car. "You have the right to remain silent…"

His words echoed in her ears, and he shoved her down the path toward his car, then pushed her into the backseat. Sadie bit back a protest as he slammed the door.

Her worst fears had come true.

Jake knew the truth, and he hated her.

Chapter 24

J ake slammed the car door and spun away from Sadie.

He had loved her with all his heart, but she had betrayed him.

Worse, his father was dead, and for years, she had allowed him to wonder what had happened to him, to hope that he might find him someday, that there would be some kind of explanation.

Dammit, he had joined the military to find him. To impress him.

But his father had been gone. Dead.

Buried by the girl he'd loved and trusted more than anyone else in the world.

Bile rose to his throat. The earth tilted and grew black, and he gripped the edge of a sycamore to steady himself. For a moment, he wavered between passing out and throwing up.

Using the techniques he'd learned in the military to mentally and physically prepare for a mission, he took slow, deep breaths, then wiped sweat from his forehead as the nausea subsided.

Sadie's confession echoed over and over in his head. She had heard the gunshot, seen his father collapse. He wasn't breathing. They had buried him.

So where was his body?

Sadie said someone had threatened her. Maybe someone had witnessed what she and her family had done.

But why dig up the grave? And what had they done with his father's corpse?

The thought of his father's body rotting in the ground with no casket or proper burial sent another wave of pain rocking through him.

Jesus, he had to tell Nick.

He walked over and knelt beside the grave. Pulling gloves from his pocket, he raked his hand through the dirt, searching for signs of bones, hair—anything to confirm Sadie's story. Maybe a button or piece of evidence from another party who'd found his father.

He shone the flashlight around the area and over the pile of dirt beside the grave, but didn't see anything. Still, he'd have a team analyze it.

He brushed dirt from his gloved hands off on his jeans, then punched in the county coroner's number and explained what he wanted.

Dread balled in his belly as he strode back to the car. He told himself not to look at Sadie huddled in the backseat, but he couldn't help himself.

Dammit, she looked so lost and vulnerable and alone.

The very reason he'd fallen for her years ago, and again over the last few days.

But her lies and betrayal mocked him, and he forced himself to close off his heart.

He was a damn fool.

He couldn't love the woman who'd covered up his father's murder.

Sorrow settled in Sadie's heart as Jake drove toward town.

"Jake, please, listen," Sadie said.

He cut her off. "Save it for your lawyer when we get to the jail," he said in a gruff voice.

Sadie's heart broke. More than anything, she hated hurting Jake. And he was suffering, that was obvious.

But what could she have done differently?

The sun was just rising over the tops of the ridges as Jake wound around the mountain. Rays glinted off the damp leaves and trees, promising a lovely day, yet Sadie had never felt more dismal in her life. Her entire world seemed to have faded into gray.

She was facing felony charges. Her career would be in jeopardy, her reputation shattered. All the good work she'd done as an advocate for needy, helpless children wouldn't matter anymore.

Even worse—Amelia was still out there, missing, troubled. Alone.

And in danger.

Jake might think she was lying about that threat, but she hadn't set fire to the farmhouse.

Although Skid could have…Skid might want to get rid of her.

The storefronts passed by in a blur as Jake made the turn to the jail, and she braced herself to be strong as he parked and escorted her inside. His cold look hurt, but he had every right to be angry with her.

He'd clung to the hope that his father would return one day, and in the blink of an eye, she'd not only destroyed that hope but desecrated his father's name.

His deputy was at the desk when they entered, and he stood. "You found Amelia Nettleton?"

Jake's jaw twitched. "No, this is Sadie."

Deputy Waterstone raised a brow. "What's going on?"

"Long story," Jake said, then stepped away from Sadie. "Let her make her phone call, then collect her personals and put her in the cell."

Sadie battled more tears as he walked out, dismissing her as if he couldn't bear to look at her again.

The deputy gestured toward the chair by his desk, and she sank into it. He took her purse and shoved the office phone toward her. Sadie debated on who to call. Dr. Tynsdale or Ms. Lettie? They were the closest people she had to family.

No, she needed a lawyer.

Chad Marshall was representing Amelia, and he needed to hear her story so he could understand the entire situation when they found Amelia again.

The phone rang three times, then a man's voice answered. "Chad Marshall speaking."

"This is Sadie Nettleton. I've been arrested, Chad. Can you come to the jail, please?"

A heartbeat passed. "Are you with Amelia?"

"No, but it's about her...and me. Please, Chad, I need to speak to you."

"I'll be right over."

Sadie disconnected the call, then clenched her jaw as the deputy led her to the cell and locked her inside.

Jake felt numb as he stepped outside. For ten years, he'd prayed that his father was alive. He'd never believed that he'd run off with another woman.

But his father had once worked Special Forces in the service, and he'd told him about secret missions he'd been called for. In the back of his mind, Jake had hoped that that had been the case then.

He'd wanted his father to be a hero.

Sure, he'd been extra hard on Jake and Nick, especially Nick. And he and Jake hadn't always gotten along. His father had practically ordered him not to see Sadie.

But he had been hell-bent on doing it anyway, because he was so damned in love with her. His father had a temper, but he also had ironclad control over himself, honed by his military background.

Of course, over the years he'd realized that if his father had gone on a mission, he would have returned or called at some point. Then the real fear had started.

How could Sadie have lain in his arms and made love to him, knowing that she and her family had deceived him?

He needed a quiet place to think. Hell, he needed to call Nick. No use in putting it off.

He punched in his brother's number, his heart hammering.

"Special Agent Nick Blackwood."

"Nick, it's me, Jake."

"Haven't heard from you in years, and now twice in twenty-four hours?"

"I know," Jake said quietly.

"If this is about the files you sent me, I'm almost to Slaughter Creek," Jake said. "I spoke with a friend of mine in biowarfare, and I may have some information."

"That's good," Jake said. "Although this isn't exactly about the case."

"Then what?" Nick asked bluntly.

"It's about Dad."

The silence was so loud, Jake could hear his own breath in the air. "What about him?"

"Just meet me out by the old mill at the river, and I'll explain."

"Jake?"

"Just meet me there," Jake said.

There was no way he could tell his brother that their father had been murdered on the phone.

God help him. At one time, he'd even wondered if Nick had gotten in a fight with his father and killed him.

But now he knew the truth.

His brother hadn't killed him. His girlfriend's sister had.

⸻

He watched the sheriff leave the jail, a smile on his lips as he thought of Sadie Nettleton going to jail.

Goddammit, that girl had been trouble.

His phone jangled, and he glanced at the number. His pulse jumped as he answered it.

"Do you have the list of everyone involved in the project?"

"Yes. In my hands now."

"We can't take a chance on any of them remembering."

"I know. I've been taking care of that."

"You've also drawn suspicion. That local sheriff's talking to the feds now. Called his brother, and he's been asking questions."

"How much do they know?"

"Too much."

"Sadie Nettleton is in jail."

"For what?"

"My guess is, covering up a murder."

"Finally. How about her sister?"

"Still missing."

"Find her. If she remembers, we lose everything."

"She's as good as dead," he said. "And so is her sister."

"What about the sheriff and the agent?"

He swallowed hard. He'd do what he had to do, just as he always had.

They would be casualties for the cause. They'd set the wheels in motion long ago.

It was too damn late to turn back now.

Chapter 25

———— o ————

S adie stared at the dingy cell walls, a desolate feeling overwhelming her. In the space of a heartbeat, she had lost it all. Her career. Her future.

Jake.

And no telling where Amelia was, or what was happening to her.

What if the man who'd attacked her and burned down her grandfather's house had found Amelia? What if he had hurt her or…worse?

She closed her eyes, willing her connection to her sister to surface. Surely, she would sense if her sister was dead.

But she hadn't known what they were doing to Amelia when they were children. Or that Amelia was upset enough with Papaw to shoot him.

The sound of keys jangling jarred her from her troubled thoughts, and she looked up to see Deputy Waterstone walking toward her cell, Chad Marshall on his heels.

The deputy unlocked the door, metal screeching as it swung open. "Your lawyer is here."

Chad stepped inside the cell, his briefcase in hand. "Are you okay?"

She nodded, although she was far from okay, and he probably knew it.

He angled his head toward the deputy. "Could we have some privacy to talk?"

Deputy Waterstone raked his gaze over her, then gave a clipped nod and shut the door, locking them in together. "Just yell when you're ready to go."

Chad stepped in front of her cot. "Is it all right if I sit down?"

"Yes." Sadie picked at a loose thread on the thin blanket on the bed, then scooted over to make room for him. "Thank you for coming."

Chad covered her hand with his. "Sadie, look at me and tell me exactly what happened."

She inhaled a breath to calm herself. Jake knew the truth now; there was no reason to hold back. "Ten years ago, I heard Amelia cry out from the guesthouse at the farm. She had been in and out of the hospital back then, and was suffering mental problems."

"I remember," Chad said.

Heat climbed Sadie's neck. Of course he did. He had attended the same high school, knew the gossip, had probably witnessed Viola's escapades.

"Go on," Chad said.

"When I heard her screaming for help, I ran out to see what was wrong. Only she wasn't alone. Jake's father, Arthur Blackwood, was there. They were in her studio...no... were they running out?" Her mind blurred, the memory confused. Had they been in the guesthouse or outside when she'd found them? She seemed to remember it both ways.

Chad patted her hand. "What was he doing at your place?"

Sadie shrugged, stewing over the question. "I don't know. He'd never stopped by before. Anyway, Amelia was hysterical. She said he was hurting her, and she shot him."

Chad frowned. "What happened next?"

Sadie sighed, the images haunting her. "He was unconscious. There was blood everywhere."

"Did you call an ambulance?"

"No—I tried to convince Papaw to," Sadie said, regret filling her. "But Papaw said he was dead, that it was too late." Her heart raced. "Amelia was out of control, had transitioned into one of her alters. We didn't know what to do. We didn't think she would survive prison, so we…" She hesitated, knowing how horrible her confession sounded. "Papaw and I helped her bury his body out by the old mill."

Chad studied her for a minute, his expression unreadable. "Jake knows this now?"

She picked at the thread again, pulling it loose and watching it unravel. Just as her life had unraveled this morning. "Jake and I have been investigating the hospital. We found evidence suggesting that patients were mistreated, that two doctors who worked at the free clinic in town performed experiments on children at the sanitarium."

"Amelia was one of these patients?"

"Yes," Sadie said, her chest aching as she imagined how helpless her sister had been. Amelia had tried to tell Papaw, to tell *her*, but no one had believed her. "So were Grace Granger and Joe Swoony."

Chad took a minute to let that digest. "Do you think Blackwood knew what was happening? That he was part of it?"

Sadie wound the thread around her finger. "I don't know. But when Amelia talked about him hurting her, now I wonder if that's what she meant. Maybe she saw him in the room with the others, or something."

"Then we can argue that Amelia shot Blackwood in self-defense," Chad said, his look brightening. "And I can probably make a deal to drop the charges of tampering with evidence against you."

"Thank you, Chad."

"How did Jake find out?" Chad asked.

Sadie rubbed her temple where a headache pulsed. "Amelia painted a picture and left it in the guesthouse," she explained. "It made me wonder if she was trying to leave me a message."

"What kind of message?"

"I'm not sure, but a man called me after I arrived in Slaughter Creek and said he knew what happened that night. He threatened to expose me if I kept poking around. Then I was attacked last night, and the man who attacked me burned down the farmhouse."

"Good God," Chad said. "Did you see who it was?"

"No, but afterward, Amelia's painting was bothering me, and I had this bad feeling, so I drove out to the mill where we buried Arthur Blackwood." Her stomach knotted. "I had to see if his body was still buried there. But when I dug up the grave, it was empty."

Chad stared at her in stunned silence. A moment later, he stood, clutching his briefcase in his hand. "I need to talk to the judge about your arraignment," he said. "Without a body or evidence, we may be able to get the charges against you dropped."

"Except that I confessed," Sadie said.

"Before or after Jake Mirandized you?"

"Before."

"Hmm, I'll see what I can do."

Sadie latched onto the crumb of hope he offered.

But she knew that even without a body, what they had done was wrong, and Jake had been hurt because of it. Worse, someone knew what had happened, and wanted her dead.

Jake parked near the mill, next to the crime unit van that had already arrived. He introduced himself to the CSU team and led them to the grave site, then explained about his father allegedly being buried there.

The agent in charge was a man named Culvert. "We'll be thorough."

"Good. I want to know why there's no body," he said. "I've called in a federal agent to work the case. He'll be here soon."

The sound of a car engine rumbled, and Jake went to meet it. But as he waited, he kept replaying his childhood in his mind, wondering how he and Nick had grown so far apart when they should have pulled together.

Because when your father left, and then Sadie broke up with you, you turned inward.

Instead of thinking about Nick and his feelings, he'd been too absorbed in his own. And Nick had been so angry with his father back then, so full of teenage rebellion.

Looking back, he realized that Nick had needed him, but Jake had abandoned him by joining the service a few months after Sadie left.

A dark sedan rolled up, and Jake almost laughed. Of all the things he'd expected out of Nick, the last was that he'd become a federal agent. At one time, he'd worried that his brother would wind up on the wrong side of the law.

When he opened the door and climbed out, Jake studied his little brother. He wasn't little anymore. He was as tall as Jake was, and just as broad shouldered, although his hair was slightly lighter than Jake's own dark brown. Jake expected a suit, but his brother wore jeans and a white shirt and a leather bomber jacket.

His chiseled jaw was just as sharp, though, his cleft chin just as prominent, his brown eyes just as serious and intense.

"Jake?"

Jake held out his hand. "It's been a long time, Nick."

Nick stared at his hand for a moment, then shook it firmly. Their gazes locked, the backlash of memories and hard feelings still there, as if they'd been brewing for the past ten years.

But in light of what he'd learned, Jake was suddenly damned glad to see Nick, to know he had some family left.

"What's this about?"

That was Nick. Straight and to the point. No chitchat.

"I have something to tell you," Jake said.

Nick glanced at the CSU van. "Spit it out, Jake."

Jake nodded. "There's a grave over there by the mill."

Nick swallowed. "Dad's?"

Jake gave another nod. "Sadie Nettleton said that her sister, Amelia, shot him, and Sadie helped her grandfather bury him out here."

Nick removed his sunglasses and cocked his head to the side. "Sadie? Your Sadie?"

"She's not my Sadie," Jake said tightly.

"She was back then," Nick said.

"Yeah, and she broke it off with me after Dad disappeared." Jake sighed. "Now I know the reason."

"I don't understand," Nick said. "Why would Sadie's sister shoot our father?"

Jake crossed his arms, then relayed Sadie's story. "The only reason Sadie came back was because her sister killed their grandfather. I told you about Grace Granger's death, then my investigation into it and what we learned about Dr. Sanderson and Coker."

"Yeah."

"It's possible that Amelia was part of these experiments," Jake continued. "Since Sadie found the files in her grandfather's house, we can assume he either knew about them from the beginning or that he discovered what had happened."

"You said that Amelia killed Dad." Nick gestured toward the river. "Are you exhuming his body?"

The air around him turned sour. "That's another problem. Sadie came back here and dug up the grave, but it's empty."

Jake expected Nick to react with shock, but instead he seemed to accept what he'd said. "The crime unit is looking for evidence that he was buried there."

"Or that he walked out of the grave," Nick said wryly. "You know our old man was just mean enough to do that."

Jake frowned at Nick's comment. He coddled Ayla, was soft on her, but his father had been cold, stern. Had treated them more like soldiers than children.

He'd accepted it at the time, but now he realized Nick was right.

Nick stowed his sunglasses in his pocket. "Let me see this grave."

Jake led him to the site and introduced him to the CSU team, then stood back as Nick studied the grave.

"Have you found any bones or skeletal matter?" Nick asked.

"No, sir, not yet," the tech said.

"But Sadie says they left a body there," Jake said. "So that means someone moved it. I'm going to search the surrounding area."

Nick joined him, and they examined the area surrounding the grave site for footprints or other evidence that someone else had been near the grave recently.

An hour later, their search had turned up nothing, so they decided to explore the old mill. Except for signs of critters digging around, the building was rotting and empty, though there were signs, including beer cans and a roach clip, that someone, probably teenagers, had sneaked inside to party.

He shone the flashlight along the edges of the rooms, noting the signs of decay, the peeling paint, and weathered flooring. In the back room, where it was darkest, he noticed a stain on the floor. Judging from the dark color and the way it had seeped between the cracks, it had been there a long time.

And it looked like blood.

Forensics would have to tell them exactly what it was. Dust and twigs that had fallen through a crack in the ceiling coated the floor near it; when he brushed these aside, he noticed what looked like boot prints as well. "Come here, Nick, take a look."

Nick walked over and knelt, eyes narrowed. "The tread on the boot looks military-issue."

Jake's gaze met his, and he read his mind. Nick thought his father might have made it out alive.

He sucked in a deep breath. "There are plenty of men who wear military boots. I have a pair, just like you do. Hell, half the men in Slaughter Creek probably served one way or the other."

"You're right. We need CSU to send a sample of the blood to the lab to determine how old it is and check it for DNA."

Jake cut his eyes toward his brother. "Sadie received a threatening call from someone, saying he knew what she'd done, and he was going to expose her. My theory is that either one of Amelia's alters moved the body, or whoever threatened Sadie did."

"Why would someone steal a body?" Nick asked.

Jake shook his head. He didn't have all the answers, but no matter how long they had to stay here tonight, or how long it took the lab, he would get them.

———————— , ————————

It had been a long night in jail.

Sadie had barely slept, and she was grateful when Ms. Lettie dropped her off some clean clothes. The deputy let her use the restroom to clean up, even offering her soap and a towel for a shower, and Sadie thanked him, praying this routine would not become her way of life.

That she could make Jake understand how sorry she was for what had happened.

The deputy brought her lunch from the diner, but she took one look at the food and felt nauseous.

She paced the cell for the next two hours, waiting for Chad to show. He'd promised her he'd schedule a hearing for the afternoon and arrange bail, and she hoped he kept that promise.

An hour later, he showed up and escorted her to the courthouse. She entered the courtroom, tensing as Jake's gaze bore into hers. Chad had arranged a meeting with the judge, hoping to get the charges dropped, but the district attorney, a thirty-something woman who, Chad told her, wanted to make a name for herself, seemed determined to go through with the case.

Sadie glanced at the seats behind her. She noticed Ms. Lettie in the background, and appreciated her support. Then she spotted Jake's brother Nick, and her stomach knotted.

He had always been good looking, but he'd grown into a handsome man. His gaze locked with hers, though, and she saw a controlled rage in his eyes.

Chad stood and spoke, and she forced herself to look at the judge. She'd testified in enough hearings to know that making eye contact was imperative in winning the jury and judge's trust.

"Your Honor, Sadie Nettleton is a forensic interviewer, not a criminal," Chad began. "Also there is no evidence that she committed a crime. The body that was allegedly buried at that grave site is not there."

The judge glanced at Sadie over his bifocals, then dropped his gaze to the papers in front of him.

DA Myra Ansen cleared her throat. "Your Honor, Ms. Nettleton confessed to the sheriff that her sister murdered Arthur Blackwood, and that she and her grandfather had helped dispose of the body. She even led Sheriff Blackwood to the grave."

"A confession my client made under duress, and without being Mirandized," Chad interjected.

"Because she was caught red-handed, digging up the grave," the DA said.

The judge turned to Jake. "Sheriff, do you have evidence of a crime?"

"No direct evidence yet, sir, but a forensic team processed the grave site—"

"Alleged grave site," Chad cut in.

Jake glared at him. "The alleged grave site," Jake said. "And we're waiting on the results."

"Do you have a murder weapon?" the judge asked.

Jake's face blanched, as if he realized he should have addressed that point. But he had been in shock, and he hadn't asked.

And Sadie hadn't offered that detail.

"Your Honor," Jake said, "Amelia Nettleton was arrested for shooting her grandfather. If she used the same gun, we may already have it in evidence."

The judge frowned at Jake. "If it's the same weapon, Sheriff?"

"Obviously I need more time to investigate," Jake replied.

The DA cut in. "Your Honor, Ms. Nettleton's sister, Amelia, was arrested for the murder of her own grandfather, then admitted to Slaughter Creek Sanitarium, from where she subsequently escaped. She is a dangerous, mentally unbalanced woman. We must take into consideration the fact that Ms. Nettleton may be hiding her sister now." Her voice rose an octave. "For all we know, she lied to the sheriff about where she disposed of his father's body to throw off the investigation and give her sister time to flee the country."

"That's ludicrous," Chad said.

The judge angled his head toward Sadie. "Ms. Nettleton, are you hiding your sister?"

Sadie licked her lips. "No, sir...Your Honor. I love my sister, but I'm well aware that she's suffering from a serious mental condition. I want to help her get the therapy she needs."

Chad started to argue, but the judge held up his hand again. "This is a complicated situation, and we're not here to decide guilt or innocence today. I'm setting bail at twenty thousand dollars." He turned to Sadie. "And Ms. Nettleton, if your sister contacts you, you are required by law to report it. Do you understand?"

Sadie nodded. "Yes, sir."

He pounded his gavel. "Court adjourned. You can pay the bailiff."

Sadie stood beside Chad, grateful he'd arranged to post bail and let her reimburse him.

She glanced at Jake as they walked toward the back of the courtroom. She wanted to beg him for his forgiveness, but he gave her a cold look, then turned and walked away.

Chad placed a hand to her back. "The sheriff had your car towed to your house, so I'll drive you home."

Sadie watched Jake leave, unable to do anything other than accept Chad's help for the time being.

As soon as she stepped out of the courtroom, Brenda Banks accosted her in the hallway. "Sadie, is it true? Your sister killed Jake Blackwood's father?"

Sadie pushed away the microphone Brenda had thrust at her. "Please, Brenda, leave me alone."

"Ms. Nettleton has no comment," Chad said to Brenda. "Now, my client would like to go home."

"I'm here to get the truth," Brenda said, dogging them as Chad ushered her toward the door. "Tell me your side, Sadie. I told you before, I want to help."

Sadie hesitated. Maybe she should tell her side, *Amelia's* side, of the story. Maybe Brenda could help her get justice.

She started to tell her to meet her at her house, but Chad shushed her. "Your legal problems aren't over, Sadie. Don't talk to anyone."

Then Chad swung toward Brenda. "Sadie has no comment, Brenda. Now move—it's been a long night."

He shoved open the door, then took her arm, and the two of them hurried down the courtroom steps.

Chad closed his car door and started the engine. "Have you heard from Amelia?" he asked as they drove away from the courthouse.

"No—have you?"

"No," Chad said. "If she calls, I'll encourage her to come to you."

They lapsed into silence as he drove around the mountain road. Sadie saw shadows all around her—Amelia's, the alters, Arthur Blackwood's.

Eyes watching her, following her. Someone hunting her down.

By the time they reached the house, she was a bundle of nerves. The ashes of the farmhouse lay in embers around her, a reminder of the loss and danger surrounding her and her sister.

She thanked Chad, then climbed out and walked past the ashes and charred remains of the furniture and belongings that had once filled her family home.

She unlocked the studio, a sense of trepidation filling her as she entered and thought about Amelia.

The doctors who'd mistreated her should be punished. But Dr. Coker was too far gone in his own dementia to try, and Dr. Sanderson was dead.

Had someone else been involved?

Anger emboldened Sadie, and she reached for the light. A faint glow spilled from the lamp across the gruesome artwork, the differences between the drawings and paintings done by Amelia's various personalities striking her.

Amelia had been hurt in the hospital, and drugged for years. A sneaking suspicion overwhelmed Sadie, and she rushed to the bathroom and checked the medicine cabinet. Several pill bottles were inside, and she took them out, examining each one. One for anxiety, another for depression, then several psychotropic drugs: Haldol, Elavil, Librium. But there were a couple she didn't recognize.

If the doctors had conducted experiments on Amelia, could the narcotics they'd given her have had an adverse effect? Had they caused her erratic behavior? Her memory losses?

What if an experimental drug triggered the voices in her head, instead of quieting them?

Trembling with the possibility, Sadie carried the pills to the studio and put them in her purse. She had to talk to someone about them.

Dr. Tynsdale had treated Amelia in the sanitarium. He had prescribed the drugs.

And she'd trusted him because her grandfather had.

Horror struck her. Had he been involved in the experiments? If so, he could have kept Amelia drugged all these years to prevent her from remembering what had happened.

She had to call Jake and tell him.

Only she couldn't turn to Jake for help now...

Suddenly something moved behind her. The floor creaked.

Then someone grabbed her from behind, stuffed a rag into her mouth, and the world faded into gray.

Chapter 26

———— o ————

Jake and Nick drove back to the sheriff's office in silence.

"I'm going to make some calls and follow up with the crime unit."

Nick gave a clipped nod. "I have to check in, too. Let's meet back in a few minutes."

Jake agreed, and Nick left the office. As he watched his brother heading toward the diner, Jake called the number for the investigator who'd worked the fire at the Nettleton house.

"What did you find?" he asked without preamble.

"The fire originated in the living room, and gasoline was used as the accelerant."

"Anything else?" Jake asked.

"We found a button in the ashes, a man's. Looks like it came from a man's shirt. Maybe a military uniform."

What did it mean? That whoever had set the fire had been wearing a uniform?

"Make sure it's logged in to evidence," Jake said.

"Will do."

Jake disconnected, then analyzed the notes on his whiteboard. The judge's question about the murder weapon bothered him. Dammit, if they had his father's body, they could remove the bullet and see if it matched the shotgun Amelia had used to shoot Walt Nettleton.

He knew one way to find out. He'd ask Sadie.

Would she tell him the truth? Hell, what did he have to lose?

Besides, the fire had been arson, which meant that someone had tried to kill Sadie. Someone who had seen Sadie and Amelia and her grandfather bury his father.

Even if Sadie had betrayed him, he didn't want to see her dead. Besides, Amelia was bound to come back to the farm sometime.

He had to find her and the person who'd attacked Sadie and put this case to rest. Find out if anyone else knew about those damned experiments.

He snagged his keys and jogged to his car. Traffic was thin, an occasional pair of headlights dotting the mountain road as he wound around the curve toward Sadie's place. More storm clouds threatened, the temperature dropping, the air filled with the possibility of snow.

The ashes and charred furniture that marked what was left of the house looked grim in his headlights as he pulled to a stop. He glanced at the guesthouse and noticed a light on, so he assumed Sadie was still awake.

Memories of their earlier lovemaking rose to taunt him, but he forced them away. He couldn't go back there, not now that he knew Sadie had betrayed him.

Nerves on edge, he parked, climbed out, and approached the studio. He hoped to hell she'd heard from her sister. He wanted this case solved so Sadie could go back to San Francisco, and he could forget her.

Wind whipped leaves around his feet as he walked up to the door and knocked. He waited several seconds, but there was no answer, so he knocked again. A dog barked somewhere in the distance, and night creatures skittered through the woods nearby, but there was only silence inside.

"Sadie?" He knocked harder, then pushed at the door, surprised when it swung open. A bad feeling tightened his gut, and he poked his head in.

"Sadie, it's Jake."

Silence. He inched inside the studio. The lamp was overturned, and several pill bottles were scattered across the floor beside Sadie's purse.

It looked as if there had been a struggle.

Cold fear knotted his insides.

Dammit, had someone kidnapped Sadie?

———————— , ————————

Sadie's head throbbed as she regained consciousness. She blinked, struggling to focus, but the room was dark, gray, cold.

A wave of nausea rolled through her, and she closed her eyes, swallowing back bile. Footsteps clattered.

The sound of metal clinked.

Ting. Ting. Ting.

The chimes began to sing.

She opened her eyes wide, terrified. Amelia had talked about the chimes before. About the sound they made.

Sadie had thought they were all in her head.

Had they been real? Or was she going crazy like her sister?

She tried to sit up, but her limbs were too heavy. Weighted down.

No, she was bound.

Terror gripped her. Where was she?

Who had brought her here?

Ting. Ting. Ting.

The footsteps shuffled again. Something metal clinked. A rolling cart?

Was she in a hospital?

She tried to think back, to remember. She'd been in jail, then Chad had convinced the judge to let her go. He had driven her home.

Jake…Jake had been in the court, but he'd looked straight through her as if she were too despicable to acknowledge. Pain throbbed in her chest, the nausea returning.

Then she heard the clock echoing in the room. *Ticktock. Ticktock. Ticktock.*

Over and over, incessantly it ticked, the sound growing louder with each second.

The footsteps shuffling. Coming closer. The rolling cart… *Clang, clang, clang.*

A chill swept over her, a fog engulfing her brain. But flashes of memory, of being in the studio, seeped through the haze. She had looked at Amelia's medications…

Something was wrong with them…too many pills. Some she didn't recognize…the combination could be dangerous.

Ting. Ting. Ting.

Suddenly a bright light shone in her eyes, blinding her. And something sharp jabbed her arm. A needle.

The room swirled. The chimes *tinged.* The clock's *ticktock* intensified like the ticking of a bomb.

"You should have listened, Sadie," a gruff voice murmured.

Sadie froze, horror hitting her. The voice…she recognized it…but it couldn't be. "Who are you?" she whispered.

A low laugh reverberated off the walls, the sound hollow and sinister.

"You know who I am, Sadie. You buried me."

Sadie gasped for a breath. Lord help her.

Jake's father was alive.

The light suddenly snapped off, pitching her into darkness. Another jab in her arm, then she felt the slow burn of the medication seeping through her.

"You should have stayed away from my son," Blackwood said near her ear. "He's not going to save you now. I'll bury you alive, just like you did me."

The room swirled, colors flashing in front of her eyes, then the gray swallowed her. Sounds echoed as if they were far away. The ticking.

The chimes.

The gunshot...

She willed herself to fight the narcotics, but they sucked her into a vortex, and she spun around in a dizzying circle, then plummeted into the cold ground.

Amelia cried out. She was screaming for help.

Sadie raced outside to her, ran to the guesthouse. She must have been having another of her episodes.

No...Jake's father was there. He had pushed Amelia onto the couch. He had a needle—he was drugging her. Amelia was struggling, fighting, crying for help...

Then she heard his voice. "Sorry, Amelia, but you served your purpose. Now it's time for you to die."

Denial robbed Sadie's breath. Jake's father was going to kill her sister. But why?

She had to do something. Save Amelia.

Trembling, she ran back to the house and grabbed Papaw's rifle. Then she hurried back to the guesthouse. When she eased open the door, Amelia was fighting. Blackwood slapped her.

Sadie froze in shock. She had to be seeing things.

This was Jake's father. He wouldn't hurt her sister. He ran the hospital that had tried to help her.

But the shiny blade of a knife glinted in the darkness.

"Too bad you took your own life," Blackwood said. His icy laugh echoed in the silence.

Amelia's head lolled to the side. Her eyes were glassy, her mouth agape, her coloring a pasty white.

Was she too late?

Blackwood reached for her sister's arm. He was going to cut her wrist...

She had to stop him.

"Leave her alone!" Sadie cried.

Blackwood swung around and waved the knife at her. His cold gaze met hers, and she realized he was dangerous, maybe even psychotic himself. He would kill Amelia, and then he'd kill her.

Then he stepped toward her. She raised the rifle and fired.

The gunshot blasted. His face paled in shock. Blood splattered.

Then the darkness swept over Sadie...

"We have to bury Blackwood, Sadie," Papaw's voice reverberated through the darkness. "We have to protect Amelia. She can't go to prison. She'll never survive."

Only Amelia hadn't killed Blackwood.

She had.

——————— . ———————

Amelia rocked herself back and forth in the art studio at the high school. It was the one place she remembered feeling at home. Safe.

Herself.

Memories of painting in this very room beside her sister flashed back. That was one thing she and Sadie had in common.

They both liked to purge their emotions on canvas.

Only her sketches were always disjointed. Sometimes childlike. Bessie, the doctors told her. Then angry and macabre—Skid. Then the sexy nudes that Viola drew.

Other times, soft and full of faded colors but wistful...the hopeful Amelia coming out.

She picked up Sadie's scarf and sniffed it, recalling the days when they were little and played together. The times they whispered secrets in the dark, talked about boys and teenage crushes and dreamed of marriage.

The times she'd been lucid.

Tonight her head felt clearer. The drugs were wearing off, and she felt...almost normal.

Go back to sleep, Amelia, Skid mumbled. *I told you, I'd take care of us.*

Don't leave me, Bessie whispered.

She's gonna tell, Viola cried.

No, she won't, Skid barked.

Yes, she is, Viola said. *She's getting stronger, and she'll forget about us.*

I won't let that happen, Skid said. *Amelia's too weak. I'll kill her before she tells.*

Skid wanted her dead...

Just like the Commander.

The memory tormented her, his harsh voice ordering her to lie still, urging her to let the others in.

Ting. Ting. Ting.

The chimes began to sing.

Time to line up, follow the Commander through the darkness.

Ticktock. Ticktock. Ticktock.

The sounds echoed in her head. But they were far away this time. As if she had traveled through time and left them behind somewhere.

I'm the ruler now, Skid said. *Amelia is going away forever.*

"Be quiet," Amelia said. "I'm starting to remember..."

No, Skid said. *Go back to sleep, Amelia. You're too weak, you need me.*

He was right. She had been weak. The drugs had done that.

But without the medication fogging her head, another voice was whispering in her mind. Warning her not to trust the others.

You have to tell Sadie, the voice said. *Sadie's in danger. You have to save her this time.*

Stop, you can't go to Sadie, Skid shouted.

Help me, Bessie cried.

Viola was humming now, *ting, ting, ting.*

"Shut up," Amelia cried. "Go away and leave me alone."

You can't do this to us, Skid said harshly. *We took care of you all these years.*

That was what Dr. Tynsdale and the doctors had told her.

But she was starting to remember differently. How the others wanted to take over, wanted to make her disappear so they could live.

Amelia shoved open the door to the art studio and ran down the hall. "Hurry, you have to tell, hurry, run..." The voice, it was growing stronger, louder, screaming at her this time. Then she recognized whose it was. The voice the others had tried to silence.

It was hers. They hadn't saved her, all these years.

Instead, they were trying to silence her for good.

Chapter 27

---◦---

Jake was in a blind panic. Who had Sadie, and what the hell were they doing to her?

Frantic, he punched Nick's number. "Sadie is missing."

"What happened?"

"I don't know, but I'm at her house, and her car is here, but she's not. There are signs of a struggle."

"Any indication of who took her?"

Jake's throat tightened. "No." He glanced around the studio, searched the table and counter, but there was no note, nothing to give him a clue.

"Maybe Amelia came back, and they took off together."

"No," Jake said. "Her car is here, and there was a struggle."

"One of Amelia's personalities could have attacked her," Nick said. "After all, you said she shot her grandfather."

That was true.

"Hang on," Jake said. "My other line is buzzing."

He quickly clicked over, praying it was Sadie. "Sheriff, this is Culvert from the CSU team."

"Yes?"

"There was no sign that a body had decayed in that grave." He paused. "But the blood you found at the mill matched your father's."

Jake's mind raced. Maybe Sadie and her grandfather and Amelia had put his body in the mill while they dug the grave. But she hadn't said that.

"Anything else?"

"We did find some other fingerprints in the mill, but they didn't match anyone in the system. Could just belong to some teenagers hanging out there. You know it's been ten years."

"Yeah, I know." Which meant they had nothing more to go on than they had before. Except he knew his father's body hadn't withered away in that grave.

He thanked Culvert, then flipped back to Nick and relayed what he'd learned.

"You know all this has got to do with what happened at the sanitarium," Nick said.

"Maybe Dad found out what Sanderson and Coker were up to and went out to Walt and Amelia to tell them," Jake suggested. "Then Amelia went ballistic and killed him."

"And someone in town saw them at the mill, or knows what happened," Nick said. "But why would they move Dad's body?"

"I don't know." Jake cursed. "If they'd wanted blackmail money, they would have asked for that long ago."

"That's a piece of the puzzle that doesn't fit." Nick hesitated.

Jake sighed, weary. Dammit, he wanted to know what had happened to his father's body. Wanted to tie up this case so Sadie could leave and he wouldn't have to think about her anymore. "Did you have a chance to look at the notes I made?"

Nick nodded. "Good work, Jake. That tattoo on Foley and Giogardi is definitely military, and from what I've seen since I joined the bureau, it's a sniper team associated with the CIA."

"Jesus."

"I know it sounds far-fetched that they'd conduct a project like this in Slaughter Creek and to children, but if you think about it, the town's pretty remote. And a sanitarium is the perfect cover."

"True. I've been thinking," Jake said. "Tynsdale must have been in on the experiments. I questioned him early on, but Sadie trusted him. So did Walt." He paused. "But he's been monitoring Amelia and Grace for years. He's prescribed their medication, so he could have kept them drugged to prevent them from talking."

"Do you have an address for him?" Nick asked.

Jake had his phone number but no address. "Hang on a minute." He searched the desk in the corner and found a small address book, then gave the address to Nick. "You check his house. I'll check the hospital."

He hung up and headed for the door, but suddenly Amelia appeared. Jake figured she would run when she saw him, but instead she launched herself at him.

"Sadie, where's Sadie?"

Jake caught her arms. "She's gone."

Amelia's eyes widened in panic. "What do you mean, *gone*?"

"Someone took her," Jake said. "There are signs of a struggle."

"It was him," Amelia said in a hoarse whisper. "He's back."

Jake's throat closed. "Who's back?"

"Your father," Amelia said. "He killed Papaw, and now he's going to kill Sadie."

———————— , ————————

Twenty minutes later, Jake was still reeling in shock. Amelia had hitched a ride with a trucker who'd put her out on the main road, and she'd walked the rest of the way.

"Your father did it all," Amelia said. "He's a bad man."

Jake's jaw hardened. She'd seemed coherent, but that statement made him pause. "My father is dead, Amelia."

"No, he's alive. I saw him at the hospital," Amelia said. "That's why I escaped. He came there to kill me, just like he killed Papaw."

It had to be her delusions talking. "Amelia, you and Sadie and your grandfather buried my father."

"I know," Amelia cried. "I don't how he did it, but he survived. If he has Sadie, he'll kill her."

"Dr. Tynsdale knew what happened that night," Jake said.

She nodded, trembling as she spoke. "Yes, but he promised to keep it secret, since I was his patient."

Jake grimaced. Poor Amelia. She had been the victim of some twisted doctors, and her psychiatrist might have been working with them to keep her drugged all these years to keep her quiet.

"He might take her to the grave site," Amelia said. "And bury her where we left him."

A chill ran down his spine. She was talking about his father, but he was thinking about Tynsdale.

"Or"—Amelia folded her arms around herself and shuddered violently—"to the basement."

"What basement?" Jake asked.

"In the hospital, it was dark—no one knew about the room with the chimes."

"What chimes?"

"They played musical chimes to hypnotize us. I don't know why, but they called us the chimes too." She clutched his arm again. "Please save Sadie, Jake."

Dammit, he needed to take Amelia in. But he didn't have time. He phoned his deputy, but Mike didn't answer, so he left a message for him to call him back, that he needed him to watch Amelia.

Desperate, he called Ms. Lettie and explained that Amelia was at the studio. "Will you come and stay with her until I find Sadie?"

"Of course—I was on my way there anyway. I'll be there in a minute," Ms. Lettie said.

Amelia curled up on the sofa, rocking back and forth, her eyes stricken. "Save Sadie, save Sadie, save Sadie…"

Jake knelt in front of her and spoke softly to calm her. "Amelia, tell me more about the basement," he said. "What was down there?"

"There's a secret door," Amelia whispered. "Near the back of the hospital. And the walls are soundproofed so nobody can hear us cry."

"How do you know that?" Jake asked.

"They told us," she said in a haunted whisper. "It won't do any good to scream, they said. No one can hear you."

"What else happened?" Jake asked.

Amelia emitted a low moan. "They tied us down and shocked us. And they played the chimes so we would do whatever they said."

"That sounds like brainwashing."

Amelia nodded, then rambled on for several minutes about the noises and lights and the drugs that had made her see things.

"Who did this to you?" Jake asked.

"The doctors," Amelia said. She covered her ears with her hands and began to moan. "Make the noises and the voices stop."

Ms. Lettie's car barreled into the drive, then she hobbled in as fast as she could. "Oh, Lord, Amelia, honey, I've been so worried about you!"

She threw her arms around Amelia, who sank against her. "We have to save Sadie…"

"I called my deputy—he should be here soon," Jake said, wondering why in the hell Mike hadn't answered. If he was off with a woman, Jake was going to fire his ass.

He left Amelia with Ms. Lettie, then raced toward the grave site. He had to hurry.

Struggling to rein in his fear, he sped down the graveled drive leading toward the river, tires spitting gravel. By the time he reached the mill, sleet was pelting the windshield.

Gun in hand, he climbed out and searched the grave site, but no one was nearby. The crime scene tape flapped in the wind, and the sound of thunder was growing more ominous as storm clouds rolled in.

He punched his hand into his fist in frustration. Amelia was mentally ill. Could he believe anything she said?

Was he wasting time, following her lead? She could be lying to throw him off.

Still, Sadie was missing, and he had to check it out, so he slipped into the mill and shone the flashlight across the rotting wooden floor, the boards creaking as he crept through the building.

But just like the grave, the building was empty.

He rushed back to his car, his conversation with Amelia echoing in his head. She thought he'd take Sadie to the grave or the hospital.

He had to check the sanitarium next.

He phoned the hospital and asked to speak to one of the security guards. "Listen, have Dr. Tynsdale paged, and if he shows up at the nurse's station, detain him."

"What's this about?"

"I'll explain when I get there."

He took us to the basement, Amelia had said. *That's where they hurt us.*

The horror of what she'd said hit him like a fist in the chest, and the worst possible scenarios pummeled him.

Sadie being tortured. Drugged.

Dead.

At the hand of a man she had trusted and treated like family.

God, he'd been so angry at her, had felt so betrayed. But he didn't want her to die.

His phone buzzed, and he snatched it up. "Nick?"

"Yeah, I'm at Tynsdale's, but nobody is here."

"Look around, see if you find any evidence of the experiments, or any signs of where he might take Sadie. Maybe he owns some other property somewhere."

"Will do," Nick said.

"I'm on my way to the sanitarium." No way was he going to tell his brother Amelia's accusations yet. Nick might be a federal agent, but he was still Jake's little brother. Jake would protect him from her rants until he found out whether or not they were true.

Jake hung up, turning on the defroster as the hail grew stronger, making visibility difficult. He cursed, braking to keep from sliding into a ditch. Headlights nearly blinded him, and he passed a couple of truckers and veered to the right to avoid a car that crossed the line.

Darkness swallowed the winding road that led to the sanitarium, the miles crawling by as he sped into the parking lot.

Jake checked his weapon, pulled his coat around him, then headed inside. Amelia had told him there was a secret entrance, that the basement had been soundproofed so no one could hear their screams.

He hoped to hell he could find it. Every second counted.

First he checked with the nurse's station. The security guard met him there, but Dr. Tynsdale hadn't answered his pager.

Jake told him to let him know if they spotted Tynsdale, then slipped down a corridor to the right. He passed several rooms where the doors were ajar. Obviously those patients didn't need as much supervision as the ones in the wing where they'd housed Amelia. He headed to the right, past a service elevator, then a series of swinging doors marked "Staff Only," then down a gloomy, shadowed corridor that looked as if it hadn't been used in years.

Praying Amelia hadn't steered him wrong, he ran his hand along a corner of the wall, searching for the hidden button to open the door. He found it a second later, and was shocked when the metal door opened.

The entrance was dark, the strong scent of chemicals filling the air. He inched down the steps, moving as quietly as possible. The sound of a clock ticking reverberated through the narrow corridor, and down below he heard footsteps, so he removed his gun, bracing himself for the worst.

Another noise sounded to the right. Metal clinking. He slowly made his way through the space to the doorway. When he looked inside, he froze.

Sadie was strapped to a gurney, her face pale, her body jerking as she tried to free herself.

Dammit.

A man was hovering over Sadie, a hypodermic in his hand.

Then he saw the man's face, and swallowed hard.

The man was his father.

———————— , ————————

Sadie twisted and fought against her bindings. She had to get away.

If she didn't, Blackwood would find Amelia, and he'd kill her, too.

"You killed Papaw, didn't you?" she asked. "You shot him."

That sinister laugh bounced through the cold room again. "Coker started having regrets in his old age and gave your granddaddy the old files. I had to take care of both of them."

"So you knew what they were doing all along?" Sadie asked. "That the doctors were experimenting on children." She jerked her head, indicating the darkened room. "Is this where you brought them? You forced all them down here and drugged them. What else did you do to them?"

"We were doing our jobs, following military orders," Blackwood said. "Coker and Sanderson thought they'd discovered a new hallucinogen that wouldn't have the side effects the drugs did in the fifties and sixties. They modified Metrazol, thinking the new form wouldn't cause convulsive seizures. It was all Sanderson's idea. He worked in biowarfare on Project Bluebird. I was with the CIA, so we formed a team."

"What kind of monster are you?" Sadie cried. "You tore apart people's families and destroyed lives. Why?"

"The government wanted to create perfect soldiers. With LSD, shock treatments, sensory deprivation, they thought they could create new identities within the children. Mind control could control them, like puppets on a string."

"Only the experiments failed, just as they had before, didn't they?" Sadie choked out. "Your inhumane treatment caused mental illness and disorders so severe that you had no control."

"We had some successes. Emanuel Giogardi, for one. He was a sniper, and he did as we commanded until the very end." He sounded smug. "And we had control," he said in a lethal tone. "We've been controlling your sister for years. Only you never knew it."

Fear seized Sadie. She remembered the drugs she'd found in Amelia's bathroom; they had kept her sister incoherent, so no one would believe her even if she did tell someone what had happened.

Dear God. Dr. Tynsdale had prescribed the drugs and monitored her sister all these years.

Had he been in on the experiment?

———————— ، ————————

Shock immobilized Jake. His father was alive.

He choked back a protest as he listened to his confession. Where was the man who had raised him and loved him?

How could he be so cold, such a monster?

Inhaling deeply to calm the rage and pain rocking through him, he texted Nick that he needed backup, then gripped his gun tighter and raised it at the ready.

Finally he stepped from the shadows. "Dad?"

His father suddenly jerked around, his eyes widening as he spotted Jake. Their gazes locked for a long, tension-filled minute. His father had always seemed ominous and powerful, a man to be revered and admired, one he'd strived to emulate.

Now gray tinged his military haircut, and the eyes that had once looked at him with love were empty, void of emotion.

Dammit, he'd missed his father for so long, had ached to see him again.

But this man was a stranger.

"It's true," Jake said. "You're responsible for hurting all those children, Amelia and Joe Swoony, Grace Granger, Bertrice Folsom, and Emanuel Giogardi. And now you're killing anyone who knew about the experiments to cover your ass."

"Did you kill my parents, too?" Sadie cried.

"Your mother overheard a phone conversation with Dr. Coker that she shouldn't have heard…she got suspicious. A pity, but I had to do something." Jake's father glared at him. "You should have stopped nosing around," he said. "But you had to come back to Slaughter Creek and reopen my case."

Jake choked back a curse. His investigation into his father's disappearance had triggered all these deaths.

"Dammit, I was looking for my father. I thought something had happened to you, but all along you were alive, destroying people's lives."

"It was a CIA project, one we hoped might benefit our country," his father said sharply. "We are military men, Jake—men who must always look toward the future and what's best for our country."

"The future that you stole from innocent children," Jake said bitterly.

His father shook his head. "Don't be such a wuss, Jake. There are casualties in any cause."

"Even soldiers have a code of ethics," Jake argued. "War doesn't justify torturing innocent children. Nothing does."

"Jake," Sadie cried. "Amelia didn't shoot Papaw—he did."

"Let it go, Jake. You're the sheriff of Slaughter Creek now. You don't want this experiment exposed. No one does."

Jake thought of Ayla, sweet, innocent, loving Ayla. This man was her grandfather, but he would never know her.

He didn't *want* him to know her.

Resigned that his father was dead to him, he took another step forward. "What are you going to do, Dad? Kill me, too?"

"I don't want to hurt you, Jake, but you have to do as I say. There are others involved."

"Then I'll find out who they are, and stop them." Jake gestured toward the hypodermic needle in his father's hand. "Drop that and turn around. You're under arrest—"

His father lunged at him, and Jake cursed. But he wasn't fast enough for his father. His father karate-chopped the gun from his hand, and it went flying to the floor, a few feet away. Jake swung his arm up to fend off another blow. Then his father raised his foot in a kick.

Rage fueled Jake, and his military training kicked in. He dodged the blow, then got in a punch to his father's abdomen. His father lunged at him, knocking him down with a body blow. The wind left his lungs, but Jake managed to roll over, and slammed his fist into his father's face. Blood spurted, trickling down his nose, and Jake vaulted sideways for the gun. His father caught him by the ankle, but Jake kicked and clawed until his fingers gripped the weapon.

His father charged him again, kicking him in the gut, but Jake curled his fingers around the weapon and raised it in his hands. The menacing look in his father's eyes knocked the breath out of him.

"You won't shoot me, Jake. I'm your blood."

Jake's hand shook, but then he heard Sadie moan his name. A second later, his father lunged toward him to wrestle his gun away. Jake pressed his finger on the trigger, and the gun fired.

His father's eyes widened in shock as the bullet pierced his abdomen, and he staggered backward, his hands clutching at his belly. Sorrow filled Jake as blood seeped through his father's shirt, oozing out between his fingers.

Chapter 28

———— ○ ————

S adie shuddered as Blackwood fell backward against the gurney where he'd bound her with leather straps. The drug he'd given her earlier was fading, but the room still looked blurry, the clock ticking so loudly it sounded as if it was going to explode.

Or maybe that was the gunshot.

Gunshot...yes, Jake had fired his gun. Had he been shot? Or was it his father?

She twisted her head sideways to see what was happening. Jake jerked the hypodermic needle from his father's hand, then spun him around and handcuffed him.

"Don't do this, Jake. I'm your father."

"You aren't my father," Jake growled. "My father was a decent man. At least I thought he was. You're a murderer."

Blackwood spit blood. "And you think your girlfriend there is better."

"Shut up," Jake snarled.

Tears blurred Sadie's eyes as the memory of that horrible night resurfaced. She had lied to Jake once, had kept secrets from him.

This time she refused to do that.

He had to hear the truth from her, not from his deranged father.

"Tell him, Sadie," Blackwood said on a grunt of pain. "Tell him you aren't the sweet little innocent girl he thought you were."

"I shot your father ten years ago," Sadie said.

Jake eyes darkened with confusion. "What? I thought Amelia—"

"I thought she did, too," Sadie said, choking back her emotions. "But I blocked out the memory. That was what my grandfather meant when he said he was afraid Amelia was remembering the details. All these years she took the rap for me. Tonight, when your father kidnapped me, my memories rushed back."

Jake jerked his father's arm, contempt in his voice. "You tried to hurt Sadie back then."

"She was in the way," his father snarled. "I was trying to help her sister. To calm her down."

"No, he was drugging Amelia to keep her quiet, and he planned to kill her and make it look like a suicide," Sadie said, determined that Jake should know the entire truth. "I found him with a knife, about to cut Amelia's wrist. That's why I shot him."

"See," Blackwood said. "Your girlfriend was no saint back then, and she's not now. So do the right thing, Jake. Help your father."

Sadie struggled anew against the bindings. "I had to stop him," she said. "I couldn't let him kill my sister."

Jake's gaze locked with Sadie's, tension thrumming between them. Then his jaw hardened, and he glanced back at his father, his expression unreadable.

Sadie's heart ached. She knew he hated her for betraying him. And he'd wanted his father back for so long…

What was he going to do now?

———— , ————

Rage, grief, anger, and a deep sadness engulfed Jake. The two people he'd loved most had lied to him, had kept secrets from him for years.

But he could not condone what his father had done.

Or let him continue killing to cover it up.

He yanked his phone from his belt and punched in Nick's number.

"I'm in the parking lot now," Nick said.

Jake told him where to come, and within minutes, Nick descended the stairs. When he saw his father lying on the floor, Nick stared at him with shock and disgust.

"It looks like you were right about our father," Jake said, his voice low, calm, nothing like he felt inside. "He's a cold-hearted bastard."

His father glared at him. "You'll regret this, Jake."

Jake shook his head. "No, you will."

Nick walked over and yanked him up.

"I'm bleeding," his father said. "Come on, Nick, Jake. You're my sons."

"You died a long time ago," Nick said.

Jake glanced at Sadie, and emotions bombarded him. She looked small, pale, trapped. At the thought that his father had tied her down and was going to kill her so ruthlessly, fury rose inside him.

He strode to her and began unfastening her bindings, but he couldn't look at her face. Hurt at her secrecy still welled inside him, yet shame filled him at what his father had done to her family. He'd watched her sister being tortured, destroying her life, killing her grandfather.

How could she ever forgive him—how could she get past that?

Sirens wailed outside as he helped her to sit up. "Are you okay?"

She nodded, although she swayed slightly, and her eyes looked weak.

"Sadie?"

"I'm fine," Sadie said. "I just want out of this place." She leaned on him for support. "How did you find me?"

"Your sister," Jake said, still unable to believe the turn of events. "She came to the studio. It was almost as if she knew you were in trouble."

"Where is she now?"

"With Ms. Lettie."

Sadie's nails dug into his arms, her voice panicked. "I think Dr. Tynsdale may have been drugging her all this time to keep her from talking."

Jake walked over and jerked his father's arm. "Was Tynsdale working with you?"

His father stared at him with cold eyes. "I want a lawyer."

Dammit.

"Jake, what if he tries to kill Amelia?"

"We'll stop him," Jake said.

"Go on," Nick said in a lethally calm tone. "I'll take care of him."

Jake nodded, then took Sadie's arm and headed toward the stairs.

———————— · ————————

Sadie held on to Jake as they hurried up the stairs, then down the hall to the outside door. Her legs felt rubbery as they walked to his car, but she had to make them work. She had to get to her sister.

She sank into the seat, her vision blurring. What if Dr. Tynsdale had found Amelia? Ms. Lettie was there, too. Would he hurt her?

Jake's cell phone buzzed, and he clicked to connect. "Waterstone?"

Sadie clutched at the door handle as he pressed the accelerator, sped away from the sanitarium, and careened around the mountain.

"Amelia, yes, I know where she is, I'm on my way. Meet me there."

"What's going on?" Sadie asked as he hung up.

"Waterstone got a call about a break-in at the high school earlier. Your sister was hiding out there, and she cold-cocked him. That's when she came to the studio and told me where you might be."

Nervous laughter bubbled in Sadie's throat. "Amelia told you where to find me?"

Jake nodded. "She sounded amazingly lucid, for what she's been through."

"The time she's been out of the hospital without her medication must be good for her."

Jake punched the doctor's number. It rang several times, then Jake shook his head. "No answer."

"Give me the phone, and I'll try the studio. Maybe Ms. Lettie will answer."

Jake handed it to her and she called her home number. It rang five times, then rolled to voice mail.

"Amelia, Ms. Lettie, we're on our way," Sadie said. "Be careful. Don't trust Dr. Tynsdale."

As she ended the call, her nerves screamed that Amelia was in danger.

Sleet pelted them as Jake wound down the mountain, and he swung onto the road to her old home. The fact that it was gone along with her grandfather sent another wave of sorrow and loss through her.

But it intensified her need to save the only family she had left.

The car bumped over the potholes and ridges, skidding twice on the black ice, but finally they made it to the guesthouse. The ashes of the farmhouse looked wet and sad as Jake parked. Dr.

Tynsdale's car was parked to the side, Ms. Lettie's station wagon by the house.

Sadie flung open the door and staggered up to the front, but Jake caught her arm before she entered. "Wait—if Tynsdale was helping my father, we have to be careful."

Sadie nodded, and he eased open the door. Just as he did, Amelia's cries echoed from the house. The lights were dim, and Sadie peeked over Jake's shoulder, terrified.

Jake drew his gun and inched inside. The front room of the studio was empty, but Sadie could hear Amelia's voice.

"Please stop," Amelia cried. "Don't do this to me anymore. I told Jake—he'll tell Sadie. They'll help me now."

Jake shoved the door open with his shoulder, and Sadie gasped when she spotted Dr. Tynsdale on the floor, unconscious.

God help them. It wasn't Tynsdale who'd been drugging Amelia.

It was Ms. Lettie.

——————— · ———————

Ms. Lettie stood with a gun aimed at Amelia.

"She killed Dr. Tynsdale," Amelia cried. "She's trying to kill me, too, and make it look like I murdered him."

At one time Jake wouldn't have believed her, but she had seemed more lucid earlier, and she had led him straight to Sadie.

And now he knew the truth. His father had tortured her and killed her grandfather. And he was responsible for so many deaths.

"Put down the gun, Ms. Lettie," Jake said calmly.

"No, I have to take care of her," Ms. Lettie said, a crazed look in her eyes. "That's my job. I've been doing it for years."

"You've been keeping her drugged so she wouldn't remember the truth about what happened at the sanitarium," Sadie said.

"You worked there. You helped Blackwood and those doctors, didn't you?"

Ms. Lettie's hand trembled. "You don't understand. They were just following orders. We *all* were."

Sadie glared at her. "Your orders involved torturing children."

"It was an experiment," Ms. Lettie said vehemently. "One that went all wrong, but we tried to help the ones who survived. That was the reason we admitted Amelia to the hospital, and I came to take care of her."

Jake inched forward. "You took advantage of innocent children and families. Instead of helping them, you lied to them, used them, then drugged them to keep your evil experiments from being exposed." Jake's fingers tightened around his gun. "But it's over, Ms. Lettie. Now put down that gun."

Ms. Lettie gave Sadie an imploring look, then tried to run. Jake caught her as she vaulted for the door to escape, then flipped her around, knocked the gun from her hand, and laid it on the nightstand. Then he handcuffed her, just as he had his father.

A second later, he rushed to Dr. Tynsdale and checked his pulse. "He's alive," Jake said, then quickly called an ambulance.

Sadie ran to Amelia, dropped down on the bed, and hugged her. "It's okay now, Sis. It's all over."

Amelia burst into tears. "I've been fighting the voices," she said. "They tried to take me over, Sadie, but I've been fighting them."

Sadie stroked Amelia's hair, pushing it behind her ear. "Good for you, Amelia—keep fighting. Maybe without all those narcotics Ms. Lettie gave you, you can finally get well."

Amelia held her so tightly that Sadie remembered when they were kids, holding on to each other when their grandmother died.

She didn't know if her sister could overcome the trauma she'd suffered from the experiment or if she'd been permanently damaged. But she vowed to do everything possible this time to make sure she received the proper treatment.

Maybe there was a chance that Amelia could have a normal life.

Maybe they both could.

Even if she had to live hers without Jake.

———————— , ————————

Jake couldn't bear to look at Sadie, not after his father had destroyed her family.

But questions nagged him. Ms. Lettie and his father had both implied there was someone bigger behind the experiments.

Maybe now that they'd been arrested, he or Ms. Lettie would fill in the details.

A siren wailed, lights flashing as the ambulance rolled down the drive. He met the paramedics at the door and ushered them over to the doctor. Tynsdale was unconscious, but hopefully he would make it.

If not, it would be another murder on his father's head.

Ms. Lettie glared at him from the corner, where he'd hand-cuffed her to the door. It was almost unbelievable that the sweet lady they'd all trusted, the woman Sadie had considered family, had been a part of this deception.

He phoned Nick, asking him to meet him at the jail. Then he turned to Sadie and Amelia.

"Considering the circumstances, I'm going to suggest to the DA that she drop the charges against both of you."

Sadie still looked pale from her earlier ordeal, but she squared her shoulders. "Thank you, Jake."

"I'm just doing my job." Still, emotions warred in his head. Sadie had taken care of her sister when she was young, and then run because she'd shot his father to protect Amelia.

If she'd confided the truth back then, what would he have done?

Would he have believed her?

Even knowing the truth now, it was hard to forgive her for leaving him in the dark.

The medics loaded Tynsdale and carried the stretcher out to the ambulance. Ms. Lettie made a low sound in her throat, as if she just realized the depth of the trouble she was in.

Jake took one last look at Sadie and her sister, then had to look away. Maybe he could forgive her for betraying him; after all, she'd acted in self-defense.

But shame filled him. How could she forget the pain and loss his father had caused her and her family?

She couldn't. It would always stand between them.

He had to finish the case—question his father and find out who else was involved in the experiment.

He unfastened Ms. Lettie from the door and hauled her to the squad car.

He had a daughter at home he needed to take care of. She was his life.

And he had done his job. Sadie knew the truth about her grandfather's death, and she and Amelia were safe now.

But he and Sadie were over.

Chapter 29

————— o —————

One week later

Jake and Nick took seats at the diner and ordered the lunch special and coffee. Jake glanced at the newspaper, frowning at the article Brenda Banks had written about his father's arrest. The entire town, even the world, now knew about the ugly experiments conducted in Slaughter Creek.

Nick had been just as shocked as Jake was to discover that their father was alive. But his brother didn't seem as surprised that he'd been part of something so evil.

They had spent the last week interrogating his father and Ms. Lettie, but both had refused to admit who had been in charge of the experiment.

"I spoke to my superior," Nick said. "There's still a question whether the CIA sanctioned the project."

"Of course they're not going to admit it, if they did."

Nick made a sarcastic sound. "That's true. But my boss thinks that Dad was following orders in the cleanup. That someone in the political arena might be involved, and that his rising political status was another motivation for the cover-up."

"Where has Dad been all this time?"

"Working undercover. Apparently the CIA thought it would be better to keep him dead. Dad had a place in DC, but they had a plant here to watch Amelia."

"Ms. Nettie," Jake said. "And whoever contacted Brenda, maybe. She still refuses to give up her informant's name." He assumed it was someone on staff at the sanitarium who'd caught on to what was happening. But it could have been someone connected to the project who'd finally decided to blow the whistle.

Either way, the informant feared for his or her safety, and he could see why.

"We still don't know who was behind the project, or how many subjects there were," Nick said. "But we're definitely investigating."

"You haven't located Herbert Foley either?" Jake asked.

Nick shook his head. "We're on that, too. He could work for the project, or he could have been a victim like Giogardi, trained to kill."

Jake took it all in, wearily. The fact that his father had escaped the grave still astounded him. Apparently he'd had some kind of tracer on him, and had sent a message to his accomplice before he'd succumbed to unconsciousness.

"What are you going to do?" Nick asked.

Jake shrugged. "I thought about resigning. But the people of Slaughter Creek have been so supportive, I think I'll stay in office."

"That article Brenda wrote painted you as a hero."

He made a sarcastic sound. Brenda had kept her word. "A hero who shot his own father."

Nick cleared his throat. "Dammit, Jake, cut yourself a break. He deserved worse than a gunshot wound."

Jake conceded with a nod.

Sadie's face flashed in his mind. She had been the protective, loving sister. And when she'd left Slaughter Creek, she had devoted her life to being an advocate for other hurting children. Brenda had pointed all those things out too.

Sadie would make a wonderful mother.

To another man's children.

At the thought, jealousy ate at him, but he had to accept that she was gone again.

Oblivious to his turmoil, Nick kept speaking. "We're setting up a task force to continue the investigation. We also think that some of the other subjects may be violent, like Giogardi."

Jake frowned. No telling what else the subjects had been brainwashed into doing, or what effect the experiment had had on them. In the government's earlier project, some subjects had become violent criminals.

"Does that mean you'll be in Slaughter Creek more now?" Jake asked.

Nick shrugged. "And if it does? Is that all right with you?"

Jake nodded. "I'll do whatever I can to help."

Then he extended his hand to his brother. "It's good to have you back, Nick."

Nick smiled, then they shook on it.

Leaving Amelia again was the hardest thing Sadie had to do. But her sister was making progress, and Sadie had hired a specialist in Nashville to treat her.

Dr. Tynsdale had been cleared of involvement, but Amelia needed a fresh start. And Tynsdale was taking time off to recover after the ordeal with Ms. Lettie.

Amelia's alters were still surfacing, but with the correct medication and a new therapist, her prognosis for a full recovery and unification was actually good. Amelia was stronger now that the truth had been revealed; she was fighting through the memories and fending off the alters, determined to become whole again.

Sadie hugged Amelia. "I promise I'll be back, Sis," she said. "I just need to tie up some things in San Francisco." Then she planned to move closer to her sister. This time she would monitor Amelia's progress herself.

Amelia wiped tears from her eyes. "You saved me, Sadie. Just like you did back then."

Sadie tucked a strand of hair behind Amelia's ear. "You saved me too." She cradled Amelia's hands in hers.

This hospital was nothing like the depressing sanitarium where Amelia'd been tortured.

It was designed like an assisted living facility, with apartment-style housing, social activities, and group and individual therapy sessions. The room was cozy, decorated in blues and greens that Sadie and Amelia had picked out. Amelia had her own studio, just like at home. Family and friends were not only welcomed, but encouraged to visit.

As a bonus, they had a gourmet coffee shop.

"I'm so proud of you," Sadie said. "You're a fighter, Amelia, so don't give up. You are stronger than the others. Remember that."

Amelia hugged her. "Will you be okay, Sadie?"

Sadie's heart melted. "Yes, I have you back now. That's all I need."

"What about Jake?" Amelia asked.

Sadie sighed. The pain was so deep and raw, she could barely breathe. But she didn't want to worry her sister. Amelia had enough to deal with. "Jake and I...just weren't meant to be."

"I don't believe that," Amelia said. "You always loved him, but you gave him up for me."

"No," Sadie said. "I gave him up because I was too afraid to tell him the truth."

One month later

Jake studied the paperwork on his desk, his mind straying, as it had constantly for the last few weeks. Sadie's image haunted him. He'd done everything he could to forget her. But how could he, when his heart was full of her?

Dammit, what was he going to do about it?

The door opened, and his brother walked in. They were both getting used to the fact that their father had been a monster.

Maybe there had been signs there all along that he'd missed. His father had been really hard on Nick...

Was there something Nick hadn't told him?

"We found out the name of the experiment. It was called the CHIMES."

"Chimes?" Jake asked.

"Yeah, it was an acronym for Children in Mind Experiments."

"Jesus," Jake muttered.

"There's more. The CIA tried to get Dad out of jail," Nick said.

"Were they successful?"

Nick shook his head. "No. thanks to the forensics work you did and the fact that you caught him trying to kill Sadie, we have him on murder and attempted murder charges."

Jake raked a hand through his hair. "Good. I hope he never sees the light of day."

A second passed, Nick's agreement palpable. "Anyway, I'm going to make it my mission to end what our father started."

"I'll do whatever I can to help."

"How's Sadie?" Nick asked.

"Sadie's gone," Jake said. "It...she has her own life. I have my daughter."

"You can't have both?"

"Our father ruined the lives of Sadie and her sister," Jake said vehemently. "He was responsible for their parents' deaths, then he killed their grandfather and tried to kill Sadie. Why in hell would she want anything to do with me?"

Nick arched a brow. "But you still love her?"

Jake glanced away. He couldn't lie to his brother. "It doesn't matter."

"The hell it doesn't," Nick said. "What happened ten years ago was messed up, but it wasn't your fault. And it wasn't Sadie's."

That was true.

Nick met his gaze. "So if you love her, go after her."

——————— , ———————

Amelia knew it was time to kill him.

It was the only way she would survive.

For so long she had thought it was the Commander who owned her. Arthur Blackwood, who'd whispered in her ear and terrified her.

That Skid and Bessie and Viola had come to help her.

But now she knew different. Bessie was she, the scared little girl. And Viola was the woman inside her who craved a man. Who wanted love and, one day, marriage and babies.

But Skid—Skid was the evil inside her. The personality the Commander had planted in her head to make her do what he wanted.

And he wanted the real Amelia to be weak.

He wanted her dead.

Then he could make Skid into his soldier.

She looked out the window at the sun shining, at the day blooming ahead.

Amelia wanted to be part of that. But if she was going to live and have her dreams, she had to silence Skid.

She closed her eyes, willed herself to be strong, then mentally took the knife and plunged it into Skid.

He screamed and cursed, but she dug the knife in deeper.

"How can you do this to me after I protected you?" he cried as blood spurted across his abdomen.

She didn't relent, though.

She had to kill him.

It was the only way she could survive.

Chapter 30

———— o ————

S adie stared across the water at Alcatraz. For so long, she'd felt drawn to that prison. Had connected with the fact that it stood alone, surrounded by frigid waters, that the worst of the worst had been incarcerated behind those walls.

That no one had ever escaped.

Now she understood the reason she'd felt that connection.

It had been her own guilt. She had been trapped by the lies and secrets.

But she was free of them now.

Except that she was still alone.

Tears pricked her eyes, but she blinked them back. She wasn't totally alone. Amelia was doing better, and Sadie was researching other practices so she could move closer to her, and they could see each other more often.

The wind picked up, the chilly mist off the water spraying her, making her shiver. Tugging her jacket around her, she headed back to her apartment.

Just as she had so many times, though, she sensed that someone was watching her.

No…she was paranoid. Arthur Blackwood might have been watching her for years, but he was in jail now. Thank God.

She and Amelia were both safe.

Still, old habits die hard, and she kept her eyes peeled for anyone suspicious as she jogged up the sidewalk to her apartment and let herself in.

The air felt thick as she entered, and she glanced around, disturbed by the faint scent of a man's aftershave permeating the air.

Was she imagining it, or had someone been in her apartment?

Grabbing her pepper spray from her purse, she scanned the living room, but she didn't see anyone. Then the whisper of a sound echoed from her bedroom.

Pulse racing, she inched toward it, angling the pepper spray in case she needed it. Darkness bathed the room, and just as she reached for the light switch, a shadow moved. Then someone grabbed her.

She tried to scream, to pelt him with the pepper spray, but he knocked the canister from her hand and threw her into a chokehold.

———————— , ————————

Jake was sweating. He had nearly changed his mind at the airport, then on the cab ride over.

But he'd spotted Sadie walking. As he watched her staring out at Alcatraz, he thought of Amelia's disturbing painting of the two little girls, locked up in the darkness.

Had Sadie felt imprisoned by her own dark memories?

Even now, he'd seen the sadness in her eyes. The haunting loneliness that emanated from her wrenched his heart.

Because he loved her.

But he had let her go; he hadn't told her. He'd allowed his pride, guilt, and shame over his father's actions to stand between him.

It didn't have to be that way, did it?

Could she forgive him for the anguish his father had caused her?

Dammit, he had to try. He couldn't leave without telling her how he felt.

Even if she told him to go away.

As he raised his fist to knock on her door, though, he froze; he heard a noise inside. One hand automatically went for his gun, but he'd left it at home because of the hassle of dealing with airline security.

Something crashed to the floor, then Sadie's scream punctured the air.

His heart thundered. Gun or not, he tried the door. It was locked, so he slammed his weight into it and busted it open. The entryway was pitch dark. As he paused to get his bearings, another scream echoed from a back room.

He raced toward the sound. Through a door, he saw Sadie struggling with a man.

The bastard had pinned her to the bed. The shiny glint of a knife blade shimmered in the moonlight streaming through the window.

Jake lunged toward the man and dragged him off Sadie. The man twisted and tried to stab Jake, but he knocked the knife from his hand with a karate chop, and it skittered across the floor. Then he saw the tattoo on his arm. He fit the description Mazie had given them.

"Foley?"

But Foley didn't answer. He swung his fist at Jake.

Then Jake punched him in the face, pinning him with his legs. The asshole tried to buck him off, but rage that Foley'd tried to kill Sadie filled Jake with adrenaline, and he punched him again.

"Why come after her?" Jake asked. "My father's been arrested."

"I had my orders," Foley hissed. "And no one called off the hit."

Jake frowned. Had Foley been one of the subjects, or did he work for the CIA?

Then Foley tried to shove him backward, and Jake's rage exploded. He punched Foley so hard that this time the man's eyes rolled back in his head.

Jake would have to wait till he regained consciousness for the answers, but for now, he had to get to Sadie.

She was struggling to get up, her ragged breathing choppy as he flipped her attacker over, removed the handcuffs from inside his jacket, and slapped them around the man's wrists. Jake checked to make sure he was unconscious and had no other weapon on him, then rushed to Sadie.

Sadie heaved for air as Jake dragged her into his arms. She couldn't believe that he was here, that he'd saved her again.

That that man had tried to kill her.

Jake stroked her back, then kissed her hair. "Are you all right?"

"Yes. Who is that?"

"The man who pushed Grace down the stairs."

"So he was helping with the cover-up?"

"Looks that way."

She clung to his arms. "What are you doing here?"

Jake rubbed slow circles around her back. "I came to see you."

Sadie relaxed against him. She had missed him so much, had wanted him with her so badly.

But she hadn't allowed herself to dream…

She realized then that Jake was trembling, and lifted her head to look up at him.

"Is your father out of jail?"

Jake's jaw hardened, his eyes slashes of black coal in his chiseled face. "No, he'll never be free again." He glanced at the unconscious man on the floor. "Foley is going away for a long time too."

Sadie gazed into Jake's tormented eyes, and all the love she'd had for him for so many years filled her. "I'm so sorry, Jake. I... know that he hurt you, that I did—"

"Shh," he whispered. "None of that matters. All that matters is that I love you."

Sadie's breath caught. "I love you too, Jake." Sadie cradled his face in her hands. "I always have, and I always will."

———————— , ————————

Jake's heart raced as Sadie fell into his arms. He closed his mouth over hers, then kissed her with all the love he had denied himself for so long.

Finally they broke apart, and he called the local police. Ten minutes later, they arrived, and Jake explained the situation, then watched as the police dragged Foley up and carted him off.

Nick was going to work this case, and Jake would help him. He also wouldn't leave Sadie alone again. Not until everyone associated with that damn project was behind bars.

Or dead.

Preferably the latter.

"Sadie," he said as he took her hands in his. "I don't want us to be apart anymore."

Emotions softened her eyes as she smiled. "I don't want that either."

"Come back to Slaughter Creek—or I'll move out here, if it's too hard for you back there."

"No, I'll come home. I want to be nearer Amelia too." A question tinged her eyes. "But what about your daughter?"

Jake's heart swelled as he thought about having the two people he loved most in his house together. "She'll love you just as I do."

Then he removed the flint necklace from his pocket and held it out to her. "I know this is crude, that it's not a ring, but—"

"I loved it then, and I love it now," Sadie whispered.

He tied it around her neck, where it belonged, then stripped her clothes and made love to her all through the night.

Jake woke early in the morning to find Sadie at her easel. She had painted over Alcatraz with a beautiful landscape of the mountains and wildflowers, and the two of them together. His sweet, beautiful little girl Ayla was walking between them, holding both their hands.

They were finally going to be together. Just as the flint had weathered storms and abuse over the years, so had their love.

That love was only stronger now; it would bind them together forever.

Sadie turned to him with a smile as she laid the paintbrush on the easel. She looked happy, at peace now, and so beautiful he had to have her again. He would never get enough.

He cradled her face between his hands and kissed her. Then her tongue flicked out to tease him, and heat flared between them. A heat so strong and intense that he slipped off her robe and made love to her again, with the sunlight pouring through the window and the colors of the flint necklace twinkling in the light.

Acknowledgments

———— ○ ————

I want to thank my agent, Jenny Bent, for believing in this project, and my fabulous editor Lindsay Guzzardo for liking my *dark*, creepy voice!

Also special thanks to my editor Charlotte Herscher, who pushed me to make this book the best it could be, and Miranda Ottowell for catching the little stuff.

For questions and technical details, a special thank you goes to my sister, Reba Bales, a licensed counselor in a psychiatric hospital, who gave me invaluable insight into the mind of the mentally ill.

And to my new friend and fabulous writer Kendra Elliot, author of the Bone Secrets series, who also answered questions regarding forensics!

About the Author

———— o ————

Award-winning novelist Rita Herron's lifelong love of books began at the tender age of eight, when she read her first Trixie Belden mystery. A former kindergarten teacher, professional storyteller, and children's magazine contributor, she wrote nine books for Francine Pascal's Sweet Valley Kids series before shifting her focus to the adult market. Since then she has written over sixty romance novels and loves penning dark romantic suspense tales, sexy romantic comedies, and family-friendly romances, especially those set in small Southern towns. A native of Milledgeville, Georgia, and a proud mother and grandmother, she lives just outside of Atlanta.

16116794R00204

Made in the USA
Charleston, SC
05 December 2012